THE ROSE AND THE AMARANTH

BOOK I
THE ROSE FLOCK

WRITTEN BY CHRISTOPHER CAIN

ISBN: 979-8-9915563-0-9

"A Rose and an Amaranth blossomed side by side in a garden,
And the Amaranth said to her neighbor,
'How I envy you, your beauty and your sweet scent.
No wonder you are such a universal favorite.
But the Rose replied with a shade of sadness in her voice,
'Ah, my dear friend, I bloom but for a time:
My petals soon wither and fall, and then I die.
But your flowers never fade, even if they are cut;
For they are everlasting.'"
- Aesop

To my children,

How could I ever explain what really happened? I could tell you verbally, sit you down and require you to listen - but no. There are simply too many details and too much emotion. And quite simply, you wouldn't believe it. Your dubious expressions piercing me as I recount these events would be distracting and I would get off track. I would forget things here and there. I must put the words on paper. I cannot risk leaving anything out, not one single fragment.

As I begin writing this, you are still in diapers. You have not taken your first steps or spoken your first discernable words. I don't know at what point in your life I will hand you this book and ask you to read it. For now, I must concentrate on recounting the incredible events that led to your arrival. I must also do my best to always be honest and candid so that when you finally take the time to examine these pages, you'll know me to be an individual who does not spin farfetched yarns or exaggerate the truth. And maybe, if I am worthy of your trust and affection, you might just believe the unbelievable.

Please understand that what I am about to write will be told as accurately as my memory will allow. The parts where I was not present were later confirmed by those who were there or can be safely assumed to be valid depictions of events. Certain liberties will be taken to fill in those few tiny gaps. The foreign languages and dialects of the people involved will be translated and familiarized to your understanding. Besides these minor forbearances to make your reading smooth and less mentally taxing, nothing will be altered or spared. There will be parts that may be difficult for you to bear, but please do me the courtesy of pushing through. In the end, I hope this story will help you to understand our place in this life and provide gratification for the questions I have not been able to answer.

The content of these pages will be a joint effort between myself and another who was there through all of it. In addition to so many unprecedented talents, he's also a competent writer. Despite the risk that you may subsequently find me mentally delusional, I am determined to tell you everything. You have a right to the truth. You deserve to hear this story.

Love,
　　　Me

PART I
A DIAMOND IN THE ROUGH

Escapists

The harvest wind sweeps across the vast farmland of central Kansas. Two deer meander outside an isolated patch of woods, sifting their noses through freshly leveled corn stalks in search of stray morsels. Within these woods, there is an ancient church. Its stone walls are consumed by ivy and eroded from ages of natural torment, yet they remain steadfast and unyielding. The building has endured for countless ages nestled amongst twisty oak limbs and foliage. Buried within the pages of early American history, there are accounts of this church discovered by travelers pushing westward. How peculiar it must have seemed to them, to happen upon this beacon of civilization in an unfamiliar land devoid of people.

Long before the Pilgrims had sunk a grateful boot into Plymouth's sandy beach, indigenous tribes worshiped, feared and marveled at this enigmatic, impossible structure, daring never to enter. Now only Mother Nature thrives within its haven. Families of squirrels, opossums and teams of mice create a rodent sanctuary within the sheltering confines of the old stone walls.

The soft glow from the setting sun seeps through dusty stain-glass windows. Marble statues with broken faces, dry rotted pews and a lonely stone altar are all that remain since the structure's abandonment. The only sounds are a moaning wind and the distant hum of a corn-picker.

Startled by a scraping noise, a mouse scurries in distress

across the cold ground. A floor stone behind the altar begins to wiggle ever so slightly. The scraping noise soon turns to a series of small thumps causing the dirt on the stone to jump vigorously. The thumping persists for several minutes until the stone wiggles loose from the ones around it.

Slowly, deliberately, the ponderous stone ascends from the floor by the force of four shaky arms. It falls aside and there is a moment of still before two heads surface from the newly revealed hole. Two children, a boy and girl, peek out into the empty church. They are terrified, dirty and starving.

With an ambitious effort the boy weakly pulls his scrawny body out onto the gritty floor and with much exertion, finds his feet. After cautiously scanning the room, he helps the trembling girl out of the hole. With just a hint of dull red light remaining, they locate the bulky wooden door leading to the unknown.

An old farmer labors into the night, bent on finishing the western acres before the day's end. Guided by the corn-picker's illuminating head beams, he plugs along row by row. A nipping breeze entices him to snap the top button on his flannel shirt and reach for his tepid coffee. Ahead, through the mist, he sees something move. The coffee cup plummets to his soiled boots. Quickly halting the machine, he rubs his eyes in astonishment. Standing before the metal monster, like deer entranced in headlights, are two children. They stand motionless and frightened, the girl clinging tightly to the boy.

1

Florence, Italy – Forty years ago.

A chill of nervous excitement careened through Benny's twelve-year-old body as he gripped the metal doorknob. Papa's private study chamber was the only room in the humble Florentine cottage that had always been off limits. The penalty for disobedience was never set in stone, but perhaps the magnitude of its harshness could be inferred by the loopy letters etched into the wood above the door…

"All hope abandon, ye who enter here."

This moment was the pinnacle of a scrupulously devised scheme that had consumed the better part of the past year. Because he had invested so much time into this project, nervousness was inevitable. So much would be for naught should Papa return home prematurely and discover an intruder within his private study.

Benny could not be certain what punishment Papa would inflict should he be caught red-handed. The verdict could encompass anything from a mild tongue lashing to instant death. His uncertainty stemmed from the fact that he knew Papa as well as say… the head chef at the Ristorante la Giostra, or the curator of the Museo San Marco, or the president of Tanzania - in short, not at all.

Benny's father, Marcello, was not a horrible father in the sense that he did not physically abuse or castigate his son. Rather, he was a horrible father because he neglected Benny much as one would neglect a leaky faucet or a creaking door. When the two were home at the same time, Marcello would retreat to his den with a bottle of grappa and a block of provolone without an inkling of acknowledgment to his one and only offspring. On rare occasions Marcello offered an aloof nod of the head, usually minus eye contact, should their paths cross in the hallway or as Benny strolled up the front walk after school, but this atypical gesture was all Benny could hope for.

To his credit, Marcello stored enough food in the refrigerator to keep Benny nourished, barely, and provided him with shelter, a bed, and an archaic color television equipped with what may possibly be the first video game system ever manufactured. He also remembered to give a birthday card every year, containing enough euros to purchase a soda or perhaps a small pack of fries. Benny never minded that this was the same card Papa had recycled for the past six years with its original uncreative message of "Happy Birthday, Benny," quickly scribbled in the bottom corner. All that mattered was that he had remembered.

The only other occasion when Marcello fulfilled his obligatory parental duties was when Benny's school counselor requested his presence to discuss his son's unique psychological condition. Benny's mental disorder, so to speak, was yet to be assigned a specific label, even after multiple evaluations from scores of distinguished psychiatrists around Tuscany. These frequent school visits rendered Papa a regular in the counselor's office. So much so that the counselor, Vincent, pretty much fit into the category of "old friend" and would uphold this role by having a steaming mug of caffe' corretto ready when Marcello arrived to discuss the latest details of Benny's uncouth behavior.

Benny would sit idly next to Papa, mindlessly wrapping and unwrapping a piece of string around his index finger, while Vincent relayed the details of Benny's inability to coalesce with his classmates.

"The children, they have been playing kickball all week. All week Benny has played nice. Then today, out of nowhere, he tackled Roberto and pushed his face into the dirt, all the while, he shouted profanities." For every identifiable symptom that related to a particular psychological disorder, Benny had another aspect to his behavior that would contradict the symptom and keep him immune to a specific diagnosis.

Only Benny knew how to classify his behavior – fake. In his own mind, it wasn't surprising why he could not be diagnosed. He had never studied abnormal psychology and had no intention of adhering to an unambiguous condition so long as his behavior merited him the one thing he wanted most, Papa's attention.

Benny's intellect allowed him to pull this off. He was a genius, at least according to his teachers and a written IQ test. At his young age, he had the mental fortitude to manipulate those around him by consciously shaping his behavior so that the desirable response would ensue. As it stood, the most desirable response for a lonely preteen was attention, specifically from a neglectful father. Every outburst in class, every disturbing quarrel with a schoolmate, every episode of schizophrenic behavior was carefully rehearsed, then executed with the perfection of a seasoned thespian.

After several years of obtaining Papa's attention in this fashion, Benny decided that the charades were no longer congruent with his ambitions. Although Papa never so much as scolded his son for these calls into school, Benny could tell that he wasn't too thrilled to be there as his schedule was probably being interrupted. Benny didn't want to upset him; this was not the intention. It was time that he came up with a new way to satiate his hunger for knowledge.

For as long as he could remember, he had been consumed with curiosity about Papa's occupation. This was something that this ghost of a man had never divulged and once when Benny had asked him about it, his evasive response was, "What I do is not something a child would understand." Asking was out. But how then could he know? After lying awake many nights in deep thought, he finally decided how he would go about finding out.

The plan was efficient, well devised, and demonstrated an impressive amount of patience and foresight, especially for a boy of eleven. It began with a little household reconnaissance.

The door to the den came equipped with an old-fashioned locking mechanism. It was one in which a large skeleton key was required for unlocking, and therefore had a keyhole of sufficient size for snooping from the outside. Though the key had been long since missing and Papa never actually kept the door locked, it provided an excellent opportunity to first understand what was happening in that forbidden chamber.

The master plan covered all the fine details and included backup plans for emergency scenarios. During the snooping phase, his most likely slip up would be making too much noise while spying. For this, he had a wily escape plan in place should Papa take note that an unwanted intruder was meddling outside the den. With youth and agility on his side, he would make a silent retreat to his bedroom where history and math books would be strewn about the desk as if he'd been studying for hours. He doubted he'd ever have to utilize this escape plan, but it put him at ease just knowing it had been established.

For the following four months, Benny's domicile was that old doorway. His knees became sore from kneeling on hardwood flooring night after night and due to the repetitive squinting into the keyhole, his face even acquired a few premature wrinkles in the form of crow's feet. Still, minor discomforts aside, there was nowhere else in the world he would rather be. In a very indirect way, this spying made him feel as though he was bonding with Papa, as if he were sharing in his activities and his life. Though this relationship between father and son was distant and one-sided, Benny had never been more content.

He found Papa's activities behind that closed door enthralling, but this observation produced more questions than it had answered. Each evening was relatively identical. Papa came home from wherever he had been all day and went directly to the bathroom. After a piss and a hand wash, he went to the refrigerator and retrieved the brandy and the cheese. He took these items to the den and closed the door. Benny allowed himself a minute or so before he tacitly took his place at the keyhole, just in case Papa had forgotten something and had to re-emerge. Next, Papa sunk into the cushiony armchair behind the desk, closed his eyes for a moment, then reopened them to pour the grappa into his tumbler glass. This glass had remained on the desk from the previous night and many nights before, never reaping the benefit of a good wash. Before getting started, he casually consumed the contents of the glass while staring at nothing in particular. It looked as though he was simply lost in thought, or perhaps zoning out after a hard day.

When the glass was empty, he poured the second round, opened his desk drawer, and produced a rectangular-shaped item wrapped in a yellowish cloth cover. He removed the covering to reveal a book that seemed to Benny as though it might have been the first ever written - as though Adam had written a biography about his life in the Garden of Eden. Papa handled this item with exorbitant care signifying its supreme delicacy. As if this individual book had not already succeeded in gripping Benny's interest, there was a second book that Papa poured over each night, and this one, he handled like a rare, one-of-a-kind artifact.

This other book, which soon became Benny's prominent point of allurement, was one that Papa took with him during his daily disappearances. It never left his side and remained hidden within the confines of the scrappy leather messenger bag that he carried day to day. At the end of each night, it was locked in a wall-safe hidden behind an old painting - a disturbing abstract of two men looking down from a cliff upon naked people depicted in suffering postures.

This book was not wrapped in cloth like the other. Instead, it was enshrouded within a heavy iron case that included a combination code for opening. Unlike the other book, this one had a black hard cover that made it appear outwardly newer, but because of the paper's yellowish hue and the extreme gentleness in which Papa handled it, it was likely similar in age to the other.

Before removing the black book from the iron case, he donned a pair of soft white gloves so as not to taint the sacred material with skin oil. He then laid the two books upon the desk, side-by-side, and frittered away the next several hours looking them over.

There was something about that black book that gave Benny the chills. Whether these chills emanated from the thrill of the moment, or an unperceived malevolence, he was not sure. He could not understand why he felt this way. Perhaps it was the manner in which Papa handled it or regarded it as though it were the Holy Grail. Perhaps it was the foolishness of a youngster, but Benny swore that the book was latching itself firmly to his desire and perpetually taunting his conscience. He maturely and patiently bottled his desire to look upon the pages of these cryptic books. He knew that if his plan were carried out as intended, his wish would come true and his thirst for sapience would be quenched.

With abiding patience, he remained outside that door for three to four hours every evening doing nothing else but watching Papa leaf through the two books with agonizing unhurriedness. It soon became clear that he was comparing them, using one as a reference for the other, or searching for something lost within their antiquated pages. After many tedious hours and five glasses of grappa, Papa ended his night. The brown book was rewrapped in the cloth and slid gingerly back into the desk drawer. The black book was placed in its iron case and locked. It was then placed into the wall-safe and locked. At this point, Benny would rise from his aching knees and stiffly shuffle to his room. After these nightly rituals he went directly to bed, excited for the days to come, and especially enthusiastic that he had spent the evening with Papa.

2

The activities that occurred within the private study were no longer beclouded. Now that the first part of the plan had been completed, Benny could now initiate phase two. Of course, all of this was leading up to the big finale – getting the chance to examine the book for himself. In order to accomplish this feat with little apprehension of being caught, he needed to establish a schedule, or a window of opportunity in which he could enter the den and examine the book before Papa returned home each evening. Thus, the particulars of the man's daily routine must be observed and documented. Unfortunately for Benny's yearning mind, this part of the plan had to wait until school let out for the summer. By the time June finally arrived, he had planned this reconnaissance phase with the scrupulosity of a veteran military commander.

The operation followed a progressive step-by-step design. Each week, Benny would track Papa a little further, taking full note of his daily routines and exact path between the house and his final destination. The only appeasing factor of this long drawn out campaign, was that Marcello's final destination was something as mesmerically mysterious as the pages of that old leather-bound book. The light at the end of the tunnel was an essential piece of the puzzle that was his father.

For the first week, Benny simply monitored the time in which Papa left the house each morning. Each morning, with impressive consistency, the man was pushing through the front door at exactly two till nine. With a hunched posture and the telltale stride of a sexagenarian, Papa shuffled to the end of the cobblestone driveway and continued down the sidewalk paralleling the street. Shortly afterward, he disappeared from view no thanks to the thicket of fire bushes inconveniently situated in the neighbor's yard.

During week two, Benny set his alarm for eight o'clock am, scooped a handful of sour gummies into his pocket for breakfast, and mounted his rust-laden ten-speed that lived most of its life toppled over in the front lawn. He pedaled the clunker to the end of the street where the road ended perpendicularly into another. On the corner, there was a little park that he had scouted days in advance. Two benches, a fountain of algae-tinged water, and several clumps of artfully shaped box elders resided at this pleasant enclave. He stashed the bike within the leafy concealment of the shrubbery and took refuge amongst a branchy grove of hawthorns. This proved to be the perfect location for spying. As he waited patiently for Papa to come strolling along, he had to take a moment to appreciate the luxury of coming and going as he pleased. Most children his age required parental accompaniment when perusing the streets of Florence. Papa surely would not take notice that his son was gone each morning, nor would he pother over his whereabouts.

It soon became clear why Papa left the house at two till nine each morning. This was because it took him exactly two minutes to stroll from the driveway to the end of the street. His consistent punctuality was reciprocated by the burgundy sedan that rolled up to collect him at nine sharp. Despite the impedance of the sun's glare across the windshield, Benny was successful in assigning an identity to the driver. He was tall, rather big boned, and decades younger than Papa. He wore clothes that were noticeably expensive and well-fitting to his portly physique, but the elegance of the garments was offset by the fact that they were several years behind the current trend. This unique attire along with the man's thick, untamed hair and pale skin made him stand out in Benny's mind as a foreigner. Once or twice over the past several years, this same man had paid Papa a visit at the house.

With a cloudy remembrance of these infrequent encounters, Benny surprised himself by recalling that his name was Paulo. Other than this slight degree of certainty regarding the man's name, he knew nothing else about him.

Week three, Benny pedaled to the Piazza Della Signoria, where he easily blended into the massive blur of pedestrians that inhabited this bustling location. Here, amongst the chaotic swirl of Florentine residents, tourists, lines of honking automobiles and zipping bicycles, he was impervious to Marcello's observation. Across the street from the piazza, there was a small ristorante that specialized in local fare, namely pastries and hot beverages. Each morning Paulo's burgundy sedan swerved through the tight traffic and screeched to a halt in a reserved parking space near the diner. The men stepped from the vehicle with Marcello clinching protectively to his messenger bag and the sacred article within.

Waiting at the ristorante each morning was a young waitress who, expecting the arrival of her daily visitors, would have hot drinks already placed upon the usual table when the men strolled in. Marcello and Paulo sat and partook in food and drink, carrying on a conversation that Benny could not hear from his outlying location. Despite the fact that this meeting occurred on a daily basis, their enthusiastic repartee put forth the impression that it had been years since they last convened.

After observing their daily practice and becoming familiar with the players in this unfolding mystery, Benny felt comfortable with following the duo further. After all, it was not the little ristorante that interested him, it was where they were going next. After paying the check, which they took turns accepting in perfect rotating order, and proffering a few flirtatious gestures toward the young blonde who had been their table attendant, the men climbed into the car and traveled northeast along via Romana toward the Arno River, where they crossed by way of the Ponte Vecchio Bridge. Thanks to the sluggish tempo of the stop and go traffic along this route, Benny was able to pedal at the same pace with minimal effort, making absolutely certain to remain at an inconspicuous distance. For another fourteen days, he tailed Papa and Mr. Foreigner to this point, again to assure that this was indeed their usual routine.

The next step in Benny's plan was to get himself across the Arno ahead of the burgundy sedan to determine where it went from there. During this phase, he vacated the house shortly after he knew Papa had been retrieved by Paulo. He followed the same daily route through the piazza to make sure they were at their customary café patio, then he rode across the Ponte Vecchio and positioned himself along a narrow side street near the bridge's terminus. In his short lifetime, he had never been to this part of the city, though it was only a few kilometers from his front door. On the first day of crossing the river, he welled with excitement as he observed from his hiding place, Paulo's car ease off the bridge and hang a left. Today traffic was particularly heavy and Benny knew that he could easily tail them further without complication. But this was not part of the plan. He had set aside another seven days to observe from this end of the bridge. His mind told him to stick to the plan, however, for the first time since he had set out on this little venture to discover the secrets of his father, logic was overridden by anticipation. He decided to hasten things a bit.

He removed his bike from behind the trash bin where it had been temporarily stowed then warily mounted the weathered saddle. Just as he had been doing before, he followed Papa at a great distance, keeping to the opposite side of the street. With each pedal along the via Dei Leoni and then the via Dante Alighieri, his pulse escalated. This impetuous deviation from the master plan, this all or nothing mentality, was a welcome alternative from the overly cautious approach he had been adhering to these past months. Now, he was experiencing a state of adventurous uncertainty unlike anything he was accustomed to, and he was enjoying every nerve rattling second.

After weaving through a labyrinth of side streets, he realized in dismay that he had lost sight of the car. Equally as resolute as he was undeterred by this little glitch, he forced himself onward, cautiously, with vigilant eyes scanning thoroughly for the target automobile.

Then he saw it, parked behind, what was the place, a museum? Yes, it was a little museum, this much Benny could decipher, but he could not find an adequate hiding spot that would get him any closer to the building without risking discovery. He could only resort to peeking around the corner of the building across the street. Upon doing this, he saw that the car was empty. The two had abandoned the vehicle and their whereabouts were now undefined. Despite this impediment, Benny was pleased with his discovery thus far and decided that it was not worth pushing his luck by hanging around. By taking the chances he had chosen to take, he was now at least a week ahead of schedule and a week closer to reaching his goal. He was comfortable leaving it at that for today. He mounted the old steel frame with the plan of returning tomorrow, early enough to see the burgundy car arrive at the museum, and watching where Papa and his friend went from there.

3

The next morning he did just that and left early enough to account for the possibility of getting lost. Yesterday, the route in which he pursued the car after crossing the Arno had been complex and not yet established in his memory. Much to his delight, he navigated directly to the museum without complication. Once he had concealed himself behind the red brick building across the street, he took a look at the little plastic watch around his wrist. By this time, Papa and company would just be departing the ristorante. Depending on traffic, Benny would have about fifteen minutes of nail-biting anticipation while attempting to appear casually indiscreet so that the occasional passer-by would not notice anything suspicious.

Each hum of an engine that came into earshot sent a shiver of excitement down his spine as he awaited the arrival of Mr. Foreigner's sedan. After three or four false alarms, the party of interest finally rolled up. It eased into the same parking spot that it had occupied the day prior, which happened to be located near the back door of the museum. When the men emerged, they made straight for the back entrance. It was the type of door that would never draw a second glance or elicit a raised eyebrow. Papa took the initiative to give three solid raps on the door, and the events to follow really ramped Benny's distress level.

The man who opened the door was perhaps the most formidable figure Benny had ever laid eyes upon. The ogrish brute stepped from the shadowed interior sporting a shaved head, dark sunglasses, black ink scalp tattoos, the physique of an Olympic powerlifter and a t-shirt bestrewn with skulls. As if these unsettling particularities weren't enough, the tattooed man toted a semi-automatic machine gun as he courteously held the door open. Despite his troubling semblance, he did possess a friendly smile as he nodded his good-mornings to Papa and Mr. Foreigner. The giant man, whom Benny decided was most congruent with a security guard, gave the general locality a visual sweep before yanking the door shut with a metallic thud. Thankfully, he had missed the curious eyes of the small boy peering on from across the street. This new discovery had contradicted all of Benny's presumptions about his father's line of work. Now, it could only be rightfully assumed that the man's occupation was of the utmost importance or maybe, he was doing something illegal.

Benny remained in his covert position for hours on end, only abandoning post once to relieve himself behind a dumpster in the adjacent alleyway. He grew increasingly hungry and thirsty but stuck to his reconnaissance plan with dogged resolve. During this long interval of time, there was little to occupy his need for stimulation. This particular area was very quiet and lightly traveled. The only activity came from the front entrance of the museum, where visitors of all ages and appearances shuffled in and out at a steady volume throughout the day. Exactly four times, the tattooed security guard emerged from his black hole to have a cigarette. He utilized his weapon to keep the door propped open as he leaned against the grimy brick wall taking drags and exhaling circular puffs of smoke. During these ten minute periods, Benny smartly refused to steal even the smallest of peeps from around the wall. After countless months of successful recon, he knew it would be foolish to ruin progress over the inability to control his curiosity. Four times, he waited patiently until the metal door clunked shut before reinitiating observance for Papa's return.

Finally, after seven hours, the door opened once more. Marcello and his comrade stepped from the darkness rubbing their eyes in defiance of the late afternoon sun. There was no significant change in the two others than perhaps the manifestation of fatigue, as if they had spent those long hours hard at work. The security guard followed soon thereafter, locking the door from the outside and following up with several aggressive tugs on the handle to assure that it had been properly secured. He nodded a cool goodbye to the others then walked off down the narrow street. Papa and Mr. Foreigner piled into the burgundy car and drove off following the same route by which they had come.

Benny exhaled a victorious breath. Phase one was now complete. He knew with certainty that Papa returned home around this same time every night. This meant that there would be no stops along the drive home and therefore, his daily routine had been fully observed and documented, except of course the goings-on behind that rusty door. Benny had now established a definite window in which he could snoop around the private study with an easeful mind.

There was just one more thing he desired to accomplish this evening to slake his inquisitive appetite. So far, he had not been able to get close enough to determine exactly what kind of a museum this was. With Papa and the others long since departed, he now had his opening. With a great deal of stiffness that could be attributed to standing in one spot all day, Benny swung a leg over the top tube of his trusty steed and pedaled toward the front entrance. There was a sign posted outside the small parking lot that read:

CASA DE DANTE: BIRTHPLACE OF DANTE ALIGHIERI, FATHER OF THE ITALIAN LANGUAGE.

Dante Alighieri. Benny had heard the name many times but knew very little about the man. He would make it a point to find out more in the hope that the answer might allow him to see deeper into Papa's mysterious life. He rode home at a casual pace just to mull things over. There was no rush to beat Papa home, because he never noticed whether Benny was there or not. He often wondered how long he could stay away before a missing child report would be called in: a few days, weeks, perhaps years? They were all equally as likely.

When he returned to the Florentine cottage, he found that Papa was sequestered in his private den as usual. This night, Benny passed right on by without stopping at the keyhole. The grin on his face was colossal. He was just thrilled with his progress so far. For the first time, he had at least some small understanding of Marcello's life. Tomorrow when the man left the house, he would take a huge leap into finding out more.

And here he was, finally, after nearly a year of fastidious scouting, standing at the threshold of the den. His insurmountable patience had made this moment all the sweeter. He paused for a tick to relish it. Papa was gone, and Benny knew without provision that he would not be back for a minimum of nine hours. His heart raced. He took one more quick glance at the discouraging message etched above the doorway and tried to pay it little mind. He turned the cold black knob and for the first time in his life, stepped into the room that had always been off limits.

4

The morning sun spilled in lazily through the crack in the crimson curtains, the rays seemingly concentrating on the wooden desk. It was as if the heavens were directing Benny to that one location. He navigated around the desk and stared longingly upon the drawer that contained the old book. Though his fingers ached to grip the drawer handle and yank it open right then, his masterful ability to remain patient in the name of covertness kept his yearning at bay. Before proceeding, he knew he must obtain a precise census of how everything was arranged in, on, and around the desk so as not to leave one infinitesimal clue of his trespassing. Fortunately, Papa kept the desktop free of clutter, decreasing the likelihood that Benny would inadvertently displace something during his investigation of the book. There was a small table lamp, a magnifying glass, the pair of white gloves, and the empty tumbler still emitting the unmistakable aroma of alcohol. These were the implements of Papa's nightly rituals. After a few minutes of careful observation, Benny decided that the thing he was most in danger of disrupting was the position of the swiveling desk chair. It was unlikely that Papa paid any note to the chair's exact place, position, and angle to the desk when he had flipped off the lamp and stepped wearily from the room each night, but it was in Benny's nature to minimize risk.

He had brought with him two items - a roll of white tape and a pair of gloves. He removed the tape from his pocket and ripped three small pieces from the roll. He knelt and placed a piece behind each wheel of the chair. This would allow him to return the chair to its exact position once he was done using it. The gloves were intended for both stealth and consideration. The desk was a polished dark oak with a surface that was sure to collect fingerprints and display them like a marquee. Would Papa notice the fingerprints of a smaller hand strewn about the desktop? Unlikely, but worth the effort of donning gloves nonetheless. Also, the gloves would help prevent unnecessary wear and tear of Papa's sacred property.

With the tape in place and his fingers veiled, he rolled the chair into a more convenient position, and with rapture, took a seat. He looked straight across the room to the doorway imagining how night after night, Papa would sit here without possessing the slightest trifle of awareness that a spy lurked just on the other side. Now it was down to business. His pulse elevated as he slid open the top left drawer, slowly so as not to disturb any contents that may lie within. To his relief, the book was the sole inhabitant of this particular space. His hands trembled uncontrollably as he lifted it from its resting place mimicking Papa's demonstration of utmost gentleness. He set it on the desk, and before unwrapping it, spent another minute deciphering the exact way in which it was swathed so that he could rewrap it in an identical fashion. He pulled back all four corners of cloth one at a time to reveal the ancient leather-bound book in all its glory. Benny swore he could hear angels singing from above in harmonious chords as the book lay there basking in his unbounded admiration.

There were no words on the front cover, only a symbol in the form of nine concentric circles. Within the thicker outer circle, there were eight more circles becoming incrementally smaller down to the center circle which was a mere dot. Benny shrugged with an air of indifference and opened the cover where he found the title and author:

The Divine Comedy: Volume 1, Inferno
Dante Alighieri

There was that name again, Dante. Clearly, as the clues would indicate, Signore Alighieri was a famous author. The sign outside the museum had made it clear that he was the "Father of the Italian Language." And of course, here was one of his works, but this revelation did little to shed light on the bigger picture. What significance did this Dante have in Papa's life? That question could be put on the back burner for the time being. Perhaps the content of the antiquated text would offer more insight. The moment of truth was now at hand. A long year of waiting and Benny sat feverishly upon the threshold of gratification. His desire was through the roof. Adrenaline coursed through his body. It felt as though he were a lion going in for the kill - the thrill of the moment, the quelling of hunger. He turned the page and began to read and would do so for the next six hours without leaving the chair.

There was an immediate hindrance. Though the book was written using Benny's native Italian language, it contained a peculiar dialect that was alien to his experience. Had the story been written in modern times, he would have sailed right through the pages, instead, he was crawling. To his credit, it did not take long to grow accustomed to the unique writing style, and his progress through the text accelerated.

The book had a total of thirty-four chapters. Dante referred to them as cantos. After the sixth hour, Benny had made it through only nine cantos. He could not read another word. Not because of mental fatigue, no, there was a much larger entity responsible for this decision to abandon the story – terror. The Inferno, he discovered, was not for the faint of heart. It contained horrific scenes, disturbing images, and graphic depictions of cruelty and torture, all in which Benny's young mind had not been thus far subjected to. Worst of all, the story took place in the one location he had been taught to fear above all others – hell. A vivid recollection careened through his brain as he closed the book with shaking hands. There was no mistaking the severity in Papa's tone when he uttered the words, "What I do is not something that children would understand." Benny wished that he had heeded this obvious warning, but it was too late now.

He shook uncontrollably as he went about returning things to their pre-imposter condition. In his state of disquietude, it was a challenge to focus on the details that he had been so careful to discern. He rewrapped the book just as it had been before, then set it gently in the drawer. His hamstrings were taut as he rose to his feet. He rolled the leather chair back to its original position, aligning each of the three wheels perfectly with the tape markers. He then angled it accordingly and pulled the pieces of tape from the floor. He took a few more seconds to seek out any biological evidence that may have littered the scene - a black hair from his head, a wayward eyelash perhaps. Once satisfied that all was in order, he vacated the room – quickly.

The hallway was full of shadow and seemed darker than usual. The little house he knew so well was suddenly unfamiliar. Sure, this was strictly a mental phenomenon but even so, it felt very real. The book was an unholy presence in these walls, and though it had likely been there for years, he had been ignorant to its existence. Now, he could almost hear the screams of the damned on the other side of that door. He looked up at the etching and could now fully understand the implication. "Abandon ye hope, all who enter." Was it a sick irony that Papa had chosen to carve those words? Ironic, because this was the exact phrase etched over the entrance to Hell in Dante's book. Either way, the phrase was meant as a warning, and one which he should have paid mind to. Because he had chosen to ignore it, the rest of his life would be defined by the past six hours.

He revisited the story over and over in his mind. It began when the main character, the pilgrim named Dante, had become lost in a dark forest. Since the author had used himself as the protagonist, it gave the story an autobiographical overtone. To add to Dante's unfortunate quandary of misdirection, every conceivable exit was blocked by a deathly creature. Fortunately, a man by the name of Virgil came to his aid. Virgil told Dante that the only way out of the forest was through the underworld, but not to fear, for he would lead the way. Devoid of suitable alternatives, Dante agrees to follow Virgil placing full trust in this mysterious man.

The pair would then descend into hell and traverse its many obstacles and horrors. Along the way, Dante seized every opportunity to speak with those souls, shades as he called them, who had been damned to this regrettable eternity. The stories told by the people they encountered were gut-wrenchingly pitiful. He discovered that the inhabitants of hell were placed in a certain level or realm based on the sins they had committed in life, and most were tortured in ways that Benny could not have imagined. The punishments became grotesquely more severe as the travelers descended deeper into the earth and Benny ceased reading once they had reached a place called, the City of Dis. This was the wicked domain in the fifth circle of hell that separated the "lesser" sinners in the upper circles from the "greater" sinners in the lower circles. It was practically a guarantee that the sadism would increase in severity once Virgil and Dante passed through Dis. This escalation was something that Benny's mind could not yet withstand.

Throughout his life, Benny had attended mass on many occasions, though only twice with Papa. His knowledge of this religion came chiefly from his school, where Catholicism was preached in the traditional Italian fire and brimstone manner. Between religion class and daily church goings with classmates, he had grasped the basic concept of heaven and hell. That was why, The Inferno, had struck him head-on like a freight train. Any time Father Riley referenced Satan or his humble abode, Benny instantly averted attention to something else, anything else. The dark angel was a being who frightened him beyond explanation, and spending infinity in his company was unthinkable. Dante not only made Benny think about hell, his descriptive narrative forced Benny to consider that it might actually exist. After suffering through only one third of the book, he had swallowed a heaping spoonful of dread. At this point, he wondered if all his effort had been in vain, because as it stood at the moment, he had no desire to reside under the same roof as that cursed object.

He walked straight to his room. Though he had not eaten all day, his hunger pangs were squelched by the knots in his stomach. There was a dead fly in the half-empty water glass he had brought to his room the night prior. He fished it out with an index finger and downed the remainder of the liquid. His body continued to tremble from the flood of conflicting emotions - excitement, accomplishment, confusion and most prominently, fear. Yearning for someone to come and relieve him from solidarity, he contemplated how nice it would be if Papa came home early today. After tracking the man's every move for so long, he knew there was no chance of this happening.
And then a new consideration struck that added another rotten ingredient to the stew of turmoil brewing in his head… Papa was sick. What sort of person spends each and every night spilling over such malevolence… night after night, page after page, torture after torture? Now, Marcello was even more of a stranger than before. Benny couldn't think of a single conceivable reason how his father, or any man for that matter, could become obsessed with such a thing.

He felt trapped in this moment. His emotions pushed and pulled from all directions rendering him nearly immobile as he huddled beneath the stiff bed sheets. The only activity he could manage was a quick sprint to the bedroom door. He slammed it obnoxiously and dove back beneath the covers. He didn't know why this made him feel better, more protected, as if the thin piece of synthetic wood would help keep the demons of hell at bay. Petty as the notion was, any measure that further separated himself from the book in the other room, would be a measure worth taking. He closed his eyes, and for what seemed like hours, relived the journey of Dante and Virgil. Somehow his brain had absorbed every element; so much so that he believed he could recite the pages word for word. At some point, he fell asleep.

He would stir awake to the muffled sound of Papa's footfalls moving about the house. His presence was neither warming nor welcoming. Indeed, this man had not changed a bit from yesterday, or the day before and so on, but now that Benny understood what sort of substance his mind craved, he was now someone to be leery of. Benny could envision Papa's every move just from the familiar sounds - the bathroom door, the clanking of bottles in the refrigerator, the door to the den. As far as Benny was concerned, that door was now the entrance to hell, labeled appropriately by those chilling words etched above it.

5

Ten days passed before Benny made his return to the den. This interval of time proved to be sufficient to acclimate himself to the book's concepts. Each passing day, the scenes from Dante's journey played out in his head, and with each virtual rewind, he gradually came to accept the idea of hell and punishment. He started by rereading the first part of the book just to ease himself back in. Now that he was well in tune with his emotions, he decided that it would be wise to take things a little at a time. He had no desire to experience such mental tumult ever again and this incremental approach would allow him to proceed without fear of disturbance overload.

By now, he was practically an expert on upper hell – the first four circles. Here, the damned were punished for the sins of the wolf. The lustful are battered by ultra storms and black tornados, the gluttons live in vile pits of muck while being relentlessly bombarded by hail, freezing rain and snow. Massive swarms of flies and hornets attack the agnostics while the wrathful spend their afterlives ripping each other apart. The hoarders and spendthrifts are forced to push around heavy boulders for all eternity.

As he read through these events again, as he pictured them in his mind, a new sensation began to creep in. It happened so slowly that he could never have seen it coming. A contented smile etched across his face. Why? Because he was beginning to find pleasure in the torment of others – the satisfaction of seeing people punished for their wrongdoing.

Just to sharpen his expertise and to make certain he understood every aspect of Dante's journey thus far, he adhered to his decision to keep with upper hell for the next few days. When those days had passed, he was more than willing to figuratively allow his mind to step through the formidable city of Dis and pass into the realm of lower hell where the sins of the lion and the sins of the leopard would no doubt be punished with unimaginable ferocity.

And this was undeniably so. In the lower circles, the severity of the punishments increased tenfold as the inhabitants had to undergo excruciating suffering. They were burned in pits of fire, frozen in lakes of ice, forced to eat each other's brains and torn apart by the various demons that lurked within these dominions. These souls would never find peace in death, for they recovered only to undergo this torture again and again for eternity. After several more months of exposure to this grisly material, Benny had fully accepted and embraced the story. It now made perfect sense why Papa loved it also. There was some sort of primal pleasure he took from the violence and before long, it got to the point where he couldn't get enough. He began craving it. Sometimes he would wake early, eagerly watching the seconds tick by on his plastic wristwatch, desperate for Papa to leave for his daily meetings at the museum. As soon as that front door shut at two till nine each morning, Benny's legs could not get him to the den fast enough.

And what about Papa? Now that Inferno was becoming so familiar to Benny, he was able to step back from its gripping confines and once again take a look at the big picture. In doing so, he realized he was no closer to discovering the truth than he had been before ever setting foot in the den. If anything, he was even farther from a point of understanding. The missing pieces were substantial: the man Papa met every day, the Dante Museum, the machine gun toting guard, and the biggest piece of all – the black book. What kind of ultra-valuable item would warrant such extreme measures for its protection? The black book was handled delicately with gloves, locked in not one, but two safes and perhaps the very reason why a guard was required to watch over the back entrance to the museum. Since this book was either locked away or kept securely on Papa's person, Benny knew his chances of getting his hands on it were highly improbable. Nonetheless, the yearning to have just five minutes alone with the book manifested as a deep ache within his gut. For now, he was stuck.

Though he was more than content sneaking into the den each and every day to study The Inferno like a seasoned scholar, the familiar inclination to learn more began its progressive return. He needed to get back to the drawing board, to come up with another well-devised plan to crack the code that was his father. It only made sense to start at the beginning, and this meant educating himself on the book's author, Dante Alighieri. The first idea came without much deliberation - visit the Dante Museum. What better place to learn about the individual of interest than his own dedicated shrine? But, as logic swept into the picture, he realized that venturing to the same place Papa went everyday was not only impractical, it was downright dim-witted. The last thing he needed was for someone to recognize Marcello's boy lurking around the museum, or to be spotted by Marcello himself. Should this come to pass, his cover would be blown for sure.

Since Papa had never bothered to equip the house with Internet, the next resort was to pedal over to the public library and obtain some information from there. However, the more he thought about it, the more he realized that this too was risky. It was a very real possibility that he would come across someone he knew or someone who knew Papa. The perceived conversation played through his head, "Marcello, I saw your boy Benny in the library the other day. He was reading a biography on Dante. I've never seen a child that young researching Dante. He's following in your footsteps, Marcello."

Finally, he figured he might just ask his teachers at school about this 'Father of Italian Literature.' Benny was under the supposition, as were most children his age, that teachers knew everything, so it was certain that they would be more than capable of providing insight. After giving it some thought, he became unconvinced that even this was such a good idea. His reasoning was that he knew nothing about Dante - except that he had written a book about hell. How would this question be received by a Catholic school? How would a teacher handle a young boy asking about such a man? This approach was just as likely to yield a simple answer as it was to elicit a phone call to Papa asking where his son had ever been exposed to such material. Either way, it wasn't worth the risk and Benny remained trapped in an ineffectual limbo land.

As it would happen, he would never learn a drop of additional information about Dante while living at the house. This was because in just a few weeks, a magnanimous mistake would be made that would change everything.

6

It was late autumn. School had since resumed and Benny had no other choice but to wait until the weekend to sneak into the den and feed his addiction. The unseasonal cold that infiltrated Florence this year had rendered Papa very sick. He was not terminally ill or confined to a bed, but the stubborn man was a visible train wreck as he insisted on going about his daily routine while battling a hideous case of the flu. Because of this, his mind seemed to have gone on vacation. He sloughed about the house like a zombie, stubbornly intent on ignoring his illness. Since his cerebrum was closed until further notice, Papa made a mistake that would finally work out to Benny's advantage, giving him the break he had been waiting for.

This Saturday morning, Benny had awoken early. He had been chomping at the bit to reread a particularly interesting conversation between Virgil and Ulysses from canto twenty-six. After a relaxing stretch he slipped his bedhead through the neck hole of a stained tee shirt and made for the kitchen. Here, he found barely enough stale cereal left in the box to satisfy his morning hunger. He sat down at the table and ate slowly so that the slim portions would last longer. Since the television sitting atop the counter had shorted out months ago, his only source of mental stimulation was watching Papa shuffle about the house as if he were sleepwalking. His body seemed as though it were on some sort of autopilot as he slid into a warm coat in preparation for his trip to the Dante Museum. The flu had been hanging tightly for over a week, and at this point, Marcello should be on the upswing of recovery. Instead, Benny noted that he actually appeared sicker today than any other day thus far. There were puffy black bags under his eyes and simply keeping his eyelids from sliding back down over his bloodshot scleras seemed a challenge. His thin white hair was in disarray as he had taken no initiative to run a comb through it this morning. He was so weak that he slumped like a haystack, unable to maintain proper posture.

"Can I help you with anything?" Benny asked bravely, not sure where the sudden impulse to speak had come from. To this, Papa just shook his head faintly, as though he had barely acknowledged the question. He feebly pulled the messenger bag over his shoulder and shuffled out the door. Under the circumstances, the man had to be commended for his punctual two till nine departure. Benny finished the last few bites of cereal while replaying Papa's response to the question, perhaps searching for some relevance within the exchange. After a moment's deliberation, he realized that there was no relevance to be found, only the unadorned truth that he had been disregarded. He was used to this, so with hardened indifference he washed the cereal bowl then trotted enthusiastically to the private study to begin spilling over Dante's masterpiece.

He opened the door to the den and nearly jumped out of his skin at the sight before him. The iron case containing the black book was actually sitting upon the desk. The wall safe and the picture that typically concealed it were both hanging wide open. Benny racked his brains for an explanation, but then he understood. Papa's absent-minded condition caused him to forget the book for the first time. Gripped with mortal fear over the possibility of being discovered, Benny slammed the door shut and flew to the nearest window with a street view. He watched with vigilance, expecting Papa to return at any second, maybe on foot or perhaps in Paulo's burgundy sedan.

A half an hour slipped by during which time he had not abandoned his lookout post from the window. Each minute seemed like an hour as the white angel on his right shoulder did all in its power to tell the red demon on his left shoulder that it was brainless to risk going back into the den today. Papa was destined to return at any moment after realizing his folly. But it was only nine thirty. Where exactly was he at this time? The ristorante. The two men would just be sitting down to warm drinks. The significance of this revelation was that there was a small time gap in which Benny could take a quick peek at the book. It was certainly not full proof or without risk, but the craving was so strong it bordered on agonizing. The angel on his shoulder offered a million logical reasons why he shouldn't do it, but the demon on the other shoulder won the battle with a simple crooked grin. Acting on impulse and fueled by stale cereal and adrenaline, he ran like a gazelle back to the den.

Today, he didn't bother with taping off the chair's position nor did he take any extra time to observe the placement of the various items around the desk. It was more prudent to his situation that he confer every available second to his examination of the black book. Besides, if Papa was too sick to remember his sacred possession, it was unlikely that he'd notice minute changes about the den. Benny knelt in front of the iron case as if it were some kind of idol, and in the next instant, his heart sunk. Amidst the exhilaration, he had forgotten that the little safe was one that required a combination in order to be opened. He gazed dejectedly at the three combination wheels, swearing he could actually hear them laughing, mocking him, reminding him that even though he was so close, he was still so far away. Each wheel contained ten numbers, and their current scrambled position resided at 716.

Desperation was now the dominant factor guiding his decisions, and he wasn't going to give up. He tried to think of what three digit combination Papa would likely use. But, since he knew next to nothing about the man, there was no use in pouring over possibilities. He would simply have to guess. What other rational alternative did he have but to begin with 000 and work up? He knew this would be painfully time consuming, but it was really his only option, unless… something came to mind that sparked a faint glimmer of hope. His hands trembled as he moved the wheels to 666. He moved his hand to the lid – still locked.

Of course not. That would have been too obvious. Papa was not that ignorant. Down, but not defeated, he returned the wheels to 000 and prepared to have a go at lady luck. Just before he started however, he had one more idea, and this one seemed so far-fetched, he ridiculed himself for even considering it.

He moved the wheels back to their original 716 orientation and considered for a moment how his rusty bike lock, the one that remained coiled around the seat post until needed, also had a three wheel combination system. During the weeks he had been tracking Papa through the streets of Florence, he was using this lock several times a day. To ease the monotony of continuous unlocking, he resorted to moving only the first of the three wheels while leaving the other two untouched. This method expedited the process of unlocking the bike and getting on his way. Did Papa have the same idea?

He took a scrutinizing survey of the numbers 716 and prepared to put his preposterous theory to the test. There was no way... he clicked the leading wheel up to eight - 816, Benny's birthday. The iron case emitted a distinct clicking noise and the top popped slightly ajar. His heart thundered with pleasure as a joyous realization swept over. In the most subtle way, Papa had included Benny in his life. No wonder he had remembered his son's birthday each year because he looked at it on a daily basis. Benny basked in this heart-warming revelation for a quick moment before his mind pulled him back to the matter at hand. He opened the lid.

While lifting the book from the case, he felt an inexplicable phenomenon of something guiding his hands, urging him onward – it felt as though he wasn't alone. With a shudder, he looked upon the black book that now lay fully exposed on the desk in front of him. Though the cover was different in material, the symbol on the front was identical to the symbol on the other book; the nine circles, which of course he now understood to be the nine realms of Dante's hell. The cover was in good condition but the yellow-tinged pages made this book appear even older than the other. Was this the exact same book? If so, why had Papa put forth so much effort to maintain its fortification? There was only one way to find out. With a racing heart, he opened to the first page. Sure enough…

The Divine Comedy: Volume 1, Inferno
Dante Alighieri

After a quick first assessment from front to back, he discovered that it was the same book and the same story, but there was one profound variation that the black book had that the other did not. In this one, following each and every canto, there were several additional pages of detailed maps and diagrams. On the bottom of every illustration was Dante's signature, which made it all too clear why this book was so valuable. These drawings were not rendered by a professional artist. They were crude in nature, but aesthetic appeal was not Dante's intention as Benny soon came to realize. He turned through every page, skimming each with rapid efficiency just to be sure that all the words and content matched the other. As far as he could tell, they did.

Canto one, the main character of the story, the pilgrim who is Dante, finds himself lost in a dark, sunless forest. Though he is desperate to leave this place, each of the three possible paths leading out are blocked by a fierce beast – a leopard, a lion and a wolf. He is trapped. But then the ghost of the long since deceased, the Roman poet Virgil, appears before Dante offering assistance. Virgil informs him that the only way out of the forest is to take another path – a path straight through the underworld. Dante, seeing no other alternative, agrees to allow Virgil to lead onward. End canto one.

The next four pages were roughly sketched maps. The first was a bird's-eye view of a vast landscape, illustrating mountain ranges, cities, rivers, seas and large expanses of forests. Benny did not recognize the names of any of these landmarks. In the mid-upper quadrant of this map was a black X, placed upon a mountain range labeled, Acheron. He turned to the next page to find that this illustration was a view of the Acheron Mountains specifically. The X was again present and now that things had been zoomed in, so to speak, it was easier to decipher its location. The map on the following page was of the same area only zoomed in much closer, focusing on a large lake situated between two mountains. And there, on what appeared to be a small outcrop of land, the X resided.

The final page before the initiation of canto two focused only on the outcrop and surrounding forest. There were three separate paths through the woods denoted by dotted lines. Each path led to the center of the outcrop where the letter X was positioned. The tiny inscription beneath the X read...

ENTRANCE TO THE UNDERWORLD.

Benny froze, gripped by a terrifying realization. It became instantly apparent what Papa and his friends were doing - they were actually trying to find the doorway to hell. The thrill of figuring it out, of finally knowing what Marcello was doing with his life was instantly eclipsed by a disturbing awareness. His stomach twisted in knots and beads of sweat materialized on his forehead while considering the significance of this discovery. The significance was that he could no longer hold out hope that hell was just a fictional location designed to scare feeble-minded humans into being good. Based on the evidence from the black book, hell was not a fantasy world. It actually existed just as Dante had described. Papa must have figured this out long ago. But had he and his cohorts succeeded in finding the entrance? Were their daily meetings collaborative efforts to decipher the exact location? Were they planning an expedition to the Acheron Mountain range in order to seek it out? And where exactly was this mountain range? Benny had not once heard the name during geography class. In canto three, there was a river by the name Acheron in which the souls of the damned were required to cross by way of ferry boat, but the other copy of Inferno had never mentioned a mountain range.

Just to confirm his suspicion, he flipped directly to the end of each canto and viewed the supplemental appendages; it was just as he had suspected. The exact path that Dante had taken through every vestibule of the underworld had been mapped out with specificity. He had also taken the time to create drawings of various people, places and creatures he had encountered along the way. All the fine details had been accounted for so that any person wishing to travel through the underworld would be guided in the right direction. But why, Benny wondered, would anyone need, or want for that matter, to take such a journey? Why would Papa…?

His thoughts stopped there. He gasped as the front door opened. There was no time to flee the den, no time to rewrap the book and lock it in the iron case. There was no time to do anything except curse himself for getting sloppy and for allowing desperation to cloud logic. When Marcello saw his son knelt in front of the sacred book, he froze with an expression impossible for Benny to read. There were several moments of silence, neither of them knowing what to say or where to begin.

Benny was downright petrified as Papa finally spoke. "Benny," he began in a weak, raspy voice. He removed a cloth handkerchief from the pocket of his wool coat and wiped his nose. "I've been very sick."

"I'm sorry," Benny interjected, but Papa put up a hand to silence him.

"I've been sick, and because of this, I made a tragic mistake. The tragedy is that you have now seen this book. You are so young, yet your eyes have beheld this priceless possession, this one object that could redefine, or even destroy the world should the wrong people discover its existence. I am glad that it has not been stolen or damaged, but this circumstance is very regretful nonetheless."

Benny could not find the words to express his apology. Even if he could, it was doubtful that Papa would be interested in sniveling justifications from his deviant son. Papa sighed deeply, remorsefully. It seemed that he was more upset with himself than the nosey sneak trespassing in his den. His next action took Benny by surprise.

Papa buried his fever-stricken face in his hand and muttered the muffled words, "No, no, no. Benny, no."

This made Benny feel as though he were two inches tall. He despised himself for bringing about such grief, though he did not understand the full extent or the reasoning behind Papa's anguish. Marcello collected himself, at least to the best of his ability and walked slowly to the corner of the room where an antique wooden chair took up occupancy. He dragged it weekly to the front of the desk and motioned for his son to have a seat. Benny complied without question. From amongst the fear and dread that currently coursed through his veins, a glimmer of optimism arose. It was obvious that Papa was about to address him, and this would be the first time in years that they would say more than a few words to each other.

Marcello took a seat in the rolling chair on the other side of the desk, the one Benny's backside knew so well after having sat there on a daily basis. This seating arrangement, an older man staring menacingly from the other side of a polished desk, reminded him of being back in the counselor's office, this time, the part of the counselor was being played by Papa.

Benny shamefully diverted his gaze to his knees, tapping them nervously with his fingers while awaiting the verdict. It seemed as though Papa was giving great consideration as to how to go about handling this situation. Finally, he said, "Benny, I would like for you to tell me everything that you have been up to, specifically as it relates to this book, and…" he opened the left drawer and removed the leather-bound edition, setting it gently next to its counterpart… "and this one. Your honesty will be the determining factor in my decision of how to handle this situation."

Benny took a long uneasy breath and decided that at this point it was all or nothing. What did he have to lose? Then, with an unsteady voice, he proceeded in disclosing the entire story. He recounted every last detail from the months of spying outside the door, to the incremental steps he took to follow Papa and his companion. He expounded on his measures to make certain the den was restored to the exact state in which he had left it. Next, he went into detail about the knowledge he acquired from The Inferno including how it had initially affected him and how it eventually drew him in with hypnotic allurement. Finally, he explained the events of this morning, how he guessed the combination, and what he found within the pages of the priceless copy.

Despite the negative energy and the uncertain state of affairs, he was actually relishing the moment. Papa had never given him this much attention before. He had never cared what Benny had to say about anything. Though Marcello listened without interruption, it was difficult for Benny to decipher his thoughts on the situation. His deepest aspiration at this point was that Papa would realize that he now shared a common interest with his son. Perhaps he would teach him more, maybe even take him along to the Dante Museum one day. In Benny's mind, nothing was more desirable than to finally establish a relationship with this man. - a man that despite his atrocious parenting, remained on a golden pedestal in the eyes of his son. When Benny had finally finished, and was satisfied that he had confessed everything, he waited anxiously for Papa's decree.

"So then, Benny," he said softly, between phlegmy coughs. "After everything you have learned, what do you suppose that my team and I are trying to accomplish?"

"I think you are trying to locate the entrance to the underworld," Benny replied so rapidly and with such enthusiasm he surprised himself.

To this, Papa nodded, not as an affirmative to Benny's claim, but more as an acknowledgement to a thought his mind had conjured during deep contemplation.

He then said to the bright-eyed boy staring from across the desk, "Benny, I'm going to tell you something," he said this with sorrow in his voice, and Benny could not understand the reasoning behind this remorseful tone. "I have not been the best father, and I make no excuses for that. All I can say in my defense is that I am sick. I'm not talking about this damned flu. No, Benny, I am sick in the head and it is because of this book." He pointed to the black one specifically. "The content within has become an obsession that consumes my life, and no matter how much I try, I cannot think or concentrate on anything else. At one point, I even sought help from, would you believe this, Dr. Pantoni, the same psychiatrist the school had assigned to you. But I did not need a professional to tell me that I had a problem because I already knew. More importantly, I did not want this problem to go away. I came to terms with my obsession and the only thing I could do was to turn this obsession into a career. I won't go into detail, Benny, but the man that you have seen traveling with me, funds my research - pays me to study these books hoping that I may discover something that will reimburse him a thousand times over. "Of course," he continued matter of factly, "the sad truth is I would have to kill him if we ever do find what we are looking for. You see, Benny, he is not the type of man who can be trusted to keep the secrets that are hidden within this book."

Benny's heart skipped several beats. Papa had to be kidding, however all signs pointed to the fact that he was being absolutely frank.

Papa went on, "Ours is a secret society. What we have learned and what we protect is crucial to the well-being of humanity." Suddenly, his eyes began to glaze over. "We have made a pact," he said as he unlocked a lower desk drawer with a key he had removed from his breast pocket, "a pact to do what is necessary to protect our secrets."

Tears began to trickle down his wrinkled cheeks. At this moment he looked so old and so tired, more so than Benny had ever seen him. He brought his hand up from behind the desk, and in it was a silver revolver. After this, everything became blurry for Benny. All of the horror from Dante's story couldn't hold a candle to the sheer dread he felt right now. There was nothing that could have prepared him for this. He was only twelve years old and about to witness the suicide of his own father, or so he thought. As if watching the scene unfold from outside his own body, he heard his father speak one more time.

"I'm so sorry, Benny," he was virtually sobbing now and his words were almost unrecognizable. "I hope you realize that this is the last thing I want to do." With that, he turned the gun not to his own head, but to his son.

Benny trembled violently when he realized what Papa was about to do. From somewhere deep within, a question arose. He did not know where it had come from. Maybe it was his brain's one last stab at gratification, one last attempt to understand this enigmatic man that was his father. Benny's last words were not a plea for his life, not a heartfelt expression of how he would love Papa no matter what. Instead, he simply asked, "Papa, what will you do if you find hell?"

The question would forever go unanswered. Marcello's unsteady finger squeezed the trigger. Benny's body instinctively lunged to the ground as the deafening shot echoed through the atmosphere. It took him a split second to assess that somehow, the bullet had not struck him. Acting on survival instinct and adrenaline, he leapt to his feet and dashed out of the den. There was another gunshot and the picture frame to his right exploded with shards of glass spilling into the air - another miss. Now it was too late for a third attempt because Benny was out the front door.

He heard Papa's mournful wail spewing from the house. And then, the gun went off one last time. Benny knew with certainty that this bullet had hit its intended target. He knew this because there were no more shots to follow. The sound of dog barking followed him as he sprinted breathlessly down the street in a state of panic.

7

Rose, Kansas – Present day.

From the time the doors open at four-thirty until ten o'clock closing, Vincent's Italian Restaurant was generally packed. In this neighborhood, Vincent's is the undisputed favorite. Its culinary reputation, along with the giant plate of fettuccine alfredo plastered to the billboard along Interstate 70, beckons to the hungry masses.

Alexis Lunden, a neatly kept waitress with a confident smile, glided through the network of tables balancing a cumbersome tray of food over her head. She was a phenomenal server, and her pretty face coupled with a gregarious personality earned her an impeccable reputation and a loyal following of repeat customers. After placing the steaming entrées on the table and garnishing each dish with a dusting of Romano cheese, Lex just happened to glance over her shoulder. Captivated, her bright green eyes widened with keen interest.

She watched as the hostess escorted three very intriguing people to her empty corner booth. Her heart started to beat a bit faster. It had been a long time, high school graduation in fact, since she had last seen them.

"Lex, you lucky dog," said Greta, catching Lex by surprise. Greta was cradling a stack of empty plates against her apron and beaming jealousy toward the corner booth. "I heard they're so rich they use Ben Franklins as toilet paper. You'll probably get a big ol' tip from the Cornfield Clan over there."

"It's the Prairie Pack," proclaimed Mary, another waitress who was just arriving for the evening. "They are no longer called the Cornfield Clan. That name was retired years ago."

Stephanie, a busser who had been working at Vincent's for at least two decades, traipsed by with pep in her step. Adding her two cents, she said, "Girls, you're both wrong. It's the Thrilling Three."

"It's the Rose Flock," Lex said, keeping her eyes fixated on the trio who were now skimming their drink menus. "A reporter on the evening news referred to them as the Rose Flock several years ago and that is what most people now call them."

"You're right," Greta agreed, "The Rose Flock. My God, is he a fox or what?"

Lex rightfully assumed that Greta was referring to Charlie Roanoke, the perceived ringleader of the Flock.

"He certainly is," Stephanie chimed, exhaling a passionate breath. "But that fox is spoken for and Jade Vandervelde is one young lady you do not want to cross."

"Remember the jogging incident?" Mary asked. "Jade beat that man within an inch of his life. He was twice her size and he had a knife."

Greta set the stack of plates on the bar and said, "He attacked Jade while she was out on an evening run and probably had scary intentions. Remember, he was later linked to several sexual assaults in Arizona and a murder in Nebraska – an absolute creep."

"He got what he deserved," Stephanie added. "Jade severed his right eye and rendered him a paraplegic. Someone told me she used his own knife to, um, make sure he would never reproduce," she concluded with a crooked smile.

Mary shivered, "I admire her, but she freaks me out. I've heard other stories."

"What about Sevastian Moskincov?" Greta asked Stephanie. "You got a thing for the short and portly or just the tall dark and handsome type like Charlie."

Stephanie thought for a moment, "The Russian Star Trek nerd doesn't really do it for me. Plus, he has a reputation for speaking his mind, speaking out of turn and speaking too much in general. I'll pass."

Though Lex barely knew Sevastian, she felt she should speak up in his defense. "Well, he is not a strapping jock or the beneficiary of physical attributes typically coveted by females but I remember he has a certain charisma. Despite his unkempt hair and the customary food stain residing on his expensive shirts, he had a whole lot of admirers back in high school."

"He certainly earned a high opinion from Charlie and Jade," Greta added. "Once they became friends, he never went back to Russia."

It wasn't just their secretive behavior or the thrilling tales of wonder that made the Flock so darn interesting, it was also their unfathomable wealth. Stories, or more appropriately, wild speculations, circulated through Rose about the means of their riches. Lex once heard from a neighbor that they dealt in online pharmaceuticals. Her hairstylist swore the three owned stock in Microsoft. Yet another popular rumor maintained that Charlie and company had invested early in electronic currency. But for all the presumptions, there was not one concrete answer as to how they had achieved such financial dominance during their teenage years.

Yes, they were rich but they weren't stingy. They gave generously to charities and donated considerable amounts of money to wildlife conservation groups. The Roanoke Public Library, which it is now called, was able to double in square-footage thanks to a sizable contribution from Charlie. Despite this charitable reputation, many thought the Flock to be pompous and greedy. This supposition might have arisen because they never accepted anyone new into their inner circle, desiring to keep the wealth amongst themselves. However, like almost everything about the enigmatic trio, this was just an assumption.

The Flock had the irresistible combination of brains, money and mystery, and that was what made the thrilling three, thrilling. In Lex's opinion, there was a fine line between thrilling and intimidating as she reluctantly approached their table. A swarm of butterflies, or collywobbles as her mother used to call them, fluttered in her stomach. The Flock was engrossed in the menu and for a moment, did not notice the pony-tailed waitress with the timid smile.

"Good evening," piped Lex as enthusiastically as possible, determined to suppress her apprehension. "Welcome to Vincent's." Charlie, Sevastian and Jade looked up from their menus with casual smiles.

"Alexis Lunden," Charlie greeted rather pleasantly. "It's been a while."

Lex was especially flattered that Charlie Roanoke knew her name. After all, they had only spoken a few times in school. Desperate to make a good impression, she fumbled for the perfect response. "That's right, seventh period gym class," she recalled, acting as though it was a difficult memory to resurrect. As though she hadn't remembered the way his triceps rippled when he did push-ups or his uncanny ability to dominate dodge ball or the beads of sweat that trickled down his sun-kissed skin after rugby. "Seems like a lifetime ago. What, five years now?"

Sevastian spoke up, apparently having no intention of adhering to the subject. With a thick Russian accent he asked, "Alexis, do you think I've slimmed down since the last time you've seen me? Answer me honestly now." His eyes narrowed at Charlie. "My friend here has been making many remarks to the contrary and I would like someone to set him straight."

Lex was taken aback by this absurd and ill-timed question. Jade and Charlie began to snicker at their chubby friend's inquiry. Supposing that Sevastian had actually put on a bit of weight since high school, she decided to do what any normal person would do in that situation – lie. "It's been a while of course, but yeah. You certainly appear trimmer than I remember."

A smile transformed across Sevastian's face as his day had just been made. "A new pill," he declared. "Taken once a day it suppresses one's appetite and boosts metabolism. I told you, Charlie," he boasted with an arrogant upward tilt of the head. "I told you I'm getting skinnier. There is more slack in my pants than there used to be."

"That's because you bought bigger pants," Charlie replied. "Anyway, it was *your* idea that I should tirelessly harass you so you'd be motivated to get in better shape. I'm just holding up my end of the deal."

"I've told you a thousand times, I had been drinking when I made that request," Sevastian snapped back. "I will never again buy middle-shelf vodka. This is what happens."

Lex suppressed an urge to giggle as the boys began to bicker back and forth. A few playful insults were thrown around before Jade redirected them back to civilized discourse.

"Sevastian! Charlie! Sorry to interrupt your charming conversation, but I'm sure Alexis has other customers. Why don't we just give her our drink order, eh?" The boys immediately cooled off and Charlie took the liberty to order a round of Italian beer for the others.

"All right then, three Peronis. Would anyone care for an appetizer?"

At the word "appetizer" Sevastian's face lit up like a Christmas tree. Scarcely allowing her to finish the question, he began to spew out his request. "I would like one order of fried zucchini, one order of mozzarella sticks, and one… no, two orders of the spicy calamari."

"You bet," said Lex, flashing him a friendly smile. "I'll be right back with your drinks."

No sooner did she turn from the table when she found herself surrounded by a mob of fellow employees. All were dying to hear what she had to say about the Rose Flock. The questions were coming so rapidly, she couldn't make heads nor tails of them. There hadn't been this much excitement about a customer since last April when the Chief's quarterback had stopped in after a training camp in Wichita. The Flock, however, were not celebrities or famous athletes. Their eminence stemmed from the compelling stories and the hearsay of the star-struck locals.

Despite the desire to mind her own business, she could not

discount the reality that her own curiosity was getting the best of her. She longed to know more about her intriguing guests, so despite a guilty conscience, she made an attempt to eavesdrop on their conversation while waiting on surrounding tables. Doing this proved useless. The three talked very quietly amongst themselves. It appeared as though they were taking every precaution to keep stray ears out of their discussion.

Charlie, Jade and Sevastian stayed for almost two hours. The substantial amount of food they had consumed would impress any competitive eater. They ate as if it was their last meal, or their first in a long time. After a polite thank you, they shuffled out of Vincent's. As Sevastian snatched a handful of peppermints from the bowl by the doorway, Lex noticed that he had unbuttoned his pants to accommodate an extra inch or so in his stomach. She then hurried to a nearby window and watched intently as they piled into a vintage Hummer and drove off into the sultry night. Her heart was still racing inexplicably.

Upon returning to their booth to collect the credit card receipt and begin clearing away empty dishes, she noticed that they had left her a note, a generous tip and a piece of candy. The note read, "Thank you for the wonderful service." A friendly note, though always appreciated, was not something new. She received them all the time from satisfied patrons and drunken businessmen. What she found to be particularly curious was the candy. It was supposed to be her job to drop off a few mints to the customers, not vice versa. It was neatly wrapped in an intricate green paper with no brand name or content description. Hesitantly, she peeled off the paper from what appeared to be a chocolate mint. Now the trivial part – to eat it or not to eat it? To eat it would contradict everything she was taught as a child about taking candy from strangers.

"Since they were so kind to leave it, it would be simply rude to let it go to waste," she thought out loud. "Oh, what the hell." She popped the candy into her mouth and instantly decided this was among the best decisions she had ever made. It was nothing less than a slice of heaven. The chocolate mint sensation saturated her taste buds with a purely perfect flavor. When it had finally dissolved, she made a mental note to find out where these delectable gems were sold.

Her impression of the Rose Flock was now altered. Giving her tables one final wipe down, she recalled how friendly they were. Her interaction with them had been smooth and comfortable, almost like conversing with old friends. Yet, it was undeniably strange that they were so blatantly secretive in their behavior. They were inconspicuously vigilant, taking heed to cease conversation each time someone strayed too close to their table. Lex found it only reasonable to assume that they were hiding something.

8

On this perfect Kansas night, lightning bugs flashed from the dark fields like millions of tiny photographers. The convertible top was down and the warm summer wind blew through Lex's almond brown hair as she headed home. It had been a good night as far as waitressing was concerned. Customers had tipped generously and she had not spilled a single drink. But it wasn't the pocket full of cash that made her spirits soar, rather the chemistry that she seemed to share with Charlie Roanoke and his crew. She just couldn't stop her mind from replaying the interaction.

At that moment she realized she was becoming infatuated, just like the rest of Rose. But that couldn't be; she was better than that. She often theorized that the arrogance and conceit of pop idols was fueled by excessively worshiping fans. These celebrity-crazed lunatics spent absurd amounts of time obsessing about the new hairstyle or the new boyfriend or the new diet of their favorite movie stars. Of course, she was nowhere near that level of obsession, but remained disappointed in herself for caring so much about three people she barely knew. Her thoughts about the evening were momentarily sidetracked as the convertible approached a familiar destination. Always happy to be home, she eased into the red cobblestone driveway of Aunt Claire's lake house.

Lex's aunt, Claire Lunden, was someone a Rose local might call a "hoot." She was a jolly, boisterous extrovert who could talk the leg off a chair. The woman was windy as April, sweet as honey and had an interesting past. Thirteen years ago, she lived in Los Angeles and played the lead role in a critically acclaimed drama series. After many years on set and nine successful seasons, a romantic relationship had developed with a co-star named Jonathan Waterhouse. She and Jonathan married in Vegas and decided they'd had enough of big city living and paparazzi harassment. It was time to live a simpler life. After the final season, they moved to Rose after signing the mortgage papers on an attractive Cape Cod on Loon Lake. It took all of eleven months before Jonathan realized that he missed the limelight. One fall morning, Claire woke up to an empty bed and an inconsiderately vague text message explaining that he had a change of heart and was moving back to LA. According to friends, the happy-go-lucky Claire didn't so much as bat an eye at her husband's unexpected departure. She loved Rose, and Rose is where she stayed.

Claire was born and raised in Staffordshire, England along with the rest of her immediate family. She graduated from the University of Exeter with a degree in drama and landed the acting job in America soon thereafter. Leaving England, however, meant separating from her best friend - her younger sister, Olivia.

Olivia, Lex's mother, was a free-spirited intellectual with a feminist edge. She reaped satisfaction from volunteering at wildlife rescues, parading about at women's rights demonstrations and reading tedious science textbooks - the ones with large pages and small words. Most of all she enjoyed tending to a postcard-worthy flower garden behind her little brownstone cottage. Claire had tried on many occasions to persuade Olivia that her gift of smarts would be put to good use as a physician or perhaps in law. Olivia on the other hand had no desire to pursue either of those paths. Instead, she opened a little sandwich shop on a busy street corner specializing in locally grown organic foods. Financially she did rather well for herself, but the monetary success fell short of the personal fulfillment attained from lowering the town's collective cholesterol and supporting the local farmers from whom the raw ingredients were purchased.

Olivia had but one serious relationship in her life and from it, she acquired three things – a lesson in fly-by-night romance, a short-lived heartache and thirty-nine weeks later, a precious baby girl. The unconditional love and immeasurable joy Olivia felt as a new mummy trumped the sting of a sudden breakup. Seven pounds, five ounces, bald with meracious green eyes, baby Alexis was more precious to Olivia than anything else in the universe.

As a natural intellectual, Olivia nourished Alexis' mind with a steady diet of education. Taking the homeschool route, she taught her daughter at a rate and level which far exceeded any that would have been offered by England's state schools. By the age of eight, Lex was practicing geometry, reciting anatomical structures and reading Shakespeare.

Alexis and Olivia were very close. Whether at the sandwich shop tending to customers or taking a morning stroll in the park, Lex was happiest in her mother's company. Perhaps her fondest memories were of Olivia's enchanting bedtime stories. On any given night as the England fog settled outside the window, she'd lay in bed while her mother spun sagas of far away lands, magical creatures and of course, a beautiful princess named Alexis. The story's end was a destination Lex could never reach. How desperately she yearned to hear the quintessential happily-ever-afters, but the sandman's tantalizing lure would never grant the privilege.

For the first decade of Lex's life, her world was filled with a plethora of good times, laughter and love – three key ingredients for a happy, healthy child. But her world would soon be turned upside-down. On a gloomy Saturday during the brunch rush at the sandwich shop, she watched in terror as her mother suddenly collapsed to the floor. In an unconscious state, Olivia laid there until the medics arrived. To her traumatized daughter, this seemed like an eternity.

After several days and numerous tests, the medical team discovered a malignant tumor in the recesses of Olivia's brain. Soon thereafter, the discovery was made that the cancer had metastasized to the spinal cord. This was a death sentence with a prognosis of less than a year to live. It might have been for the best that she died the very next month because it hastened the inevitable. She also avoided the suffering, which was predicted to increase with each passing day. These thoughts, however, did little to comfort Lex. She took it as hard as one could take the unexpected death of a mother and a best friend. Claire was Lex's guardian. Following the funeral, she helped her heartbroken niece pack up for the start of a new life in the United States.

To Lex, it had all seemed so long ago; the little cottage in Staffordshire, the sandwich shop, the bedtime stories and her mother's warm embrace. All that remained were cherished memories and an English accent which remained razor sharp thanks to hanging around Claire. As days went by, and the activities of her new life forced those memories farther into the back of her mind, it sometimes seemed like it had never happened at all. She reflected on this as she sat on the porch swing with Aunt Claire and watched a white moon rise over Loon Lake.

"How was work tonight?" asked Claire as she took a sip of coffee, wincing in pain from the scalding beverage. Lex wondered why her aunt insisted on repeating this absurd tongue-burning ritual night after night.

"About the same as always, except…, Aunt Claire, you've heard of the Rose Flock, haven't you?"

"Most peculiar buggers in town, who hasn't heard of them? Why do you ask?"

"They came into Vincent's tonight and I served them. I'll agree they were a little peculiar, but quite charming overall."

Aunt Claire showed minimal interest. "I heard they were snobby."

"Oh, that's what everybody says about rich people," Lex stated somewhat defensively. "In fact, they were polite, pleasant and good conversationalists. I really enjoyed them." Claire remained unimpressed as she continued to stubbornly sip at the smoldering decaf. "I have a very good sense of character," Lex added very matter of factly.

"It's a pity you didn't use your good sense of character

with Jonathan," Claire joked. "You could have stopped that trainwreck of a marriage before it started. Oh, and speaking of which, have you heard the new song, "Trainwreck", by Annie Marie Bailey?"

Lex nodded, "I heard it during my drive to work this afternoon. A disconcerting title but a beautiful tune."

"It certainly is," Claire agreed. She then asked hopefully, "Would you sing it for me?"

Lex replied with a guilty grimace, "Forgive me, Aunt Claire, I'm a bit knackered for a porch swing solo. Perhaps tomorrow?"

"I'll hold you to that," Claire promised. "You don't sing for me as much as you used to. I dare say you would put Annie Marie Bailey to shame with that angelic voice of yours."

Lex laughed. "And that is why I'm declining to perform. I don't wish to make Miss Bailey look bad."

It was, by most anyone's standards, a perfect evening. A cool breeze whisked off the lake, taking the edge off the humidity. Fireflies danced over the grass and down near the shore. The silhouette of a pair of swans traveled slowly across an inlet before disappearing behind a patch of cattails. The moon and its reflection on the lake provided an ethereal glow over it all. Lex was happy to be there with her aunt. Even though Claire's personality and physical appearance differed from Olivia's, she could still catch a glimpse of her mother from time to time.

As the minutes lazily passed and Aunt Claire's coffee mug had been long since emptied, Lex realized that she was still dwelling on the Flock. By this time, the encounter had been rehearsed in her mind about a hundred times. She remembered every look, word and gesture that had been exchanged. She was unsure why the three had successfully stirred her interest so profoundly but assumed that it would soon be forgotten after a good night's sleep. Little did she realize the folly of her assumption.

9

Lex had a dream that night unique to anything her mind had ever generated. It began as she was cradled like a small child, held aloft by a soft cloud. With sleepy eyes, she gazed upward to the midnight sky of twinkling stars and hazy galaxies. A peaceful lullaby filled the air. The omnipresent notes were pure and perfect, as they seemed to rain down from the heavens. Her senses became saturated in complete relaxation. Everything felt so real – a little too real.

Suddenly the cloud around her began to dissipate. The precious barrier between earth and sky was fading quickly, yet she remained at ease. Once it had vanished, she instinctively stretched her arms outward like a fledgling on its maiden flight and began to soar. It was the most amazing sensation she had ever felt within a dream. Above, there were three moons, two of them crescent and one nearly full. The lunar trio cast a placid illumination on the landscape below.

Floating over this breathtaking land, she observed crystal ponds, emerald forests, and in the distance, dark snow-capped mountains. Ahead, a peaceful glade came into view. The sole occupant of this grassy clearing was an ancient willow, projecting its labyrinth of branches upward as if reaching out to her, beckoning her to come down. In a state of absolute bliss, she pulled her arms in and began an exhilarating swan dive. She came to a gentle landing near the tree. A fresh breeze rolled across the earth sending symmetric ripples through the grass and rustling the branches of the massive willow. Although she was now grounded, the weightless sensation remained.

Suddenly a human figure stepped from the shadows of the tree into the moonlight. Upon recognition of this mysterious stranger, her jaw dropped before turning upward in a cheerful smile. "Charlie?" she cried. "Where are we?"

"You're dreaming," he replied.

"It's hard to tell this is a dream, everything's so real."

"I know," he said. "This is no ordinary dream. I figured this would be a good place for us to talk."

Lex cocked her head with interest, "Talk?"

"There is something you possess that makes you unique to any other person who has ever existed. You have hidden attributes, rare qualities hidden deep within - a diamond in the rough if you will."

"I don't understand," she replied.

"At this point, I don't fully understand it either," he said cryptically. He turned his gaze toward the sky with moonlight twinkling in his eyes. "The universe is an amazing, unfathomable thing." He then looked into the eyes of the dreamer and said warmly, "I know very little about you, Alexis, but the one thing I do know is that you are here because you are supposed to be. There are forces of nature that work in mysterious ways, ways that are premeditated and manipulative. I've always had this theory that the universe is a living, breathing entity and as such, must function like all other living things, that is, to assure its own survival. And therefore…here you are."

Lex smiled over the lunacy of it all. "I have no idea what that means," she declared honestly.

"Maybe not, but you will. We all will I assume."

Abruptly, a fog rolled in and the world began to evaporate. The soft grass began to transform into a linen bedspread. "I don't want this to end," she pleaded.

She heard his voice once more. "We'll meet again, Alexis."

"Charlie, you don't have to call me Alexis, you can call me

Lex. Charlie? Charlie!" She opened her eyes to the morning sun pouring through the open windows. "No!" she beckoned. "Come back!"

She closed them again, desperately trying to grasp any remnants of the dream, but it was gone. With glassy irises, she lay there for a few moments in utter stupefaction. The feeling she had just experienced was beyond words and beyond this world. With the sensation being steadily whisked away by the lake breeze pushing in through the bedroom windows, she could only focus on the last thing she said to Charlie. "You don't have to call me Alexis, you can call me Lex," she muttered contemptuously to herself, "Of all the stupid things to say."

10

Saturday morning was usually a time for veggie omelets, scrolling mindlessly through social media and relaxation. This morning, Lex decided to deviate from her standard routine in order to preserve the remaining images of the dream. She feared that stimulation of any kind would interfere with the hint of nirvana that lingered. She filled a bowl with cornflakes and took it to the front porch swing so she could watch the boats on the lake while eating. This morning, like every other Saturday, Aunt Claire was at her weekly appointment with the massage therapist. It was a tinsel town tradition that she had no intention of giving up.

Saturday mornings also meant gymnastics practice. Although Lex was not taking classes during the summer semester, she still met with her team once a week to keep the edges sharp. Gymnastics were a major part of her life thanks to Olivia's persuasive influence. As a child, Lex would quickly choose reading and studying over physical activities, but her mother must have seen potential in her scrawny little bookworm.

"Alexis, darling, you need to exercise your body as well as your mind," Olivia had said while literally dragging her reluctant daughter to the first gymnastics lesson. It only took a few more sessions before gymnastics transformed from a mere Tuesday evening appointment into a passion. After thousands of handsprings, aerial cartwheels and perfectly stuck landings, young Lex had found herself amongst the most competitive gymnasts in Staffordshire.

By ten-thirty her gym bag was packed and she was on the

road to Wichita. The thirty minute drive to the college was quality down time to relax and let her mind wander through thoughts. Of course today, it didn't wander far from the dream.

What did it mean? she thought. *Why was it only Charlie and not the others? What was the meaning of all that universe mumbo jumbo? How on earth was it so real?*

The questions might have strung all the way to the Wichita city limits if a green road sign had not derailed her train of thought. It simply read,

County Road 13 Next Right.

This was not just any road as she was fully aware. County Road 13 wound back through an ocean of corn, wheat and soybean fields, and ultimately to the mansion of the Rose Flock. "I can't believe you're even thinking about it," she said to herself in a punitive tone. "You're going to do it aren't you? You'd better not. You'd better..." At the last second she whipped her car onto County Road 13 with the rationale of taking the scenic route, but deep down there was no denying her true intention.

Frustrated, but driving onward nonetheless, she continued to mutter self-disciplinary slurs. "I can't believe what I'm doing. This is one step away from stalking them. Next thing you know, I'll be camping out in the bushes with a pair of binoculars and a long-range camera." She had no intention of going up to the door and saying hi, but the dream made her desperate to see Charlie again, if only one more time. Maybe, just maybe he would be outside and she could catch one quick appeasing glimpse. As guilty as she felt about the decision to pull a casual drive-by, she kept on going in that direction as if some unseen force was compelling her to do so.

As the black sports car crested a small hill, she could see the massive stone mansion in the distance. It had been many years since she had been this way and looked upon this grand structure. It was an architectural anomaly straight out of the Renaissance.

This awe-inspiring home was certainly remarkable, but the real attention grabber was that Charlie had been only eighteen when he hired a renowned French architect to design and build it. It was a truly impressive home that begged the question - where is the line between mansion and castle? Many stories in height, its solid walls of white marble glistened in the morning sun. Kissing the blue sky in a glorious display of vertical dominance were four cylindrical towers of varying structural design. Each tower was adorned with scores of winged sculptures that were slightly indistinguishable from Lex's vantage point. Nothing could be more out of place on this windswept prairie. Surrounding the mansion were desolate grass fields stretching to the horizon with intermittent patches of trees sprinkled here and there.

As she drew near, she slowed the convertible just enough to remain somewhat inconspicuous. A surge of excitement shot through her body when she noted three familiar figures in the front yard. There were large leafy oak trees and thick rows of boxwood shrubs impeding her view, but she was still able to acquire enough quick peeks to determine what Charlie and his crew were up to.

With a white two-piece covering a tanned body, Jade was laid back on a lawn chair reading a book while Charlie and Sevastian seemed to be practicing some sort of martial art. They battled each other almost rhythmically with long wooden broom handles in what seemed like a friendly combat scenario.

In the blink of an eye, the mansion was in her rear view mirror. The drive-by was quick and inexplicably satisfying. *The dream made me do it*, she thought. *Who knows, that might be the last time I ever see them.* That consideration enticed her to try for one more quick glance. She looked back over her shoulder.

At that very second, Charlie wheeled around and looked directly at her. Taking advantage of his distracted opponent, Sevastian slammed his broomstick across Charlie's hand. Charlie's stick was expelled through the air and he began shaking the sting from his fingers, all the while his eyes remained fixated on the car. Sevastian threw his arms up victoriously. Lex gasped, turned back to the road and stepped on the gas.

"Oh my god," she said to herself now feeling like a bleeding idiot. "How did he...? It's like I called out to him. But he couldn't have possibly recognized me. He doesn't know this car. He doesn't really know me." That thought mollified her angst as she turned back onto the main road toward the city. She decided at that point to wash her hands of Charlie and his preposterous Rose Flock. She cranked up the music and tried to forget about the dream.

11

Sunrise, sunset – the summer days were rapidly passing. This prompted Lex to take advantage of her free time because the final semester of college was quickly approaching. She spent mornings training at the gym and evenings relaxing with friends. Afternoons were always reserved for tea and Banbury tarts with Aunt Claire.

Several times a week, she would drive to Sunnybrook Stables to see her oldest and dearest friend – a dappled palomino named Boc. Boc was a "welcome to America" gift from Aunt Claire when Lex first arrived here all those years ago. During her childhood in Staffordshire, she became quite an equestrian enthusiast and on several occasions competed at an annual dressage meet in Scotland with a beautiful Friesian that belonged to her mother. After Olivia's passing, the horse was sold to a family friend. As far as Claire was concerned, buying her heartbroken niece a new horse could only result in a positive outcome. She was right.

The name Boc was an acronym which stood for Blue Oyster Colt. A young Lex thought that it was a clever play on words, not to mention a proper memorial, to name her new horse after her mother's favorite band. These days, Boc was too old for aggressive riding, but he still had the juice for relaxing trots along the wooded trails behind the stables. These summer rides were therapeutic and they allowed Lex the opportunity to think, relax and breathe the fresh prairie air.

On a long ride, she would often ponder her plans for the future. For the time being, the dream was medical school; in particular she longed to specialize in oncology. Influenced by what had happened to her mother, it had been a prominent goal to be in the mix of groundbreaking cancer research. If for some reason medicine didn't work out, she had but one alternative – open her own boarding stable. There was no doubt a drastic difference in income between the two careers but happiness was paramount. Money or no money, she didn't need the finer things in life. As long as there were family, friends, free time and enough cash to pay the bills, she would be completely satisfied.

Like many singles in their early twenties, there was the dream of love and romance. She spent a great deal of time in a reverie about her wedding day and sifting through many possible faces of a future husband. She imagined nestling beside him watching the Caribbean sunset on their honeymoon or picking out a house together. She wondered how many children she would have and what they might look like. What would their names be? She bemused herself with the thought of being the quintessential soccer mom, lounging in a folding chair next to all the other parents at a Saturday morning game. Would she succumb to driving a minivan and living in a cookie-cutter neighborhood full of neatly primped lawns and clean vinyl siding? She wouldn't rule it out. For some reason the typical American dream of white picket fences and yellow Goldendoodles seemed inexplicably appealing to her. Sometimes she would fall so deep into thought that she lost track of time and location. Fortunately for this daydreaming jockey, Boc had walked these trails a million times. He would never allow them to get lost.

By the time fall semester rolled around, Lex was anxious to return to school and finish her pre-medical biology degree. Despite all that she had so far accomplished in the academic realm, a Mount Everest still loomed on the horizon, standing between her and a diploma. This immense obstacle was a class by the name of Advanced Concepts in College Calculus. Lex hated math. It wasn't that she lacked the intelligence to do it, rather, the motivation. She had been putting off this particular class for three and a half years, and now it was crunch time – take it, or not graduate.

Two weeks into the new semester, she found that her fear had been legit - calculus was killing her. It was an innate loathing of the subject coupled with a bad case of "senioritis" that gave her a difficult time reaching deep within for the incentive to study the material. Her brain, as if on strike, simply refused to accept this unwanted knowledge. The evening before the first big exam found her a nervous, unprepared wreck. She was a bat on a sticky wicket and worst of all, she had to work.

"I hope I can get out of here at a reasonable hour," she said to Greta, looking to score a little sympathy. Greta was also in college and could certainly appreciate the stress of a looming exam. These were the nights that, in accordance with Murphy's law, you would always be the last server on the floor.

"The last few Tuesdays have died down early anyway," Greta said encouragingly as she loaded a serving tray with a colorful array of drinks from the bar. "I'd bet you'll be out of here by nine."

Lex sighed, "I hope you're right." With a hint of contempt in her eye, she regarded a gathering of five middle-aged women cackling chaotically over a fresh round of martinis. "But those ladies over there, table twenty-three, might as well have brought their tents and sleeping bags, because they've been camping out the entire night so far. I have a feeling they'll be here until we close."

Greta's consoling expression abruptly changed to one of delight. "Lex, look who just sat down at your empty table!" Lex turned to see. All of a sudden, the butterflies returned, the repressed images of the dream burst free, and the unexplainable excitement thundered through her like a freight train – it was Charlie and Sevastian. "I'm jealous," Greta said, snapping Lex from her trance. "That's one good lookin' boy over there."

Lex giggled, "I'll be sure to slip Sevastian your number."

"Not Sevastian," Greta retorted in good sport. "Charlie! Although I wouldn't mind dating a rich foreigner like Sevastian Moskincov. With all that money I could surely put up with a little pudge."

Lex laughed and decided that she was very happy to see them. Besides, what better way to take her mind off the exam than to be distracted by Charlie's eyes, or smile, or… she inhaled deeply and took a moment to gain her composure.

"Charlie and Sevastian, right?" she greeted cheerfully. Of course, she knew full well who they were, but decided to act as if they weren't important enough to be certain. She was already worried that Charlie had spotted her that day she drove by his mansion.

"Hello," said Sevastian cordially. He then got right to the point, "I would like a bottle of your finest chianti and three orders of mozzarella sticks to start."

"Sevastian is on a diet," Charlie informed Lex with an energetic grin. "Tonight, he's only getting three orders of mozzarella sticks instead of five."

"Oh, spare me your sarcasm!" Sevastian growled, emphasizing his irritation by shaking his fist. "I need some fried food every once in a while. I haven't had any for…," he thought for a tick, "it's been at least a year."

Lex could have easily informed Sevastian that he was mistaken. It had been only two months since that fateful evening when she had the mind-boggling dream. She remembered their appetizer order to a tee: fried calamari, fried zucchini, fried mozzarella. This proved once again that she was uncharacteristically obsessed. She felt irritated with herself for having zero control over her infatuation.

"We requested to have you as our server, Alexis," said Charlie. "You did such a good job last time, we figured we might as well leave good enough alone, right?"

Lex smiled appreciatively. She could see that Charlie at least remembered something about his last visit. "I'll try for a repeat performance," she graciously replied.

Their stay at Vincent's went much like the last time. Charlie and Sevastian ordered an outlandish amount of food and gobbled it up like ravenous wolves. Lex wondered how Charlie kept such a lean physique. The way he ate, at least tonight, would make any nutritionist cringe. Even Sevastian should be morbidly obese rather than moderately portly with the way he devoured multiple plates of buttery clam linguini. The two were certainly a conundrum and they were doing exactly what she hoped they would do – distract her from tomorrow's daunting task.

"Where's Jade tonight?" she asked as she dropped off their check, knowing it was really none of her business.

"She wanted sushi and we wanted Italian so we split up," Sevastian answered while massaging his belly, as if to manually aid the digestion process.

"Alexis, this will no doubt seem unusual for me to ask you this," Charlie began slowly with an air of reservation. Her heart raced. In that split second she thought of a million different things that he might possibly ask her. And then, "Do you have any metal in your body?"

"Um... I'm not sure I understand," she replied, trying to mask her initial expression of *What the...?*

"Sometimes when a person breaks a bone badly enough, a metal plate or rod must be inserted for supplemental support. Do you have anything like that?"

"No, not at all."

"What about metal caps on your teeth?" he continued.

"No metal caps either," she answered knowing there must be a legitimate reason why he would ask such a bizarre question. "Why do you ask?"

"Never mind," he stuttered, seeming a tad humiliated. "Please forget I mentioned it." His next task was to quickly change the subject. "Anyway, Alexis, I can't help but notice that you seem kind of distant. Don't get me wrong, your waitressing tonight was totally on point but perhaps your mind is elsewhere? Is something troubling you?"

Although she had been putting forth a strong attempt to veil her anxiety, the effort had apparently been a failure – that, or Charlie was profoundly intuitive. "Is it that obvious?" she asked, somewhat embarrassed. "Yeah, I'm not going to lie, I have a calculus exam tomorrow and my comprehension of the material is not quite where it needs to be." Charlie and Sevastian exchanged a quick glance before bursting out in an unexpected tirade of laughter.

"Wonderful!" Charlie exclaimed.

"What an amazing coincidence," Sevastian chimed in before downing the final swig of his ale.

"Wonderful?" she asked almost defensively. "I'm terrible at calculus. I'm not even sure I can pass the course."

"You're in luck," Charlie reassured her in a comforting tone. "It just so happens that Sevastian and I are calculus experts. If you'd like, we'd be glad to help you."

She might as well have watched her winning lottery numbers pulled right before her eyes. "Really? You will? I...I mean I won't be off until late tonight. I don't want to inconvenience you."

"No inconvenience," he calmly replied, sliding back in the seat and casually interlocking his fingers behind his Jayhawks' ball cap. "We'd be more than happy to tutor you, as long as you don't mind driving out to our place."

Lex was beside herself. At this point the last thing on her mind was the exam. All that mattered now was that Charlie Roanoke had just invited her to his mansion. "No, I wouldn't mind at all," she answered, voice saturated with gratefulness. "I think it would behoove me to take any help I can get. I can't thank you enough."

He smiled. "Do you know where we live?"

Lex had to fight to keep a straight face before responding. "I have an idea but refresh my memory."

"We're on County Road 13. Ours is the big place just past Garlough Cemetery – you can't miss it."

The boys departed soon thereafter, leaving in their wake an outrageously large tip, towers of empty plates and an awestruck waitress in an excited frenzy. In a split second, Lex had gone from a nervous wreck to a state of effervescent bliss. According to popular rumor, not since the abduction of Sevastian Moskincov had an outsider been allowed into Charlie Roanoke and Jade Vandervelde's inner circle. She couldn't help but wonder about the intended purpose of their invitation. As thrilled as she was, everything was working out almost too perfectly. She hoped this wasn't too good to be true.

12

The Range Rover cruised along County Road 13 toward the mansion, windows down, hard rock riffs pouring into the night.

"Why does it have to be calculus?" Charlie asked his Russian buddy who was slumped down in the passenger seat due to a painful belly ache. "I hate calculus."

"Maybe you should let Jade teach her," Sevastian suggested. "After all, she's way better with numbers than you are."

"If this plan is to work, I think I should be the one to earn her trust," Charlie said. "Anyway, I've been looking for an excuse to better myself at limits and continuity. It shouldn't take us more than three months to get a good grasp on it – right?"

Sevastian perked his head up with an irresolute grimace. "What do you mean, *us*?"

"Remember, I said that *we* were experts at calculus - *we*. Besides, I don't want to take this on alone. We'll be study buddies," he said, giving the Russian a playful fist to the shoulder. After a moment's deliberation, Sevastian finally nodded in tentative agreement.

"Alright then, I believe that I'm up for this task. After all, it's not like we don't have the time." At this comment, they both had a hearty chuckle.

Charlie then said, "I felt like an absolute fool asking Alexis about the metal. I wonder what she must think of it."

"I was wondering why you brought that up already," said

Sevastian. "Or at all for that matter. What difference would it make if she has a crown on her tooth anyway?"

Charlie shrugged, "I don't know, I just thought that it may have been an issue, but I guess you're right, what difference would it really make? Maybe I didn't think that one through."

"Well either way, at least we don't have to cross that bridge," Sevastian observed while allowing a muffled belch to punctuate his thought.

The Range Rover turned into the long cement driveway and rolled to a halt along side of the vintage Hummer. Its presence indicated that Jade had returned from High Thai. Charlie glanced at his watch. "I assume we have at least an hour before she arrives. I'm going to enjoy a hot shower before we leave."

"I'll just hang out in the kitchen until you're ready," the Russian said. "You do realize that we didn't get dessert tonight?"

"I still can't believe it," Charlie asserted as the two strolled up the walk toward the front door. "Alexis Lunden of all people. Who would have ever guessed?"

"There is something special about her," Sevastian perceptively stated. "I can't wait to see how this will play out."

"We'll find out soon enough," Charlie said as he courteously held the front door for his friend. The two shuffled inside. A low, rumbling echo drifted over the fields as the door closed.

13

Lex showed up nearly two hours later so excited that she almost forgot why she was there. After parking, she took a moment to marvel at the house. Now that she was up close, the structure's true grandeur was fully divulged. It was no doubt an impenetrable fortress – immune to anything the open plains of Kansas could conjure. Torrential rain, fierce wind, or even the terrifying funnel would not likely put a dent in this place. She snatched her book and calculator from the front seat and strutted excitedly up the long sidewalk, consciously suppressing the urge to skip. Arriving at the massive oak door, she half expected to see an ugly gargoyle door-knocker but was greeted instead with a modern glowing ringer. She took a deep breath and pushed the button.

Seconds later, the door opened to reveal Jade wearing a pink tank top and fitting yoga pants. She displayed a pair of very defined arms and shoulders. Her long black hair was pulled back in a sleek ponytail. With ocean blue eyes, she peered at Lex fixedly over a glass of milk.

"Hello, Alexis. I hear the boys are helping you study for a big exam."

"Yes, they were kind enough to offer," Lex replied. "I just hope I'm not being a burden."

Jade laughed then said, "Believe me, you'll be helping Charlie more than he's helping you." Lex wasn't quite sure how to take that, but by Jade's cheery tone, she was certain that it couldn't be a bad thing. "Please come in," Jade offered, motioning her inside. "I've heard a lot of good things about you over the years. I'm just disappointed that we haven't really gotten to know each other very well."

Lex was taken aback by the warmth and friendliness displayed by Jade Vandervelde, the girl preceded by such a tumultuous reputation. "Thank you," she replied flustered, then stepped inside, "I feel the same way."

The majesty of the room in which she now stood rendered her nearly breathless. Never in a million years would she have imagined that anything like this existed in Kansas. The prominent attraction was the immaculate golden chandelier hanging overhead. It radiated a dazzling glow on a neoclassical mural of mythical creatures that covered the domed ceiling. Serpents, mermaids, cyclopes, griffins, flying horses and winged deities, all basked in the illuminating splendor. Exotic trees inhabited every corner of the room, guarding floriated marble walls adorned with arabesques and vivid tapestries. A collection of professionally rendered portraits were hanging on the wall beneath an enormous Roman numeral clock. Among them were faces of Socrates, Homer, Copernicus, Albert Einstein, Nikola Tesla, Carl Sagan, Doctor Martin Luther King, Junior, Pelé and Neil DeGrasse Tyson. Lex guessed that all of these people had probably influenced the lives of the Rose Flock in one way or another.

The floor, like all of the walls, was made of large marble ashlar - its buffed sheen reflecting all of the foyer's brilliance. To the right, a grand staircase where an ornately designed carpet runner of greens and blues led upward to an arched hallway that branched off in many other directions. With moonstruck eyes, Lex realized that the foyer alone was probably larger than Aunt Claire's entire house.

Ahead, through an arched corridor, there was a dining hall. The archway was bordered on both sides by two interesting marble statues. On the left, a perfectly proportioned woman in the nude stood with her arms upright in a defensive stance. Her body and face represented pure feminine beauty, but her refined grace was overshadowed by an evil tangle of snakes that seemed to portray hair. The marble hero to her right, also in the nude except for a pair of sandals, thrust a mighty sword across the corridor entrance toward the neck of the viper-headed woman. Perhaps the outcome of a practical joke, a pair of comically misplaced gym shoes hung ridiculously from the sword, bonded together by frayed strings.

From Lex's limited view of the dining hall, she could see that the centerpiece was a lengthy granite table. It had the capability of comfortably seating twenty and was a definite overkill for a household of three. Soft moonlight spilling in from somewhere above cascaded off its polished surface. The tabletop was supported by statues of Spartan soldiers, teaming up with brawny granite arms to collectively bear the burden of the ponderous rectangular slab. Poised olive trees, with their lush foliage neatly trimmed, bordered the side walls. At the head of the room was a vacant stone fireplace the size of a tool shed. Jade stood by unobtrusively as Lex took it all in.

"How long does it take you to clean this place?" Lex asked wide-eyed, rousing a subtle smile from Jade.

"We have a crew in here once a week," Jade replied with a grin. "It takes fifteen people nearly the entire day to finish, but they do a… what is it that you British folk always say…brilliant job."

"Brilliant indeed," Lex concurred.

"So then, Alexis, I'd love to give you a tour, but Charlie requested that he do the honors. I'll let him know you're here." She then produced a cell phone from her pocket. "Please don't think of me as lazy. It's just that he could be anywhere, and in this house 'anywhere' mustn't be taken lightly." Lex nodded understandingly as Jade quickly spoke to her phone, "Call Charlie." Startled, the girls wheeled around as some futuristic cosmic cellphone tune popped up from behind.

"Alexis! So glad you could make it!" Charlie greeted with more enthusiasm than expected from someone who was about to spend hours poring over math books.

"Hi, Charlie," she reciprocated. "Seriously, I can't thank you enough. This is really nice of you guys."

"It's really no problem. In fact, you could say that calculus is a specialty of mine," he mentioned before Jade chortled derisively and rolled her eyes. "Something you'd like to say?" he asked with an exaggerated expression of inquisitiveness.

"Since when was calculus *your* specialty?" she asked tauntingly.

"Oh please," he protested. "Are you seriously comparing your calculus knowledge to my calculus knowledge? That's like comparing Larry, the village idiot, to Stephen Hawking."

"Well then move aside Larry because my motorized chair is rollin' out," said Jade as she bounced up the stairs. "Stephen Hawking, ha! Now I've heard it all." She waved goodbye to Lex. "Have fun studying," she called out before the dark hallway swallowed her up. Charlie crossed his arms and smirked as if amused by Jade's playful banter.

"Shall we get started?" he asked. Lex sighed and forced a half-hearted nod. She was in no mood to study, but very thankful to be working with a tutor rather than pounding the numbers on her own. "The library is my preferred study room," he said. "It's quiet, relaxing and we have access to thousands of different books."

"You have a library in this place?" asked an astonished Lex.

"Sure do. It's right this way," he declared with a hand motion toward the dining hall. "Follow me."

She became more flabbergasted with the mansion's mammoth interior as she trailed Charlie like a puppy dog through what seemed like an endless expanse of rooms. Each was striking and unique. One room had a glass ceiling that offered a clear view of the night sky. In the center of this room was a sparkling fountain with tamed ivy vines crawling around its wall. Standing within the crystal water was a man of solid gold. Upon fatigued shoulders, the grimacing man supported the intense weight of a planet nearly three times his own size. *Is this statue made of real gold?* Lex wondered, having not the audacity to ask. If so, she couldn't begin to speculate its value.

Greeted by a perpetual whooshing sound, she and Charlie strolled into the adjoining room to the spectacle of a giant pendulum. The lustrous rod was attached to the ceiling high above and swung back and forth over a yearly clock which, adhering to the popular theme, was gold. The face of the golden clock, which lay parallel with the floor, portrayed a Trojan battlefield, and was festooned with engravings of soldiers, horses and ancient armaments all engaged in a combat scenario. Lined up around the circumference of the circular timepiece were three hundred and sixty five soldier figurines. Each golden warrior was hand-carved and completely unique to its comrades.

"This is a Foucault pendulum," Charlie explained to Lex while she gazed upon the device as if it were the most interesting thing she had ever laid eyes on. "A machine of this nature works with the earth's rotation. Each day, the next poor soldier in sequence will eventually cross into the pendulum's arc and fall victim to his unavoidable fate." As it was now mid-September, she observed that nearly three fourths of the little soldiers had already tasted this fate. The rhythmic swishing of the pendulum rendered her a tad hypnotized, and it wasn't until Charlie gave her sleeve a gentle tug that she finally turned away.

The next area was a sharp contrast to everything she had seen so far. The fitness room was very modern and just one more testament to the Rose Flock's incredible wealth. This workout facility put to shame any health club Lex had ever seen. There were two levels to the room. The top level contained treadmills, stationary bikes, stair machines and elliptical trainers. The lower level was dedicated to free weights and weight machines. All of the equipment, of course, was top of the line. Massive flat-screens hung in various locations around the room, each one connected to a central sound system. Perhaps the most incredible feature was the lap pool, which was not located in the ground, but suspended high overhead covering the length of the ceiling. Thick glass held the water high in the air and allowed the swimmer to look down on the exercise room and even catch a glimpse of whatever was on the big screen. The pool also provided a visual ambiance, as it sent rippling reflections of light down upon the workout area. After crossing the fitness room, the two passed through a series of glass doors and were soon greeted with a therapeutic, earthly smell.

"Welcome to the living room," Charlie proudly declared. Lex was quick to recognize his play on words. He called it the living room because everything in it was living. Covering an area the size of half a football field, this room was a replica of a South American rainforest. Exotic trees stretching all the way up to the glass ceiling were bristling with colorful birds, tree frogs, and even snakes. The floor was covered with soft dark soil and plants. A gravel path led Charlie and Lex through the lush vegetation to a sparkling pond teeming with tropical fish.

"Among other foolish extravagances, we have a trampoline room, a movie theater, a planetarium and the north tower is basically a big climbing wall with an automated belay system," Charlie mentioned as Lex circumspectly eyed a green snake inching its way across an overhead branch. "It would be my pleasure to take you through all of them, however, your exam is top priority and time keeps on slipping, slipping, slipping into the future," he sang playfully, stirring a smile from his guest.

"This living room, as you call it, is beyond astonishing. I couldn't imagine how any other room could compare to this," she told him as they passed through another series of doors, departing the living room to a lorikeet's serenade. In a moment, they entered the library and she found her mouth hanging agape in absolute marvel. "I stand corrected," she uttered in a spellbound trance.

The library resided within the largest of the four towers, so the room was cylindrical in nature. Every inch of wall was covered with books, seemingly millions of them. A spiral staircase was positioned in the center of the tower and permitted access to five different levels of books. Each level had its own catwalk and a rolling ladder mounted on circular tracks so every book was within reach. Far above, in close proximity to the ceiling, there was yet another level with a grated floor – a mini observatory. There were four windows permitting access to the night sky, each with its own telescope. Elaborate charts of celestial bodies covered the observatory walls, making an ideal alcove for studying astronomy. The library was a reflection of vast intelligence and lust for knowledge. Even to acquire this many books, and to sort and place them, was a feat in itself.

"I know books are old-school, you know, with the internet and all," Charlie said. "But I just have a thing for the hard copies. I guess you could say I'm a collector."

Lex was so preoccupied with looking up that she hadn't yet taken note of the comfortable study area that had been thoughtfully established. In a large stone hearth, oak logs popped as they fueled a roaring fire. In the center of the room there was a black leather sofa, loveseat and armchair surrounding a fancy glass table. Upon the table was a stack of calculus books, calculators, three matching laptops, enough sharpened pencils for a whole classroom of students, three fancy cups and a steaming kettle of tea. Yet another subtlety that slipped her observation was Sevastian, who was cozily perched in the armchair flipping through a book on derivatives.

"Oh hello, Sevastian," Lex greeted. "I see you've selected an appropriate book for this evening's endeavors."

"Just warming up my brain for a long night of studying," he reciprocated with a dimpled grin. The words "long night of studying" hit Lex like a sledgehammer. Immediately her yawning mechanism was triggered and she felt the need to rub fatigue from her eyes.

"Don't worry, Alexis," Charlie said as he seized the tea kettle from the table and began pouring. "This will keep us all wide awake."

"What is it?" she asked with a flicker of interest.

"It's called cicadaweed tea," he said, "but don't let the name fool you. It's unbelievably delicious and very effective at keeping you awake. Please, try some." After a moment's hesitation, she was prodded onward by Charlie and Sevastian's anxious expressions.

I can't believe I'm about to drink something called cicadaweed, she thought, selecting a steaming cup from the table and slowly raising the aromatic drink to her lips. Charlie and Sevastian looked on, eagerly awaiting a verdict. She took a sip letting the soothing liquid caress her taste buds. A smile of satisfaction arose from behind the white china cup, and her green irises widened in exultance. "This is the best tea I've ever had, and I'm English." she declared. "Why haven't I heard of this?"

"Not many have," Sevastian replied. "cicadaweed is a little hard to come by."

Almost instantaneously this mysterious brew had rejuvenated her mind and sharpened her senses. She felt bright-eyed and bushy-tailed. Suddenly she became ready and willing to take on the world... the world of calculus anyway. "Is this stuff legal?" she inquired half jokingly.

To this Charlie laughed, "Certainly is. Cicadaweed is exceptionally beneficial to mind, body and spirit – it's all those antioxidants you know." The boys helped themselves to a cup as the three sat down to begin what would be a six-hour study session.

14

The minutes faded into hours as Charlie and Sevastian tirelessly guided Lex through the taxing world of advanced college calculus. The cicadaweed tea turned her brain into a magnet that attracted and retained every detail of information. As the once roaring fire faded to a mere flicker and the oak logs were reduced to glowing embers, the three were still going strong. Every now and then as the night marched on, she reflected on how profound it was to actually be here with Rose's elite.

Seven melancholy chimes from a clock in another room announced the arrival of dawn. Lex found herself a trifle disappointed that her time with Charlie and Sevastian was on the downswing. In good fun Charlie tossed his pencil, now just a stub, into the fireplace. "Well, I think that about takes care of it," he said victoriously as he fell back onto the couch.

"Mission accomplished," added Sevastian, completing his sentence with a deep yawn. "I think you now have a good handle on this subject, Alexis."

Lex was thrilled with how well everything had worked out. Several hours ago, calculus was a python, slowly constricting its body around her sanity until near suffocation. Now it seemed nothing more than a simple class. She never imagined understanding the basics of calculus let alone learning the material for the entire semester in one night.

"Thank you a million times over," she said gratefully. "Tell me, do you help everyone this way? I mean, you barely know me, yet you invited me into your home and spent your entire night teaching me this dreaded subject."

"We enjoy helping others when we can," Charlie said as a deep rumbling from Sevastian's stomach surfaced like an earthquake. "Good point, my friend. We can't send Alexis off to an exam on an empty stomach. I'm thinking, let's see, eggs and pancakes?"

"I have to admit that sounds delightful," Lex answered. In reality, she wasn't really hungry as the cicadaweed tea had satiated her appetite. She was, however, looking for any excuse to stay with Charlie and Sevastian just a little longer. Sevastian on the other hand was ready to chow down and the excitement on his face at the mention of pancakes was the confirmation.

The three began the journey back through the labyrinth of rooms until they came to a tidy, contemporary kitchen. Sure, it was beautiful and spacious, but Lex expected something exceptional like everything else thus far – perhaps a robot that prepared food or a talking garbage disposal, but this was just an ordinary kitchen.

Charlie motioned for Lex to have a seat at the island. "I'll go ahead and see if Jade would like to join us." Sevastian didn't hesitate to fire up the stove while Charlie pulled a phone from his pocket and sent a text to Jade informing her that breakfast preparations were underway. After trekking through just a small portion of this place, Lex fully understood the logic of employing a phone for easy communication. Jade appeared a few moments later with flannel pajamas and a sleepy expression but still looking like a perfect ten. She greeted Lex like an old friend and slid onto the neighboring bar stool.

Lex took an envious look at her and noted how beautiful she was, even right out of bed. Neither movie stars nor supermodels could hold a candle to the natural beauty of Jade Vandervelde. Truly, this "Helen of Troy" was downright unblemished. It seemed only natural that men would be swarming her way like moths to a flame. Jade and Charlie certainly made a beautiful couple and Lex couldn't help but be a little envious. At least she assumed they were a couple. Thus far, however, she had seen no evidence to prove it one way or the other.

During the next hour before she had to depart for class, which suddenly wasn't such a big concern, the four sat in the kitchen feasting on eggs, pancakes and fresh fruit while the Kansas sun made its presence known through the kitchen window. The conversation flowed like the sweet mimosas that Sevastian had concocted. Champaign before an exam was a first for Lex. Perhaps if she did well on the cursed thing, a celebratory glass of bubbly would also be in order.

The discussion revolved around Ms. Lunden as if she were the center of the universe. She thought this peculiar but couldn't deny that it felt good to win this kind of attention from three people of such imposing repute. Charlie and company wanted to know everything - aspirations, interests, hobbies, friends and family. She told them all about her childhood in England and the tragic loss of her mother. She told them about Aunt Claire but chose to leave out that minor detail about her acting career. Lex was enjoying being center stage for once, besides Claire had already had her time in the spotlight. The Rose Flock remained fully entwined in her stories, and with unwavering expressions of interest, hung on every word.

Although few and far between, she was able to squeeze in a few questions of her own, but avoided anything pertaining to their business or how they came to afford all of the luxuries within the mansion. She assumed that this information would be volunteered when the time was right. After all was said and done, and the breakfast dishes had been relieved of their contents, the three had somehow managed to remain a complete enigma, disclosing scant information about who they were or what they do.

The time finally came when Lex had to leave for class. After bidding farewell, Jade departed to her room to catch a few more hours of sleep. Sevastian was not long to follow after he made sure that all pots and pans were devoid of spare morsels.

Displaying his gentleman-like qualities, Charlie escorted Lex to the door.

"I know I've said it a million times already," she said sincerely as she placed a hand, which trembled for some reason, on the smooth golden door handle, "but thank you so, so much. I don't think I've ever had anyone do me a grander favor. I am grateful to the both of you."

"It was our pleasure," he said with a smile as he opened the door allowing the September breeze to sneak in. "If you think of it, let me know how you did."

"I sure will," she promised.

They stood there for a moment, seemingly on the brink of a goodbye hug before she reluctantly turned and walked away.

"Good luck, Alexis!" he called after her. She turned and flashed a confident smile as he shut the door.

She reached the car and tossed her book and calculator into the back seat, then climbed into the driver's chair appreciating how the cool leather felt against her legs. She heard the front door open again, and, as if she hadn't just spent an entire night at his side, smiled affectionately at the sight of Charlie Roanoke.

"Hey, I forgot something!" he called to her.

"Yes?" she called back curiously.

"I've been calling you Alexis all night. I forgot that you wanted me to call you Lex. Sorry 'bout that." He then shut the door leaving Lex's brain spinning in disbelief.

15

There was little doubt in Lex's mind that the only time she had ever asked Charlie to call her by that name was in her dream. Even though it had been several months, the words she had said to him right before she woke up were still vivid. "Charlie, you don't have to call me Alexis, you can call me Lex." She remembered how silly she felt about saying this. Perplexing though it was, she had no intention of confronting him about it for fear of appearing mental. There had to be a logical explanation. Maybe sometime during the long night of studying she might have mentioned it, but certainly did not remember. Driving to campus that morning, her head was filled with memories of her extraordinary evening, Charlie's shocking comment and most of all – calculus. It seemed ironic that one of the most enjoyable nights of her life was spent studying.

The exam came and went and the long hours had paid off. Lex strutted from the classroom unable to repress a self-assured grin. She knew she had aced it even before the grades were posted. If any doubt had lingered about the validity of Charlie and Sevastian's devoted character, it was now entirely extinguished. Still, she could not rid her thoughts from the ever intruding question – why her?

The grades were online a few hours later and confirmed her premonition of a perfect score. Not only was her test faultless, she also nailed the taxing extra credit problem earning her the highest grade in the class. She strolled gaily through the bustling college parking lot beside herself with excitement and a subsequent sense of reprieve. Her Mount Everest, calculus, had been climbed, conquered and now she stood on the summit looking at a downhill journey to her diploma. As the afternoon sun sent its soothing rays down from an ocean blue sky, she smiled contentedly as she came to realize that the class that had caused her so much worry was not going to be a problem after all. An even grander feeling was that she had presumably befriended the Rose Flock.

She wanted to drive straight to the mansion and throw her appreciative arms around Charlie and Sevastian but at the same time, did not wish to wear out her welcome. She thought about calling or texting but remembered that phone numbers had not been exchanged. Choosing to exercise some self control, arduous though it was, she decided to wait a day or two before casually swinging by to thank them. But what to do in the mean time to divert her mind from the irrepressible craze of the Rose Flock? As if to answer this question, Mother Nature sent a breeze laced with the hint of autumn rustling through her long brown hair. Suddenly she was reminded that she had not seen old Boc for several days. A relaxing ride sounded really good.

Later that afternoon, Lex and Boc reached the shady frog pond that meant they were at the halfway point along their eight mile loop. Boc had a little extra bounce in his step today, as if the happiness radiating from his rider was contagious. For the entire ride, Lex had been developing her return strategy to the mansion. Every detail had been elaborately rehearsed. Her plan enveloped everything from the exact day and time her revisit would occur, to the engaging outfit she was going to wear. Most importantly, she thought about what to say. She wanted to relay the news about receiving the highest grade in a forthright manner without coming off as pretentious. Maybe a gift would be suitable- but what?

"What do you get somebody who has everything?" she asked Boc. "A thank-you card is most definitely in order but what else?" At that moment, a particularly plump squirrel with a cheek full of acorns bounced across the trail a few yards ahead. "Of course!" she shouted gleefully, "a gift certificate to Vincent's!"

After the ride, she planted an affectionate kiss on Boc's snout, and then set off to Vincent's for the gift certificate and the drugstore for the thank-you card.

16

Lex returned home to find Aunt Claire hauling in groceries from her car. Upon seeing the black convertible pull into the driveway, Claire nearly dropped a bag of milk and orange juice.

"My god, Alexis, where have you been? I was very close to calling the police!"

Lex felt quite irresponsible as the sharp words rattled her like a gunshot. Sure, the invitation from Charlie and Sevastian had been unexpected and the entire night was spent productively, but she should have remembered to inform her aunt. She felt very disappointed in herself for being so negligent.

"Oh, Aunt Claire, I am so sorry," she apologized wholeheartedly. "I honestly cannot believe I didn't text you."

Aunt Claire shook her head. "How much was that phone of yours? Let's see… forty extra per month tacked onto my phone bill for three years? Quite a pricy piece of tech to neglect. Where were you last night?"

Lex was stewing in a pot of regret. She pictured her poor aunt sitting up all night worrying herself to death and calling every ten minutes. Lex had purposely left her phone in the car so as not to be distracted from Charlie and Sevastian's vital tutoring. She searched for the right way to adequately express her apologies but found herself wrapped tight in Claire's comforting arms before she could say anything at all.

"I'm just glad you're okay," Claire said with a sigh of relief.

Lost for words, Lex could only come back with, "I'm so sorry."

"Well, make yourself useful and help me carry in the rest of these groceries," Claire ordered, taking a collected breath. "That will give you something to do while you explain just what the bloody hell you were doing last night." Lex smiled at her aunt's resilience and happily snatched a bag of "Fancy Feline Cuisine" from the trunk.

It took the rest of the afternoon to fill Aunt Claire in on every detail of last evening with the Rose Flock. She listened with keen interest as Lex told her about their house, their personalities, their uncanny calculus knowledge and the triumphant conquest of the exam. By the time she had finished with the entire rundown of events that had taken place, the groceries were unpacked, the tea and Banbury tarts had been consumed and Claire had just put a ham in the oven for dinner.

"You should really go over there tonight and thank them," Aunt Claire suggested as she peeled a sweet potato.

Lex nodded hesitantly, "Yeah, I'd like to, but they're probably sick of me by now."

"Oh please. I've seen you nearly every day for the last eleven years, and I'm not sick of you. Besides, if you don't let them know about your exam soon, they'll assume you did poorly."

"Splendid point," Lex enthusiastically chimed, looking for any minor excuse to nudge her judgment toward returning to the mansion sooner rather than later.

"Why don't you go now? This ham will be a few hours anyway," Claire suggested. That was all the persuasion Lex needed. In an instant she was bounding up the stairs two at a time so there would be no delay in showering and preparing her outfit. It took quite a while to make sure everything was just right. When she finally returned to the kitchen to collect the gift certificate and card, Aunt Claire let out a whistle.

"Marilyn Monroe is back from the dead," she announced, full of jest. Lex had straightened her hair, applied make-up, put on a prismatic summer dress and doused her skin with an expensive lotion designed to enhance one's natural tan. She looked like a million bucks. The sight of her would turn any head in a public place, but the look on her aunt's face illustrated disapproval.

"Is it too much?" Lex asked.

"Maybe if you were going to a formal dinner party, but perhaps a bit overdone for dropping off a thank-you card."

"You know, you're right," Lex agreed, now a bit embarrassed.

"You're a natural beauty," Claire assured her. "Trust me, you don't need all those bells and whistles to catch Charlie's eye."

That remark made her wonder why she had gotten dressed up in the first place. Why did she care so much about looking so perfect for the Flock? Was this an unwitting attempt to impress Charlie? Sure, he was handsome, smart, and rich, but making an impression on him in particular had never crossed her mind – or maybe it had. But what difference did it make anyway? He was with Jade.

With a sheepish smile, she trotted back up the stairs and returned a few minutes later with her hair in a tidy braid, most of the makeup removed, a USA Gymnastics tee shirt, a pair of soccer shorts and sandals.

Aunt Claire nodded with satisfaction. "Now that's beautiful," she declared genuinely.

Claire accompanied Lex to her car. "If you'd like, you could invite them over for dinner tomorrow night," she offered.

Lex's eyes brightened. "Really? The thought had crossed my mind but... you don't mind?"

"Of course not," Claire replied warmly. "They sound like an interesting lot. Besides, after all of their help, dinner is the least we could do in return."

"I'll extend the invitation," Lex promised as she pushed her thumb print against the ignition panel making the well-maintained six cylinder purr. "Thank you, Aunt Claire."

17

As Lex stood before the hulking front door, she was even more excited than the night before. She pushed the glowing ringer and waited eagerly.

"Be there in a minute," came Sevastian's voice from the doorbell's communication speaker. In fact, it took nearly two minutes until the sound of footsteps could be heard from the other side. With a deep rumble, the door hoisted open and there before her was Sevastian with a friendly smile upon his face.

"How did you do?" he asked with much curiosity and a thick Russian accent. The excitement within Lex was comparable to a volcano ready to erupt. Finally, the pressure was too much.

"Only a perfect score and the highest grade in the class!" she blurted out - so much for modesty. "I'm sorry," she apologized with a smile that wouldn't abandon her face. "I didn't mean to sound boastful. I'm just so relieved."

"As you should be," he replied without any inkling of disdain for her proud attitude. "The others will be delighted to hear of your success. Please come in."

She gladly stepped into the foyer which was no less impressive the second time around.

"We have been working all day and now we are enjoying a Kansas sunset," he said as he led her from room to room toward the library. Again, she fought the urge to ask what it was that they were working on as he continued – "I'm sure you wouldn't mind unwinding a bit, eh?"

"Certainly not," she replied." After a whole week of stress over one exam, I should say that a good bit of unwinding is much needed."

When they arrived at the library, happy memories of the night before were rekindled. She followed him to the spiral staircase in the center of the room and they began their ascent. After an exhausting climb, they reached the top level where the observatory was located. Although she did not fear heights, the astronomy loft in which they now stood made her nervous. All that separated them from many stories of free fall was a thin metal grate. Sevastian opened a small door and ushered her out to the roof.

In this house, there seemed to be no space that went unused. Lex shook her head and grinned upon observing that the surface of the roof was host to an exhibition of recreational devices. There was a basketball court, a tennis court, a hot tub, several hammocks and a set of pull-up bars. Her attention shifted from the rooftop amenities to a row of four lawn chairs lined up near the western edge. She could see that two were vacant and the other two were occupied by Jade and Charlie. *Is the extra chair for me*? she wondered. *Did they know I was coming back*?

"Congratulations, Lex," Charlie said as she approached.

"Congratulations? How do you know? Perhaps I did terrible and only came here to apologize for wasting your time."

He chuckled flippantly at this. "Not likely. Besides, I would expect nothing less from such an intelligent individual. Let me guess, perfect score?"

"Well, yes," she verified, again trying not to sound immodest. "I just wanted to stop by to thank you and Sevastian for your help." She dug into her purse and pulled out the card and gift certificate.

Sevastian was quick to recognize the Vincent's logo on the gift card. "Is that what I think it is?"

"Just a little thank-you. It's nothing really, but I know how much you like Vincent's."

Sevastian snatched the gift card from Lex's hand with astonishing velocity and grinned like a child on his birthday.

"Super-duper! Fifty dollars to Vincent's!" he announced exuberantly. "I would be willing to go right now if anyone else wants to join me."

"Very thoughtful, Lex, and you're most welcome," said Charlie, blatantly ignoring his friend's hunger-driven enthusiasm. He passed the card on to Jade and offered Lex a seat.

"How about a cold one?" Jade asked as Lex selected the empty chair next to her.

"Well, only if you don't mind," she answered, quite ready to kick back with a brew.

Jade rummaged through the icy cooler and took roll call. "We have wheat ale, pale ale, oatmeal stout, hefeweizen…."

"Hefeweizen sounds perfect. Thank you."

"And now prepare yourself to participate in one of our favorite activities," said Charlie. "We call it, drink beer and watch the sunset. Listen closely to the rules. To be successful in this endeavor, you must sit back in the chair, sip on a beer, and watch the sunset."

"Sounds rough, but I think I'm up for the challenge," Lex said with feigned trepidation, settling into the comfy lawn chair. She took a sip of beer, a deep breath, and was immediately absorbed in late summer's rapture.

There was complete silence now as the four sat side by side watching the orange fire-sphere drop below the pomegranate horizon. This however was not an awkward silence, rather an unspoken bonding between Lex and her new friends. For once in a very long time, all the concerns and worries that she had carried evaporated into the eventide. A sense of renewal and peace cloaked her mind. Unfortunately, this revitalizing serenity only lasted for a few minutes before a familiar voice shattered the quiet.

"So, did you guys want to use that gift certificate tonight or…?"

18

The next evening, Aunt Claire was storming about the kitchen like a whirling dervish and Lex was doing everything in her power to subdue her aunt's tension. Charlie and Jade had happily accepted Claire's dinner invitation but Sevastian ruefully declined as he had a flight out of Wichita earlier that morning departing for St. Petersburg. Every year he returned home to visit family, but for Sevastian, who looked distraught over missing out on a free meal, the dinner invitation could not have come at a more disadvantageous time. Claire's hands were noticeably trembling while she and Lex shucked corn.

"They're really wonderful people," Lex offered, attempting to pacify her fidgety aunt.

"I'm sure they are," Claire answered. "It's just that those three have been the talk of the town ever since I can remember. And I'll never forget the Jade Vandervelde trial – do you remember how badly she battered that man? He looked as if he had taken a flying leap off of a ten story building and landed face first – and now I'm having dinner with the girl. They're mysterious people, always have been. Filthy rich with no apparent means."

"Oh, that reminds me," Lex interrupted, abandoning her corn shucking responsibilities in order to cuddle the chocolate Burmese who had found his way to her lap. "This may sound like an odd request, but please don't ask them about their jobs. I don't want them to think that we're only interested in their wealth and success."

"Seems strange to me that they can't talk about their business," Aunt Claire observed. "Do they have a meth lab in their basement? Constructing nuclear weapons perhaps?"

Lex giggled. "Certainly not... at least I don't think so. Either way, I would just appreciate it if you didn't bring it up."

"Don't get your knickers in a twist," she replied lightly. "My lips are sealed."

It was seven o'clock on the tick when the Range Rover rolled into the driveway of the lake house. Charlie and Jade stepped out onto the crimson cobblestone to the alluring aroma of Claire's sumptuous feast. It was now harvest season in Kansas and she took advantage of the fresh fruits and vegetables offered at every farmer's market around town. Tonight's specials included sweet corn, tomato and mozzarella salad, baked potatoes and the ever-succulent steak kabobs grilled to perfection with a medley of garden veggies. It was a meal fit for royalty – or at least Charlie and Jade.

Lex bounded to the door to greet her guests. "Hey guys! Long time no see. Please come in."

"This is such a beautiful house," Jade said as she stepped inside carrying a cherry pie. "It's right on the lake and it's so cozy."

"Yeah, I've always loved it here," Lex said, feeling flattered.

Jade wasted no time greeting her with a warm hug – just like they were old friends.

Charlie too was carrying a pie, except his was apple. He said, "I know you told us not to bring anything but Sevastian insisted on baking these pies. I think you'll really enjoy them. He's quite the hash slinger." Much to Lex's surprise, not to mention delight, Charlie also surrendered a hug then gazed around at the snug, shabby-chic interior.

Claire burst from the kitchen like a cannonball. "Hello there you two!" she boomed. "Welcome!" Charlie and Jade introduced themselves to their peppy English hostess and handed off the pies. Earlier, Claire had inadvertently parched her angel food cake by neglecting to remove it from the oven in a timely manner, so now dessert was back on the menu.

Lex watched with felicity as the relaxed personalities of Charlie and Jade coalesced to perfection with Claire's ostentatious persona. The three immediately hit it off and the ensuing conversation did not cease for the rest of the night.

During the meal, Charlie, Jade and Lex listened bemusedly as Aunt Claire ranted passionately about the county's poor decision to erect a mega dairy at Rose's southern border.

"If the city grants the construction proposal, the whole town will smell like cow shit," Claire fervently remarked. "I like fresh country air as much as the next person, but with hundreds of dirty heifers under one roof, it's bound to be the origin of quite an unbearable stench."

"Better than a slap in the face with a wet kipper," Lex reminded her aunt, trying to get Claire to change to a topic more befitting for the dinner table. Claire missed the hint and kept right on ranting.

During the lengthy monologue, Lex's attention was focused on Jade, who for some time had been intently studying Claire with a visage of abiding curiosity. Finally, Claire shoveled a heaping bite of baked potato into her mouth, offering an opportunity for Jade to finally speak.

"Claire, I don't mean to digress, but something has been really bugging me." Aunt Claire looked up with interest. "I know I've seen you before or even know you, but I can't figure out where or how."

At this statement, Claire perked up in her chair and batted her eyes rather proudly. Here we go, Lex thought with an eye-role as she observed her aunt morph from cordial host to Hollywood big shot; as if Dr. Henry Jekyll was being pervaded by Edward

Hyde. Lex knew that she missed certain aspects of the glamorous life, one of these being public recognition. Sure, Lex was proud of her, and even thought it riveting to be the niece of a famous actress, but sometimes the excitement could rouse Claire into bouts of egocentric reminiscing.

"Well let me see, my dear," Claire replied, feigning uncertainty. "Have you ever seen the series, Love, Lust, Desire?"

Jade's eyes widened exposing the full circumference of her cobalt irises. "Of course, you're Claire Lunden, also known as Marsha Wellington! How did I not make that connection earlier? I can't believe it – Rose of all places. Love, Lust, Desire was so binge-worthy I actually watched it twice.

Lex observed Claire restraining her zeal and play it off like Marsha Wellington was no big deal.

"Well, I did win a Golden Globe for the role but our director was so incredible and the cast had such chemistry, it would have been impossible not to."

"Lex, you didn't tell us that your aunt was a famous actress," Charlie remarked.

"Guess I just haven't gotten around to it yet," she replied.

Jade then began firing off questions as if from a machine gun. Lex had no idea that she had such a kick for sleazy, romantic shows. For the remainder of the meal, the conversation revolved around Aunt Claire's thespian exploits.

Pompous though she could sometimes be, Claire usually knew when to wrap things up. She was well-mannered enough to understand that remaining in the spotlight for too long can breed contempt from those who aren't interested in the discussion. While collecting dinner dishes to make room for the dessert settings, she changed the subject by carelessly posing the one question that Lex had begged her not to ask.

"So, Charlie, Jade – what is it that you do for a living?" As soon as the question escaped her lips, she cringed as Lex's look of displeasure reminded her of the folly. Despite the unspoken tension now reverberating between the Lundens, Charlie and Jade did not exhibit an ounce of bother over the question.

"Well, for one thing we're authors," Charlie coolly replied. "Jade has written a book on the history of Scotland, a beginner's guide to martial arts and several books on outdoor survival. And as for me – are you familiar with the author P.J Stockton and his series of mystery novels for kids?"

Aunt Claire nodded titillatingly. "They're the latest craze in youth literature. You can't go anywhere without seeing them for sale."

"That's me," Charlie continued. "P.J. Stockton is my penname. The whole endeavor started when Sevastian foolishly bet me that I couldn't write a better mystery novel than our AI program. One thing led to another and the next thing I knew "The Igneous Oyster " was published and flying from bookshelves as if each copy had its own set of wings. I still marvel at how a silly bet turned to such a lucrative income."

"*You're* P.J Stockton?" Lex asked, unable to restrain giddy excitement at this newfangled revelation.

"Yes, but unlike our gracious hostess," Charlie continued sending a nod in Claire's direction, "I'm not cut out for photos and autographs, which is why I remain as anonymous as possible. I dare say that the two of you are the first in Rose to see the cat out of the bag."

"Your secret is safe with me," Claire vowed while conveying pies from the kitchen to the dining room.

For a moment, Lex believed she had finally seen through Charlie Roanoke's veil of ambiguity. His literary prosperity would no doubt render him a multi-millionaire, especially with the last five of P.J Stockton's novels lingering on the New York Time's best seller list. His selected alias would explain the secretive behavior. Yet even with these variables affirmed, there were holes in the equation. Even a great gaggle of the world's wealthiest authors could not collectively afford everything that the Rose Flock possessed. Lex knew for a fact that the possessions within the mansion soared into the billions of dollars. In addition, Charlie had erected his mansion when he was a mere teenager. P.J Stockton had only been on the scene for the last several years. Lex was convinced that he was still dancing around the whole truth. But then again, he did answer Claire's question with the phrase, "Well for one thing."

What was the other thing? She wondered. Just like the previous morning, when she had eaten breakfast with Charlie and company, the truth was guilefully bypassed without resorting to downright lying. This was the craft of the Rose Flock, and one which they had mastered. But why the delusion?

"Yet another celebrity in our midst," Lex said, beaming over-exaggeratingly. Repressing the Nancy Drew within, she decided not to dig any further - at least for the time being.

But as she was about to stand to retrieve the dessert pies, a bone-chilling noise torpedoed through the atmosphere as a stack of saucers came crashing to the wood floor. A thousand white shards were dispersed helter-skelter in every conceivable direction. The two cats that had been dozing at Lex's feet fled the room for their very lives with erect ridges of back hair. Lex and Jade leapt from their chairs and dashed to Aunt Claire's side. Charlie had remained in his seat at the table, and Claire stood behind him looking down with what appeared to be terror.

"What is it?" Lex asked with urgency.

Aunt Claire could only point to Charlie who seemed just as alarmed as everyone else and completely oblivious to the dark blood stain that was saturating the fibers on the back of his white polo shirt.

"My god, Charlie, you're bleeding!" Lex shouted. Quick yet gentle, she pulled the bloody shirt up over his head. A trio of gaping vertical slashes extended from his neck all the way down to his lower back. Several portions of these grotesque gashes were crudely scabbed. It looked as though he had been mauled by a grizzly bear. A generous chunk of scab was hanging fastidiously from the center wound, and this appeared to be the origin of the blood-letting. The wounds needed medical attention in the worst way, stitches in particular.

He remained silent for a moment and appeared to be in a state of fraught rumination. Finally, with what was obviously an impulsive twisting of the truth, he mustered a response. "I was out in the garden today when I tripped over the sprinkler and fell backwards onto a pitchfork that I was using to move mulch. It actually looks worse than it is," he said, attempting to make light of the situation.

Claire finally broke from her petrified trance as her nurturing instincts kicked in. "Charlie, these wounds must be tended to. You are in my house so I will not allow you to object," she said with motherly authority. "Lex, run upstairs and fetch me some bandages, gauze and antibiotic cream from the bathroom cupboard."

Lex nodded and hastily complied with her aunt's request.

"I told him he needed stitches, but he can be very stubborn sometimes," Jade stated.

Charlie who had all the while been blushing from his embarrassing predicament rolled his eyes at this. "Claire, I'm sorry about all of this trouble. I feel like I've ruined the evening. I'll replace those plates."

"Nonsense," replied Aunt Claire. "Follow me into the kitchen and I'll get that wound under control. Afterward, we can all head out to the front porch, have dessert and forget about the whole nasty incident."

In addition to the requested items, Lex returned with a tee shirt from her room so Charlie would not have to sport the blood-stained polo for the rest of the evening. The group migrated into the kitchen and watched with sporadic cringes as a thoroughly humiliated Charlie allowed Aunt Claire to doctor him up. After the bandages were in place and the antibiotic cream had been applied, Charlie squeezed into Lex's shirt.

"Little tight," he said with a coy grin. Lex smiled with a flirtatious semblance. This ploy of retrieving a snug shirt had been premeditated and she did not suffer an insinuation of guilt for seizing the opportunity to see his defined musculature protrude through the soft fabric.

"I think that's the biggest shirt I have," she lied. Claire, apparently on to her niece's scheme, flashed a mischievous glance before announcing, "I guess that'll just have to do. Well, who's ready for pie?"

The remainder of the evening passed swimmingly. As the four lounged on the front porch eating pie and drinking tea, the golden moon ascended with eminence and Charlie and Jade entertained their hosts with extraordinary stories. Some of these tales were so outlandish, Lex would not have believed a single word had it come from anyone else. Among other noteworthy feats, the intrepid duo reminisced over their K2 summit, elaborated on their humanitarian efforts in west Africa, and explained how they had made significant contributions to astrological research. It seemed inconceivable how much the two had accomplished during the short span of their lives to date.

A mellow clang from an indoor clock escaped through the open window reminding those on the porch just how much time had slipped by. As the remnants of the temporal beacon fluttered through the night air, Charlie and Jade offered their parting farewells. After they delivered a heartfelt thank-you to Aunt Claire, Lex accompanied them to the Range Rover. The uncertainty over when or if she would see them again left her disenchanted.

"Tonight was wonderful," Charlie said as he gave Lex a friendly hug. "We must do it again sometime." Jade seconded that claim then climbed into the passenger seat.

"I've really enjoyed hanging out with you both," said Lex with dolefulness in her voice she could not conceal.

"We feel the same way," Charlie continued. "So then why should we stop hanging out? The state fair is going on this week.

Jade and I were going to shoot down there tomorrow just for something to do. Interested?"

Not wishing to mimic a child upon hearing the alluring ditty of the ice cream truck, Lex fought back the urge to jump for joy. "I have to work tomorrow night, but not until five-thirty. Will that be okay?"

"Sure thing," he said. "Pick you up tenish?"

She nodded happily. "See you tomorrow then."

Charlie and Jade waved goodbye as the Range Rover cruised off into the September night. At that moment, Lex concluded she had successfully passed their initiation. She had been accepted into their inner circle where unspeakable wonders surely awaited, or so she guessed. Despite the grandeur of this new cognizance, a bothersome inquiry lingered in her brain. After hours of conversation, this night and the one before, she had learned so much about them but somehow understood less. How could three accomplished people who seemed so genuine, exhibit such obvious deceptions? She decided, if only for her own temporary appeasement, that the reason for their lack of full disclosure must be justifiable. The uncertainty and doubt was rapidly shoved out of her mind because all that mattered was that the thrilling three might soon become the fascinating four.

19

After the state fair, Lex, Charlie and Jade were inseparable. Whenever in each other's company, everything seemed right with the world. Lex was regularly receiving kudos about her sweet natured disposition in which she was often compared to "a breath of fresh air." In turn, she was drawn to her new friends by the sheer fact that they were utterly intriguing. The more she got to know them, the more interested she became in knowing more. She discovered that Charlie and Jade, though far exceeding any standard of conventional normality, turned out to be more down to earth, more human than she had once thought. With this new insider's perspective, she was able to gather more knowledge of their accomplishments and personalities.

She finally allowed herself to give in to Charlie's charm and just accept that infatuation was inevitable. However, there were things about him that left her somewhat leery. It all started at Aunt Claire's dinner party, where he had lied, in her best judgment, about falling onto a pitchfork. He had also not told the entire truth about his means of fortune. The contradiction was between his authentic disposition and his apparent deceptions. In other instances, he would come off as the most easy-going, carefree bloke this side of the Rockies; but with closer inspection, he seemed to be perpetually searching for something. He was hardworking but rarely busy. He was serious yet lighthearted. He was brilliant and industrious but never demonstrated exactly how. These mysterious attributes only succeeded in accentuating his appeal, which attracted Lex like a bear to a honeypot.

Jade was much simpler. There was no mistaking anything

she said or did. She functioned with tell-it-like-it-is candidness, no matter what degree the truth might flatter or offend its recipient. Her every thought and opinion was made perfectly clear. Because of this frankness, Lex would often use Jade as a personal "mirror-mirror on the wall." She had an unwavering source of honesty at her beck and call, and whether the topic was people, current events or simply a third party opinion about a new hairstyle, she would consult Jade. Despite all of this, Lex could not muster the courage to confront her about Charlie's falsehoods. Perhaps she was in on the whole scheme, whatever the scheme may be. Was she under Charlie's reign? Sworn to secrecy? Protecting some vast wealth of information at his request? Lex knew for certain that there was more to the Rose Flock than they were willing to unveil and couldn't help but wonder if Jade would tell all if specifically asked. Either way, Lex knew she would never ask. She didn't want to jeopardize this new relationship by sticking her nose into something that wasn't her business.

When Sevastian returned from Russia, Lex soon discovered that he had his own set of riveting hobbies and a one-of-a-kind personality. He was assertive, dogmatic and sometimes out-and-out overbearing. He was the only one who would stand against Jade in a debate. He loved to talk, loved to eat and loved to playfully harass Charlie whenever the opportunity presented itself. Lex might have found these little quirks vexatious if not for his overall good nature and the fact that his intentions were well placed. Like Charlie, he was a blast to pal around with, but for different reasons.

As if he had a split personality, Sevastian could morph from a "mouthy Molly" into a stoic artisan in the blink of an eye. At heart, he was a liberal arts virtuoso. His first love, even before food, was music. There wasn't a wind or string that he could not play or did not own. On the harp and piano he was a prodigy. An entire row of shelving in the library served the responsibility of housing dozens of binders filled with music he had composed. In addition to excelling in music, he was also a gifted painter. Lex came to notice that the entire mansion was bestrewn with his art whether in the form of a wall-sized mural or a life-like portrait, which were his forte.

The others in the mansion would argue that Sevastian's claim to fame was not the heavenly chords he sent reverberating throughout the corridors, nor was it his spellbinding artwork. Charlie and Jade would both agree, because each adored a good meal, that Sevastian's specialty was cooking. Almost daily, a refrigerated truck would roll into the driveway with a fresh batch of delicacies imported from anywhere and everywhere around the globe. The others were granted the luxury of a five-star meal on a nightly basis from an accomplished chef whose culinary aptness rivaled the world's most famous cooking gurus.

As if all of this wasn't enough, Sevastian was also a master craftsman. No matter the material, be it wood, metal or stone, he could carve it, craft it, or build it. His workshop within the mansion was second to none, containing every conceivable implement of craft. Within the walls of his sawdust-laden domain, he made furniture, jewelry, cutlery and even medieval weaponry. He sold his goods online for a noteworthy profit. His specialty, and most lucrative source of income, was wooden sleighs, or troikas as he called them, designed to be pulled by a team of horses. Lex discovered that he was among an elite few who designed such transit. Each sleigh was carved from the finest lumber and demanded several months of diligent labor to complete. The finished product was of unmatched perfection. The waiting list for these world-renowned masterpieces was of such depth, that he would never be able to fill every order should he live ten lifetimes. The wealthy buyers of these troikas were known to offer double or even triple the price to get their name moved up the waiting list. When asked how he was able to pursue all of his hobbies to such an elite level, his simple answer was always, "time management."

Charlie's mystery novels were a monumental success. Jade's how-to guides saturated every bookstore. Sevastian's handiwork yanked in scores of cash along with many triumphant returns from various art expositions. Lex saw a lot of money coming in and a lot of money going out. Oversized delivery trucks were frequent visitors. They dropped off new appliances, workout equipment, the latest high-power telescopes, microscopes and even exotic pets for the living room. At times it was quite the fiasco, like visiting New York's Grand Central Station. Amidst the cleaning crews, food caterers and moving men hauling in the next golden statue, it was sometimes difficult to find a quiet corner to curl up with a book, even in a house of such leviathan proportions. On that remote hundred acres along County Road 13, there was rarely a dull moment and Lex was delighted to be part of the excitement.

20

Since becoming entwined in the world of Charlie Roanoke, Lex was spending so much time at the mansion that she had nearly forgotten about her old friends. In particular, Autumn, who always sat highest on the best friend totem pole, had been a daily denizen of her voicemail. There were now two parts to her life – "before the Flock" and "after the Flock." Most everyone in the "before the Flock" category would testify that she had dropped off the face of the planet. She had no intention of kicking her old friends to the curb, but her new lifestyle had a habit of distracting her from obligatory correspondence. Autumn refused to go down without a fight. Her tenacious efforts paid off as she was finally able to pry Ms. Lunden from her busy schedule of school and hanging out at the mansion. They met up at the local sports bar one night after Lex had left Vincent's. The hours slipped away as the friends caught up over free margaritas, courtesy of the three single guys that had been hovering around the bar all evening.

"Wow, that's just remarkable," Autumn proclaimed with wide-eyed elatedness after Lex had finished telling all about the Rose Flock and how she had become inducted into their exclusive circle. It was late on a Friday night. The bar was starting to empty incrementally as the tipsy hoards shuffled out the door leaving behind piles of empty beer bottles and stripped wing bones. Lex and Autumn had been so preoccupied by gossip, they did not hear the bartender's last call announcement. "Tell me more about Charlie," Autumn requested as she prodded a tequila-saturated lime around her empty glass with a straw. "You said he was adopted?"

"Yea, actually it's a pretty interesting story," Lex began. "Apparently, he was abandoned when he was very young. He had been dropped off at the home of Robert and Ella Roanoke."

"Hmm, a mysterious baby in a basket, just like in the movies," Autumn observed.

"No, I think he was something like five or six when this happened - a little big for a basket," Lex replied with a smirk. "I really don't know too much about the Roanokes other than Robert was a career farmer and Ella used to run the pastry shop on Shellaveve Street; and they were pretty old of course. I guess they had searched extensively for whoever had abandoned Charlie, but never did figure it out. During the search, they had taken him into foster care and as time passed, they became attached to their little stray and were able to adopt him. And if that's not weird enough for you, get this. Little Charlie did not speak a word of English. Robert and Ella spent quite a bit of money on language tutors. They eventually got him up to par with other kids his age so he could be enrolled in kindergarten."

Autumn's face radiated with intrigue. "What language did he speak?

"Greek," Lex replied. "Ancient Greek to be exact."

"You're right, that is weird," Autumn remarked.

The conversation was put on hold for a moment as an employee, clearly anxious to go home for the night, snatched the empty glasses from the table with deliberate haste.

"Very peculiar indeed," Lex continued after the employee had ventured from earshot. "I'm ashamed to say that I didn't get this information from Charlie. I was snooping in the mansion's library one afternoon and decided to peruse the book collection. In doing so, I happened upon a series of scrapbooks and diaries from Ella Roanoke. She had kept detailed accounts of her life. It was there that I found the diary containing the information about Charlie's mysterious appearance. It seems his first moments of fame were at an early age. The story of an abandoned child near Wichita, Kansas who spoke ancient Greek was enough to get national attention. The story was actually published in Time Magazine. To this day, the whole event is still an unsolved mystery."

"Why not just ask Charlie what he remembers?" Autumn asked.

"I hope that one day I can," Lex replied. "But as of now, I'm not on that level with him. I think I'm always a little nervous to overstep my boundaries with the Flock." *And,* she thought to herself, *I'm not sure if his answer would be entirely truthful anyway.*

Autumn just shook her head in amazement. She uttered the word, "fascinating," as all the lights came on with pupil-agitating luminescence. Employees with brooms began pouring from the woodwork.

"Oh, and one more thing," Lex quickly added, "The diary also mentioned another child who was abandoned at the same time and had been adopted by another family in the Rose area. Ella, however, did not go into detail about that other child. I hope to find out more about that as well."

"Where are his parents now?" Autumn asked. "The Roanokes I mean."

"Both have passed away," Lex replied. "Charlie inherited the land and the farmhouse, which he tore down and built the mansion in its place."

"Is that where all the money came from? Collecting life insurance after Robert and Ella died?" Autumn proposed.

Lex was quick to reject this theory. "Most definitely not. According to Charlie, the Roanokes were rather poor. I doubt very seriously that they had a multi-billion-dollar life insurance policy."

The disjunction in chatter allowed the girls a moment to glance around the bar and realize that they were the only two remaining, apart from a scraggly kid with a broom and their waitress who was addressing them from across the room with an impatient stare.

"Where does the time go?" Lex asked as they stood and

stretched their legs, which were quite stiff after several hours on a rigid barstool.

"It certainly flies when you're having fun with an old friend," Autumn said. The sleepy twosome shuffled outside, selected Wednesday for the next rendezvous, hugged goodbye, and split off in opposite directions toward their respective vehicles.

Lex had been chomping at the bit to check her voicemail. She was hopeful that someone from the mansion had called.

"You have twelve messages," said the automated voice in its usual enthusiastic tone.

Once again feeling ashamed of herself for lacking a considerate bone, she listened to eleven demoralizing messages from Aunt Claire who was wondering why she hadn't come home from work at her usual time. Each message was more urgent than the one before and each was a brazen reminder that she needed to inform Claire when nightly excursions were to occur. The final message was one that rejuvenated her spirit and brought a smile to her face. It was Sevastian proposing a horseback ride tomorrow. Lex giggled at his amusing intonation which was yet to get old. She happily fired up the engine and headed for home, all the while intensely pondering on the proper apology to her aunt, who would predictably be watching from the bay window when she rolled into the driveway.

21

December arrived like a pack of wolves and the fields of central Kansas now hosted a blanket of pearly snow. Gratefully, Lex finished her final semester of college with an impressive collection of A's – including calculus. The class she had feared most had come and gone and gone well thanks to Charlie and Sevastian. On the afternoon of her graduation ceremony, it felt as though the weight of the world had been lifted from her shoulders. As the dean handed her a leather-bound diploma and her name echoed throughout the crowded arena, she glanced into the audience and saw the proud faces of Aunt Claire, a handful of high school friends, and of course, the Rose Flock. Before stepping down from the stage, she stopped for a moment to take it all in and bask in this magical blip of her life.

After the excitement, the tears, the speeches and the bittersweet goodbyes of the graduation ceremony, Aunt Claire surprised Lex with a post-commencement party at her favorite restaurant, The Birch Club.

"Have I told you how much I adore you, Aunt Claire?" she asked jubilantly as Claire guided her toward the reserved party room. As the Lunden family breached the threshold of the fancy glass doors, applause discharged like cannon fire. Lex was overcome with emotion upon observing the large gathering of friends who showed up to celebrate her accomplishment. As salty drops tumbled down blush cheeks, she threw her appreciative arms around Aunt Claire. Through the tears, she saw Charlie, Jade and Sevastian looking on with proud smiles.

During the feast, Lex made her rounds and made it a point

to converse with everyone. She couldn't help but giggle when overhearing the attending waitress mutter to another server, "This is the sixth, no seventh time I've refilled his bread basket."

"Who?"

"The chubby one with the funny accent."

"Seven times? Seriously?"

"Literally seven times."

Meanwhile, Charlie and Claire were in deep conversation about the proper way to care for rose bushes, Jade was modeling her designer shoes for Autumn, and Sevastian was entertaining an assembly of giddy gymnasts by transfiguring his linen napkin into a swan. All seemed right with the world.

Many fun-filled hours glided into history. The satiated guests, full of New Zealand lamb chops and Pinot Noir, said their goodbyes and began to filter out. This was when Lex finally got a chance to talk to Charlie. All evening she had been desirously awaiting this moment.

"So, the hero of the day has at last come to pay me a visit," Charlie said, taking the terminal swig of his potent Sambuca.

"Just saving the best for last, as they say," she reciprocated with a sheepish grin.

"Your aunt is quite the chatty-Kathy," he said with a laugh. "Honestly though, some of the best conversation I've had in a long time. I really enjoy her."

"She thinks an awful lot of you too," Lex assured him while scanning the room for the rest of the Flock. Much to her dismay, they were nowhere to be seen. "Did Jade and Sevastian leave?"

"Yeah, they left while you were talking with your calculus professor. They didn't want to interrupt your conversation, but no worries. Anyway, we were hoping you'd be able to come by our place tonight."

"Tonight?" she repeated with a spark.

"So, here's the deal. Now that you've graduated college, I…we want to be the first to offer you a job before you get snatched up by some other lucky employer."

Her heart began to race. "Are you having a laugh?"

"This is on the level," Charlie answered.

"Seriously?"

He nodded.

Was she finally going to find out exactly what Charlie and his friends were hiding? "A job doing what exactly?" she inquired as the floodgates of her brain opened sending a tidal wave of suspense careening throughout her body.

"I think in this case, show is better than tell," he finally said after a tick of deliberation. "That is if you don't have other plans. I heard a few of your friends talking about going to the city for the after-party."

"That was the plan, but then the wine kicked in and suddenly everyone became too tired, so my schedule is clear," she assured him, having no desire to do anything but seize this newly presented opportunity.

"Excellent! It's a date then," he happily declared. She detected an uncharacteristic jitteriness in his tone and knew whatever he had in store must certainly be prodigious.

Before leaving the restaurant, she and Charlie thanked Aunt Claire for planning such an exquisite soiree. She also remembered, for once, to make known the plan so that Claire wouldn't be up all night in consternation over the whereabouts of her niece.

A sharp-dressed employee manning the entranceway offered his thanks for choosing The Birch Club as Charlie cordially held the door for Lex. A chilling wind heaved its way inward in competition with the warm blast of garlic scented air escaping into the parking lot. As if he was her personal chauffeur, Charlie opened the Range Rover's passenger door for his job candidate. With a discrete smile fueled by a contented heart, she climbed into the leather seat just as a light snow began to fall.

22

The tension in the vehicle was thick enough to cut with a knife. During the journey back to the mansion, Lex tried every angle, every trick in the book, to get Charlie to disclose more information about his job offer. Yet no matter which way she asked, or how she pleaded for just a little hint, he would not budge. His only response was an easygoing grin as he navigated along the slick roads. Finally, to add insult to injury, he changed the subject by illustrating the differences between The Birch Club's lamb chops and Sevastian's recipe. After ten minutes of excruciating tedium, he wrapped up with the conclusion that Sevastian's chops were the better of the two based mostly on his marinating techniques. For Lex, most of this rambling distraction went in one ear and out the other. Finally, after what might as well have been a road trip to Canada, the mansion came into view.

Jade and Sevastian were chatting zealously around the granite table in the dining room as she and Charlie strolled in shaking snowflakes from their hair. Overhead in the entranceway, she noticed the pair of tennis shoes that had been hanging from the sword of the naked marble man had been replaced by a red bra. Normally a sight such as this would have sent her straight into a giggle fit, but with this mysterious job offer looming on the horizon, she barely paid it a second glance. Sevastian was chowing down on a giant helping of rocky road ice cream topped off with a box of Milk Duds. Apparently the raspberry truffle at The Birch Club had not succeeded in placating his sweet tooth. Upon noticing the new arrivals, they perked up in their chairs. Lex could sense that something big was about to happen owing to the unspoken excitement percolating the room.

"Are you really offering me a job?" she asked as she pulled out a chair next to Jade and glided into a crossed-legged position.

The three exchanged expectant glances before Charlie answered, "We are, but you should know this job has absolutely nothing to do with your degree. Anyway though, I think you'll find it most appealing."

Lex was on pins and needles. Of course, her plan was to attend medical school, but after witnessing first hand the success of the Rose Flock, she figured it couldn't hurt to keep her options open.

"Here it is straight," Jade began. "We all think you're an amazing person. We have to be very selective as to who we bring into this business. For us, it's more about finding someone with the right qualities and personality rather than a specific type of degree or background."

"Right qualities?" Lex asked.

Jade nodded, "Intelligence, for example and empathy, selflessness, creativity. Above all you must be trustworthy."

"And you are all of those things," Sevastian added.

"Literally," Jade continued with emphasis, "you are the only person for this job."

Lex felt herself blushing. She was taken aback by the adamant praise.

Charlie continued, "To put it another way, Lex – you're a diamond in the rough."

At these words, the memory of the incomprehensibly life-like dream illuminated her brain. She remembered clearly that he had used that exact metaphor while he stood beneath the willow tree. Before she could make heads or tails of this, Charlie, as if still inside her head, offered a shocking comment. "You're thinking about your dream, aren't you?"

She could only imagine the stupefied expression that must have ensued. Held in the vice grip of shock, she could not convoke a response.

"You'll have quite a few surprises coming your way," Sevastian forewarned. "Might as well sit back and enjoy the ride."

"How did you know about the dream?" she finally blurted louder than intended. Jade gave Charlie an uneasy look.

"I think that may have been a bit untimely, Charlie," she said.

"That's okay. It's all part of the experience," he replied lightly.

The perplexity aggregated inside Lex's head and the pot was about to boil over. Her brain was parched from confusion and thirsted desperately for enlightenment. Before she could speak, the three unanimously rose from their seats and motioned her to do the same. "Allow us to show you the office," Charlie said.

"The office?"

"We run our business from the house," he explained.

"I thought I'd seen every room in this place. I don't recall an office."

"That's good, because it's not meant to be easily discovered," he said while situating his hand on the small of her back. He guided her out of the dining hall while the others trailed close behind with sprightly gaits.

23

The four began a brisk saunter through all of the rooms that had become so familiar to Lex. Onward they went, through the pendulum room, the living room, the gym, the kitchen, the indoor pool, through corridors and down hallways – until they finally arrived at a room that had never really caught her attention. She had noticed it of course, even studied a few hours here one day when Sevastian's bassoon practice had driven her from the library, but it wasn't so remarkable compared to the other rooms. It was like the lobby of a hunting lodge, only a bit smaller. The furniture was hand-crafted from pine logs, probably Sevastian's handiwork. Paintings of wild geese and emerald-headed mallards populated the walls. A bookshelf housing various texts about wildlife and the great outdoors stood in one corner, and a stuffed bobcat in another. The main attraction in this room, like many others in the mansion, was a large stone fireplace that circumscribed a monstrous fire. Several photographs sat upon the dark-wood mantle. One in particular drew Lex's attention; a darling eight-year-old Charlie in an off-centered ball cap flanked by an elderly couple. Robert and Ella Roanoke, she concluded. All in all, the room was neat and cozy, but didn't exhibit the qualities she would have expected from an office.

"Is this it?" she asked.

"Our business is confidential," Sevastian commented with an air of importance. "You would not suspect anything unusual about this room. So, in order to get to the office, you must start here." With that, he traipsed over to the fireplace and glanced back as if to make absolutely certain Lex was watching. Right before her eyes, as if observing a magic show, he hopped into the raging inferno and vanished amongst the flames. Lex was floored.

"It's not a real fire," Jade quickly pointed out. "With help from our friend, technology, we were able to create a hologram fire," Sevastian's face popped back into view.

"I am the great and powerful Oz!" he announced.

Charlie rolled his eyes. "That one never gets old."

Jade continued, "We've even installed heaters in the mantle that blow hot air. We must be as convincing as possible."

Lex was desperate to understand what kind of secret was vital enough to warrant the use of a hologram fire. Jade hurried to the false fire, and as if this was a run-of-the-mill routine, disappeared within the flames. Lex met Charlie's eyes with a half-hearted smile. "Shall we?" he asked as he took her hand.

She was still rather apprehensive. "I suppose," she replied while approaching the hearth with solicitude. As she stood before the roaring flames, she had to appreciate the realism of this facade. If she hadn't witnessed the other two go first, she wouldn't have thought it conceivable. Just a few paces from hearthside, the flames seemed so real. She deliberately outstretched her hand and sure enough, it went right into the conflagration without complication. She surrendered a nod, inhaled a deep breath, and closed her eyes. Hand-in-hand they stepped into the flames.

Sevastian and Jade were waiting on the other side each displaying a satisfied grin. Sevastian gave Lex a courtly pat on the shoulder as if to commend her bravery.

"Well, this is interesting," she observed. The four stood shoulder-to-shoulder in what appeared to be nothing more than an extension of the fireplace. The floor, walls, and ceiling were made of bricks and coated with murky soot; surely just another measure taken to ensure realism. The small recess was dirty, cramped and unexceptional. Standing idly in this incommodious dead end, Lex was now more confused than ever.

"Watch carefully," Sevastian instructed. "This is the next

step, or should I say – brick."

He squeezed between Jade and Charlie positioning himself in the corner. Glancing back to make certain she was paying attention, he knelt down and pointed a round digit to the bottom brick in the left corner.

"Start here and go up one, two, three, four, five… are you getting this, Lex?"

"It's not rocket science," Jade remarked impatiently.

He ignored her and continued. "And over three – one, two, three." The brick at which he had arrived upon looked identical to every other, but as he administered a mild tug, it started to wiggle free. When he had completely removed it from the wall, Lex could see a black button in the newly revealed opening. Charlie nudged Lex toward the button.

"Will you do the honors?" he asked. She nodded and gave the button an examination before conducting a good solid push. She jumped in bewilderment as the entire back wall began to move away, emitting a grinding rumble as it went. It slid backward to reveal a stone staircase leading downward into an aphotic abyss.

Bubbling over with suspense, she carefully trailed the others down a very long set of stairs. Each step conveyed them farther and farther from the fire light. Just as darkness became complete, they had reached the bottom. Sevastian's voice broke through the opaque atmosphere.

"It's right around…here it is." There was a click and a series of bright lights flickered on in succession down a long hallway. The hallway ended fifty feet ahead into a dingy, moss-covered wall. Seeming a bit out of place in the eerie corridor was a gleaming metal door in the left wall about fifty paces ahead. The four of them made quick work of the short jaunt from the stairwell to the door. Upon arrival, Lex took note of the security panel in which a code was needed. Jade punched in a long strand of numbers and the device beeped in acceptance.

As the door glided open, automatic lights sprang into action offering Lex her first view of something so unbelievable, so astonishing, she nearly fainted. All of the mystery, the secrets and the suspense had come down to this moment. "This can't be real," she heard herself saying, as if undergoing an out-of-body experience. "It just can't be."

The Flock shared a mutual laugh while watching her initial reaction when she finally saw how they earned their fortune.

24

"Welcome to the office," Charlie exclaimed with a presenting gesture of his outstretched hand. "Also known as the ice cave."

Lex's eyes sparkled as they reflected the shimmering phosphorescence of thousands and thousands of diamonds. There were so many it was staggering. The nickname "ice cave" could not have been more fitting as the room truly appeared to be iced over. The entire spectacle seemed so far beyond the bounds of possibility that her brain would not accept the notion that these were authentic precious stones.

A series of desks ran along the far wall, which housed a row of computers, a plethora of loose papers and pens, and enough binders to stack to the ceiling. On the adjacent end of the room were workbenches plentifully bestrewn with various diamond cutting machines, tools and microscopes. Everything in between was an unfathomable ocean of lustrous diamonds. There were shelves of them along the walls and many aisles of display cases dividing the room. Cases upon cases of breathtaking stones were situated in every available inch of space. Some of these brilliant baguettes were the size of softballs, each clear and perfect as a raindrop. While Lex gawked around the room completely speechless, Jade took the liberty of retrieving a swivel stool from a nearby workbench.

"I'm sure you'd like an explanation," she said.

Lex couldn't have agreed more. She noticed the seat and was quick to take a load off. Her whole body was shaking with excitement.

Charlie put a hand on her shoulder. "Sevastian will handle this one," he said. "This is his domain, as he is our master diamond cutter."

The enthusiastic Russian didn't hesitate. He hustled to a nearby display case that housed five gargantuan diamonds. "Lex, have you ever heard of the Star of Africa?" he asked.

"I can't say that I have," she replied.

Sevastian continued. "It is the largest cut diamond in the world. It's part of the British Crown Jewels and weighs just over five hundred and thirty carats," he informed her as he proudly raised his hand to present the largest one on the left. "I call this the Star of Sevastian. It weighs one thousand six hundred and forty carats."

Lex had a finite understanding about diamonds, but she did know that a simple ten carat diamond, if the clarity and cut were just right, could emulate the cost of a dream home in the Hamptons. She was exceedingly astounded by this as the source of the Rose Flock's boundless wealth was coming into light.

Sevastian went on. "It's impossible to put a price tag on this diamond because, you see, it is the very definition of priceless; priceless because it is the single largest diamond in this world making it one of a kind."

"And if you had to put a price on it?" Lex asked just to satisfy her own burning curiosity.

"Relative to other famous diamonds that have been purchased over the years," Sevastian answered, "the Star of Sevastian could be purchased for, let's say, several billion – maybe more. There is more value sitting in this very room than the entire North American continent- and that, my friend, is no exaggeration."

"Where do diamonds of this size come from?" she asked in bewilderment.

"Sorry, Lex," Charlie interjected, "but I have to withhold that information for now. I know that may seem inconsiderate, but we must proceed through this one step at a time."

She didn't know where to go from there. So many questions were swarming in her mind, yet her vocal cords were paralyzed.

"Of course, the largest diamonds are just trophies of ours," Sevastian pointed out. "If you look around, you will see that the majority of these stones are the typical size of what you would find in a common jewelry store – and that is where we make our money."

"Who do you sell them to?" asked Lex.

"We have buyers all over the world," Jade answered. "Popular jewelry chains, small companies, private collectors. In addition, we own and operate multiple online stores. In order to preserve our secrecy, the majority of our diamonds are filtered through Sevastian and Sevastian's father - sort of like money laundering but, um... legal and with diamonds. It's a massive enterprise and a tedious operation for just three people, which is why we hope you'll help us."

"What would you need me to do?"

"You would learn how the entire business operates," Jade explained. "This includes understanding policies and regulations of exporting these diamonds to foreign countries and all of the security measures involved in doing so. In addition, you'll need to learn market mechanics, economic relations, financial accountability, how to run our online stores, and even how to properly cut diamonds."

"But I've never had experience with any of those things," Lex admitted feeling slightly overwhelmed.

"They can be learned with just a few months of training," Charlie said reassuringly. "Soon your diamond knowledge will rival the world's top enthusiasts. Your lack of familiarity with the field does not concern us. In our business, there are more important attributes to a potential employee than experience."

"What do you mean?" she asked.

"Look at the Star of Sevastian," Charlie instructed as the four gazed upon the world's largest diamond. "Obviously, we don't have a common production. It all comes down to the origin of the stones. When we show you where they come from, you'll understand two things. First, you'll see why we need someone like you, someone we trust, to work for us. Second, you'll understand why we take extensive measures to remain secretive and anonymous. Over the past few months, you have proven to be competent, strong-willed and trustworthy, which as we said earlier, are the most important attributes one needs for this job. And, if I may say so, I feel that we are all pretty good friends. Who better to work with than a friend?"

Lex was overwrought. This entire situation was so outrageous she had trouble thinking clearly. Why her? Why was she the right person for this kind of work? Despite Charlie's claim that she was notably trustworthy and a good friend, it seemed only fitting for a thriving diamond empire to bring an expert onboard. "I'm flattered," she professed to no one in particular, "but if I am truly your choice, why must I be kept in the dark about your diamond source?"

Charlie was quick with a response. "Two words, – shock overload."

"I'm not sure I follow."

"Let me put it to you in another way," Sevastian interposed. "This little business of ours is nothing compared to what awaits you."

"Sevastian, I'm surrounded by a universe of diamonds - countless billions of dollars. How could anything be bigger than this?"

Sevastian looked to Charlie for an answer to this question. Charlie obliged by taking the reins. "In the end, I believe you'll understand my decision to hold off on this revelation of our "diamond mine" so to speak. But in the meantime, your desire for knowledge will be pacified by an extraordinary gift – the gift of freedom."

"I don't understand," Lex conceded. "Am I not already free?"

"Most people believe they are," he said. "In fact, we are very much confined by heavy chains. In America, the phrase "land of the free" is drilled into our heads from early childhood until we become brainwashed patriots. There is nothing free about America or the rest of the world for that matter. There is nothing free about life in general. We are all constrained by so many rules, regulations and laws, that our lives can hardly be considered free. It can be argued that these governing rules work for humankind and are a necessity to prevent chaos. This may or may not be true, but in either case, don't be blinded by the notion of being free. Furthermore, there is a much bigger limitation to freedom than our world's governing bodies."

Lex cocked her head, "And that is?"

"Let me show you," he said. He walked over to a shelf of particularly dazzling, golf ball-sized diamonds and selected the pick of the litter, then proceeded to place the stone upon a metal table. His candidate was a stone of such clarity and beauty, Lex could not take her eyes off of it. At that moment, she desired nothing more than to stare in admiration at this masterpiece.

"This one is Sevastian's magnum opus," he stated. Before Lex could say anything, or even blink, he snatched a sledgehammer from behind the table, raised it above his head, and swung it down upon the diamond with such force that the beautiful stone cracked, sending pieces helter-skelter about the room - one of them landing on the leg of a dumbfounded Lex. Jade and even Sevastian seemed completely undaunted by this premeditated act of ruination.

"Why did you do that?" Lex asked belligerently. She was so troubled by this heinous violation of pure beauty that her harsh tone could not be restrained.

"It's only a rock," Charlie calmly replied.

"That rock could have fed a third world country!" Lex continued, consciously surprised at how much Charlie's destructiveness was vexing her.

He just smiled. "It certainly could have," he agreed.

"Maybe several countries. But don't worry my young humanitarian, we have fed many starving families around the world."

Allowing him no room to continue, she hammered on. "Not only that, but you could have sold the diamond and invested the money - maybe bought another mansion."

Charlie's expression suddenly went serious. His trap had been sprung. "Why?" he asked. "How many mansions does a person need? You've seen this place, what other ridiculous excess could we possibly squeeze in here? No, there's nothing else we need; nothing that money could buy anyway. The three of us have traveled the world. We've done and seen things that most people only dream about. We have every material item we could ever desire. We have billions upon billions of dollars sitting in multiple bank accounts in many different countries. We have stepped beyond the domain of success into a realm of financial immortality. Sounds wonderful, doesn't it? Sadly, however, with our monumental success came a grim realization - from excess wealth grows an empty void. We began to realize that material possessions are only pieces of plastic or metal or stone. What do they really mean? Don't get me wrong, we have indulged, and continue to indulge in every conceivable extravagance. This house and everything in it is a testament to that. You can say we live life to the fullest, and certainly to the extreme. We are gluttons. We swim in a sea of luxury and comfort – expensive cars, hologram projectors, people who clean our home, indoor swimming pools. Yes, these things are enjoyable, and yes, it's great to catch a plane to Switzerland any time the mood strikes, but after a while the thrill of material luxury wears off. Once you are able to see beyond money's confining grip, new horizons come into view.

I smashed the diamond to illustrate two points. One, that Jade, Sevastian and I are no longer controlled by valuable material goods; two, that you still are. Don't take that as an insult. It's simply a demonstration of how people are not free because they are completely controlled by money and survival. Everything revolves around it whether we want to admit it or not. We all need to make a living to provide for ourselves and our families so that is exactly what we do. In the process, we fail to see the bigger picture. We involuntarily miss out on the most valuable opportunities life has to offer because we're working so hard just to get by."

"Forgive me for being puzzled," Lex cut in, "but I'm not sure I understand what you mean by valuable opportunities."

Charlie ruminated for a tick. "We are a unique breed," he said, insinuating Jade and Sevastian. "We are unique in that we possess both the desire and the means to search beyond mankind's conventional knowledge of life. Everyone talks about learning the secrets of the universe – who we are, where we came from, how it all started. Science has toiled over these questions for centuries but continues to come up short. Religion claims to explain it all but fails to provide proof beyond faith. You may be wondering why we are so interested in the secrets of the universe. You may also be surprised at how certain I am that the answers are within our reach. When we show you where the diamonds come from, you'll understand why we may be closer to solving these timeless riddles than anyone else before us."

In Lex's mind, his newly revealed desires were both confusing and intriguing. As if the ice cave wasn't shocking enough, he was now throwing this "secrets of the universe" mumbo-jumbo at her. "How long must I wait before you show me where the diamonds come from?" she inquired.

"Two weeks," he said. "And remember, we have…"

"You have your reasons, and I trust your judgment," she interjected.

Charlie's warm smile demonstrated that he was pleased with this remark. "Back to your gift of freedom," he continued as he paced around Lex like a piranha circling a chicken leg. "You now understand that a person cannot be free while confined by the restraints of finances."

Her heart rate sky rocketed. She could see where this was

going. She rotated clockwise in the swivel stool, keeping a skeptical eye on him as he paced her perimeter.

"We want to relieve you of the heavy burden of financial slavery. If you work for us, you will not get a paycheck. Instead, you will receive our bank account number and have unlimited access to all of the money you could possibly want." Her eyes widened with exhilaration as he proceeded. "I know you're excited about this, Lex, because any normal person would be. To deny that is a lie. Also, I know you'll politely refuse the offer because you feel that you don't deserve it. But please understand that you'll be doing us a tremendous favor by helping with the business. During the next two weeks, before we reveal the rest of our secret, we want you to get acquainted with the business and enjoy your new financial freedom. Pay off any debt, buy a new car, donate a million dollars to cancer research – whatever your heart desires. But most importantly, take the time to decide if this is what you want to do. It's not medical school, but I promise, if you choose to work with us, you won't regret it." He looked happily at his two companions and then at Lex who was still trying to comprehend everything that had just been put on the table. Her pulse had soared, her palms were sweaty, her mind raced. This was huge.

"That's enough for one night," said Jade. "The poor thing has got a lot to think about."

"I couldn't agree more," Charlie concurred, helping Lex to her feet. "Graduation ceremony, party at the Birch Club, big job offer – been one hell of a day for you. Come on, I'll drive you home."

The four vacated the ice cave and proceeded back through the series of secret obstacles by which they had entered. After stepping out from the hologram fire, Jade and Sevastian shook Lex's hand and extended their congratulations for taking everything so well. They then departed the room leaving her alone with Charlie.

Her next move was as involuntary as a heartbeat. Without saying a word, she wrapped her arms around him and laid her head upon his chest. Was there any other gesture of appreciation that could be more fitting for the generosity she had just received? She was surprised at how natural this felt. After a slight pause, and possibly a bit of deliberation, he hugged her back. His expression was an ambiguous mixture of uncertainty and content, although Lex could not see his face as her cheek was nestled into his cotton shirt. Little did she know this hug was more than a simple gesticulation of gratitude; it was an unspoken contract that bound her to this new life. She was now entirely enmeshed in whatever Charlie had in store, desperately hoping he wouldn't let her down. There was no turning back now.

"So this is what you've been hiding," she said. "This is what the Rose Flock is all about. You are all truly fascinating in every sense of the word."

He nodded. "Yes, Lex, this is what we've been hiding, but the diamonds and the wealth aren't what we're all about. Soon you'll understand that this is something we do for more important reasons. I know it's difficult to fathom, but there's still so much more."

Basking in the simple pleasure of each other's company, Charlie and Lex walked back through the network of rooms and out to the snow-covered driveway where the dependable Range Rover was patiently waiting.

25

During the drive home, Lex marveled over the fact that her whole world had flipped upside down in just an hour. In a way, it seemed as though she really was experiencing freedom for the first time. And how could she not feel this way? College was finished and apparently so was any concern over money. With these two cumbersome burdens removed, she felt as though she could just float away. The incessant smile upon her face told the tale.

The colorful glow of Christmas lights reflected off the Range Rover's glossy paint as she and Charlie rolled through a picturesque neighborhood straight from a Currier and Ives piece. Smoke cascaded from every chimney, ornament endowed Christmas trees adorned every picture window and families captivated by the sudden accumulation of powder, built snowmen in their front yards. There was nowhere else in the entire world Lex would rather be just then – in Charlie's company in beautiful Rose, her home. She positively apotheosized the Flock. They had become such good friends and role models. It could easily be assumed that they thought the same of her. Why else would they ask her to join their diamond company?

When they arrived at the restful lake house, Charlie escorted her to the front door, just like he always did. The chilly north wind kissed the exposed skin around her neck enhancing the desire to hurry indoors. "Want to come inside for a moment?" she asked hopefully. "I'll make tea."

He nodded. "Selfishly yes, I'd love to, but you need some time alone to mull everything over. Oh, and I have one more gift for you."

"I think you have already spoiled me beyond all reason," she commented as he pulled an antique pocket watch from the breast pocket of his coat. He gently took hold of her hand, opened it, then placed the watch upon her palm. She could only stare blankly at the antiquarian timepiece, unsure of his intentions.

"This is the greatest of all gifts," he said. "Not the watch itself, but what it represents."

"Time?"

"Yes."

"So, time is the greatest of all gifts?"

"In two weeks, it will make more sense to you," he promised with an assuring nod. "In the meantime, keep it safe."

"I will," she assured him.

"One other thing," he added as Lex reached for the door handle. "Please don't tell anyone about what you've seen tonight. I realize that your aunt will want to know and so will your friends, but I need you to keep it a secret until the two weeks pass and you know everything. Is that cool?"

"Mum's the word," she pledged with a smile. At this time, Charlie acknowledged his companion by simply staring directly into her eyes. He seemed lost in them for a moment, hypnotized beyond his own consent and held against his own will. Lex could not help but involuntarily blush.

"What?" she asked. "Is there something in my teeth?"

"No, it's not your teeth," he answered, "It's your eyes. I've never seen eyes of such resounding green."

"So I've been told," she replied with a sheepish grin. "I got them from my mum. Her eyes were green also."

"Yeah," Charlie said with a trace of uncharacteristic bashfulness, "they're like artwork. Green like an ocean of emeralds."

Her smile spread instantly from cheek to cheek. "That was very poetic."

"I'm just saying," he finished, breaking gaze and looking to the ground, seemingly embarrassed. "Anyway, think things over and give me a call when you've reached a verdict. I truly hope you decide to take us up on the job offer. Or at least give it a try for a while and see if it suits you."

"Just to be thorough, I'll sleep on it," she said, "but I think my mind is pretty much made up."

Charlie could not disguise his felicity after hearing these words. "Wonderful!" he declared, "simply wonderful!"

After a goodbye hug and saying "thank you" so many times that it bordered on obnoxious, she watched with a full mind as the Range Rover's taillights disappeared into the powdery night. She was floating on clouds and couldn't repress a squeal of sheer delight. Sleep would be impossible tonight. She was so worked up from the evening and simply dying to know the unimaginable surprise that would come at the end of two weeks. Inhaling several deep breaths of December air, she gave herself a moment to regain composure before heading up to Claire's room to say goodnight.

26

On his way back to the mansion, Charlie was all business as he conversed on the autophone with Jade. "Everything is going as planned," he mentioned. "She didn't totally freak out, which is a good sign."

Jade's voice resounded over the vehicle's speaker system. "Did you ask her to keep it a secret?"

"Yeah, no worries."

"I worry," she dolefully replied after a long pause. "Not that Lex will tell anyone about our secret, but I worry for Lex herself. This feels so wrong... so deceitful."

Charlie dropped his head in shame. "I was hoping you wouldn't say that because, well, I thought the same thing. But what choice do we have?"

"None other I guess."

"It still astounds me every time I think of it," he said, regaining a salient smile. "Alexis Lunden - the cute little bookworm in the front row of our ecology class. The star gymnast. Did I ever tell you she sat right in front of me at our high school graduation? Who would have ever guessed in a million years that... well you know."

"She's wonderful," Jade replied with an insinuation of caution, "but heed my advice – don't get too attached. We needn't any confounding variables. Remember, we made a pact to do what has to be done." Jade couldn't see Charlie's unsettled reaction when she advised him to "not get too attached."

Finally, he added, "I just hope she'll come through. It's a

lot to put on her shoulders."

"Literally the weight of the world," Jade inventively included before the two disconnected.

"She's right," Charlie said to himself. "There is no room for error. Attachment is a confounding variable and I won't allow it to interfere."

27

For Lex, the next two weeks were so eventful that the days just cruised on by. She had yet to experience a single boring moment. There was always so much to do and learn and it felt as though she had regressed to childhood, once again taking in a brand new world. The grand revealing of the diamond business had altered her life almost completely and she had no qualms about immersing herself in this new exorbitant lifestyle.

After the first week, the others must have predicted she would be in it for the long haul. Acting upon that notion, they furnished a massive upstairs room, at the time only used for storage, into a luxury suite fit for royalty. Each of the housemates added their own touch to her new living chambers.

The room came equipped with everything a girl could want. The centerpiece, handcrafted by Sevastian, was a king-size canopy bed with heavy orchid drapery concealing an immaculate mahogany frame. The sturdy frame held a mattress so voluptuous you'd swear you were sleeping on air.

In addition to the bed, the tenacious Russian had labored into the small hours of each night in order to complete the room's main attraction. The finished product was a mesmerizing mural of gargantuan proportion covering the entire ceiling. The masterpiece stole Lex's breath away every time her irises gazed upward. The theme was wild horses and there were hundreds of them sowed about the panoramic terrain. Entwined within the mountainous landscape were sparkling ponds, evergreen forests, grape arbors, woodland birds and grass covered prairies. There were so many subtleties that she discovered something new each time she studied it. Although the painting was one continuous countryside, a different season was assigned to each separate quadrant of the ceiling. If one of the horses happened to occupy two different quadrants, he might just have his hind legs on lush green grass and his front legs in deep snow. As if the changing seasons didn't add enough multiplicity to the piece, each seasonal-themed quadrant was also equipped with both a day and night section. There were suns, stars, moons and clouds. Owl silhouettes grazed moonbeams with their outstretched wings in the night sections, doves dotted the sky in the daylight portions. The painting was so intricate, one would guess that it would have taken a lifetime to complete. Lex found that one of her favorite pastimes was examining the mural to discover Sevastian's hidden surprises.

The latest of these surprises revealed itself one evening after she had finished an exhaustive session with Sevastian learning the fine art of "girdling" diamonds. Mentally and physically spent, but not entirely sleepy, she decided to disregard The History of Diamonds, a shoddy old textbook Charlie had given her to read, and instead slip into the paradisiacal world populating her ceiling. She found that lying in bed to study the painting was not a good approach as the drapery overhead obscured her view. To alleviate this dilemma, she decided to try her luck by testing the durability of the bed. As if more primate than human, she utilized her gymnast dexterity to shimmy up the bedpost and flip her nimble body into the hammock-like comfort of the canopy. Should the structural integrity fail, the only repercussion would be a freefall onto a cushiony mattress – a consequence she thought would be most exhilarating should it come to pass. The canopy, however, showed no evidence of succumbing to her weight and now she had a closer, unobstructed view of all the wild horses her eyes could behold.

Directly above her bed, a riveting subtlety snagged her eye. Purposefully positioned into the background dimension, a dapper stallion of glimmering black stood majestically beneath the shaded haven of a cypress grove. This singular horse held two distinct differences to every other in the mural. For one, he was the only black horse and two, he had a rider. The only human in the picture had an unclear identity due to the large scale distance from the foreground, but Lex held little doubt about the subject of Sevastian's intended representation. The female rider had long brown hair, creamy skin and a flowing azure frock fitted to a thin body. The semblance between herself and this mystery rider was undeniable. With her image permanently imprinted in the landscape, she was now absorbed in the mural both mentally and physically and this pleased her. She adored the painting and it had earned Sevastian a special place in her heart.

Jade's contribution was the oak wardrobe. Medieval in appearance and standing twelve feet tall, it was certainly a spectacle to behold. The true awe, however, lay within. During the past months of their blossoming friendship, Jade had picked up on Lex's favorite clothing designers and preferred style. This was to be the basis of the wardrobe's contents. On the other side of monstrous double doors, there were nearly fifty new outfits, including shoes, sunglasses, jewelry and hats all tailored to Lex's exact specifications. Assuredly there were thousands of dollars spent on the new vestments and at least as much on the wardrobe itself.

Finally, there was Charlie, who of course added a modernistic touch to the room. He had installed a radically contemporary entertainment center which encompassed a gargantuan hologram television, the newest video game system, and a two petabyte memory drive containing nearly every movie ever made. The wall-sized screen doubled as a computer monitor with voice-activated everything so Lex was able to peruse the web without tying up her hands.

She was deeply touched by the generosity of her friends and also very grateful. But, at the same time she couldn't help but feel guilt's insistent bite. It was not clear to her why they were giving in such abundance. Perhaps they were catching her up with their own indulgence, leveling the playing field so to speak. Or maybe they were just happy to have an excuse to burn some cash. The reason, for now, would remain speculatory. Every time she asked, they would always offer the same response - "It's just a little token of appreciation for your help with the business."

Then there was the matter of Aunt Claire. How was Lex to explain this drastic life alteration while adhering to her promise to keep Charlie's secret? She couldn't lie to her beloved aunt, only distort the truth a little. Instead of particularizing about the ice cave, the billion dollar enterprise, and her new found wealth, she went with a more streamlined approach. She simply told Claire that the Rose Flock was responsible for operating the websites of several renowned diamond companies – the truth. They needed another body in the operation – the truth. There was an extra bedroom in the mansion – the truth. Living in the mansion was too sweet a deal to decline – positively the truth.

Though it was a foregone conclusion, and only a matter of time before a girl Lex's age would fly the coop, Aunt Claire was saddened by the news of her niece's intended adieu. Claire was a wee bit on the old-fashioned side and the idea of living in the same house with two boys was not the arrangement she would have chosen for Lex. Her fondness of Charlie and company at least allowed her to appreciate the decision, but she had offered her opinion that Lex should not be bogged down by anything that would sidetrack medical school. When Lex notified Charlie about Claire's uncertainty, he devised a clever scheme to change her mind and seal the deal. It was time to return the dinner favor.

The plan played out like clockwork. Jade hand delivered to Claire a formal invitation to dine at the mansion which she accepted without hesitation. After a feast of pecan crusted whitefish, a guided tour through the fantastical array of rooms, and the pleasure of watching her favorite movie, Breakfast at Tiffany's, in the home movie theater, Claire was convinced that this profound utopia was indeed the perfect place for her niece.

28

Even with the Aunt Claire dilemma resolved, Lex was still busy as a beaver. Besides the perpetual back-and-forth trips between the mansion and the lake house in which she was incrementally shifting her belongings, there was an endless array of other matters to occupy her time and attention. Primarily she was learning to be fascinating, and she was assuming the role rapidly. Charlie, Jade and Sevastian helped free her from the cocoon, the prison that had confined her until now, to reveal her full glorious potential. Though this was partly accomplished by the allotment of financial freedom, she discovered that it wasn't so much the money that altered her, rather, it was the new mindset she had acquired. Sure, it was surreal not batting an eyelash when paying off the looming car loan, or buying Boc the latest and greatest equestrian gear, but other than a few minor forbearances here and there, she had little motivation to go on a grand shopping spree or buy an island in the Caribbean. Perhaps Charlie was right when he claimed that your entire outlook of life changes when money is no longer an issue.

Much like a sugar cube dissolves in liquid, she began to coalesce with her housemates as she participated in the activities around the mansion. She spent mornings and evenings with Sevastian learning the ins and outs of the online stores and how the diamond business operates. She was put in charge of what they called "The Mediterranean Sector," which required her to learn Greek. She was gung ho about finally adding another language to her unilingual repertoire. With Sevastian's untiring assistance, she was astounded at how fast she was picking it up. Within the first few days, she had already completed exercises in the advanced section from her Learn to Speak Greek in Just Six Weeks workbook.

Every afternoon, she exercised in the mansion's gym. In particular, she just couldn't get enough of the suspended pool. Swimming laps back and forth along the ceiling was the closest thing she had ever felt to flying – with the exception of her enigmatic dream of course. After a pleasant sit in the steam room and a rejuvenating shower, she met up with Sevastian to resume diamond cutting lessons. After inadvertently defacing her fifth million-dollar diamond of the afternoon, she would apologize and promise to do better the next time.

The rest of the day would be spent pursuing a new found desire to train her brain. She found learning to be extremely enjoyable when you could select your own subject, do it at your leisure and not be tested over the material. Many hours slipped away each afternoon as she studied over a cup, or cups, of cicadaweed tea. Subjects that had never before captured her interest like meteorology, physics and astronomy were suddenly magnetic.

Every evening after Sevastian's gourmet feast of the day, Jade invited Lex out to the rooftop to meditate in the soft snow. It was both exhilarating and lulling to perch cross-legged on the roof's edge while impenetrable winter attire deflected the arctic blasts. Whether the girls remained in a state of silent rumination or got wrapped up in a philosophical discussion, the result of these ecopsychology sessions was a thoroughly rejuvenated mind, body and spirit.

Time spent with Sevastian and Jade was an honor and a privilege, but her favorite times of all were spent with Charlie. Anything from washing dishes to bird watching was more enjoyable when he was around. Every moment they were together, their bond grew.

Interwoven within the plume of this new exciting life were uncertainties that kept rearing their ugly heads. It was a constant battle to keep these monsters at bay. As hard as she tried to do so, they always found a way to break free. Every amicable moment spent with Charlie was overcast with looming questions that were slowly gnawing away at the trust she had for him. She was desperately inquisitive about the diamonds, their origin in particular. Clearly, the Rose Flock had some source that nobody else on earth had access to. Other questions - the origin of cicadaweed tea, the mysterious mint candy, Charlie's puzzling childhood and why Greek?

The most pressing question, the one that had been driving her delirious, was how Charlie knew about her dream. He had vowed that all of her questions would be answered after the two weeks were up, but it was hard for a curious individual like Lex to wait that long. On the final evening of that extraordinary fortnight, she would finally succumb to the agony of being kept in the dark.

29

Thirteen days had elapsed since Lex's first trip to the ice cave. In that short time, she had gotten a good handle on the diamond business, succeeded in becoming semi-fluent in Greek, acquired noticeably improved abdominal muscles from a disciplined regimen on the "Power House Abs" machine in the mansion's gym, and annexed a new overall appreciation for life. To add to her felicitous state of mind, it was now three days before Christmas – a holiday which she had always placed on a pedestal above all others. At this point however, she was more excited to find out what her friends had in store for her tomorrow, than for Christmas day itself.

That night found the four of them at Vincent's, huddled around a back-corner table talking quietly amongst themselves. This was the very place at which Lex had recently resigned employment now that it was no longer prudent to pour drinks and take food orders for a living. The restaurant was packed to the gills with patrons boiling over with holiday spirit. Merry clamor rang out from every angle as guests laughed the night away with family, friends and wine. Not a single employee passed by without casting a star-struck glance toward Lex and her companions. Even the staff that had been her good friends displayed an aura of awe when stopping by the booth to pay her a hello. She noted how enrapturing it was to see things through a celebrity's eyes. It was satisfying to now be on the other side of the fence, which of course was the side with the greener grass.

She watched her friends shovel forks full of pasta into their mouths as if there were no tomorrow. How three worldly people of such intelligence and awareness could make every meal resemble a lion pride devouring a zebra carcass was beyond her. Her head was a teapot ready to spout steam from two weeks of agonizing patience. She knew she didn't have a prayer of getting the big answers until tomorrow, but she figured in the meantime, she could at least get answers to a few other enduring questions. "Okay I'm sorry but I'm just going to ask," she stated with a playful note, so the question would not be taken as offensive. "How in the world can you guys possibly eat so much food in one sitting?" The others, both surprised and amused by the sudden inquiry, glanced at each other as if this were the first time they had realized the oddity of their behavior.

Finally, Charlie, with his quick-witted humor replied, "Jade and I have hollow legs. Sevastian has a fat belly. Plenty of room for food storage." Everybody laughed at this except Sevastian who blithely chomped away at his veal marsala. Judging by his subtle contemplated air, Lex knew he was already planning Charlie's payback. She secretly enjoyed the boy's ceaseless game of one-upmanship.

"Here is something else," she continued. "Forgive me if this question is intrusive, but I can't help but wonder why you keep the diamond business going. I mean, the three of you are by far, the richest people in the world..."

"The four of us, you mean?" Charlie interrupted, his words muffled by a mouthful of crab cake.

"Yes, well...," she replied unpretentiously, "what I'm trying to say is that you...I - I mean we, have more money than could ever be spent in ten lifetimes. Wouldn't it be worth our while just to stop the business altogether and have all the free time in the world?"

"That's a very savvy question," Jade replied, "and I have two answers. First, Sevastian loves to cut diamonds. If this pastime were taken from him, he would certainly go through some sort of depression. But obviously that isn't the main reason. We can't just pull out because, well, because of the consequences of pulling out. Our business is a major supplier for the world's diamond market. If we were to just withdraw, our departure would have a serious impact on the global economy."

"That's right," Sevastian added. This was the first time he had offered any comment since his entreé had been placed on the table. "However, we do have a long-term plan for eventually weaning ourselves out. When we first started into the industry many years ago, we had not accounted for the rapid growth of the company or how difficult it would be to stop the ball once it was rolling."

"Yeah, I guess that makes sense," said Lex.

Charlie swallowed the last few drops of whatever cloudy red liquid was in his wine glass then looked at her in the same excited way that he did almost two weeks ago, before showing her the ice cave. "I'm sure you're well aware that tomorrow marks two weeks since we promised you'd find out the origin of the diamonds," he said quietly as another curious waitress passed just a little too close for his comfort. Lex nodded enthusiastically. "Well, my friend, tomorrow you'll get your chance. I speak for all of us when I say how sorry I am to have kept you in suspense this long. Again, we just needed to ease you into this whole thing to see how well you would handle it. Honestly, we couldn't be happier. You've resisted the temptation to use the money foolishly, despite my instructions to do whatever you wanted with it. The money that you did spend was well within the boundaries of reason. Quite frankly, you seemed more interested in the leisure activities that we love so much and not at all interested in burning green. This confirms that you are the perfect person for this job."

Before she could say anything, Jade broke in with an announcement so urgent, she nearly choked on a bite of butternut squash. "Lex, it's seven thirty!" she cried out pointing to her watch as if a bomb was about to go off.

Lex gasped and looked at her phone, "Already?" she said in disbelief, leaping from her seat so quickly she knocked over her water glass. In all the excitement, she had forgotten that she was due at St. Paul's church in less than thirty minutes for a Christmas concert. She had been a member, more so the backbone, of the church choir since moving to Rose and her tardiness would undoubtedly put a few gray hairs on the head of the choir director.

A few weeks ago, Lex had been lured to the library by the dulcet tones of a violin playing Ennio Morricone's "Gabriel's Oboe." Up to that point, she had been too shy to sing in front of Sevastian because of his staunch musical idealism. Although she had plenty of confidence in her vocal abilities, she still felt the bite of trepidation when the urge came to join in on one of his practice sessions. This time, however, the necessity was irresistible. As if driven by all nine muses at once, she simply walked up behind him and began singing. The perfectly controlled notes that outpoured from her vocal cords hypnotized Sevastian to the point where he could no longer pull the bow across the strings. She finished the next three verses in a spellbinding acapella, not at all oblivious to the fact that her singing was impressing him. This impromptu performance had attracted the others to the library where they watched and listened, thoroughly surprised by this gift they had no idea she possessed. Since then, Charlie, Jade and especially Sevastian would not miss an opportunity to hear her sing. Tonight would be no exception.

"We've gotta move!" Charlie urgently declared as he popped from his seat completely unconcerned that half his plate was still covered with delectable fare. Even Sevastian, whose plate was not entirely clean, jumped to his feet with purpose. He pulled two crisp Ben Franklins from his pocket and slapped them into the hand of their passing server.

"No change," he said as the waiter's face glowed with appreciation.

The four hustled out the door and into the vintage Hummer. They succeeded in making the twenty minute drive to St. Paul's in fifteen, allowing Lex just enough time to change into a breathtaking heather gown which matched the other two soloists.

While the star of the show resigned to the lower church quarters to warm up her vocal cords, Charlie and the others located Aunt Claire. She had selected the front pew, the dream seats, and for the past half-hour had been shooing people away like gnats in order to save them. The church was quickly reaching capacity and she was very relieved when the others had finally arrived.

The next ninety minutes were a rapturous oeuvre for all who had come to listen to the timeless Christmas hymns sung by the St. Paul's choir. Lex had stolen the show with her angelic solos and sealed the deal with an effectual high E in the crowning verse of the final song, Oh Holy Night. During that one sound note, a few members of the audience had been brought to tears. There was not a soul in the entire congregation that had not been gripped in some way by her unprecedented gift.

Aunt Claire and the others convened with Lex in the snow-dusted parking lot after the concert had concluded. While soft flakes fell on their hair, they chatted for a few minutes, conversing about the particulars of the show and praising the wonderful music selection. After discussing plans for Christmas day and a plethora of goodbye hugs, everyone departed the church and headed for home.

30

Later that night, twelve booming chimes resonated throughout the mansion and found their way into Lex's bedroom. Although this particular clock made an hourly racket, she was yet to ascertain its exact location. This served as a reminder that there were still places in this behemoth house that she had not yet discovered. Right now, as she and Jade were nestled amongst the cozy covers of her bed while The Christmas Carol played on the wall-sized television, she had no yearning to venture out into the mansion's drafty corridors in search of this ethereal timepiece.

The Ghost of Christmas Future stood eight feet tall and thanks to cutting edge technology, protruded from the television as a demonic hologram. Even Lex, who had viewed this film annually for as long as she could remember, felt a little jumpy as the hellish phantom floated about the room.

"This is my favorite part," Jade declared as her hand dug into a bowl of popcorn the girls were sharing. She emitted a devilish laugh as poor Ebenezer Scrooge at wits' end, dropped to his knees in mortal terror and whisked away the thin blanket of snow from his own gravestone. Though it intrigued Lex to see the great pleasure Jade took in this single disconcerting scene, she could hardly pay it a bit of mind, as there was a more pressing matter occupying her thoughts.

"I'm definitely jazzed about tomorrow," she said.

"Huh?" Jade uttered inattentively as her focus remained on a grief- stricken Scrooge.

"The big surprise!" Lex elucidated. "The source of the diamonds. Remember?"

"Oh yeah, thanks for reminding me," Jade said, finally

prying her eyes from the movie and transposing regard to her friend. "I need to fill you in on tomorrow's agenda."

Lex's conscious was filled with the expectation of wonder the next day would likely deliver. "What's the game plan?" she asked, utilizing all her willpower to maintain an unruffled composure.

"What I'm about to tell you will sound strange," Jade warned. With all Lex had so far witnessed from the Flock, she maintained credence that whatever Jade was about to say, would be unlikely to surprise her. "First thing in the morning," she continued, "you and I are going shopping at Outdoor Surplus for some comfortable trail shoes. I've noticed that you don't own a pair."

"You're right," Lex cut in. "That does sound strange; but no more so than a swimming pool in the ceiling, a hologram fire, or an entire room of tree snakes."

"Can't argue with that," Jade frankly observed before continuing. "Afterward we'll go to the salon. I know it may seem comical that egocentric beautification is part of the big plan but remember there's a reason for everything. You told me the other day that you could use a trim and a highlight. It would behoove the both of us to have this done before we… get to the big surprise. Afterward, we'll come back here where I expect Sevastian will have a delicious holiday feast prepared for all of us. I believe it's roast turkey, ham, cranberry salad, you know, the usual Christmas entrées. After the meal I hope we, especially you, can find time for an afternoon siesta because tomorrow evening you'll need to have all your wits about you."

"Why will I need to have my wits about me?" Lex asked quickly, attempting to catch Jade off guard in hope that she would prematurely spill the beans. Jade answered with a shrewd grin that seemed to portray the timeless saying, "You have to get up pretty early in the morning to get one by me." This new information was indeed bizarre and left Lex feeling farther than ever from reaching a viable prediction about tomorrow's big surprise. She racked her brains to place these new puzzle pieces in any kind of cohesive arrangement, but as hard as she tried they would not fit together. Trail shoes? The salon? How do these two things relate to diamonds?

"Alright well, I'm going to bed. Big day tomorrow," Jade said as her bare feet found the stone floor and Ebenezer Scrooge called merrily to a boy in the street instructing him to purchase the prize turkey from the vendor a few streets over.

"Sure thing," Lex replied as she watched her intriguing friend exit the room. "Goodnight and thank you," she called after her.

Jade halted abruptly and turned back with a warm smile. "Thank you for what?"

"For making my life so wonderful," answered Lex sincerely as she caught a gleam of, was it guilt? in Jade's expression.

"Oh, um, think nothing of it," Jade said as she pulled the door shut.

31

That night, Lex tossed and turned. Although she desperately wanted sleep to find her, it would not come. This insomnia was plausibly due to the anticipation of tomorrow's surprise coupled with too much caffeine at the restaurant earlier in the evening. Nevertheless, she was restless and willing to try anything to achieve slumber.

Thinking back to a comparable experience in her childhood, she recalled her mother giving her warm milk in order to make her drowsy. She also knew that Sevastian had been to the grocery store yesterday and that several gallons of milk were available in the kitchen. It was worth a try. She climbed out of bed and cloaked herself in a wool nightgown. The mansion was always cold, especially in the winter.

She shuffled out of her room and into the hallway. An eerie silence engulfed her as she hurried past portrait after shadowy portrait of Sevastian's design. They were resplendent by day and haunted by night as their eyes seemingly followed her every footfall. She had never been one to scare easily, but with the Ghost of Christmas Future's image lingering in her memory, she traversed the spooky corridors very hastily this night.

Finally, she arrived at the stairs leading down to the first floor and ultimately, the kitchen. Directly across from the stairwell entrance, was a large, Victorian-style window that offered an all-inclusive view of the snowy, moonlit fields behind the mansion. She stopped there and took a moment to appreciate the starry sky and the bright white moon of this early December morning. She could always count on Old Man Winter to ease her senses.

In the midst of turning back toward the stairs, she happened to catch sight of a tiny glimmering light, a miniscule flicker from outside. She turned back toward the window to see a little fire on what appeared to be a torch. The torch was being conveyed by a dark figure, which from her vantage point was small and ambiguous. Following directly behind the first figure came two more torch-baring shadows. Although she could not positively identify who composed this mysterious fire parade, she surmised that it had to be the Flock because they seemed to have come from the mansion. She watched with abysmal curiosity as the procession persisted through the deep snow toward the patch of trees in the distance. After many minutes, they arrived at the trees, and then disappeared amongst the branches.

For the next few minutes, her mind filed through a million possible explanations which eventually produced a frustration headache. She was certain that the people she just saw must be Charlie, Jade and Sevastian. But wait, what if it wasn't? She wondered if the night walkers were intruders, thieves perhaps. Finally, she concocted a logical plan of action. She would go by Charlie's bedroom. If he was there, she would warn him of the trespassers. If he was not there, then it was likely he and the others who were the anonymous night walkers. The plan made perfect sense. But then, just as she took the first vaulting stride toward Charlie's room, the tiny dots of fire re-emerged from the trees and her attention was diverted back to the window.

It took the strangers much longer to make the return trip. They had traveled out with such vitality, and now, they shuffled along like a pack of coyotes exhausted from a long, unsuccessful hunt. As the dark strangers finally reached the mansion, they vanished from Lex's view. From somewhere on the first floor, she heard the faint sound of a door opening, footsteps, and voices. Without a second thought, she descended the stairs. Her heart galloped tempestuously. Her instincts were saying that something was amiss. At the base of the marble stairwell, she stopped to listen. There were muffled voices coming from the direction of the kitchen. She stepped quietly and cautiously beginning her pursuit toward the unknown. Utilizing keen observational tracking, she followed an indistinct trail of wet footprints and snow clumps. The lighting was meager, as the mansion was always kept on an energy-efficient regimen from midnight to seven. Still, with the dim illumination from several small lamps along the way and an occasional beam of moonlight from an overhead window, she could just make out tiny puddles of blood on the stone floor. Following the snowy, bloody trail and the sound of sporadic voices, she found herself standing at the kitchen door. It was cracked open allowing beams of bright light to spill out. Ever so heedful, she peaked through the opening only to observe an extraordinarily disturbing spectacle.

There before her was Jade and Sevastian. An unusual hooded garment made of heavy brown material, a cloak of sorts, was worn by each of them. The two were utterly unrecognizable. Jade wore no makeup. Her hair was pulled back in a scraggly up-dew. Dry dirt veiled her face and hands. She seemed tired, beat up. Sevastian was unmistakably worse off and his battered guise turned Lex's stomach. She covered her mouth to restrain a cry of horror.

His face was littered with gashes, bruises and dried blood as if he had tangled with a large animal. Then with Jade's assistance, he rolled up his sleeve and began to remove a mess of bloody bandages from his arm. When the dressing had been shed, a horrid, gaping wound was now the center of attention. Lex was now on the brink of losing her supper as crimson skeletal muscle projected from the open gash.

Jade retrieved a cup of sanitizing alcohol and a medical stitching kit from a nearby drawer and immediately set to work. Sevastian, as if completely undaunted by the whole thing, peeled open a banana and began to chomp away while Jade proceeded to stitch him up without the benefit of anesthetics. Perhaps what disturbed Lex more than anything else, was the fact that they were treating this little operation as if it were a run-of-the-mill occurrence. Neither of them showed any outward indication of bother over this scene from the pages of a horror story. It wasn't until they started into a friendly discussion about plans to update the library's computerized book catalog, when her curiosity finally got the best of her. She pushed open the door and entered the kitchen.

32

They could not mask their surprise at Lex's arrival nor could they conceal their unease. Within the first few uncomfortable seconds, she understood full well that this was something she was not intended to see.

"Lex! What are you doing up so early?" Sevastian asked, attempting to be blasé but failing miserably. There was urgency in his tone. Lex felt tears welling in her eyes at the sight of her mangled friend along with the blatant secrecy of the situation.

"What happened to you, Sevastian?" she asked meekly. The delayed response only meant that the others were not ready to be truthful.

Finally, after what seemed like an eternity of awkward silence, Jade spoke up. "He had an accident with a diamond cutting tool down in the ice cave. Don't worry though, he'll be just fine after I get a few stitches in him."

Lex knew perfectly well that there was more to the story and she let this much show through in her facial expression. She had felt the same way about Charlie's supposed pitchfork accident. Part of her assumed that the Flock had a legit reason for these ongoing mendacities, but the other part could no longer stand being the outsider. Feeling defeated, she decided not to ask about their peculiar clothing or for more details in regard to Sevastian's injury. "I hope you'll be okay," she said solemnly without incorporating eye contact. "I was just getting some milk." No one spoke as she went about her task. She was feeling dispirited. As close as she thought she was to the Rose Flock, there was obviously much more that they were hiding.

Finally, as the mug was topped off with cold white milk, Jade finally succumbed to whatever guilt she must have been carrying. "I'm so sorry, Lex," she began in a pleading tone. "I know you're not stupid. Of course, we're lying and yes, we're hiding things from you. Please understand there's little choice. If I were to fully divulge the details of this little situation, you wouldn't understand; not because you lack the intelligence, but because you lack the experience."

"What do you mean by that?" Lex asked honestly.

"I can't say anymore," Jade replied as apologetically as she had ever come across. "I want to, but Charlie, he…" Her sentence faded into an inconclusive oblivion. Then, catching everyone off guard, a voice from behind picked up where she left off.

"But Charlie has his own set of plans and we must follow them explicitly," Charlie chimed as the others wheeled around at his stealthy entrance.

Lex wondered how long he had been behind her. Had he followed her down the dark hallway? Had he witnessed the entire encounter with the others? Was he buying time outside the kitchen door while desperately concocting another implausible excuse for their bizarre antics? She then took note of his clothing. The brown cloak matched those worn by the others and his overall condition looked slightly worse than something the cat might have drug in.

Despite his dirt-stricken cheeks and matted hair, he displayed his usual exultant tenor. "And when everything is said and done, our dear friend Alexis will understand why Charlie's way was logical under the circumstances." He concluded his claim with a smile and a placement of his dirty hand on Lex's shoulder.

"Please trust us," Jade added imploringly.

"Yes," Lex replied. "I do trust you. It's just that sometimes it's hard to be the newcomer. But I do understand. I promise."

"You weren't supposed to see this," Charlie said. "However, since you have, please don't freak out about Sevastian's wound. Although I can't yet tell you how it happened, I can honestly tell you that it was an accident."

"Well thanks for that bit of reassurance," Lex said jestfully. "I imagine he wouldn't have done it on purpose."

"Indeed," he said with a wink, then proceeded to Sevastian's side. The Russian's head hung in shame, as if he were disappointed in himself for having undergone this "accident."

"How's the arm, buddy?" Charlie asked.

"Looks worse than it really is," said Sevastian. "It will make for a cool scar. I've heard that chicks dig scars."

Jade screwed up her face and leered him, "Chicks dig scars? No, you clown. That's an urban legend. Girls dig abs, not ugly old scabs."

"Right," Charlie said. "But you, my friend, could have all the abs in the world and you still couldn't get a girl, so it really doesn't matter."

They all laughed at this typical Charlie-Sevastian exchange, including Lex who couldn't help feeling better now that Charlie was here. Once again, just like always, his presence was like a warm blanket on a cold day.

"In just a few short hours, you'll know everything," he then said to her, peppering his tone with seriousness. There will be no more secrets, no more mysteries."

She was surely relieved to hear that, but now, after taking in Sevastian's injury, she was gripped with concern. For the past thirteen days, she had imagined this big surprise as something wonderful and splendid. Now her expectations were overcast with premonitions of danger.

Charlie suggested that she return to bed as it was only four in the morning. After heating the milk, she said goodnight and left the three to do…whatever the hell it was they did in the small hours of the night.

The long trek back to her room allowed her time to replay the kitchen scene again and again. No matter which optimistic angle she tried to take regarding what she had just seen, she couldn't find any solace from this new anxiety. She slid into her room, pushed shut the wooden door, and hurried over to the comfort haven of her bed. She removed her robe and crawled underneath the warm, silky covers. As her eyes closed, a smile forced its way across her blush cheeks. Despite it all, there was no denying that the Rose Flock injected plenty of excitement in her life. Whether it was an antique pocket watch or a nasty arm wound, it was always something, and something interesting. Soon, she fell into a deep sleep.

33

Dark clouds hung low over the winter forest. Plumes of snow spouted upward with each turbulent wind gust. Icicles dangled from overhead branches and clinked together like frozen wind chimes. A lone white owl peered down from a twisted tree limb with vampiric eyes. An indistinct sound arose from the distance sending the bird into flight. The sound grew louder.

A giant black horse ripped through a snowy thicket shattering the serenity. The creature's immense stature and rapid velocity did not hinder his ability to navigate through the labyrinth of unyielding tree trunks, powdery thorn patches and frozen streams. Upon his back, crouched low and safe from the danger of decapitating branches was a female rider. She was riding bareback and her soft white hands grasped tightly to his neck. Her indigo dress unfurled behind and rippled in the wind like a cascading river. The horse's powerful strides kept the pair airborne for so long, he might as well have had wings. There was perfect harmony between human and beast.

Ahead, sparkling sunlight broke through the trees, and then, suddenly, it was a summer afternoon. The horse and rider galloped onward through an emerald prairie incognizant to the dramatic change of atmosphere. Soaring overhead in the dazzling blue sky was a flock of white egrets, serenading the dashing duo with a symphony of squawking. Their outstretched wings eclipsed the bright sun and their shadows glided along the soft grass.

Then, amid the birds' distinct calls, came a tapping noise. At first the sound was squelched by the wind and the skyward voices but it grew increasingly louder, then overbearing. The rider let go of the horse and brought her hands to her ears. The motion was ill-timed as the horse cleared a large boulder. The girl, engulfed in a swarm of blue fabric, was hurled from the animal's back. Now the only sound that prevailed was her thundering heart as she plummeted toward the earth. And then…

Lex sat up in bed so fast that she nearly gave herself whiplash. She was breathing heavily with beads of sweat trickling down her forehead. The momentary rush was interrupted by a persistent tapping at the bedroom door.

"Yes?" she called out, flustered. A muffled voice came from the other side.

"Lex, may I come in?" It was Jade. Lex took a deep breath, used the sheet to wipe the moisture from her face, then tucked her pillow hair behind her ears.

"Sure, come in."

The door creaked open and Jade popped her head in. Lex noted that she was pretty again. Not that Jade Vandervelde was ever remotely close to anything less than stunning, but she had obviously cleaned up from her nighttime escapades.

"Are you ready for some fun?" she asked with a Cheshire cat grin.

Lex's heart rate remained elevated, but it was the remembrance of the day rather than the interesting dream that was now the culprit. "Oh, I'm more than ready," she replied as a surge of excitement plastered her like a tidal wave. With youthful vitality, she leapt from bed en route to the wardrobe.

"Meet me down in the foyer in, say, fifteen minutes?" said Jade. "We'll grab some breakfast on the way to the store."

"Brilliant," Lex agreed as Jade slipped her head out of the room and closed the door.

Lex made herself ready quickly, but before leaving the room she stopped to cast an appraising glance at the ceiling. There, standing in their usual spot amongst the shady cypress trees, were the black horse and the rider in the blue dress. She smiled, then, as if the oil-brushed images were alive and receptive, she said, "Hope to see you again soon."

34

Jade and Alexis started the morning with bagels and chai lattes from Caffe' Parlatto. In good spirits, they chatted merrily as snow began accumulating on the sill of the window by which they sat. The next destination was Outdoor Surplus. Although the store was packed to the rafters with last minute shoppers, Lex was able to sift through the rubble that used to be the shoe section and uncover the perfect pair of trail shoes. This particular pair was warm, durable and even flattering to a lady's foot. The best part of all was that wearing them felt much like walking on pillows. This was top-of-the-line footwear confirmed by an outlandish price tag. Two hundred and sixty dollars was a lot to pay for shoes, and though she had no need to concern herself with such a trivial amount of currency, she couldn't help but cringe just a little when the cashier swiped her credit card.

Next came the salon. Jade treated Lex to a trim and highlight, a facial, a pedicure and even a massage. After all was said and done, Lex decided that this wonderful experience might just become her new Christmastime praxis. The girls strolled from the building looking and feeling like a million bucks.

The final task before returning to the Range Rover, which was waiting in a side alley a few blocks away, was to place a few hundred dollars into the shiny red bucket of the bell-clanging Santa on the corner of Waterman and Market - as if this task might somehow negate their self-indulgent morning.

"As you always say," Lex mentioned to Jade as they trotted felicitously along the snow-laden sidewalk, "we are truly spoiled."

"You've got that right," Jade agreed as a nipping breeze pushed from behind. "That will be entirely evident when we get back to the house."

She was right. Returning home was a prime example of how well-off the four really were. Walking through the door, the unmistakable aroma of roasted turkey greeted the girls like a warm hug. In the dining room, Charlie was pouring glasses of milk, cranberry juice and hot apple cider. The spread was divine as the table was suffused with numerous mouth-watering dishes. It seemed like enough food to feed an army, but with the appetites of her three housemates, Lex supposed there would not be so much as a crumb left to scrap.

Sevastian appeared from the kitchen pushing a rolling cart that rattled with additional food dishes. He smiled after noticing that the shoppers had returned and were already seated at the table.

"This looks wonderful, Sevastian," Lex said. "How did you prepare this massive feast in such a short amount of time?"

"We master chefs never reveal our secrets," he proudly remarked.

"The master chef had quite a bit of help," Charlie added as he proceeded to light the candles that were artfully positioned around the table. "Hope you're all hungry."

The answer was obvious as the three started into the meal like a pack of hyenas. Lex shrugged her shoulders and started fiercely devouring her garlic mashed potatoes just to fit in.

The wine and conversation flowed in unanimity as they heartily dined. The happy banter first addressed the diamond empire's successful week. This conversation somehow turned from record profits to heckling Sevastian about his tacky Christmas tie, and then deviated into plans for Christmas day. Three smiles briefly turned to frowns when Lex informed them that she would spend the majority of the special day with Aunt Claire. Although her friends understood completely, they were truly thwarted that their newest family member would not be participating in their festive celebration until later on Christmas night.

"And speaking of Claire," Charlie said as he dished a fourth helping of marshmallow yams. "There's something I've been meaning to ask you, so while I'm thinking of it… how exactly did your aunt end up in Rose? I mean, of all places, right?"

The question was concise and seemingly innocent. Lex shouldn't have given it a second thought had it not been for the prompt silence of the others. As Charlie delivered the inquiry, silverware had been placed on the table, chewing had ceased and three pairs of eyes settled heavily on her. Her instincts were throwing up red flags, telling her that this was something that the Flock deemed very important – for whatever reason.

"Well," she began, trying to conceal suspicion, "I don't know for certain. Actually, I've asked her that question several times, but strangely she always acts somewhat evasive."

"Strangely?" Charlie prodded.

"Well, yes, 'strangely' because as I'm sure you know, she is customarily an open book. At first I thought the relocation from Los Angeles to Rose might simply be a bitter memory of her ex-husband, but she loves talking about him – I mean she loves the opportunity to tell anyone who will listen about what a thick-head he was. It's strange that she shies away from any reminiscence of her life. Yet, every time I ask, she acts, um... different, even a little nervous." Charlie and the others nodded with keen interest. Lex could almost hear the gears in their brains attempting to crank out an answer to this riddle that was obviously very important to them. "May I ask why you want to know?"

Charlie shook off his unyielding stare as if he had just popped out of a contemplative trance. "Oh," he said, "just curious."

That was the answer Lex expected and didn't want. Of course he was curious, that was obvious. What she really desired to know was why he was curious to such a profound degree, and the others as well. "Sorry I couldn't answer your question," she apologized while starting in on the cranberry salad that had been tantalizing her taste buds during that unexpected conversation. "If you really want to know, I'll try and ask her again."

She thought she might hear a "don't worry about it" or a "it's no big deal," but instead Charlie replied with a, "Sure, if you don't mind."

It should have taken the better part of two hours to finish that meal, but in "fascinating fashion" the four had reduced the Christmas fare to scraps and bones in a matter of forty minutes. They slouched back in their chairs, full and satisfied. Sevastian was still managing to pick at a butter roll.

"That's what life is all about," Charlie said with a smile of repletion.

"Eating?" replied Jade.

"Yes, ma'am. I now believe the reason I was put on this earth was to eat food," he sarcastically declared.

The others chuckled lazily out of politeness but lacked the energy to requite his remark with anything more. The crackling fire and full stomachs made eyelids heavy and heads groggy.

"Should we leave this mess for the cleaning crew and pay them a little extra?" Jade finally asked.

Lex was by no means in any mood to clean up dishes, but she thought it was the least she could do. "I'll be happy to clean up," she lied, then stood wearily and began stacking empty plates in her arms - second nature after years of waiting tables.

Jade quickly rose to her feet. "You'll do no such thing," she said. "I've been pampered all morning anyway. I'll clean up."

Charlie was the next to rise. "Look, we'll all help and get this mess knocked out in ten minutes."

Sevastian made a feeble attempt to absolve himself from any post-meal responsibility by submitting the old adage, "In Russia, it is not customary for the cook to clean." This was shot down in mid air and once the others were able to pry him from his chair, the clean-up effort was underway. Soon enough, the dining room and kitchen were back to their neat and tidy state. Soon after, Jade and Sevastian departed for a comfortable place to curl up and take a nap leaving Charlie and Lex alone in the kitchen.

"I have a surprise for you in the library," he said as he gave the stove and counter a final wipe-down. "It's not the big surprise that you'll get in a few hours, but I think you'll like it."

"I'm sure I will," Lex said without a doubt in her mind. They flipped off the kitchen lights and headed for the library.

She was pleased to see that there was a toasty fire burning in the library's fireplace. The simple stroll from the kitchen was enough exposure to the mansion's drafty hallways to secure her appreciation for the searing flames.

"Please, sit down," Charlie offered, motioning her toward the comfortable couch. She obliged his request and watched with curiosity as he retrieved a blanket and brown paper package from a nearby drawer. "An early Christmas present," he said.

"Could this possibly be a book?" she slyly guessed as he placed the gift in her hands and took a seat next to her.

"I can't fool you," he replied. "The question is – what book is it?"

With a smile of gratitude, she ripped the package open. Upon revelation of its contents, her eyes promptly glazed over and her heart melted. In her hands was a children's book called Molly the Mouse's Christmas Adventure. This very tale had been her utmost favorite as a child. Every Christmas Eve back in Staffordshire, her mother would read her this story just before bed. It had become a Christmas tradition, but one which had been lost after Olivia's passing.

A tear hung from the corner of her eye as she threw her arms around him. "How could you have possibly known about this? Like my dream, you must have the capability of getting into my head."

He smiled. "I'm glad you like it. But alas, I am not the miracle worker you think I am. In truth, I was talking to your aunt a few days ago and we happened into a conversation about how Christmas was your favorite holiday. One thing led to another and the topic of this book came up. After I hung up the phone, I got online and ordered a copy."

"It doesn't matter if it was magic or eBay, you are still a miracle worker in my opinion," she assured him with a smile that would not subside.

He threw the blanket over the two of them. "And now of course, after years of waiting, you will hear the story once again."

She wrapped herself in the blanket and laid her head on his shoulder as he opened the book and began to read.

The heat of the fire, the soft leather couch, the comfortable blanket and Charlie's soothing voice sent Lex into a state of deep relaxation. Though she desired to hear how Molly the Mouse helped Santa save Christmas, she was soon overpowered by sleep. Within minutes Charlie's voice became a palliative reverberation in her head – and then silence.

35

Jade and Sevastian were peering around the corner of the library's entranceway, spying. Their eyes cast foreboding glances at the pair on the couch. As a sleeping Lex snuggled closer to Charlie, their expressions went from concerned to unsettled in a hurry.

"Be careful, Charlie," Jade whispered so that only Sevastian could hear. "The risk is too great."

"He's beginning to like her a little too much," Sevastian quietly remarked.

Jade nodded. "Yeah, I've noticed that too. I hope he knows what he's doing." With that, the two slipped away quietly.

36

Hours later, Lex opened her eyes and was for a moment, slightly disoriented. Batting the sleep away with her fluttering eyelids, she quickly regained bearing as the multi-hued blur above morphed into ten stories of books. Sleepily, her head lifted to see Charlie sitting in the armchair next to the couch. He was reading a National Geographic magazine and sipping a cup of tea. Once again, he was wearing that strange brown cloak. He smiled when he saw she was finally among the conscious.

"I was about to wake you. You've been asleep for almost four hours."

"Really? What time is it?" she asked drowsily.

"Five after five," he replied. She rubbed her eyes and sat up, surprised to have actually slept that long. "That Molly Mouse can really take care of business," he said sarcastically.

"Yeah, sorry about that," she stammered. "I really wanted to hear the story, but I just couldn't keep my eyes open." She finished the apology with a deep yawn.

"That's okay," he said. "I'm glad you're well rested. That was the plan, wasn't it?"

Her scrutiny remained on Charlie's clothes. "What is that you're wearing?"

"These are the most incredible garments that have ever been stitched together. Despite their appearance, they are very expensive. They'll literally last for hundreds of years before they finally begin to fall apart. They keep you cool in the summer and very warm in the winter. And best of all," he said with a grin, "they never smell bad no matter how dirty they get. They are made from the wool of a rare sheep. As a matter of fact, I had an outfit tailored to fit your frame." He reached behind the armchair, grabbed a pile of clothes and handed them to Lex. Skimming her hands across the material, she understood right away what he was getting at. They were very pleasing and almost ensnaring to the touch. She wondered if this was part of the big surprise.

"Thanks," she said. "So, what's on the agenda for this evening?"

"Oh, not much," he answered, "Just the immaculate finale after two weeks of abiding patience." The way he said it made her skin tingle with expectancy. "But I have a few final requests before we go. Again, strange as they may seem, they all have a purpose. First, I need you to go to your room and change into the clothes I just gave you. There is a shirt, a pair of pants, socks, gloves and a heavy hooded cloak that goes over everything. There is also a pair of boot covers. Put on your new trail shoes and place the boot covers over them."

The image that had been established in Lex's imagination for a few days now, was that the Rose Flock was veiling an incredible diamond mine, a breathtaking utopia of precious stones sparkling from slick cavern walls like stars in the ebony sky. The unconventional clothing was fitting for such a damp, dark setting like this alleged cave of wonders. Before she could spin more illusions of guesswork into her web of impractical expectations, Charlie continued pitching his oddball requests.

"There's a pen and paper in the drawer of the nightstand by your bed. You must make a list of all your appointments in the next two weeks. A dentist appointment, lunch with your aunt, no matter what, write it down. Or at least make sure they're all updated in your phone's calendar. Oh, have all your computer passwords been saved?"

She nodded.

"Okay good. Finally, bring the pocket watch I gave you. Once you're dressed, and the list is made, meet me back down here in the library and we'll be on our way."

"You don't have to ask me twice," she said as she eagerly leapt from the couch, breaking free from its cushiony confines. She hustled out of the library and as soon as Charlie was out of sight, took off in a dead sprint up the stairs en route to her room. She returned twelve minutes later, much longer than her goal of five minutes, but decided it might be in her best interest to spend a little extra time to assure the list of appointments was accurate.

Charlie's eyes sparkled when she returned to the library and his intentional, or unintentional ogling did not evade her notice. The chestnut-hued material of her cloak brought out the natural glow of her soft white skin and rosy cheeks. Her long brown hair glimmered as it reflected the firelight. In that moment, in the plainest of clothes, she looked like a goddess – as Charlie's exultant expression would have her believe. This interchange of longing admiration only lasted an instant before he recovered his professional air. Though this was a probable slip-up on his part, she could not have been more pleased that his true feelings may have momentarily escaped the confines of repression.

I look like Friar Tuck," she said. "But you're right. I've never felt more comfortable and, well, able. I feel like I could complete a floor routine, climb Everest and cross the Sahara all in this one outfit."

"Yep, you truly could," he agreed as he found his feet. "This is the only thing to wear where we're going. So… you ready?"

"That's a silly question," she replied.

"Do you have the pocket watch?" he asked.

She nodded.

He took a deep breath, as if he were nervous too for some reason. "Let's do it then."

37

After the events of last night, she was not entirely perplexed when they began their journey in the mansion's back yard. "Where are we going?" she asked as the icy wind pattered against the exposed skin of her face.

Charlie raised a finger to the lone patch of woods about a kilometer away. This also did not come as a surprise. "The answer lies within those trees."

They began their footslog across the white landscape. The setting sun slung dazzling red rays from behind a purple cloud creating a placid ambiance. A freezing wind blew quickly and powerfully as there were no obstacles to hinder its progress. Off in the distance was a deer family grazing on the scarce vegetation beneath the snow. A flock of crows, also scavenging for food, kept a watchful eye on Charlie and Lex as the two trudged by.

"They're beautiful birds," said Charlie, "majestic and mysterious. I've always had a thing for crows. Interesting how these creatures have been the cornerstone of dark literature for millennia. From Aesop to Poe, and many in between, crows are typically used to symbolize death. Carnivorous scavengers are never allotted a fair reputation I suppose."

Splendid point, Lex thought to herself. But whatever he was going on about, crows perhaps, was not holding a candle to the anticipation of what might be hidden in this little patch of woods that was drawing nearer with each avid step.

Finally, they reached the tree line and that was when she first noticed it. Hidden way back amongst the skeletal, leafless collection of crooked old trees, was a structure of some sort, but her vantage point allowed her to decipher nothing more. Locating a narrow trail, utilized predominantly by deer as told by the multitude of frozen hoof prints, Charlie led her into the woods. A minute later, they had arrived at what she believed to be the final destination. Her first thought was to turn back.

It was a church, an archaic one at that. Its primordial stone walls supported an eerie network of dead vines, and bird nests. Massive oak trees, as if they were bodyguards, stood imposing and impenetrable around the perimeter. This was just as likely a scene from a Robert Frost poem as it was from a Stephen King tale. She committed to saving her questions for later and tip-toed behind Charlie toward the decayed, wooden doors. Despite an inconvenient encumbrance from the breeze, he managed to heave them open and when the two stepped inside, Lex decided she'd rather about-face back into the arctic chill.

The inner sanctuary was eidolic and dismal. The dreary red glow, the sun's final effort on this December evening, seeped in through dusty, stained-glass windows upon dry rotted pews, broken stone statues of indiscernible people, and a solitary stone altar. She couldn't imagine what in the world they were doing in a place like this. For all of the thousands of ideas that had crossed through her mind in the past two weeks, not one had come remotely close to this.

"Lovely," she said, not at all serious as she gazed around vigilantly, half expecting to see an apparition. "What's the history behind this place?"

"To be honest with you, Lex, I'm not sure," he replied. "After digging through archived newspapers at city hall, I found out that it was last used by a Protestant congregation more than a century ago. There was no record of who built it or how long it had been here before that. I have a strong suspicion that it's probably thousands of years old."

"That can't be right though," Lex said, somewhat confused as to why he would believe this. "That was the Native American era. They didn't build churches."

"No, they did not," he answered mysteriously and left it at that. "Follow me this way."

A shuddersome feeling engulfed her as she followed him down the center aisle toward the stone altar that stood front and center, as if it had some superiority in this dreaded place. When they reached the altar, he gently lowered to his knees and slid his fingers between two flat stones on the floor. With a mighty effort, he hoisted the larger of the two right out of the ground.

Fueled by excitement and a sense of adventure, Lex's heart thudded wildly when she saw a stairway leading downward.

"You seem to have a knack for finding secret passages," she said.

He acknowledged with an accomplished grin before motioning her to follow. They made it down exactly ten steps before confronting a familiar obstacle – a heavy metal door with a glowing security panel. This modern mechanical hatch was a direct contradiction to the timeworn staircase which it guarded. Charlie punched in a complex code that differed from the one that Lex was trying to memorize for the ice cave. She was not looking forward to memorizing another long set of numbers, but at this point, it was the least of her worries. The panel emitted a high-pitched chirp and a circular red light switched forthwith to green. The door slid into the wall smoothly, revealing more steps. After the door had receded, a series of small lights, one mounted to each step, flashed on in succession spiraling downward around a center pillar toward an unknown terminus.

Before they fared onward, Charlie ran back up the stairs and slid the floor stone back into place. Now the current location felt very much like a tomb.

"Remember," he called breathlessly after toiling with the cumbrous slab, "we must take every precaution to remain secretive. Soon you'll understand why."

Step by anxious step, she trailed her leader down the steep, circumvoluted stairwell. The further into the earth they progressed, the colder it got. The air became permeated by a dank, dewy smell.

The supernatural aura coupled with an overwrought nervous excitement sent a shiver so deep into her body that it rattled her bones.

When they finally reached the bottom, she was once again befuddled by the paradoxical location. They stood side-by-side in a small room with a dirt floor. It was a dead end. There were no doors, no passageways, and no other points of interest except for one small pool of water encircled by a ring of matte black boulders. Peculiar enough, the pool seemed to have an underwater light source causing it to glow with an attractive aqua tint. As the two approached this mysterious centerpiece in this unsettling room so deep beneath the abandoned church, she could see that there were steps leading down into the water.

"I know what this is," she said with a flare of excitement. "This is a hologram pool. Right? Like your hologram fire?"

He chuckled and put his arm around her. "Great guess, but wrong. Sorry."

She cocked her head in confusion. "Well then, what is it? I can't imagine that we're going for a swim. It's freezing down here."

"May I have your watch?" he asked composedly. She reached into the pocket beneath her cloak and pulled out the little gold timepiece. "Note the time."

She looked at the watch. "Five forty-two."

He took the watch from her hand and placed it gently on one of the rocks surrounding the pool. "Well, this is it," he mumbled hopefully before exhausting a deep breath. "No turning back now. I hope you'll trust me on this."

She nodded as her pulse quickened. "I wouldn't be here if I didn't."

Without further delay, he took her trembling hand then hopped over the rock onto the first step that led down into the pool. It was then that she realized, to her immeasurable dismay, that they really were going down into the water. Just the thought of this gave her goosebumps. At this point however, after everything she had so far been through, after the nail-biting suspense that had gripped her tightly ever since she had met Charlie, she was not going to argue. With a firm grasp on his hand, she stepped over the rock and into the pool. She closed her eyes and tensed her muscles while waiting for the water to fill her shoes, but it never did. "I thought you said that this wasn't a hologram."

"It's not," he said.

Lex reached down to touch the water-like substance. As her hand made contact with the surface, she couldn't believe her own senses. It felt like water except… it wasn't wet. She swished it around and pulled her hand out, watching drops trickle back into the pool. Wide-eyed and bewildered, she nodded to Charlie indicating that she was ready to continue onward. Together, they took the next step, then another, then another. She felt the strange medium press against the outside of her clothes just as water would. Soon they were up to their necks. Then suddenly, she became devoured by an irrepressible sensation of, well…she wasn't sure. Everything became blurry and evanescent. The sounds from the room turned to a dull echo and her mind went blank. The weight of her eyelids was overbearing. They closed. Her body went limp and her head sank beneath the surface of the pool.

38

Lex was now a ghost, a spirit, a shadow. Her physical body vanished as the entire universe began to sail by. Her mind slipped through space and time. Everything that had ever existed flowed through her; the universe, black voids, blinding light, galaxies, stars, planets, molecules, cries of desperation, pandemonius screams, laughter, peace, serenity, life, death and then nothing – an infinite ethereal nothing. From that nothing arose an angelic lullaby starting ever so softly, stirring her consciousness. She began to remember and recall something that happened eternities ago. A church, a glowing pool and someone she had cared about. Her body became sodden with pure relaxation. Then a sense of surrounding took hold. She was sinking beneath water, yet still breathing. The water then began an inexplicable transmogrification into air, all the while keeping her body weightless and suspended. The subtle lullaby grew louder and her brain rekindled distant memories. She was able to recall that this was the same song from her perfect dream. She opened her eyes but remained in a sleeping catatonia, watching as a white cloud began to engulf her hovering body. It became thicker and cradled her, seeming to lift her upward. Small lights began to materialize from the darkness, then three big lights. They were blurry for a moment, but soon it became clear that they were stars sparkling in the night sky. The three larger lights focused into moons. As she gazed upon the beautiful heavens, the space below faded into a brilliant moonlit landscape. A cool breeze kicked up and it was then she realized that yes, this was exactly like her dream. The cloud suspended her high above the earth. The wind whipped through her hair and the lullaby echoed across the night sky. For a moment it felt as though she was alone, but whose hand was she holding? She looked over, only to find that nobody was there. "Are you here, Charlie?" she asked, feeling his grip but not able to see him. As the voice flowed from her lips, it echoed magically through the atmosphere.

Charlie's voice came soon after in the same echoing manner. "I am here, Lex, but I've got to let go of your hand now. Don't worry though. I will be with you until you awake. Enjoy."

With that, she felt his hand pull away and the cloud began to dehumidify. She felt no fear. Looking down at the stunning landscape, she remembered these same mountains, forests and fields from her dream. Her body started to move forward and soon she was soaring rapidly through the sky in absolute euphoria. This time, everything was more real. This time, somehow, she wasn't dreaming.

Ahead, the giant willow tree came into sight. Then suddenly she stopped, hovering in mid-air like a human kite. Whatever gravity-defiant force that had been holding her body aloft vanished and she began to plummet downward. Faster and faster toward terminal velocity she fell, overcome by an immense thrill that trumped any consternation of impact. As the earth approached at seemingly light speed, she innately understood that her life was not in peril. When her body finally made contact with the soft grass, she felt no impact. Again, she seemed to be floating.

She wondered if Charlie would be waiting for her beneath the towering tree like in the dream. Utilizing the light from the three moons, she peered into the weeping limbs in hope of spotting his familiar silhouette. She saw nothing but the gentle dynamism of green leaves fluttering in the night wind. Then, once more, an oppressive urge to fall asleep crept over. She felt it careening through her head like a tidal wave but used every ounce of fight to hold out for a few more seconds just in case Charlie were to arrive. This battle was lost expeditiously. Her head fell back into the grass. The ground turned to snow, then water, then ashes, and then something soft and pleasant. The wind disappeared and the lullaby faded into the infinite void. It was silent now. Everything went black.

39

"Alexis, wake up."

Lex heard the voice ricochet around the inside of her head but did not comprehend it. Soon, there were more sounds - bird songs, wind and rustling leaves. She felt the pleasing warmth of the sun upon her face. Her eyes cracked open to observe a dark silhouette leaning over her, eclipsing the bright sunlight. As her pupils adjusted, a familiar smiling face came into view.

"Charlie?"

"You've got that right. Not bad, eh?"

"Wha…what just happened?" she asked, disoriented and terribly confused. He did not answer right away but assisted her in sitting up.

They were sitting amongst lush grass on a rounded hilltop overlooking a misty forest with trees of monumental breadth. The large willow, the one she had seen in her dream, was only a few paces away. In the distance, several stone towers projected over the forest canopy. The temperature was pleasantly warm, an absolute contrast to the harsh wintriness that plagued Kansas.

Finally, after allowing her a moment to regard the surroundings, Charlie spoke. "You have just experienced what I like to call a sliver of heaven," he said. "The best part is, every time you go into the pool, the same thing happens; and let me tell you, it never gets old."

She had no idea what he was talking about or where they could possibly be. In fact, this was the very first time in their acquaintanceship that she became fearful of him. Whatever just happened, the pool, the out-of-body experience, and this alien location, could only be the result of some sort of drug consumption. It had to be, there was no other rational explanation. The idea of being drugged unknowingly and unwillingly did not sit well. She wondered how long she had been out of her mind, so to speak, for Charlie to bring her to such a place. "Impossible. This is just impossible," she muttered aggressively. "I'm going to need an explanation, Charlie, this time no more secrets."

He remained reposeful despite these obvious misgivings. "When I first brought Sevastian here all those years ago, I was not prepared with a good explanation. He didn't really handle it well and I regretted my lack of preparation. But then I came to realize that there is no way to explain this. The fact of the matter is, you just won't believe it; nobody could believe it. I just ask that you'll allow me to guide you step by step. You'll come to find out that everything I tell you is the solid truth, no matter how crazy it may seem."

She shook her head doubtingly. "Alright then, tell me the truth. What happened when we went into the pool? How was it so much like the dream that you somehow knew about? And, and… where the hell are we?"

"I will answer your questions as they come," he said. "First the pool. I haven't the slightest idea how it works. All I know is when someone steps into it, they fall asleep and slip into a state of… well, bliss. When they awaken, it's always inside the hollow trunk of that willow tree, which by the way, has another pool. The pool in the trunk of the tree allows us to get back to the church. Though I don't know how this is accomplished or the precise physiological effects it has on our bodies, I can bet that there is probably a scientific explanation."

She looked at him as though he might benefit from some time in a mental institution. Despite the clear fact that she was not buying his explanation, he went on.

"The point I'm trying to make is that there is no such thing as magic. Let me introduce you to a term I'm sure you have not heard before – acanthary. Acanthary is the ability to use biological organisms, namely plants, to achieve enhanced mental abilities. An acanthar is a person who has learned to use plants to accomplish things that are seemingly magical in nature. The pool is a tremendous feat in acanthary. To my knowledge, it has never been matched or recreated."

Lex cursed herself for not packing her phone while speculating whether or not 911 would actually work in this strange location.

"Let me ask you this," he went on. "Ever heard of an acanthus?"

She nodded and gave her best answer, though she was not remotely satisfied with his explanation thus far. "Acanthus is a plant, right?"

"Correct! Acanthus is a genus of flowering plant. The word can be traced all the way back to ancient Greece."

"What does this have to do with anything?" she prodded as rudely as she had ever done with him.

He continued calmly despite her impertinent attitude. "This leads us into your second question about the dream you had this past summer. The answer is all acanthary. With the help of some very wise teachers and a common water plant, I have learned to invade the dreams of others. Not only that, but I can shape the dreams any way I want. I plan to teach you how to do these things too, that is, if you're willing to learn.

Finally, Toto, it doesn't take a wonderful wizard to see we're no longer in Kansas. This will sound unbelievable but…" he paused for a second, seeming almost uneasy to continue, "Lex, you and I are no longer on, or in, the same world with the church and the pool. Remember down in the ice cave when I went on about the secrets of the universe? For years I have been trying to find out how and where…"

Lex leapt to her feet, driven by all the pent up frustration. "Bloody hell, Charlie!" she interrupted. "Do you actually expect me to believe that?" She glared down at him vindictively. "How thick do I look? Are you really trying to get me to believe that we are in a different world and that the pool was a… a portal to get here?"

He nodded. "Yes, that's exactly right."

"Oh, that's just amazing, isn't it?" she yelled, throwing her arms up to accentuate her intended sarcasm. She cupped her hands around her mouth so that her voice might reach the valley below. "Hey, all you little fairies and elves, we have a real nutter here. Does anyone know where I can find Merlin? Perhaps he'll use his magic walking stick to beam me back to Kansas. Can anyone hear me? Dragons? Goblins? Anyone?"

Charlie patiently waited until she was through. "I know how your mind works," he said calmly. "You require solid, indisputable, scientific facts to accept this situation as authentic. Trust me, your skepticism is natural and I never expected you to believe it right away. Please bear with me and I'll show you everything you'll need to understand and believe."

"I don't see how that's possible," she combated with a huff, crossing her arms opposingly.

"Listen, I've been through that pool literally hundreds of times, and still find myself in awe and disbelief of this seemingly impossible reality. Sometimes I half expect to wake up in a bed somewhere and realize that this was all a very elaborate dream. But as you can plainly tell, neither of us are dreaming."

She didn't know what else to say. Every conceivable emotion was filling her head and it was overbearing. Charlie seemed to have all the angles covered. She knew that she could stand here all day and quarrel with him, but that would be pointless. At this junction, there was no choice but to go along with everything, at least until she could find a phone and call for help. She brushed the stray pieces of grass from her wool cloak and allowed a prolonged kiss from the warm sun. She then asked her kidnapper while spitefully eluding eye contact, "Well, what's next then?"

He jumped to his feet, seemingly content that she was willing to follow him a little farther. "See those towers beyond the forest?" he asked, pointing skyward to the goliath citadels that were erected to such a height that they penetrated the clouds. "That is the city of Crow - and my home."

By now, she was growing accustomed to his onslaught of ludicrous ascertainments. "The city of Crow?" she repeated mockingly.

He smiled and gawked toward the prestigious towers, with allegiance radiating from his face. "The most powerful and respected city in the world. That's where we're heading. It's a pleasant walk."

Lex deducted that he was either out of his skull, or, just maybe, telling the truth. Just this single instantaneous notion that the preposterous information he just conveyed could be true, made her question her own sanity. A portal to another world? Not likely, even for Charlie Roanoke.

40

In similar fashion to the loyal dog who trails his master anywhere without inquest, she began following him down the grassy hill to the tree line of the giant forest. This confirmed her long established supposition that she would probably follow him wherever and whenever. There was something about him, there always had been, that she could not resist or refuse. This something existed as an alluring spell he had over her, as if he were a snake charmer and she were a snake. She wanted to bite, to strike, to fight back and demand a no-nonsense explanation, demand to be taken home, demand that he let her return to the simple life she led before he came around, but she couldn't bring herself to do it. Though he had deceived her in the past, and she was certain he was lying to her now, somehow an unwavering trust remained.

Thickset grass blades nipped at their calves as the two descended the hillside following a narrow dirt path. The air, although comfortable and pleasant, had just a hint of chill, as though spring had just overthrown a frosty winter or summer was relinquishing its life for autumn. She took a deep breath and greatly enjoyed the sensation.

"What you have just experienced is pollution-free air," Charlie informed her. "No cars, factories, or power plants around here."

She nodded but refrained from rolling her eyes, feeling that she needn't convey her frustration any further for now.

As they drew nearer to the trees, she found herself recycling the word "impossible" in her mind over and over. From a distance, they had the semblance of giant sequoias, which was impressive enough, but now that they were but fifty yards away, she noted that these trees were much, much larger than anything she had ever seen or known about. This was her first dose of reality because she knew without provision that there were no plants like these in her world. This thought made her body tremble. Still there was that little voice reminding her that Charlie was sage, sharp and swank, capable of seemingly anything - like concocting this grand hoax. She was not yet ready to believe that she was treading anywhere but logical.

They entered the forest following a lengthy navigation around the base of a tree so monstrous, she decided that there would be little difficulty fitting a cruise ship inside the hollowed trunk. This thought engaged her mind as the full splendor of the woodland haven swallowed her in. She halted dead in her tracks and raised a hand to her mouth. Her eyes widened to the size of dinner plates and gleamed with wonderment. She knew that Charlie was observing her reaction as they entered the forest, and though she wanted to maintain her image of malcontent, there was no controlling her actions upon seeing this glorious, impossible place for the first time.

Unlike the deciduous forests of North America to which she was accustomed, this forest floor was not strewn with brown leaves, dirt or scraggly underbrush, rather it was blanketed by thick emerald grass glistening with pearly dew. Giant boulders were sprinkled throughout, and they were not gray limestone or unremarkable slabs of igneous, but polished onyx. Luminous bands of sunlight pierced the treetops meeting the cool mist resulting in a multitude of rainbows. A crystal river snaked through the trees. Somewhere up ahead, there was the unmistakable gushing of a waterfall.

"You'll find that everything is bigger here," Charlie mentioned.

"You don't say?" she replied in a spellbound state.

He gave her sleeve a gentle tug breaking her from the

trance and the two set off following the river's edge. With each step she became more taken by the mystique of the forest. As the misty air caressed her skin, the peaceful babble of the river whispered in her ears, and the brilliant colors shined all around as if inside a giant prism, something rekindled deep inside that she thought had been long extinguished – her adventurous spirit. This was the same spirit that kept her outside all day exploring the moor near her grandfather's house when she was a child. Back then the world was brand new and exciting and everything was worth investigating. As it happens, familiarity breeds boredom and after a while the world became less interesting. Though she had always retained an adventurous nature and a will to explore, she, like most others, had gotten absorbed in life's routine. Now it was all coming back. Once again, she felt like a child, exploring her world for the first time. Suddenly, and quite contradictory to her initial feelings about this strange place, she did not want to leave. At that moment she wished to remain forever among the therapeutic domain of the giant trees.

Shortly, the pair came upon a woodland lake which sprawled out placidly at the terminus of the waterfall. Plumes of mist and crystal droplets spouted upward as water met water. Illuminated by the light of Helios and possessing the clarity of glass, the lake offered an unopposed view straight down to the bottom, many meters in depth. It was as clean and untainted as any body of water Lex had ever come across. Its brilliance was enhanced by the bank of translucent white stones that looked vaguely familiar. A triple rainbow stretched from the sky to the base of the waterfall as if it had been purposefully positioned by whichever artist had painted this masterpiece. She felt as though she was not worthy of treading in such a place, as if she might be trespassing in a territory that belonged to a higher being. And if she should be struck down this instant for having overstepped her boundaries, she supposed that she would die happy for just having caught a glimpse of what perfection really was.

"The water here is so pure, you can drink right from the

lake," Charlie said. "Something that is unheard of back on… well the other earth. By the way, did you notice the rocks we're standing on?"

"Yes, the rocks," she began as she observed them crunching together beneath her disguised boots. "My God! Diamonds!" she exclaimed in revelation. "So this is where you get them? This is your secret supply?"

"I don't remove them from this forest," he explained. "It's too perfect here. I can't bring myself to alter a single characteristic, not even the removal of a few stones." He knelt down and retrieved one of these diamonds, in the rough of course, but Lex knew from her scant experience that this one had the potential to be one of Sevastian's finest works. Charlie eyed it almost longingly and returned it to the exact spot from which it had been resting. "Diamonds are as common in this world as corn in Kansas. Though I don't remove them from this forest in particular, I have plenty of other reservoirs at my disposal. In this world, diamonds are useless."

"Really? Why?"

"No means to craft them," he expounded. "Around here diamonds are only good for looking at."

"It just doesn't make sense," she continued. "I thought diamonds were formed underground by intense heat and pressure. How is it that they just lay upon the surface?"

"That very question speaks volumes to how old this place is. And if you want to dive deeper, we can postulate that the inner workings of this particular earth may function differently from the other. Perhaps the core is more active, driving matter up and out at higher rates. Perhaps the mantle is thin and unimposing to surfacing diamonds. Perhaps underground temperatures are different. It's really hard to say."

Lex was dissatisfied with yet another vague and uncertain explanation from him. Maybe he should have had his ducks in a row before bringing her here. But then again, she thought, not even Charlie can know everything.

"No matter where my travels take me, I'm always happy to return to this lake," he said, maintaining a curious focus upon the waterfall. She followed his gaze to the base of the falls where she discovered exactly what he was looking at. Whatever, or whomever, was there behind the wall of thunderous liquid, existed as an undistinguishable shadow, or silhouette of sorts. Was it just one, or two? It was hard to tell. It was as if some creature had been stirred by their presence, perhaps awakened from sleep. She didn't know what to think, or if they were in any immediate danger, so she looked to Charlie for direction as to what they should do next. He answered this request without words, but with a sharp whistle.

First one muffled splash, then another as two separate and still indistinct beings dropped into the lake, disappearing for a moment among the bubbly white turbulence of the waterfall. Then she saw them torpedoing toward her beneath the water's surface with fish-like grace and hydrodynamic efficiency. But they weren't fish, so she initially surmised, they were women. But wait really? Who, I mean what…? She wanted to get these thoughts across to Charlie, but before she could, the two strangers surfaced directly in front of them not more than an arm's-length away.

Two girls, late teens by the looks of them, bobbed effortlessly with gentle and rhythmic undulations of their legs and pelvises beneath the water. They were both possessive of an unnatural beauty as if they did not belong to a mortal world - the kind of untainted perfection that all artists strive to capture in their sculptures and paintings of angels and holy deities but can never quite achieve. Their bright eyes gleamed. Pale cheeks with rosy hues seemed to capture and reflect the sun's light much as the moon would do when it was full and glorious in the heavens. Everything about them was beauteous and symmetric from their unblemished faces to their modest breasts which were fully exposed and bordered by dripping locks of dark hair. Their expressions exhibited excitement over the visitors who had happened upon their lake. This, however, did little to quell Lex's unease. This unease stemmed not from their friendly smiles, but from their belly navels downward. Each had what appeared to be two separate legs, but it also appeared that these so-called legs were covered with not skin but, no doubt, scales. Their feet were long and webbed, not like the mermaids from her childhood fairytales, but more like amphibious beings –gorgeous, mystifying, half women half water creatures.

She found her own legs involuntarily trembling as the darker-haired of the two offered a fond welcome to Charlie spoken in Greek. She raised a moist hand to him, dripping with the lake's purity. He took it and kissed the top. The other repeated the hand offering and Charlie obliged this one too with a kiss. Lex's vision suddenly became blurry, barely allowing the acknowledgement of two concerned faces staring up from the water. She wanted to ask Charlie to help her sit for a moment because she was not feeling well, but whatever utterance came from her vocal cords was nothing more than a few rambling fragments of nonsense. Soon it was hard to stand. Her final cognition before plummeting heavily to a bed of diamonds was a breast and a rainbow.

41

She had fallen hard, so hard in fact that the sharp diamonds had succeeded in puncturing the skin on her right shoulder upon impact. The painful throbbing awoke her. At this moment, she expected to awake in her bed back at the mansion to the realization that this had all been a deranged dream, however, that inclination was quickly put to rest when she surveyed the two water beauties looking on with grave concern.

Charlie had pulled her to his lap, cradling her body protectively against the abrasive rock bed. There was the warmth of seeping blood beneath the cloak but this minor discomfort was easily ignored by the pleasantness of being held by Charlie.

"This was the shock overload thing I was telling you about," he said. "Maybe now you can begin to appreciate our decision to ease you into things one step at a time."

She stiffly found her feet. This was a forced action because she did enjoy his embrace, however, she remembered that she was supposed to be mad at him.

"Rather big step that was," she mentioned, referring to the amphibious goddesses. She then regarded them sort of uneasily, feeling she was probably obligated to do so. "I'm sorry for that," she apologized. "I've been feeling a little…" she glanced at Charlie with narrowed eyes, "out of sorts today. My name is Lex." This apologetic introduction was met with silent stares of misunderstanding, and before Charlie could remind her, she realized her folly and repeated the apology to the best of her ability in Greek.

"You are beautiful, like a flower," said the brown-haired

girl, stirring Lex's positive energy with the compliment. "My name is Daphne. This is my sister, Iris. We are daughters of the sea god and guardians of this lake."

"Charlamos has told us all about you," said the black-haired Iris. "You are just as beautiful as he has described."

Lex caught an innuendo of embarrassment in Charlie's sheepish smile. *Was he really talking about me?* she wondered in her usual modest mindset. If so, the notion was exalting to her ego.

Iris continued, "I can see you carry the burden of doubt," she said to Lex as though peering deep into her soul. "Charlamos tells us everything, but there is one secret he keeps - where you come from. He assures us that his reasoning is just, and we trust him entirely."

"He has always been a friend," Daphne said trueheartedly, "not only to us, but to the gods we serve and the land in which we all share. Though we have only just met, dear Lex, I can clearly see several truths in you. Deep down you trust him as we do, though currently, this trust is clouded by disorientation to your surroundings. Despite this disorientation, I assure you that you belong here."

Where is here? Lex thought as Daphne went on.

"There are forces all around which humans cannot discern. These forces are in the air, the earth, the trees and the water. These forces, the spirits of this world, are more in harmony with you, Lex, than any being we have ever encountered. Though the significance of this harmony and your arrival is not clear, the very idea that you are now among us is encouraging."

They spoke with an ageless wisdom and understanding of nature's inner workings – as if they were the first creatures to inhabit the earth. Did this mean they were older than they looked? So many new possibilities were surfacing and Lex was struggling to sort out the impossibilities. Each minute that passed in this exciting place further reshaped her understanding of what impossible really meant.

Their message was clear, but she could not comprehend its

implication. She could, however, appreciate their pinpoint diagnosis of her faith in Charlie regardless of this bazaar situation he had put her in. Did that also mean they were accurate in their assertion that she did indeed belong to this world despite being a newcomer? As of now she couldn't know, but she would certainly ponder this claim in the days to come. And though she didn't know how to reply to such a deliverance of so-called truths, she put forth the friendliest smile she could muster under the given circumstances.

"Thank you for your insight, old friends," Charlie said warmly. "Alexis has been through a lot today, and I'm sorry to say, she still has much to see and do before she rests her head tonight. Therefore, we must travel onward to Crow. I promise we will not stay away long."

Daphne and Iris sent the travelers on their way with fond goodbyes and glances of hope and excitement. They flung beads of crystal droplets with their fish-like fins as they dove beneath the water's surface.

"You sure handled that well," he said playfully as the woodland lake passed into the distance.

"What are they?" Lex asked.

"Naiads," he said, "water nymphs if you'd like. Offspring of gods. Ancient, immortal beings. There are many of these creatures throughout this world. Their purpose is to protect the domain in which they inhabit, be it a forest, a lake, a meadow, a mountain, an ocean, etcetera, etcetera. I think of them as nature's guardians. I also think of them as my friends. Though the gods typically don't interact with humans directly, they will consult their children. This means that being in good standing with the nymphs means being in good standing with the gods. Should the time come when man must look to the gods for help, this alliance will be most important."

"I'm sorry, Charlie," Lex interjected more politely now, remembering that he had supposedly sung her praises to Daphne and Iris, "but it sounds as though you are reading directly from a

Greek mythology book. I'm not going to lie and I'll say this in all due respect; despite what I've seen so far, I still think this is some kind of trickery on your part."

"I know," he replied acceptingly, "but for the time being remember one thing in particular that you have just observed - the resemblance of this world to the world of Greek mythology. The concept will be important as you begin to understand more."

She nodded. That was all she could do in her overwhelmed state of being. The two didn't say much else as they made their way through the giant forest toward Crow.

42

Ahead, beyond the tree line, was sapphire sky and open land. There were faint voices from somewhere in the distance accompanied by the fluttery melody of a flute. The pleasing aroma of smoke and cooked meat weaved its way between the trees to greet them as they approached the forest's edge. Clearly, they were nearing some form of human establishment.

Stepping out of the forest and into the light, Lex was smothered with surrealism. Before her was a sight so impressive that anything she had seen before failed to rival it. She halted in her tracks, fell to her knees, and did her best to take it all in. "Charlie, have we gone back in time?" she mumbled, unsure of her own sanity.

"No," he replied, "but we have arrived at Crow. Nice view, eh?"

They were standing at the edge of a soaring cliff looking down upon a magnificent city unlike any she had ever seen. There were no cars, no stoplights, no billboards or skyscrapers. The streets were not of pavement, but of dirt or stone. Treading these streets were horse-drawn chariots, various livestock and crowds of people wearing attire foreign to Lex's familiarity. The multitude of buildings that constituted the city's very framework were manufactured of brilliant marble blocks, voluminous pillars, and hefty wooden beams.

Despite the overload of captivating items to observe, there were things that stood out above all others. Near the city's center was a coliseum of enormous proportion and indescribable perplexity of design. Each pillar, statue, or marble slab that had been collectively assembled to create this architectural marvel, were likely to weigh several tons apiece. It was flawless in design and symmetry and made Lex strive to imagine how such a thing could be created without the use of modern machines. The coliseum was astonishing because of its sheer size, but there was another structure in this great city that was even larger - much, much larger.

The castle of Crow, a titanic fortress so prevailing that even the fury of the gods was unlikely to blemish it. It surged skyward like a mountain and acted as the city's central hub. Its black shadow engulfed over half the city creating a sort of giant ying-yang appearance from their current vantage point. She had never in her life seen a building this large, this high and this solid. She had always been enraptured by all the wonders of the ancient and modern world, and now, after setting eyes on the castle of Crow, there was a brand new wonder that transcended them all.

Beyond the castle were hydrangea-blue waters extending toward the horizon, where it met the white clouds and purple sky creating a kaleidoscope-like ambience. Wooden fishing skiffs, row boats and large trading vessels dotted the harbor, congregating near the port docks. She could just make out an assemblage of people unloading goods from a large vessel with towering white sails. From her high perch on the cliff, everyone looked like tiny ants, scurrying about with a purpose.

"I think this is a good time and place to commence with my explanation," Charlie announced energetically. He took a seat in the soft dirt along the cliff's edge and dangled his legs loosely over the steep drop-off. Lex sat beside him ensuring care and concentration so as not to slip over the edge and take an unwanted plunge to an early grave. Her face showed a mix of awe and desperation as she looked to him for more answers.

"You asked if we've gone back in time," he began. "Well, that is not the case."

She suddenly and most obtrusively interjected, surprising herself with the irritated tone. "I wasn't really serious. In fact, the only thing I'm serious about is getting back home." She shook her head hopelessly while speaking. "Whatever this is Charlie, whatever you have done is not fooling me. Something doesn't add up." The enchantment that the forest had cast upon her had now subsided. She was getting worked up again and had yet to dismount the emotional roller coaster. The Naiads were one thing, but this grand scene below was another entirely. Perhaps the key factor that afflicted her mind was the mounting evidence that she really was not in her own world. "I know what kind of money you have, Charlie. With that kind of wealth, you have the power to do anything. How did you accomplish all of this? Be honest with me because I'm tired of all the secrets." With that she propagated a vehement scream of frustration that echoed multiple times over the city before it seemed to disappear out to sea. This behavior was completely out of character, but she had never been in such a situation.

It was in Charlie's nature to be patient and understanding. He gave her a moment to cool down before doing the only thing he could do – proceed with his justification. "All of this is beyond anything I could ever create with money," he resumed, cringing just a bit in anticipation of another outburst. This time she kept quiet, staring out at the distant mountains in aggravation. "The reason why we couldn't have gone back in time is because there are creatures here that never existed in our world. Naiads for example, or," he paused, "Cyclopes."

Lex's response to this was an incredulous roll of her eyes.

"Before you ask any more questions," he continued, "I should tell you what I know about the pool. Unfortunately, I don't have all the answers. I only hope that you might offer your intelligence to assist me in my quest for the truth."

Before he could proceed, a new sound arose- a muffled sobbing. Lex had her head between her knees, in tears. He scooted close and put a consoling arm around her. "I just don't know what to make of all this," she bawled. "One moment I'm fine and then the next I'm overcome by complete doubt. I mean, everything seems real. That city surely seems authentic, the forest looked real enough and those women back there didn't seem to be wearing costumes." She sniffed and wiped her eyes with the sleeve of her cloak. "Since we've arrived at…wherever it is we are, I've been thinking of every viable rationalization as to how you've done this. The fact is, I can't find a rationalization, which leads me to believe that you are telling the truth. If that's the case, then I have no choice but to believe that we are in another world, and that idea is so utterly ridiculous that it makes me cry like a blubbering idiot."

He gently rubbed her shoulder. "Sevastian cried for three days in a row," he said jokingly, or maybe not jokingly at all. "He might have gone on forever had he not taken a break to eat."

She managed to crack a smile but failed to find solace in his humor. "Lex, if I can offer you any advice right now, it would be this: whether you believe me or not, at least try to enjoy the moment. Do whatever it takes to achieve a bit of composure. If you want to pretend you are dreaming, by all means go ahead. The fact is that once you hear the story of how this all came to be, then you will fully believe it, but in the meantime, don't let doubt and disbelief ruin the experience."

She thought about that for a moment, actually, many moments before eventually coming to realize he was right. Whatever was happening seemed as magical as one of her childhood fairy tales. Why should she not take pleasure in it just because she didn't believe it? She took a collected breath and gently nodded a "go ahead."

"Thank you," he said as he started into something that, just by his tone, she could tell was of great significance. "I am about to tell you a true story. This story is so astounding that our very connection to the universe may be entwined within its words. I must warn, however, that once you hear it, you must keep it a secret. The problem with knowing something of this magnitude is that absolute disaster would most likely ensue if the wrong people found out. After I am through, you will possess insight into something that nobody else in existence knows about, save myself and two others. Here we go…"

43

Charlie's task was to enlighten Lex without nudging her volatile mind over the edge. She was teetering between acceptance and meltdown and he had to choose his words scrupulously. The inquisitive green eyes of his companion were staring at him, longing for answers.

"I want to reiterate the point that I made before," he started. "There is no such thing as magic. All of this," he pointed first toward the remarkable city below, then to the forest behind them, "is backed by a logical explanation. This is not like the fairy tales, or the movies, or every other countless story in which there are orcs and wizards, elves and dragons. No, Lex, there is no magic, there is only chemistry. The pool that brought us from the world that you know is the work of…let's say a brilliant chemist. Remember what I told you about acanthars and acanthary?"

She nodded.

"As you may have noticed from the trees behind us, there are plant species in this world that do not exist in the other. When certain plant species are ingested, their biological components intermingle with the cellular components of our bodies, most significantly, our brains. I have spent years collecting different varieties of these plants and bringing them back with me through the pool. Studying them under a microscope has yielded mind boggling discoveries. The plant's unique biological features are what allow humans to perform acts that are seemingly magic. Keep in mind, however, that not everyone has developed the ability to perform these acts."

"You are dipping below my radar," she said honestly. "Can

you give me an example?"

"Certainly," Charlie obliged. "In fact, you have already been in contact with two of these plants. Does the name cicadaweed ring a bell?" A manifestation of interest materialized on her face as he proceeded. "The cicadaweed plant is very common in this world, which is why, even though you ask on a daily basis, I have not revealed my cicadaweed source until now. In this world its tea is a popular drink. Its effects on the mind's alertness are tremendous and undeniable. In the other world, it has no equal.

You'll surely find my next example even more interesting," he declared, "because you have already fallen victim to its effects – and I use the word 'victim' lightly. That little chocolate mint I left for you at Vincent's, you remember, don't you?"

"It was the most delicious candy I've ever eaten," she assured him.

"That piece of candy was made with an ingredient that only comes from a certain body of water in this world. You are yet to be familiarized with the geography here, but far to the west of Crow is the Sea of Poseidon. Native to that sea is a water plant called yebillok. Yebillok is the culprit behind your dream, which of course occurred the same night you ate the candy. All that is necessary for dream invasion, as I like to call it, is the tiny root from the yebillok plant. I cut it in half, bake one piece into the candy so that my host, if you will, will consume it, and then I eat the other piece. That night you and I were connected by the fibers of that tiny root. If you had the know-how, you could have created a dream for me."

This new revelation sparked an instant suspicion as red flags began popping up in Lex's mind. Sure, Charlie had delivered his dream invasion explanation with an air of gusto and innocence, but she was certain that he had just unconsciously slipped. First, he had just confessed in so many words that the candy was a premeditated ploy to invade her dreams. Second, the dream he had chosen to create related to this world specifically. Third, that night at the restaurant in which he had given her the candy was the first time they had crossed paths since high school. As a result, two possible explanations emerged. That fateful summer night at Vincent's, he either picked her at random to be the recipient of his little acanthary trick, or, and the more likely culprit, she had already been identified and targeted before he and the others even stepped foot in the restaurant. If the latter were true, this would not only be slightly disturbing, it would also confirm her long upheld suspicion that everything with the Rose Flock had worked out a little too perfect to be mere happenstance. But even with this new incriminating evidence, she still hadn't the slightest idea how or why he would single her out specifically. Since the jury was still out, she quickly made the decision not to question him right then and there. She would store this information as ammunition so when the time came, she would have the resources to launch a full on assault and achieve victory by getting the whole truth from him. She masked these misgivings by putting forth her best poker face and casually proceeding with the conversation. "Interesting," she said, "but that still doesn't tell me how you are able to shape my dreams."

"It's complicated," he replied after a moment of deliberation. "It would take all day to explain in detail what I know about the whole process. Dream invasion is a little ahead of the game, however, to illustrate my point, I can give you a quick, basic lesson in acanthary."

He leapt to his feet and scanned the area. His gaze landed upon a plot of colorful wildflowers several paces away. He hurried to the patch and selected a small yellow one. Returning to Lex's side, he reclaimed his seat in the dirt holding tightly to his find.

"The first step in becoming an acanthar is to access the areas of your brain that you do not usually, if ever, access. You must utilize the neuron and nerve connections that course between your mind and the rest of your body. A popular myth back in the other world claims that a certain percentage of the human mind is unused. I've studied the field of Neuroscience thoroughly and found that this is not necessarily true; but to this day, there are still parts of the brain whose functions are not fully understood. With modern brain imaging techniques, we have also learned that individuals vary in which areas of the brain they use more often."

"I have heard that too," Lex interjected, unsure what he was getting at.

He continued, "Many theories have been formulated about what the brain could accomplish if these lesser-known regions were accessed, or harnessed if you will. For example, in the other world there are a handful of people who claim to be psychic, communicate with animals, or have a sixth sense that allows them to see spirits. The list goes on. Maybe these people are frauds and just want to get themselves some attention...but maybe some of them are telling the truth. Perhaps the secret to their supposed special ability is that they have somehow unlocked doors within their brains that lead to more advanced functions.

In this world, like the other, the people who can access these brain regions are few and far between, however here, it is a learned skill rather than a fluke, and the ones who can do it are able to teach others. Tapping into those specific brain regions, along with the right plant is the key to unlocking your mind's full potential. And thus, you have the basis of acanthary."

"Do you think I will be able to learn?" she asked dubiously, as if she should even be entertaining the notion.

"I'm sure of it," he replied, noticeably delighted over the question. "Everybody has different levels of mind capability. Anyone can be taught, but it comes more naturally to certain people. Let me give you a demonstration. I want you to close your eyes and imagine that you have an itch on your head."

"But my head doesn't itch," she said, grinning over the madness of it all.

"Just close your eyes and imagine it does," he instructed. Although she felt ridiculous, she did as she was told. He whispered softly in her ear, "Concentrate on your scalp. Feel it with your mind."

She focused dogmatically on her task, first by taking note of the minor sensations that might be itches in their infancy. She zeroed in on these areas with her brain and before long the delicate tingles transformed to sensations just imploring to be scratched. She soon gave in, eliciting a cool smile from her teacher.

"I feel as though I'm in a shampoo commercial," she declared with a light-hearted laugh.

He nodded approvingly, "Good work. I know it must seem silly, but that is how you learn to consciously connect your mind to your body. Now let me show you what happens when we take this concept a few steps further." With that, he plucked all the golden petals from the flower he was holding and discarded them into the wind. They fluttered over the cliff and down toward the city like a swarm of tiny insects. Lex observed with interest as he crumpled the stem into a little ball and popped it into his mouth as if it were candy. His sour expression denoted a displeasing piquancy. His next objective was to find something sharp. He located a section of thorny branch within arm's reach that had disjoined from a nearby bush. Then to Lex's surprise, or horror for that matter, he removed a large thorn, plunged it deep into the skin of his forearm, and ripped downward several savage inches before removing the pointed object. Blood then began to cascade from the incision like water boiling over a kettle. Lex was stupefied.

"Why on earth did you do that?" she cried, finally able to channel her mortification into words.

"Just watch," he answered, calm as ever. A few seconds slipped by and she was once again awestruck. Right before her eyes, the jagged wound began to close. The exposed blood dehydrated into a crimson powder that blew off with the wind. Before long, there was little evidence that the injury had ever existed. "See, no magic at all, just the learned ability to hasten the body's natural healing process."

"So, you're immortal then?" she asked breathlessly.

He shook his head. "Certainly not. I've practiced this

technique for many years and at best I can mend small skin punctures and cuts. Large injuries, like the one on my back, I cannot heal with this method though I'm confident that someday I'll be able to. Also bear in mind that these are simple external wounds. There is only one man that I've ever heard of who could cure both external and internal wounds, rendering him nearly invincible."

At this junction, Lex was still not convinced of anything. Her senses were tenured by curiosity and despite it all, she was sort of enjoying this experience. Determined to find some flaw that would expose this grand charade, she continued to prod him for clarification.

"How does all of this plant and mind stuff tie in with the pool?" she asked.

Charlie did not answer right away. Instead, he glanced around to make certain no one was in close proximity. After a thorough observation, he slipped his hand beneath his cloak and carefully withdrew something that she could tell was of grave importance. It was a small black stone, round, shiny and inexplicably beautiful. He held it delicately, as if his life depended on its safe keeping. He allowed her to look it over, and although there was no evidence that anyone else was nearby, he commenced with his explanation tacitly. "Let me assure you, this stone is the most valuable possession we could ever own."

"Why?"

"Without it, the pool does not work. The reason you and I were able to come to this earth, and the reason we will be able to go back, is because the stone entered the pool with us. If it had not been in my possession, the pool would just be water and both of us would have been soaked. It still amazes me that so much can be attributed to such a small object," he stated rapturously, ogling over the little stone. "Everything that I have, every wonderful memory and priceless experience I owe to this. This, dear Lex, is the legendary Stone of Manult."

"What is Manult?" she asked.

"The appropriate question would be – who is Manult?" he corrected. "Manult was the greatest acanthar to ever live and the man responsible for creating this stone. In this world, much like the other, it is common practice to teach our children of notable people and events. These teachings become stories. The stories become legend and over considerable spans of time, truth blends with fiction. The stories of the great acanthar Manult have been passed down from generation to generation, enthralling all who hear them. Few men have had such an impact on the people of this earth."

"So you're saying he existed, but the stories about him may be false, or distorted over time?" she asked, feeling a trifle confused.

"Yes. The point that I'm trying to make is that sometimes it's difficult to decipher factual historical events from exaggerated events. The Manult stone," he raised the occult object a bit closer to Lex's eyes, "is much like the Arc of the Covenant. Both of these objects exist in legend. Both have been extensively sought after through the ages. Both have consumed and sometimes claimed the lives of those who become obsessed with finding them. And, neither have been found. Well, until…" He completed the thought with a dignified grin as he meticulously twirled the stone around in his fingers. "Truthfully, I never believed it really existed, until the day it came into my ownership."

"Two questions, Charlie. First, why did Manult create the stone? Second, I'm terribly curious as to how you ended up with it?"

He nodded, thought for a moment, then answered, "Of all the legends about Manult, the most popular is the story of the stone. It tells of an unmatched accomplishment in the mystifying world of acanthary and it just so happens to be a great love story.

Manult used his extraordinary acanthary skills to achieve many things. He created portals, conquered armies, tamed wild beasts, mastered healing, it was even said he could fly. Of all these spectacular achievements, the creation of the stone was the most notable. He made the stone so that one could instantaneously travel from one place to another. This is why for millennia, kings of the world's great cities have sent scores of soldiers in search of it. Owning the stone means having the ability to transport large armies in a split second, providing a major advantage in times of war. To be honest with you, Lex, the powers of this stone are way beyond my understanding. The only thing I know with certainty is that it gets us from one earth to the other and I'm happy to leave it at that."

"Will you tell me the story of the stone?" she asked, remembering that he had mentioned it was a great tale of love.

"Unfortunately," he proceeded, "it would do the story no justice to tell you now because in order to fully appreciate its implication, you must first become more familiar with this world. I do promise that as soon as I feel you're ready, I will tell you."

"Alright then," she said, supposing she understood his point. "Can you at least tell me how you found something that others have not been able to find for thousands of years?"

"With pleasure. Look below us," he instructed as he pointed toward the city. "Do you see the large road in the middle, the one that leads directly to the castle?"

She nodded.

"It all started there; the incident that I will never forget – the one that altered my life so completely."

Lex foresaw a story coming on. As if Nature was cued to set the stage, a dark cloud crept in, blocking the sun and plunging the land into rayless shadow. A brisk gust cascaded into Lex's body, whisking her mind away to that fateful night a long time ago in a world she barely knew.

Hand of Fate (part 1)

Only once every three hundred years does it occur, the moment in time when all three moons are concurrently full. The streets of Crow explode with activity as the festival to commemorate this prodigious event is in full swing. Myriads of bonfires embellish the streets in a conflagration of haunted luminescence, only to be outdone by the emissions of moonlight spilling down from the midnight sky. The most accomplished acanthars in the known world have been summoned to keep away any clouds that may hinder lunar gazing. They have so far been successful but their workload has been light as the gods have granted the city of Crow a clear and perfect sky. There are thousands out this night - eating, drinking, dancing and singing. There are storytellers and street performers, fire dancing and choir groups. Spirits soar and laughter runs rampant. Jubilant voices echo from the castle walls to the Andromeda Sea, and all the way to the city's far reaches where metropolis meets farmland and eventually wilderness. Those who are fortuitous enough to be alive during this age, cherish every moment, because nobody here will live long enough to experience it again, save the great gods looking down from the sacred mountain.

Tonight, hierarchy is ignored, dictatorship is placed on the back burner, and social classes ebb from existence as the poorest of citizens eat, drink and converse with Crow's elite. During this festival, there is no distinction between royalty or vagrant, rich or poor, soldier or artisan, king or beggar. Above all, the full moon festival symbolizes equality and balance among all things.

Each moon has a name and a story. Archea, the largest of the trio, leads the lunar procession across the sky each night and represents Nature. Encompassed within her symbolic domain are the earth, the animals, the sky, the trees, rocks and mountains, the universe, the unknown, and the absolute power the elements have over all else. The other two moons are visually comparable in size to each other. Artemis, the moon to directly follow Archea, exhibits a mysterious bluish hue and is representative of the gods, their children and their ethereal ascendancy. The final moon, Enuma, glows brightest among the three and symbolizes man and the promise he holds to consummate greatness. Enuma's gleaming characteristic is said to be a result of the sun god, Apollo, concentrating his radiant beams upon man, a race he greatly favors.

The full moon festival is funded by the royal families, and not a single particle of wealth was spared to ensure its grandiosity. Amidst the chaos of planning and participating, one royal family has not realized that two of their own children have breached the confines of protective custody and have wandered away on their own adventure. A young boy and girl, each of only five years, proceed unaccompanied through Crow's bedlam-ridden streets.

It began as a quest for sugary treats. The streets are chock full of vendors who have carts of homemade cakes and exotic candies of every conceivable color and flavor. It was of minimal ado for the rambunctious cousins to fill their stomachs with these mouth-watering goodies and quickly ascend toward sugar high. With their energy levels on full and two wooden play swords that had been graciously bestowed by a street entertainer, the boy quickly pursues the girl through a labyrinth of encumbrances. They weave through the masses of people, between legs, over haystacks and under carriages, jumping, screaming, rolling, and every once in a while, falling. Every now and again, the boy's tenacity allows him to catch up to his target, and a mock sword fight would quickly ensue. Following several minutes of intense combat, a few finger smashes, and some uncomfortable jabs to the abdomen, the girl again sprints off.

The sugar-driven energy of a child can only persist so long

before that unavoidable crash and it is the girl who first succumbs to her weariness. Following their final battle, an exhaustive skirmish in front of a pig roast to the amusement of a group of drunken townsfolk, the girl darts into a shadowed alley to hide from her aggressor and catch her breath. In his determined pursuit, the boy abandons the safety of the festival and enters into a world of murky obscurity.

He creeps along slowly, maintaining vigilance in this unsettling environment. He is certain that his cousin will leap from the shadows at any instant and have the better of him. Deeper and deeper he tracks, stepping idly over a motionless body that expels a powerful stench of wine and vomit. Next, he is startled by the lustful moans of a man and a woman, huddled together in the nude, rolling about the damp ground in inebriated animalism. He pays them little mind, for he is committed to a singular goal - proving that he is the better warrior.

Ahead, the alley makes a sharp left. The boy tiptoes around the corner, clinging tightly to the wooden sword ready for anything, or so he thinks. What he sees in that next moment is something utterly unexpected and a sight he will never forget for the remainder of his life.

Like a vision from a fairytale dream, bright beams from all three moons converge upon a single spot in that dead-end alley. Standing among this heavenly glow like some sort of god, is a mystifying old man. His kind face of weathered skin is accented by his wavy black hair and long, thin beard. He bears a cloak of resounding blue that exemplifies his eminence. He is entrancing, and perfect, and is devoid of anything that might bring forth fear in a child. The man's irrefutable allurement bewitches the boy who cannot help but to approach, just as the girl has done.

With twinkling eyes of wonderment and curiosity, the children gaze upward at his smiling face. He says nothing but reaches out and gently takes the girl's wooden sword; she offers no resistance. He twirls it around in his hands several times, inspecting it as if to appraise its craftsmanship, then he says in a voice as calm as a summer night, "This is a mighty sword, Jadenhara. You must be a mighty warrior to handle such a blade."

"How do you know my name?" she asks.

"It would only be fitting for a beautiful girl to have a beautiful name and I cannot think of a more beautiful name than Jadenhara," the old man contests. "It was a lucky guess." The girl giggles in delight as he continues his appraisal of the little play weapon. "Would you mind if I improved your sword?" he asks. The girl shakes her head with an unfaltering smile.

He holds the sword away from his body with two hands, as if making a sacred offering. Then, before the bedazzled eyes of the children, the wooden sword begins to emit a faint glow like a firefly's beacon, then quickly and steadily ascends through the ranks of luminosity until it shines with such clout, they may as well have been staring into the sun. The children can barely maintain observation but cannot bring themselves to look away. The blinding cylinder that had once been a sword of plain wood begins to extend laterally on both sides, all the while keeping its perch upon the man's open palms. Once it reaches its desired length, it explodes with a light of such blinding radiance, the children instinctively shield their eyes.

The light wanes as quickly as it had come, seemingly sucked up into nothingness through a pinhole in the air. With the eye-stinging sensation no longer an impediment, the children turn to see an unfeasible phenomenon. The sword remains within the guardianship of the old man, though it is no longer composed of rickety, splintered wood. Instead, it is a masterpiece of the purest silver, reflecting two dumbfounded faces from its mirror-like surface. There has never been, nor ever will be, a more perfect weapon in existence – the sword - living somewhere between flawless art and deadly potential. And then, it is placed back into the hands of the child Jadenhara without a moment's reconsideration. She looks it over breathlessly, taking certain care to avoid the razor-sharp edges. Without words, her glowing blue eyes convey her gratitude.

"Keep it in a safe place until you are old enough to use it," the old man instructs the girl, who nods with sincere affirmation.

"Me next, me next!" chants the boy, unable to contain his excitement.

"For you, young Charlamos, I have an even greater gift," the old man says in a way that verges on metaphysical. The boy does not care how the stranger knows his name, as he is blinded by anticipation for this "greater gift." The old man opens his hand, which was clearly empty a moment before, and presents the boy with a small, shiny rock of obsidian hue. A tidal wave of disappointment washes over the boy, drowning his high hopes. The wise bestower takes note of the dissatisfaction. "Charlamos, take this stone to the western end of the city. Locate the dirt path up the cliff. Once you have made your ascent, cross through the forest. On the other side there is a meadow where a willow grows. Inside the trunk is a pool of water. Throw the stone to the bottom. When you have done that, go into the water and retrieve it, then you will have your true gift."

The boy reaches out and half-heartedly accepts the stone. Upon doing so, he feels a sense of something beautiful, terrifying and unexplainable course through his body. The feeling is precipitous, yet to the contrary, enduring.

Suddenly, a roaring voice booms from behind. The children jump and turn to see a group of Crow Soldiers bearing torches of dancing flames. "Here they are," the lead soldier shouts back to the others. Charlamos succeeds in concealing the stone within the pocket of his upper garment before the men approach. Obliging the king's orders, they have come to retrieve the boy and girl. "You gave your family quite a scare," the lead soldier says in a friendly, yet commanding voice as he gently takes each child by the arm. Concerned over what the soldiers might do upon finding the old man, the boy spouts the first thing that comes to his young mind.

"Do not arrest him. He did nothing to harm us."

The soldier and the others give a swift yet thorough

observation of the silent ally before asking, "Arrest whom? There's nobody here."

In the dead-end alley, surrounded by high walls, the old man has evaporated, or so it seems to the children. The moonbeams have moved on leaving only the soldiers' flickering torches to provide guidance. The only sounds are distant echoes from the main streets.

As the children are led back to the safety of the castle, the boy is consciously devising a plan to escape to the willow tree and claim his gift. Despite the all-encompassing fanfare of the full moon festival, the children are too busy replaying in their minds, the magic they had just witnessed. Although each is ravished in thought, they cannot disregard the baffled voice from the head soldier. "Jadenhara, where did you get that sword, child?"

44

The spectacular scene Lex was picturing in her mind began to dissolve as Charlie wrapped up. The story had answered many questions and produced as many more.

"Cousins - you and Jade are cousins?" she uttered in bewilderment. For some reason, she took this as very good news. It also absolved the lingering guilt she felt about having such strong feelings for Charlie while he, so she had assumed, had been in a relationship with a girl who considered her a friend. "So you never found out who the old man was?"

"Never saw him again. After years of replaying that night in my mind, I have come to only one obvious conclusion. Jade and I were meant to be in that exact alley, at that exact moment in time."

"Why do you think that?"

"I believe the answer has yet to reveal itself."

"What about the gift he promised you? What was he talking about?"

Charlie pondered that for a moment. "I can't be sure. I often think that the gift was the other world and all of the knowledge and opportunity it has offered me. Recently, however, I can't help but wonder if my true gift is…" he stumbled over his words abashedly. "Let's just say I've gained some wonderful friends out of the deal." He made this flattering remark with an obvious insinuation toward Lex - obvious if only she had been paying attention instead of organizing her thoughts.

"Tell me if I've got this straight, Charlie. A complete stranger gives you a magical stone…"

"Uh, remember, no magic here," he reminded her.

She continued undeterred by the interjection. "Then you and Jade go to the willow tree, into the pool and all of a sudden you're in another world."

He nodded. "The first time through the pool was a terrifying experience. The blissful music and the amazing feelings were there, but after that was over, we awoke in a pitch black hell. Imagine waking up on the floor of that basement room in the church, not knowing where you were or what to do. We were only five. We had never been without our family's care for more than a few hours. It was beyond traumatizing to be trapped in a cold, dark place without any clue as to how we got there or how we could get out."

"Why didn't you just come back to this world through the church's pool?" she asked.

"We would have, had we not lost the stone," he assured her. "Somehow during the confusion, I had dropped it. Blind to our surroundings, we felt all along the ground for it. The only thing we found were dirt floors, stone walls and a staircase that dead-ended into a stone ceiling. Eventually we resorted to venturing into the pool, but when the stone is not in hand, the pool is just water. Not only were we scared, confused and miserable – we were also wet."

"I can't imagine how awful that must have been," she said consolingly, feeling genuine empathy over the situation.

"Pretty rough experience for a couple of kids," he declared with a "what doesn't kill you makes you stronger" insinuation.

"How long did you stay down there?"

"Hard to say. Seemed like an eternity but Jade and I came to the agreement that it was probably three days."

"How did you finally manage to get out?"

"Well at some point I knew and even accepted that I was going to die. I had wedged myself between the top step and the ceiling, drifting in and out of sleep and hoping that the inevitable would come sooner than later because the cold, the hunger and the fear were overbearing. It was during that time when I heard a distant, unrecognizable humming and felt infinitesimal vibrations. The vibrations eventually increased in magnitude causing tiny bits of dirt to fall from the ceiling onto my face. I laid there for hours and observed as the sound faded then returned over and over again. Every time it was at its loudest, the dirt again fell from the ceiling. Finally, enough dirt had fallen to produce a minuscule crack from which I could see a trace of light. It was then I realized that I might be able to push through the top. I called to Jade for help. We were weak, but still managed to force that stone out of the ground."

"And the rumbling sound?"

"It was a corn picker," he replied, "piloted by none other than Robert Roanoke, the man who would later adopt me."

The pieces to this immense puzzle were falling into place for Lex as the mysteries that shrouded Charlie's past were now being unveiled. "The Roanokes adopted you and the Vanderveldes adopted Jade."

He nodded in affirmation. "It was quite an ordeal. Imagine two children popping up in Kansas speaking ancient Greek. We were all over the local newspapers - even made the national news, or so I was told."

"So, then what?" she asked, prodding him for further enlightenment.

"The transition process is sort of blurry. I remember being very confused, even violent at times, while learning to live with my new family. According to Robert and Ella, I learned everything quickly, the language, the customs, and a whole new life. By the time I had finally adapted to life in America, I had accepted the fact that my old life was gone for good. Besides, I was having too much fun. I really enjoyed working on the farm and going to school. With all the new friendships and activities, I had pushed the past into the back of my mind. I guess it was Jade who ultimately made me come back."

"I can't say I'm surprised by that," Lex said, now very

familiar with Jade's power of persuasion.

"Indeed," he said. "We had always stayed close. The Roanokes and Vanderveldes were good friends. Both families were farmers who were getting up in age. Euchre nights were Tuesdays and Fridays, and every Sunday they got together for lunch. It was during these engagements Jade and I would get to see each other."

Nostalgia

It is a sultry Sunday afternoon. The early summer rains have allowed the Kansas corn to achieve full potential this year. Their coarse leaves rustle against one another in the breeze, rippling in succession across the fields as if a stone had been cast into a giant emerald pond. The aroma of chicken and dumplings tiptoes through the screen door and out to the front porch of the Roanoke house. The boy and girl, now fourteen years old, sit complacently on the swing anxiously awaiting the meal that has produced these mouth-watering fumes. They welcome the refreshing breeze as they have not yet exchanged their uncomfortable church attire for something more befitting to the humidity of the day. Though side-by-side, there is no present conversation. The boy is engrossed in a thick novel and the girl eyes the distant patch of woods with a solicitous air.

"Charlie," the girl suddenly says, "why haven't we ever discussed our past?"

Charlie is taken aback by the comment. For close to a decade, he has shut out the horrifying ordeal of what he termed "the black hole." After this prolonged mental repression, he has nearly managed to convince himself that the whole thing never happened. "What are you talking about?" he asks nonchalantly, knowing full well what she means.

Jade fixes her blue eyes on him and he feels the weight of her conviction. "Please don't play this game. I know…" she pauses to make sure nobody else was around then continues in a commanding whisper. "I know you remember what happened. The city, the old man, the pool… I used to think I was crazy, like I had imagined the whole thing, but the fact is, it happened. I can't deny it and neither can you. Why haven't we ever talked about it?"

He sets the book down, calmly, trying to keep composure in hope that he will successfully calm his imperious cousin. He did not expect her to bring this up so abruptly, and truthfully had no desire to discuss it again. He is at ease in his new life and is a trifle concerned about his own sanity. However, Jade's current confirmation of those dreaded and baffling events prove that either they are both mental, or it really did happen. It's clear to him that this issue has been welling up inside Jade for some time and for whatever reason, she had chosen this moment to let it boil over.

"Okay," he replies quietly. "What do you want me to say? Whatever happened to us, whatever means we came to be here defies all logic. But yeah, it happened. You and I both know it, but what do you propose we do? Go back? Relearn a language? Reappear out of nowhere and attempt to find our place among a society that we know absolutely nothing about?"

"How can we carry on with the rest of our lives without knowing for sure?" she rebuts. "We should go back, if only for a few moments. Please. It's something that has been weighing on my mind for years."

He looks out toward the unearthly patch of trees with certain trepidation. "If you remember, we lost the stone," he says, desperate for a legitimate counterpoint. "I'm not sure we could go back even if we wanted to."

"It must be in the church. We can use flashlights to look for it. We'll find it."

Ella's voice beckons from inside the house. "Charlie, Jade, lunch time."

"Tonight then?" Jade quickly offers, more as a demand than an inquiry. "Meet me at the church at eleven."

"No," he responds, quite set in his decision.

"But..."

"No."

Jade has always exerted a certain dominance over poor Charlie. He realizes this later that evening as he sits apprehensively at the desk in his room, staring blankly at his favorite poster - a beautiful and thought-provoking depiction of the solar system. Jade has opened his mind's version of Pandora's box – lifted the floodgates, released the hounds. He has no control over the torrent of memories that are pouring into his head. It is all coming back in astonishing detail. Repressed memories leapt from the crevices where they had remained dormant for years. Although his mind tells him no, his heart says that perhaps this is worth considering. At ten-thirty, he finishes a lengthy, heartfelt letter to Robert and Ella. The basic premise is that he would be gone for a while, but not to worry for he would return safely. He has not had enough time to produce a practical alibi and hopes to come up with something useful by the time he returns. As of now, his greatest wish is that the stone will not be found and he will return this very night to shred the letter.

He places the note on the crisply made bed with the feeling of guilt slashing through his insides. His parent's health has been declining and he hopes this unexpected departure will not antagonize their condition. Trying not to think too much into it, he stuffs a ragged leather backpack with a few snacks and a change of clothes. It is nearing eleven and Jade is never tardy. After donning an old brown poncho, dimming the lamp, and snatching a flashlight, he slips out his bedroom window while two opposing entities, excitement and fear, wage an all out war within his mind.

"And?" Lex asked inquisitively, yearning for the story's continuance. It seemed as though he was satisfied with his decision to stop here. He made good use of his hand as a sun visor, squinting intently toward the castle. "What are you doing, Charlie?"

"From up here, the castle acts as a giant sundial. I've gotten caught up in the story and neglected to remember that you and I have an appointment."

"An appointment?"

"At the kapeleia. It's our version of a bar, or tavern," he clarified as he found his feet. "We're due there very shortly."

"What about the rest of the story? You still have quite a bit of explaining to do."

"The whole purpose of this appointment is to continue the explanation, except now I'll have a bit of help."

She had no choice but to shrug her shoulders and follow her shepherd, who seemed to be intent about moving on.

As the two carefully descended the precarious pathway of the rocky cliff, she surprised herself and apparently Charlie as well, with a sudden bout of laughter.

"I wasn't expecting that, at least not this early in the game," he asserted.

"It just hit me," she adduced with a visage of gaiety, "your real name is Charlamos. I don't know if I can get used to that."

45

The rugged dirt trail meandered down the cliff and transitioned into a refined trail when it hit level ground. That narrow trail transitioned into a wider path which turned into a stone road that gradually widened. When it got to that point, Charlie and Lex were entering into the heart of Crow.

Most of the city's infrastructure, save the castle and the coliseum, followed a similar design. The farmers' dwellings and the majority of the small houses and barns on the outskirts of the city were made with wood, mudbrick, or clay. As the pair trekked farther into the city, the building design became more durable and elaborate. The inner-city architecture was of limestone or marble blocks, enormous cylindrical pillars and tiled rooftops. The walls of most public buildings, be it a bath house, a gymnasium, a courthouse, a fountain house, or one of the many glorious temples, were graced with sculptures of animals, people and other various creatures of which Lex had never seen before.

They passed by an attractive amphitheater, carved into the side of a grassy hill. Upon the sturdy wooden stage, musicians and bards had gathered in what appeared to be an informal rehearsal. There were instruments and scripts, singers and costumes. Several dozen citizens were scattered throughout the stadium-style seating along the hillside, observing the practice session. Behind the amphitheater was a vast expanse of land confined by a gray stone wall. Everything within the wall was either a cypress tree, a statue, or a tombstone. Lex was to learn that this necropolis was just one of many throughout the city.

The only visible modes of transportation were horseback, chariot, or walking. There was so much of each going on, Lex and Charlie had to have their wits about them so as not to collide with the many four-legged beasts and chariots zipping here and there without any apparent regard to speed limits or the proper side of the road. Lex's eye for equine species allowed her to discern that the horses in this world were similar to the horses in the other, except that the ones here were, on average, much larger.

The citizens of Crow were out and about in full force, and the sight of them was engaging. Right away she was able to decipher the contrasting garments of the various social classes. The destitute were wearing shambles of clothes, raggedy scraps and remnants of what once might have been a presentable tunic or toga. They were standing, sitting, or laying here and there accepting handouts, usually in the form of an unfinished piece of fruit or the slim remains of a rib bone. Their matted hair and long beards provided padding against the uncomfortable ground on which many of them were resting. They reminded her of the modern day homeless.

The majority of the populace was dressed similar to Charlie and Lex, that is, nothing fancier than a wool cloak, a modest shawl, a short or long tunic, leather sandals or boots, or any combination thereof. She guessed that these people were of the working class. Though their garments were functional and well mended, there was no comparison between their plain brown, off-white, or gray attire to the vibrant hues of the group that was obviously royalty.

The privileged nobility traveled in small groups, usually gender specific. Whether man, woman, or youth, the members of Crow's royal families walked tall, proud, and displayed like peacocks the eye-catching colors that confirmed their aristocratic prestige. Though the particular style of clothing was near exact to everyone else, the royalty furnished their vestments in ways that necessitated attention and envy. Lex noted that the noblemen wore tunics just like all the other men of Crow, except theirs had been dyed of crimson red, midnight blue or forest green, and embroidered with symbolic designs of crows, wolves and other various creatures of intimidation. They wore sturdy leather belts with gold or silver daggers hanging off their hips. Some wore metal headpieces in the shape of fig branches or laurel leaves.

The royal women were perhaps the most eye-catching of all. They seemed to possess a unique beauty, much like Jade, with their smooth olive skin and their glowing black hair. They were charismatic and feminine but at the same time, displayed a sort of fire within, as if willing and able to go to war if called upon. These regal enchantresses had thoughtfully clad themselves in feminine variations of tunics and togas that were more dress-like than their male counterparts. Silky material, died with hues throughout the entire color spectrum, danced across the stone streets as if the spellbinding garments breathed their own life. The predominantly sleeveless style allowed an appraisal of lean, muscular arms that were ornamented with bracelets and shimmering bands that coiled upward like gold or silver snakes. The women's fingers and toes were embellished with rings of silver. Gorgeous laurel leaf bands sat fittingly upon proud heads. Whenever Charlie and Lex encountered a group of nobles in passing, all members made sure to render a quick and courteous bow to Charlie. He would always reciprocate with a courteous dip of the chin. These continual exchanges only fueled Lex's perplexity.

A half a dozen men approached rapidly, and they were so engrossed in some riveting conversation, they nearly plowed right over Lex. She had to leap to one side to avoid them, narrowly escaping sinking her boot into a pile of steaming horse dung. Two of the men turned and offered a hurried apology before scurrying onward to catch the others and rejoin discussion. During this brief interaction, she had caught snippets of their conversation. The topic these men were discussing matched the topic on the lips of everyone else out and about today, and coincided with the declaration on the scrolls that were posted on every available building, statue and wagon in sight. She could tell that something extraordinary was about to take place in Crow, and the individual who was responsible for all the stir went by the name...

"Who is Xenogorus?" she asked. "Is he like an evil pirate or something?"

Like everything else thus far, Charlie's answer was not as direct as she would have hoped. "This city is set apart from all the others in this world because we alone have a coliseum. This makes Crow the epicenter for popularity among all people who like a good sporting event. To compete against other skilled soldiers in front of thousands of amped-up spectators is the quickest way to climb the popularity ladder. Competing is one thing, but to win is another. Earning the title of grand champion ascends the victor to god-like status in the eyes of man. Talk to any one person in this city and they will tell you that they dream of one day competing for glory, and in a way, immortality. The coliseum has turned peasants into heroes and proven that even the mightiest of warriors can be brought down by weaker fighters with bigger hearts. Within its circular walls, epic battles have taken place, legends have been made, blood has been shed, and lives have been lost. In short, a fight day is about as exciting as it gets.

Recently, a new hero has emerged and differs from all others before him. His name is Trigonous. He conceals his identity by arriving to battle in a hooded black cloak, and fights with three different weapons. To master one weapon is impressive, to master three, as Trigonous has done, is unheard of. Ever since he first arrived on the scene, he has been challenged by every elite warrior this city and all the other great cities have to offer. So far, he has not lost a single battle – not even close. Now, because of Trigonous, the excitement and anticipation for a fight day has increased tenfold. The coliseum fills to capacity each and every time. People flood into Crow from all over the land to witness this famed warrior in action. The many hundreds of people who did not arrive in time to secure a seat, resort to standing outside the coliseum just to listen."

"This all reminds me of boxing or that mixed martial arts stuff," Lex expounded. "Interesting that no matter what world you're in, human nature is the same. We love good sport and it seems we're drawn to violence."

He nodded in agreement. "An accurate observation. And it's true, a fight day at the coliseum is not much different from pay-per-view boxing. There are anywhere from five to ten "lesser" fights that all lead up to the main event. These fights take place every one-hundred days. The rulers of each city select their best warriors to travel to Crow and compete for their city's honor. Once the contenders are chosen, their names are added to a list which is delivered to the Queen of Crow. She alone has the exclusive privilege of matching up the fighters and putting together the schedule."

Lex cut in. "So each contender uses the weapon he has mastered. Are there any weapons that are forbidden?" she asked, trying her best to see the whole picture.

"Any weapon is allowed as long as it has not been enhanced by acts of acanthary," he replied.

She wasn't sure exactly what that meant. Her next question: "Which city does Trigonous fight for?"

"The only embellishment to Trigonous's black cloak is a small design in the mid chest area - the Crow crest. This of course means he represents Crow, but no one knows who he is, where he lives, where he trains, or how he gets into the coliseum without being seen. Trigonous is virtually invisible until it is his time to fight. Following his victories, he seems to disappear into thin air. Some say he isn't human."

"Does he finish off his opponents? That is, err, does he kill them?"

"Surprising though it may seem, he does not execute his competition. He does, however, carry out a unique victory ritual. When his competitor has been subdued, he forces them face-down in the dirt. He then carves the Greek letter theta deep into the skin of their back to serve as a lifetime reminder of defeat."

"Sort of inconsiderate," Lex mentioned. "Guess it beats a public execution though."

"True," he agreed. "Sadly, as you have intuitively observed, it's in our nature as humans to be captivated by violence, and sometimes you have to give the crowd what they want."

She realized then that several minutes had elapsed since she had posed the question that catalyzed this entire discussion, and she still had no clue about this Xenogorus character. She relayed this thought to Charlie who recommended with a sympathetic nod.

"In your current circumstance, there is no simple explanation. Not just yet. If I had flat out told you who Xenogorus was, it would have meant nothing without the understanding of the coliseum and Trigonous. Now to give you some gratification; Xenogorus is a cyclops from the city Harond." He paused, as if anticipating some sort of disgruntled response of skepticism. This time, she made no motion to interject. "Cyclopes and man have had a delicate relationship for thousands of years. To put it bluntly, we don't care much for their lifestyle nor do they care for ours. In this world, when that happens, we typically adhere to the "live and let live" principle."

"In our world, that would be unheard of," Lex submitted.

"Very true. And this is not to say that there have never been wars, or significant conflicts, but they have occurred less frequently throughout our history."

"I like the idea of peace," she said honestly, knowing this statement was cliché.

"I couldn't agree more," he reciprocated. "So, the city of Harond is the northern-most city of this world. It lies on the doorstep of the dreaded Acheron Mountain range. It is cold and dangerous - perfectly suited for the Cyclopes race. As it is with every city in this world, Harond has its warriors who journey to Crow to have a go at overall victory. The Cyclopes have produced the most deadly fighter to ever challenge Trigonous. He goes by the name of Xenogorus. Many predicted Xenogorus to be the first to defeat the undefeated. And so it was yesterday, a fight day, that an epic battle occurred between the deadly cyclops and Trigonous.

Twenty minutes into the fight, after a praiseworthy display of physical endurance and weapon skills, Trigonous had the irate cyclops fighting for his reputation and his life. The giant was being toyed with as if he had just learned to fight yesterday. The crowd howled with laughter at his futile efforts to dismember Trigonous with his enormous chain weapon. Finally, after being humiliated to the point of madness, Xenogorus mustered every last ounce of energy and channeled it into one mighty attack. This powerful surge must have caught Trigonous by surprise as the cyclops successfully managed a brutal strike to the arm of his hooded opponent. Fighting with only one arm leveled the playing field but only temporarily. Trigonous was still able to manage a victory but after the injury, it was hard fought. This was the first time in Trigonous' history where he showed vulnerability."

"According to the scrolls posted everywhere, the two are to fight again tomorrow," Lex observed.

"A truly unprecedented occasion for the coliseum," he replied with fiery enthusiasm. "The Cyclopes, who traveled such a distance to arrive here, asked for a rematch. This request, along with the magnitude of excitement during the fight, prompted the Queen to bend the rules, or should I say, the tradition, and give Xenogorus another shot. You, Lex, will be lucky enough to witness a first ever rematch midday tomorrow. Needless to say, anticipation for this event is at its pinnacle."

Lex couldn't really get excited for this epic rematch because she was still too captivated by everything else. In her mind, a battle in the coliseum was not nearly as interesting as two naked Naiads living in a woodland lake, or an inter-world gateway, or astounding mind capabilities produced by exotic plants, or a mysterious stone or… her thoughts were put on hold when something snagged her eye. She and Charlie were now passing a bustling market that occupied the space between an armory and a smaller building that exhibited the Greek word for "POTTER" above the doorway. Here, vendors displayed wooden carts full of colorful fruits, seeds and nuts, thick slabs of meat on the bone, headless slimy fish, handmade vases and pots, a myriad of fabrics, and other various goods. Everything was housed under a network of wooden trellises covered by large white awnings that rippled lazily in the breeze. Despite the overwhelming activity that was taking place, one person in particular stood out. Maintaining a statue-like idleness beside a circular stone well, was a haunting specimen of a young woman. With hollow eyes, she traced Lex and Charlie's every movement. It wasn't just her lack of motion or her piercing gaze that was concerning, it was also the manner in which she was clad. Not so much a cloak as it was a dress, the black, shapeless material extended from her pale neck all the way to the dirt on which she stood. Her long, stringy hair matched the dreary color of the unappealing garment and it hung from her head like a curtain in the window of an old house.

When she and Lex locked eyes, it was as if nothing else existed for that brief moment, as if the other hundred or so people that scurried about the market just faded into silent oblivion. During this interaction, Lex was overcome with discomfort and unease. Contrary to the urge to continue looking upon this zombie-like figure, she broke gaze and turned to Charlie. She caught him in the process of nodding politely to a clique of noble women who beamed in ecstasy at his celebrity acknowledgement.

"Charlie, who is that girl over there?"

"You say something?" he asked, returning his regard to her as the clan of well-dressed beauties moved onward emitting high-pitched giggles like a flock of songbirds.

She was attempting to be discreet by avoiding further eye contact. "The girl in black next to the well, she's staring at me as if I had a tail or something."

He stopped suddenly, his calmness vanished. "Which one?" he asked with more concern than she would have expected in the given situation.

"Turn slowly," she instructed, "seven o'clock... only one wearing black."

Charlie, attempting to conserve Lex's effort of inconspicuousness, pretended to survey two soldiers on horses as they passed by, and then slowly shifted his gaze to the stone well. "I don't see her."

"What?" Lex spun around to see that the young woman had stolen away. "Hmm, she sure took off in a hurry. Definitely gave me a looking-over though."

He gave the area a thorough scan. "Oh well, nothing to fret about, I'm sure. You may find that being the new girl in town and also traveling in my company may render you the object of investigation by curious onlookers. Anyway, we're finally here."

46

They had arrived at the doorstep of a rather unimpressive little building - only in the sense that there was nothing fancy or outstanding about it. Summing up the exterior were weathered stone walls, two cloudy windows, one with a jagged crack and a squatty hay pile slumped to the left side of a rickety wooden door. In similar fashion to every other public building, the identification was etched above the door – Kapeleia.

Lex tailed Charlie through the front door into a cozy tavern of Greek composition. Only a trace of sunlight was able to squeeze through the opaque windows, leaving the collection of irregular-shaped candles the responsibility of providing illumination. To the left, was a bar made of white stone. On top of the bar sat several rows of clay pitchers, each with Greek lettering that Lex understood to say "wine" and "mead." Attached to the wall near the bar was a stone mantle which supported a hefty stack of bronze cups. An entryway, or exit depending on which way you were going, was located behind the bar. A steady stream of smoke and the aroma of cooked meat lofted steadily from the back room.

There were many tables scattered throughout the main area, arranged in such a way that lacked any kind of uniformity. Each table was hand-made, not mass produced, and differed in height, color and size. Though the room was dark, Lex noticed that the table in the back corner, the one obscured by shadows, was occupied. Due to the covert location, she had a feeling that she and Charlie were about to join whoever was already sitting there. She squinted hard, attempting to discern the figure barely visible by candlelight. As her eyes adjusted, she could just make out an unmistakable silhouette. This instantly brought a smile to her face. Full of happiness, she dashed toward the table.

"Sevastian!" she greeted avidly. The Russian, clothed in a wool cloak, was quick to his feet upon her swift approach. She managed to get an arm around him, pulling him in for a hug. For some reason, it was reassuring to look upon a familiar face during this crazy experience. This meeting proved to be the confidence booster she needed. Charlie strolled up, greeting his mate with a smile and a nod.

Sevastian placed a hand on her shoulder and looked her square in the eyes. "I want to assure you that all of this is real. It's not a joke, nothing is staged. I wish I had realized this sooner so I might have better enjoyed my first time here. "Also," he added quietly, "please understand that it was not my wish to miss your first time through the pool. Sadly, due to other engagements, I had no choice. So, how are you handling everything so far?"

The three sat down. She answered with an exhaustive smile, "Let's just say I'm in desperate need of further explanation. Other than that, I am simply astounded."

"Did Charlie introduce you to his goldfish?"

"If you mean Daphne and Iris, then yes."

"I'll tell you one thing," he continued with a tone that reeked of sarcasm, or authenticity, it was hard to tell which, "If either of those gorgeous creatures were at all interested in me, I'd have no trouble dating a fish." Charlie guffawed at this absurd remark while Lex fought to repress that mental image.

"What engagements were you talking about?" she asked the Russian after getting her thoughts back on track.

"Tonight, at the castle, a celebratory feast is being held in honor of tomorrow's rematch at the coliseum," he explained. "I'm not sure if... Charlie, have you told her about that?"

"One of the few things I've explained thus far," Charlie confirmed.

Before the conversation could advance, a shadow draped

across the table as if a storm was rolling in. An abominable woman of hefty proportion was approaching, wheezing repugnantly and rattling the floorboards with her heavy footfalls. After her exhaustive passage across the small room, the woman required a moment to catch her breath before addressing the three. During this fragment of time, Lex noted several interesting features.

The woman was beastly and had no business wearing something as revealing as the grease-stained toga, which was obviously two separate togas delicately pinned together. She looked like a giant marshmallow, ready to burst open and spill gooey contents all over the room. Her face was puffy and contorted. Her beady eyes were disproportionately tiny, giving the appearance of two black marbles stuck in a lump of pie dough. She had Albert Einstein's hair, Porky the Pig's mouth, and Grizzly Adam's beard – No, Lex thought to herself. Must be the lighting. She looked closer. Nope, not the lighting. That's a beard. She made the assumption that this woman was probably kind-hearted and felt bad about these initial demeaning observations. When the woman began to speak, Lex was once again reminded why she should never assume.

"Good day to my favorite customers!" the lady boomed in Greek.

"Good day, Delias!" Charlie and Sevastian greeted in synchrony.

Delias's attention shifted directly to Lex. "Who is this?" she asked with obvious indignation. Judging by her malcontented expression, there was no denying that Delias was not happy with her presence.

Charlie offered a submissive introduction. "Delias, I'd like you to meet our friend, Alexis."

Lex nodded timidly. "Hello."

"I have never heard a name as strange as Alexis," she blatantly stated, for some reason directing the comment to Sevastian specifically. Lex's Greek was still coming along, but what she thought she heard next was… "It must mean - plain as manure." She had never been so enraged and looked to the boys for any sign that this was some kind of joke, but both exhibited flabbergasted facial expressions confirming that Delias' statement was intended to be malicious rather than comedic.

Lex spoke up defensively, "Well, I think you're very rude, and I don't appreciate…"

"You don't adore this girl, do you?" Delias obtrusively butt in, once again addressing Sevastian. Sevastian's face scrolled through several different shades of red. Meanwhile, Charlie was doing everything in his power to refrain from erupting with laughter. At least *he* was enjoying himself.

"Of course not, lovely Delias," Sevastian replied in a mockingly poetic tone, "it is you, and only you whom I adore." This assurance elicited a smile from the bosomy troll.

"Why should I worry? My Sevastian would want nothing from such a common girl. What may I fetch to ease your thirst?"

Lex's jaw dropped in disgust. "Excuse me," she blurted out in perfect Greek, "just who do you…...?"

"Rabbit and your finest mead," Sevastian quickly spouted, cutting short Lex's self defense for a second time, and evading an impending conflict.

Delias nodded felicitously and said, "My favorite customers, you two," conveniently neglecting the fact that there were actually three. "Foregoing the luxuries of the castle to partake in our wine and mead. So very generous." She shot Lex one more scrutinizing glare then stampeded off to retrieve the requested fare.

"What is with that woman?" she demanded, completely repulsed and offended.

"She has a thing for Sevastian," Charlie pointed out.

"And she's, um, socially challenged," added Sevastian. "She will say whatever is on her mind. A real piece of work, that one."

"So, you just humor her then?" Lex asked.

"Yes I do – and for two reasons. First, her mead is the best around, so we want to stay in her good graces. But even more, she scares the living hell out of me and I fear the physical repercussions of upsetting her. She could smash any of us flat as a crêpe."

"The real truth is," Charlie added, "that Sevastian doesn't mind her company because by comparison, she makes him look thin as a rail!"

At this, there was an outpouring of laughter. Even Sevastian, who had been the butt of the joke, jiggled hysterically with delight. As a warning, Charlie cleared his throat. The others instantly regained a nonchalant composure as Delias returned with three bronze cups overflowing with syrupy mead and a dented tin plate stacked high with greasy rabbit legs. All the while she kept a peripheral eye on where Lex's hands resided in proximity to Sevastian.

47

"Where to begin?" Charlie wondered aloud after Delias had retreated back through the smoky bar-side doorway. He looked to Sevastian who was currently preoccupied with picking through the mountain of rabbit legs in search of the juiciest selection.

"How about I ask a question and you answer," proposed Lex who had been chomping at the bit for a straightforward question and answer session since she met Charlie.

He nodded and said, "Splendid idea. Ask away."

"Alright then, beginning on a larger scale, tell me about this world. You've already made it clear that you don't know where it is or how it came to be, but certainly you must have a theory. Is it likely we are…on some other planet, or is it a creation of acanthary, a parallel universe maybe?"

"No doubt another planet," he replied without equivocation. "Because you can't create an entire planet from plants. And a parallel universe…, does anyone know what that really means? I've dabbled in theoretical physics but it's not my strong suit. Maybe Hawking's followers understand the concept better. In my mind, the parallel universe idea was invented by science fiction writers so that they could justify other worlds in their stories."

"Not to rain on your parade, Charlie, but the parallel universe theory is about as cliché and overused as the "portal to another world" concept," she contested as if she were once again out to disprove this so-called reality.

He nodded agreeably, took a long drink of mead, then said,

"What you say couldn't be more true. An interplanetary gateway in the form of a mysterious portal is about as typical as it gets. I assume this is why the moment I informed you that the pool in the church was some sort of gateway that connected this world to the other, you automatically concluded that I was full of…what was it that Delias said… manure? When Sevastian first came here, he too found the concept laughable."

"Okay I get your point," she said as she poked irresolutely at one of the rabbit legs with her index finger, wondering whether or not to give it a taste. "It's unfortunate that the two worlds just happen to be connected in such a manner, because it makes it more difficult for the newcomer to swallow. I'll put that thought aside for now. Hopefully as I become more familiar with this world, it might begin to make more sense. So, you believe that this is another planet entirely?"

"Without a doubt," he continued. "Why do you imagine that we have such a passion for astronomy? All of our expensive telescopes and star charts, observing the sky night after night, keeping absolutely current on all the new discoveries of the universe. Do you now understand what we are attempting to do?"

She shook her head blankly, realizing it was pointless to rack her brain for an answer that he would momentarily disclose.

"We've spent years charting every prominent star that appears over this world. Every detail is accounted for, including their type, size and relationship with one another. We then bring these charts back through the pool and up to the astronomy loft in the library where we…"

"Look for the same stars from our world," she finished, finally getting it.

"Exactly," he said. "Though alas, we have not yet been able to locate these stars. This isn't surprising as there are countless trillions of them. All we can do for now is keep searching."

"What happens if you do find it?" she then asked. "Let's just say that one night in the astronomy loft, you look out across millions of light years and you find this planet in a remote solar system in a remote galaxy. What will you do then?"

He shrugged indifferently, "Absolutely nothing."

"Well then, why all the effort?"

"We are curious people," he replied, looking to the Russian who confirmed this claim by rendering a sharp, astute nod. "At this point, in our primitive understanding of this reality, we wouldn't know what to do if we did find this planet in some remote solar system in some remote galaxy…. we would just simply like to know. Knowing something like that could account for one piece in a much larger puzzle."

"What do you mean… larger puzzle?"

"You know how I'm always talking about those timeless questions – when, how, where and why? Do you remember when I said that the answers may be within our grasp? Uncovering the ultimate truth has become an obsession for us – me in particular."

Lex ceased the opportunity to intervene. "What makes you think the answers to those timeless questions are within your grasp?"

"After traveling between this earth and the other, an obvious truth became incontestably evident. That is, we are unique. You, me, Jade and Sevastian. We possess…" he glanced around and lowered his voice to a mere whisper. "We possess the one stone that allows us, and only us to travel between these two earths. Because of this, we have opportunities for knowledge that nobody else has."

"How can that be true?" she demanded, pressing him as though he were on trial. "The church in the woods has been there a very long time - much longer than you've been alive. Clearly, somebody else had access to the pool before you."

"No doubt about it, but whoever had the stone before us, whoever built that church… well let's just say their time is over and our time has begun."

"You say 'whoever' like you don't know where the stone came from," she challenged. "Didn't it belong to the old man in the alley?"

"Yes, but you know just as much about him as the rest of us," Charlie calmly replied as he gnawed on a piece of meat. "And for some reason, he felt that it was time to pass the stone to someone else."

"So let me get this straight," Lex said while rapidly clicking her nails across her empty cup, "you don't know where in space this planet exists, you don't know how the gateway works and you don't know anything about the old man who gave you the stone?" She attempted to be as amicable as possible while recounting the information. She wanted them to understand that her intent was not to be demeaning, only thorough.

"When you put it like that," he said, "we sound utterly clueless. Let me fill you in on what we do know."

"Please." She invited while finally mustering enough temerity to make an attempt at a rabbit leg, feeling that her chance to eat was quickly slipping away. The bone pile in front of Sevastian was towering, and only a few edible morsels of meat remained.

"Okay," Charlie began after thinking over his best approach. "For the sake of conversation it will be less confusing to you if I refer to the other world, the one with Kansas, as Earth A. I will refer to the world in which we now occupy as Earth B."

"I figured this world might have some fancy name," she submitted jokingly, "Like…" she deliberated on something that might be typical, "like Fantasma or Pandora." The others chuckled at her regaling attempt at wittiness.

Charlie said, "Those names would seem as likely as a magic portal, but in this world, as in the other, it is just referred to as Earth."

"Sorry," she apologized with a grin. "You were saying?"

"There are undeniably many connections between Earths A and B, which cannot be dismissed as mere coincidences," he explained. "On Earth A, there are two famous books written by the Greek poet Homer. You know them both very well – The Iliad and

The Odyssey. These famous stories are among the first accounts of Greek mythology, written over three thousand years ago. And as it happens, these books are perhaps the most significant link between the two earths."

"How?"

"I don't need to go into detail about the contents of these two epic poems because you have already read them. So, here's where it gets interesting. On Earth A, The Iliad and The Odyssey are considered pure fiction, nothing more than a creative story by a gifted bard named Homer. The battles, the heroes and the terrifying creatures are believed to be made up. Here, however, on Earth B, Homer's accounts of King Odysseus' adventures and accomplishments are actual history. All of the people that Homer mentions in his writings, are all people whose existence in this world are very well documented. The same goes for the creatures Odysseus encounters throughout his travels – gods and goddesses, nymphs, deadly sea monsters, harpies…"

"And cyclopes," Lex added, easily recalling their earlier discussion about Xenogorus.

"And cyclopes," he corroborated as he shifted positions in his chair. "Not only was Odysseus the most famous and influential king this world has ever known, every one of the creatures we just spoke of certainly exists or existed in this world as well. Now it gets even more interesting. Although the people and the creatures of Homer's writings exist here on Earth B, all of the locations, be it Ithaca, Troy, Pylos, or Ismaurus just to name a few, exist, or did exist on Earth A. Why he decided to use entities from both worlds is a mystery, but the fact that he did leads us to deduce one certainty."

With avidity, Lex completed his thought. "That Homer has traveled between the two worlds," she stated, certain of her insightful conclusion.

"That's right," he chirped, supplementing his remark with a golf clap. "To further confirm this theory, we have done a good deal of research and easily came to discover that Homer lived on

Earth A at approximately the same time that the people who make up his writings were alive here on Earth B. And if that's not enough proof, the time period in which Homer lived on Earth A, was the exact same time that the Greek language was introduced to the people here on Earth B."

"You mean the people here haven't always spoken Greek?" she asked.

"No. Before the time of Homer, this world spoke a different language. The history books here make many references to the introduction of the Greek language and most attribute King Odysseus as the one responsible. The new language fascinated the ancients. It was far more advanced than their original primitive language, and the people of the time quickly adopted it. Even the gods began to speak the tongue."

Lex asked, "Do any of these Earth B history books make mention of Homer?"

"Not one," said Charlie. "In fact, even on Earth A, very little is known about him. Even the time period in which he lived is disputed amongst scholars. It's not entirely certain that Homer was the man's real name. What's more, we're not entirely certain to which world he actually belongs. It's just as likely that he was native to this world and traveled to Earth A, where he learned the Greek language and brought it back here. This unfortunate ambiguity prevents us from learning much about him."

"It could also be that Homer and Odysseus were the same person and one of those names was an alias," Sevastian added. This was his first contribution to the conversation since the food had arrived.

Lex racked her brains to make sense of this. "So, Odysseus and Homer could have been the same man because he, or they, were alive during the same time period on both earths?"

"Yes," Charlie said.

She continued, "At that point in history, which you said was about three thousand years ago, this man crossed from one earth to the other, though we're not sure which was his native earth, and brought the Greek language with him?"

Charlie and the Russian nodded a confirmation.

"During this time, he wrote The Iliad and The Odyssey. And these two books are proof that he had traveled between the two worlds because all of the characters lived in this world, and all of the locations exist in the other. Is that right so far?"

"Exactly right," Sevastian confirmed.

"If all that is indeed the truth," she said, "there is just one little problem. Every connection between Earth A and Earth B revolves around ancient Greece. Based on this fact, one would guess that the connection between the two worlds would lie between the willow tree and somewhere in Greece, not the willow tree and Kansas."

"Good for you, Lex," Charlie applauded. "And over three thousand years ago, Kansas existed only as a dense wilderness. It seems highly unlikely that Homer departed from Greece, sailed across the Mediterranean Sea, then the Atlantic Ocean, docked his ship on the east coast of what is now North America, and trekked fifteen hundred miles through harsh wilderness to the old church. If Homer was indeed native to this world, it would seem equally unlikely that he came to Kansas via the portal in the church and made the reverse trip over to Greece."

"There must be another pool," Lex concluded."

"That is conceivable," Sevastian put in calmly, "but according to our studies of the Manult stone, we are led to believe that there is only one stone, and one gateway."

48

The windows to the outside burned a sleepy crimson, denoting that dusk was at hand. The front door creaked open and three bearded men clad in dirty cloaks shuffled inside. They found a table and fell into their seats heavily, exhausted. By their appearance, Lex surmised that they were probably farmers, stopping in for some food and drink after a hard day in the fields. Delias managed to squeeze herself through the doorway by the bar and greeted each of them with a lop-sided smile. Speaking Greek, the men gave Delias their orders and to Lex's surprise, she understood every word. Secretly, she was proud of herself for taking on this language so absorbingly, and with such expedition. There was one Sevastian Moskincov to whom her success could be attributed, because he had tutored her patiently and methodically. She put this thought on the backburner for the time being, realizing that she needed to seize every opportunity to obtain answers. Charlie had been flighty lately, as though he was not content to stay in one place for too long. To make matters worse, more people were accumulating within the little kapeleia, making privacy an issue. Who knew how much time she had before he was off and running again? She began her next round of questioning with haste, moving on to a separate topic after understanding that the connection between the two earths was still an unsolved mystery.

"Why is it that after thousands of years, humans on this earth still live in such a primitive society?"

"Phenomenal question!" Charlie exclaimed. "I'll leave this topic to Sevastian. You see, Lex, one of his many occupations here in Crow is chief historian. He has learned more about the past fifty-thousand years than anyone before him, I think. This job is tedious and highly revered. But most importantly for us Earth A folks, we have a man constantly digging through the archives looking for connections between the two planets."

Sevastian dove right in following Charlie's flattering introduction. "It would seem logical that after fifty-thousand years of documented human existence, that this earth should be in the clinches of a super technological era far beyond anything our primordial minds could comprehend. Or, contrarily, humans might have been expected to devour the earth's resources like a swarm of locusts, leaving nothing but desolate ruins incompatible with life. But as you can plainly see, we remain locked in antiquity. Everything here is in perfect balance and there are three contributing factors that make it so – environment, gods, and tradition.

Let's start with environment. As you will soon learn, there are six great cities, twelve smaller cities and a handful of small villages that make up the bulk of human habitation on this earth. Surrounding each of these human establishments, and in the case of Harond, a Cyclopes establishment, is a vast wilderness. You see, in this world the wilderness is truly untamed and dangerous. It's only after great human sacrifice that villages and cities are able to exist. Once a human habitat is established, it can only expand so far before it meets an impenetrable barrier – the beasts of the wild. It is likely that you may become acquainted with these beasts as you spend more time here."

Yet another comment that Lex was forced to take with a grain of salt.

"Take Crow for example. The sea and the farmland provide food, but these are our boundaries. Obviously, we cannot expand into the sea, and beyond the farmland are forests teeming with danger. This small stretch of land is all we have."

Lex noticed that Charlie was maintaining keen observation of who might be encroaching on this top secret conversation. As more citizens took up occupancy at nearby tables, Sevastian's vocal volume became increasingly stifled. At this point, he had reached a mere whisper.

"On Earth A," she added, attempting to match his quietness, "nothing, especially limited boundaries, stops humans from breeding and extending our territory."

"Which brings us into tradition," he explained. "Here on Earth B, the ways of old are highly honored and respected. One such timeless tradition is for a couple to produce only one offspring. If the child is male, he will be named by his father, a girl is named by her mother. The name usually has ancestral significance. The couple will stop with one child and devote themselves to his or her upbringing. It is a beautiful thing that most children here are well cared for.

The other limiting factor here on Earth B when it comes to having children is money. There are no government assistance programs available to help parents who can't afford to feed their children. A family understands without provision that they must find a way to feed themselves or starve to death. As rich as this city is, it simply doesn't have the resources to accommodate an exploding population."

"To put it simply," Charlie supplemented, seemingly eager to add his two cents, "wilderness limits human expansion and therefore humans limit their own offspring."

"That explains environment and tradition," Lex pressed on. "So, what about…" she almost felt silly saying it, "the gods?"

It was now Charlie's turn to drive. "When people think of Greek mythology, the Olympians are usually the first thing that comes to mind. Eleven great gods living atop the sacred mountain, drinking nectar, eating ambrosia and ruling the universe. Zeus, king of the gods, his wife Hera, and the others - Demeter, Dionysus, Apollo, Ares, Hermes, Poseidon, Hephaestus, Aphrodite, and Athena."

"Aren't there twelve Olympians?" Lex questioned.

"Well, yes, and no," he replied. "You see, the twelfth

Olympian, the goddess Artemis, lives in her own castle atop her own mountain."

"There is also Hades, god of the underworld," Sevastian added, "and scores of demigods that inhabit the earth, like Daphne and Iris."

"Here is why the gods are a contributing factor for limiting human expansion," Charlie resumed, returning to the point he was trying to make. "Take the Naiads as an example. If the people of Crow even tried to expand our territory into their sacred forest, Daphne and Iris would likely invoke deadly consequences against the destructive trespassers. Remember, almost every natural location, be it land, water, or air, has the protection of the nymphs."

"Just one more example to supplement Charlie's thoughts," Sevastian said. "This brings us back to Artemis. We've mentioned her several times already, but she is exceptionally important to Crow and the conservation of natural order. Lex, can you recall what you have studied about her?"

Lex surprised herself with the ease of her recollection. "The goddess of the moon. A virgin goddess, protector of children and animals. Daughter of Zeus and sister of Apollo." She said it as though she had memorized it for the purpose of taking an exam.

"Precisely!" Sevastian raved with felicity. "As the protector of animals, as you have just so stated, Artemis would never sit idly by while humans hunted a certain species to near extinction. To please her, we must take from the land no more than what we need. On Earth A, humans are the only creatures, the only, who take much more than they need. By doing so, they skew the natural balance. This is how ecosystems are destroyed and species are driven into extinction. Should Earth A have had the fortune of an overseer such as Artemis, humans would not have had the opportunity to inflict so much damage.

And as you just recalled, she is indeed a protector of children. She is the very reason why the one child custom began in the first place. You see, Lex, many millennia ago, no such tradition existed. Human population began to explode within the great cities of this world. Due to nature's barriers, as we have just discussed, man had no way to extend his property beyond the city. Thus, the cities became overpopulated. Disease ran rampant. Hunger and starvation were the status quo. There was much crime and violence as people were prepared to take any risk in order to feed themselves and their families. Royalty could not safely leave the confines of the castle for fear of being robbed at dagger point or ran through with a spear. This state of being went on for hundreds of years. They were despicable times, our dark ages. Sadly, through all of the madness, it was the children who suffered the most. Innocent souls brought into the world by those who had no means to care for them.

Just when this so-called dark age reached its apex, Artemis intervened. As a punishment for hundreds of years of human negligence, she bestowed a deadly plague on each of the great cities. The sickness claimed the lives of many thousands, reducing the human population to a mere fraction of its original census. Amazingly, not a single child died.

Artemis presented herself to the ruler of each city and explained the reasoning behind her actions. She forewarned each king or queen that if humans could not find a way to properly care for their children, that death would again come on swift wings. It was because of this devastating blow to society that we started the one child tradition. Ever since, humans have held their children in the highest regard. We do not dare abuse them, starve them, or neglect them for fear of the punishment Artemis might inflict. And there you have it, Lex," he said in conclusion, "Environment, tradition, gods."

"That is why we still wear togas, still read by candlelight, and still live without the luxury of nonstick Teflon," Charlie enumerated.

At this junction, Lex had to take a moment to appreciate the unique situation. It was surreal to be sitting here in this particular place with these particular boys talking about gods and planets and portals. This reminded her of the night Charlie and Sevastian had lent their calculus expertise. There were so many occasions during that long study session when she just couldn't believe she was actually there. She rested her chin on the palm of her hand and watched for a moment as Delias shuffled from one table to another, grinding the soles of her poor sandals into the floor and wheezing heavily from the effort. Lex knew their time at the kapeleia was coming to an end, so she slipped in one last question. "Have any of you seen one of the Olympians?"

The boys shook their heads.

"Then… forgive me if this is out of line, but how do you know they exist?"

"This is a valid question, and no, it is not out of line," Charlie assured her. "On Earth A, when one asks… 'how do I know God exists?' the typical response is, 'Oh, you just have to have faith.' I assume the basis of your question is to determine if the Olympians exist in faith, or actuality. The answer is that they truly do exist, there is no question about it. Now, the trick is to separate the truth from the fiction. First the truth. The gods are immortal and possess eternal youth."

"How do you know for sure?" she asked, desiring an example of such an outlandish ascertainment.

He coolly replied, "Lex, within the castle Crow, there is a collection of books and scrolls that dwarfs any collection you have ever seen. Of course, humans have been around for plenty of time to accumulate such a collection. I will make it a point to show you the books I'm about to reference sometime in the near future, but for the time being, you'll just have to take my word for it.

The castle's library is arranged in chronological order according to the time period in which the books were written. The oldest books are kept in a special room, each wrapped in a leaf from the giant fie plant for preservation. The historians of old kept detailed accounts of all activities in and around Crow – including the creatures that live in the surrounding forests. Within these ancient pages, there are detailed drawings of two Naiads that dwell in a woodland lake. These drawings appear in hundreds of books throughout the ages."

"Daphne and Iris," Lex exclaimed.

He nodded with a grin. "Let me assure you, and Sevastian can back me up on this," he said looking to his buddy for confirmation, "those beautiful creatures look exactly as they did fifty thousand years ago, and forty thousand years ago, and thirty, and… you get my point. This is how we know that they possess immortality and eternal youth. I can give you many more examples, but since you have already had the pleasure of meeting them, I figured you would appreciate that one the most."

"Truly," she agreed.

"How the whole immortality thing works, I could not tell you," he said almost regretfully, as if ashamed that there was yet another aspect of this world that he could not figure out. "As you have read in your mythology books, the god's main food source is nectar and ambrosia. Perhaps these plants, in some form of acanthary that is unknown to me, are how the gods maintain their immortality. The only location of this food source is the forest that surrounds Mountain Olympus, and it is very well guarded. Unfortunately for humans, the penalty for taking the fruit from the forest is an eternity of pain and suffering. There have been those who have made an attempt to get their hands on nectar and ambrosia, but to my knowledge, no one has ever succeeded."

"From the top of the cliff, I saw many temples around Crow, obviously for worshiping the gods," she said. "Exactly what kind of relationship do humans and gods have with one another?"

"The belief in this world, and I cannot back this up with solid proof, is that the gods created man in the likeness of themselves, but without their powers and immortality. Why did they create man? - not sure. But since they did, they act as our overseers. As in the story of Artemis and the killing plague, they intervene in human affairs when they see that it's necessary. There are numerous accounts in the history books of them doing so, especially Artemis."

"Why Artemis?" Lex asked.

"Whether the task was appointed to her by the other gods, or whether human activity is a unique interest, I cannot say. We humans are especially respectful, and might I add, fearful of her. She can disguise herself as almost anything. It is said that she has spies in the form of plants, animals and particularly birds. You never know when she is watching or what she will do if you upset her. Again, this is why we treat our children and environment with such reverence. By doing this and worshiping her and the others within the sacred atmosphere of our temples, we please them."

Lex found Charlie's explanation enthralling, but especially confounding at the same time. One minute he was declaring that everything has a scientific explanation, and the next, he was going on about immortal beings transforming themselves into different entities in order to spy on a race which they themselves created. For all his assurances that science was behind it all, it sure seemed like magic to her. Perhaps, she thought, I should do some serious thinking about what the word magic really means. Is it an all-encompassing term for the unexplainable or is it...? Oh, who knows?

"Here is something that may be of interest," Sevastian mentioned. "Though we do not have the time to go into details, Artemis has recently made contact with our queen. This occurrence is unprecedented and enigmatic. Only once before has a god..."

He was cut short as a barrage of wheezing breaths engulfed the air along with the stench of body odor mixed with flowery perfume. Much to Lex's dismay, both for interrupting Sevastian and the sheer fact that the woman was wretched, Delias had returned.

"Another round of drinks for my favorite customers?" she boomed causing Lex to tense up in fear of being struck by the wobbly blanket of skin that hung from her underarm.

"That will be all today," Charlie respectfully declined. With that, Sevastian pulled out a little brown bag with a drawstring and removed three copper coins. He handed them to Delias whose face lit up like a meteor entering Earth's atmosphere.

"Always so generous, you two," she exclaimed, again neglecting to mention the third. She was breathing heavily, seemingly on the verge of tears. "Thank you. Thank you." She bowed her head several times then waddled off to a nearby table.

"Where to next?" Lex asked as they stood to leave. "You can't deny me more answers."

"Another date," replied Charlie with a grin. "This time, a bit grander."

Lex looked from Charlie to Sevastian, then shrugged wearily as they began to weave through the crowded tavern toward the front door. All around, she heard murmurs and whispers. One name that she overheard at almost every table they passed was "Charlamos." Obviously, Charlie was well-known around here, but why? As they left the tavern and stepped out onto the quiet street, now nearly dark, she was determined to find out more about the mysterious Charlamos.

49

The three companions strolled side-by-side along Crow's main road. The sight of them bemused Lex. It was as if they were in some sort of ancient wool-cloak posse, prancing about the city in their imposing hooded vestments. They were making toward the castle, and with each step, she was accorded more visual illustrations of how things on this earth existed on a much larger scale. The castle, Crow's most prominent landmark, was a mountainous fortress to say the least. It was erected to such a lofty altitude, that only half of it could be seen from their current orientation. The other half was deluged by the accumulation of whitish-gold clouds, as if it were being sucked into the heavens through a skyward vacuum. One could only guess how much farther the castle extended above the billowy ceiling. The height was just one grandiose aspect of the man-made mountain. The other preeminent particularity was the magnitude of the perimeter. She was under the supposition that the whole town of Rose could hide itself within the castle's inner sanctuary. Overall, it seemed beyond the bounds of possibility that something this behemoth could be constructed without the aid of…the gods, acanthary, magic perhaps? Certainly not without Earth A's modern machines. She was ravenously curious about this marvel of ancient engineering, but there was another question that took precedence.

"So, Charlamos," she said whimsically, "where exactly, if you don't mind me asking, do you fit in? That is, what is your occupation here in Crow?"

"I am commander over the Crow Soldiers and a member of the Queen's high council," he humbly replied, making himself sound less imperative than he probably was. "My duties include overseeing the training programs for all eligible soldier candidates, assigning duties to the few that actually make it through their program, and of course as a soldier myself, I see to it that Crow is well defended."

"Don't allow him to downplay his status," Sevastian interjected. "Charlie is notoriously the greatest soldier in Crow's history. In addition, he is responsible for reopening the Hall of Providence and producing the most elite army this world has ever known. Every soldier you see around the city, believe me, has earned the right to call himself a soldier. The training they must go through to become one is not for the faint of heart. Most do not make it. Because of this, our army is smaller than all of the others in this world. However, history has taught us that wars are won by skill, not by numbers."

"Ever think of having a go at Trigonous?" Lex asked Charlie, impressed by the prestige of it all.

He said unequivocally, "No desire."

"What is the Hall of Providence?" she then asked to no one in particular.

Sevastian, who was noticeably keen on the matter, spoke up instantaneously. "The Hall of Providence is where a candidate for Crow Soldier first begins his journey. It is within this room that he is assigned his weapon and ultimately his destiny. Here, the man does not choose his weapon, the weapon chooses the man."

"How does that happen?" Lex asked.

"One cannot say for certain," he ruminated vaguely. "We like to think the gods have a hand in the destiny of each individual who sets off to become a soldier of Crow." He said this as if in deep resolve over the mystique of it all.

"Is Jade a Crow Soldier?" she then asked.

"Traditionally," Charlie replied, "there has never been a female soldier in Crow. That's not to say that she doesn't possess the skills to give any of Crow's elite warriors a run for their money." His statement was tinged with an obvious fondness.

"I can't believe I haven't yet asked, but with all that's

happened...where is Jade? Lex wanted to know.

"Jade's situation is unique," he began. "As you know, she's my cousin. Obviously, this means she's royalty, but interestingly, she chose to marry a commoner."

"What? Jade's married?" Lex blurted, taking no heed to restrain the volume of her flabbergasted reaction.

"It's very unusual for a noble female to marry outside of nobility," he explained in a purposefully quiet voice, as if reminding Lex that hushed was the appropriate tone of conversation. "Unusual, though not unheard of. As we all know, Jade marches to the beat of her own drum."

"Swept off her feet by a strapping farm boy from Taras Argos," Sevastian said. "It just goes to show that love is not subject to the confinement of social class."

"Well put," she replied, commending his insight with her head still shaking in disbelief. "Is she with him now?"

"Yes," Charlie said. "They live on an olive plantation. It's harvest season and the two of them have a lot on their plate right now. The window of opportunity is small, so they're forced to work around the clock to collect all the produce. She's very sorry she couldn't be with you when you came through the pool."

"Two lovers picking olives by moonlight," Sevastian poetically included.

"If a noble marries a commoner, does the noble relinquish his or her birthrights?" asked Lex.

"Certainly not," Charlie declared. "In fact, not only is Jade still very much part of the royal family, she is also a member of the Queen's high council. And perhaps most importantly, she is an undercover guardian of Taras Argos."

"What does that mean?"

"Taras Argos is the farming village just north of here, a brisk ten minute walk. Think of it as a suburb, or more significantly, Crow's life blood. Ninety percent of our food comes from its farms and plantations. Though the village is patrolled day and night by soldiers, Jade offers an even greater level of protection. Disguised as a common farm girl, if you will, she has an exclusive insight into everything that happens there. Bottom line – if Jade is in Taras Argos, Taras Argos is safe."

Lex couldn't continue with her questioning, though she yearned to know more. This slab of information was almost too big for her brain to wrap itself around. Jade, married? She was like a sister, and this was like finding out that your sister had gotten married and didn't tell you. There was just one more thing she desired to know before allowing the issue to be temporarily set aside. "What's his name?"

"Who?" asked Charlie.

"Jade's husband."

"Elias."

Now that dusk was at hand, the streets were nearly deserted, a sharp contrast to the hustle and bustle that was going on before Lex and Charlie had entered the kapeleia a good hour earlier. The sun existed as a mere expulsion of crimson, spilling over the shadowy mountains on the western horizon. There was a certain tranquility that consumed the sleepy streets as the trio pressed onward toward the castle.

Two men bearing the Crow crest upon the breasts of their white togas, were in the process of making the streets suitable for travel after dark. One man sat atop a brawny horse pulling behind it a sturdy wood wagon. In the wagon there were rows of oil lamps, each containing a wick for lighting, a handle for hanging and enough fuel for the night. Placed at equal intervals along Crow's main drag were metal posts, each with a dangling hook for receiving the handle of an oil lamp. The horseman halted his steed when the trailing wagon was positioned beneath the desired hook. The man on the wagon aptly lit the lamp with a flaming torch and used the wagon's elevation combined with his own outstretched arm to hook the lamp onto the post. Lex watched with interest as they repeated this task again and again with the aptitude of having performed this responsibility on numerous occasions.

With the auxiliary light, she was now able to focus on her

surroundings. Deep ruts from horse hooves and chariot wheels threatened her ankles' well-being. All the trade dwellings were now closed, their interiors pitch black through dusty windows. The fire from the lamp posts cast a flickering glow upon the posters announcing tomorrow's fight, which were tacked upon every building in sight. Lonely chariots and wagons lined the street taking refuge amongst the shadows. A group of people shuffled past in a hurry, chatting rambunctiously about Xenogorus and Trigonous.

As the excited voices of the passing group faded behind, the alluring tones of a choir became audible from somewhere up ahead. The music was a meditative chanting, much like that of old-world monks. Lex had never heard such a profound conjoining of voices. The music grew louder as they neared a temple that she found to be of particular attraction. Earlier, she had spotted it from the cliff top, and the sun's rays seemed to settle more on this specific temple than any other building in Crow. This made her think that it might belong to the sun god, Apollo. Now that they were right in front of it, she saw that she had been mistaken. This was evident by the incredibly gigantic statue residing near the temple's main entrance.

She knew the being's identity right away as she gazed upon this breathtaking woman many stories in height. In one arm the goddess held a newborn child, in the other, a hunting bow. On her head was a marble crown with winding leaf designs. Her hair was long and wavy and her hollow eyes stared off to the horizon, gazing omnisciently over the city's rooftops out to the distant forests. Nestled among the thick robe at her feet was a dainty fawn, portrayed as basking in the goddess' protection. Lex did not even need confirmation from the others because there was no doubt in her mind that this was the statue and profound temple of the moon goddess, Artemis.

The temple's design was akin to those of ancient Greece or Rome, with many cylindrical pillars supporting an impossibly massive rooftop with elaborate sculptures sprawled over every square inch. There were no walls to obscure an outsider's interrogation, so Lex walked her gaze up the marble stairs to the congregation of white-robed figures within. These individuals were the source of the pleasing, and deeply spiritual harmony. Men and boys of all ages formed a circle several rows thick surrounding a fountain of sapphire liquid. The water seemed to glow enchantingly as several streams shot upward from the base pool in a perpetual glorious flow. It was a sight to behold and she had to stop, if only for a moment, to quench her eyes' desire to observe the spectacle. Seeing for herself one of these immaculate temples made her realize that the graphic re-creations in the history books or movies did little justice to the true splendor of the sacred shrines. In addition, the overall atmosphere created by the crisp nightfall, the enrapturing voices of worship and this foreign city, made the mysterious ceremony seem downright magical.

She looked to Sevastian knowing he, above all, would value the singing. When it came to the musical arts, nobody could identify and appreciate this kind of purity like he could. With his head tilted back, eyes shut and an easy smile, he was drinking it in, lost in the perfection.

"They meet every night at sunset," he quietly explained, noticing Lex's attention had befallen him.

"It's so beautiful," she stated lustfully. "She's beautiful - Artemis."

"She surely is," Charlie agreed, stepping to Lex's side and looking upward toward the soaring deity. "Every city in this world has dedicated itself to a specific god or goddess. Ours happens to be Artemis," he explained as though he was star struck in the statue's looming shadow. "I just hope for the chance to one day look upon her with my own eyes."

Lex deliberated for a moment then said, "You said she lives on her own mountain somewhere, could you not just pay her a visit?"

He shook his head. "It's not quite that simple. One doesn't

just pay Artemis a visit."

"Oh," she replied, having no more understanding of the implications of his words than before he said them.

The three watched for a few minutes, absorbed in the splendor of it all, then, like always, Charlie was there to call them back and urge them onward.

The amplitude of the voices gradually faded into silence as they continued toward the castle. To the left there was a horse stable connected to a quaint private residence. Utilizing the light from the streetlamps, a man and boy were piling hay outside each stall as the burly creatures hung their heads over the gates, diving snout first into the crunchy banquet. Beside the stable sat another flat-stone cottage. The window presented a slightly obscure view of an older man and woman sitting at a table drinking from metal goblets, dining on fruit and bread. Next in the row was a weapon smith's quarters and then a sleepy three-story inn, where two welcoming candles burned on either side of the front entrance. Another little kapeleia stood adjacent to the inn. This casual observation of Crow's intricacies was exciting to Lex, feeling as though she was a time traveler traversing a city that by all accounts should be part of an ancient civilization. However, had she not been so unduly regardful, she may have overlooked the frightening silhouette in the alleyway between the inn and the kapeleia, and relinquished herself a heap of anxiety.

Just barely visible among the consuming darkness of the alley, was that strange girl whom Lex had seen following her every footfall in the marketplace earlier that day. Then, the girl spoke in a voice that sounded more like the whispering wind than human tongue. The words, "Alexis. Sacred flower. Defender," echoed throughout the street. To Lex, the voice seemed uncomfortably loud against her eardrums, but strangely, no one else seemed to have heard anything at all. Just a step ahead, Charlie and Sevastian were walking onward oblivious to this supernatural verbalization. With an accelerated heart, she shot her hand forward grabbing the cloak of the nearest friend, locating the backside of Sevastian.

"Look! There she is!" she cried out somewhere between a whisper and a scream.

"There who is?" Charlie demanded, eyes darting wildly in every which direction. The stranger in black was no longer visible at this point as she had retreated into the shadows.

"The girl I was telling you about in the market. She's hiding in that alley. Didn't you hear her calling to me?"

"No. I didn't hear anything. Not a girl's voice anyway."

"Well, she didn't exactly call to me. She made a statement. It sounded like she was whispering in my ear - really strange."

Unease began to etch its way across Charlie's face. "What did she say?"

"She said my name and then something about a sacred flower. Then she said "defender."

"What the…?" he asked, eyes narrowed in disbelief. "You're sure?"

"Charlie," Sevastian said quickly, now seemingly troubled, "no offense my friend, but how could she have made that up?"

"Yes, I'm sure," Lex confirmed. "But what does it mean?"

Suddenly a switch flipped in Charlie's brain and his stunned reaction was overtaken by criticality. His response was something Lex had never seen before and certainly did not expect. Quick as a wink, he produced from beneath his cloak a fierce weapon. The thing was essentially a short metal staff, perhaps three feet in length, with a blade on each end. Each blade resembled the basic curvature of a samurai sword. He then, quick as lightning, spun the weapon. The rotational torque increased the length of the staff by another three feet thanks to an ingeniously designed collapsible handle.

This prompted Sevastian to take action. Lex was bewildered to see that Charlie was not the only one carrying a weapon. Sevastian brought forth a battle axe with a double-bladed head and held white-knuckle tight to its bronze helve. Before she could be gratified with any sort of explanation, Charlie nodded toward the alley and Sevastian bolted into the murky shadows between the buildings.

"What the hell is going on?" Lex demanded nervously. "Am I in danger?"

"I shouldn't think so," he answered, eyes fixed straight ahead and listening attentively with his head cocked to one side. "This is… just a precautionary measure." His response was flimsy and implausible.

Before she could object, the Russian blasted from the alley breathing heavily. "I didn't find anyone!" he called out as he approached. "Dead ends into a stone wall. There's a side door to the tavern but it's boarded shut." He turned to Lex. "Are you sure that's where she was standing?"

"Positive!" she assured him. "Who is she? What's going on?"

"Someone knows Lex is here," Charlie informed his friend as if he hadn't already reached the same conclusion.

"But how can that be?" Sevastian asked.

"Okay seriously," Lex growled," What is going on?"

"Someone knows you're here," Charlie said quietly, "Someone who shouldn't." His statement gave her the chills. Before she could follow up however, he added one more thing. "Lex, I promised to be up front and honest with you, and I have every intention of holding true to my word, but there are many things about this earth and your situation that you don't understand. Be it the case, if I explained why we are stupefied by what just happened, our explanation would mean nothing to you."

"But…" Lex started to protest before Charlie silenced her by placing a hand upon her right shoulder.

Looking her square in the eyes with utter sincerity, he said, "As soon as I can, I will teach you the implication of the words you just heard. It goes deeper than what you may think. In the meantime, I promise you this," he said in earnest, "as long as you are with us, nothing, and I mean nothing, will harm you." Somehow, per usual, he had managed to convince and comfort.

Once again, her yen for knowledge had to be repressed due to an overall lack of familiarity about anything this side of the portal.

Charlie and Sevastian stowed their respective weapons and the group slowly resumed forward progress, each glancing back several times at the vacant alley. Not unnoticed by Lex, they were now positioned on either side of her in a bodyguard-like manner.

"There's something almost paranormal about that particular alleyway," Sevastian muttered to himself. At that moment, Lex became aware that this was the same alley in which Charlie and Jade had met the old man and acquired the Manult Stone.

50

Soon, they arrived at a crossroad with the option of going left toward the coliseum, right toward a long stretch of marble cottages or straight into the main entrance of the castle. A steadfast bridge constructed of thick logs and massive rock slabs stood firmly over a sparkling moat separating the street from the castle. Armed soldiers with varying weapons patrolled along the bridge and in front of the grand arched entranceway to the castle. From here, Lex could see a whole other city beyond the castle door. Surrounding a stunning courtyard of breathtaking flowers and shrubbery, were what seemed to be ancient apartment buildings, built with the ever popular white stone and wood. It was too dark to see much beyond that.

Charlie put an arm out to halt the others. "Alright Lex, I'll see you at dinner."

"Dinner? Wha…you're leaving?"

"I have some business to tend to. Don't worry though, you're in good hands." Giving her a nod goodbye and his buddy a trusting smile, he headed off toward the castle without any further delay. As he crossed the bridge, unease crept over Lex like an invisible phantom. Even though Mr. Moskincov was a dear friend, he didn't offer the same feeling of comfort as Charlie did. His prompt departure didn't appeal to her at all. She turned to the Russian with the stare of a lost puppy.

"In order to get into the castle," said Sevastian "you need either be royalty, a Crow Soldier, an employee of the royal family, such as a gardener or chef, or have special permission from a member of the royal family. The kingdom is made up of different social classes, as I'm sure you've taken note of."

Lex wondered if this was all part of the master plan or if he was just going with the flow. She nodded and watched as Charlie crossed the threshold into the castle boundaries. Each soldier that he passed rendered a sharp bow or nod in reverential acknowledgement of their head soldier.

"The tip of the sword," he continued, "are the royal families. There are four ancestral divisions which can be traced back tens of thousands of years to the original founders of Crow. The genealogy isn't important for you to know now...or ever unless you get really bored and need something to do." He gave a hearty snort. "Charlie and Jade belong to one of these families. The royalty acts as the kingdom's governing body. They provide law, protection and many other services to the lower classes, who pay taxes for these services. But not all royal members are valuable assets to our society. Some simply sit back and enjoy the luxury of, how do you Americans say, being born with a silver tongue?"

Lex giggled. Sevastian was always making attempts at popular metaphors and failing miserably. "Born with a silver spoon in one's mouth," she corrected.

"But you don't have to be born of royalty to become so," he continued. "It is perfectly acceptable for a commoner to be married in. This helps keep the gene pool umm… fit to swim. Here it is in a nutshell. King Astrapedes died, tragically, a while back leaving his daughter, Queen Palas, the sole ruler. She is a good queen and does well ruling Crow. She is beautiful and kind, but equally as dangerous if her laws are not obeyed. Stay on her good side and you can't go wrong. The Queen has one daughter, Phaedra, who is the heir to the throne. She will marry... someone from one of the other royal families, thus giving each family equal opportunity for overall leadership of Crow." He began to walk, motioning Lex to follow.

They hung a sharp right toward the avenue of little houses sheltered by the enormous castle wall. After passing by several of these puny marble dwellings, puny as compared to the castle anyway, they stopped abruptly in front of a nicely kept cottage that in no way differed from all the others in the long line of residential establishments.

"Most of the castle employees live outside the castle," Sevastian explained. He pointed all the way down the street, where the look-alike houses extended into the distance before becoming obscured by the night. "These homes nearest the castle are where most of them live. Also, those who are not born of royalty but have made it through the trials to become a Crow Soldier, have the option of living within the castle, but may choose instead to live with their family outside the walls. As it stands, I happen to be both a soldier and an employee. Although I have every right to live within the castle, I find that it suits me well to escape the congregations of aristocratic arrogance once in a while." With a contented smile, he nodded his head to the cottage in front of him. "Welcome to the house of Moskincov," he proudly stated.

"Congratulations," Lex said as they strolled briskly up the trampled dirt pathway toward the front door.

"For?" Sevastian questioned.

"For making it through the training to become a soldier," she elaborated, duly impressed. "I hear it's tough."

He had a hearty laugh at this, all the while conveying a facial expression that seemed to say, "You have no idea."

"And you work for the royal families as well?" she asked.

"Indeed, I do," he declared with a smile. He pulled a black metal key from underneath his cloak, one of many on a laden circular ring, and used it to unlock the small, yet hefty wooden door. "Soon, you too will be. That is, as long as it suits you."

This heightened her curiosity as they slipped into the home.

A bit to her surprise, the single-room residence was very small, and with absolute contrariety to the mansion back in Kansas, lacked any kind of expensive or excessive décor. That's not to say it wasn't a cozy little nook. Glowing embers sizzled in the little fireplace. A hand carved bed and dining table coexisted neatly in the same small area. Beautiful paintings of mountains and seascapes were tacked to the walls. The floor was hard packed dirt and the smell of potato stew lingered in the air. As Sevastian proceeded to light several oil lamps, Lex took a seat in one of the four wooden chairs surrounding the dining table. Upon the table was a pitcher of cloudy water and a glass. Sevastian filled the cup and handed it to his guest.

"Thanks," she said. "So, the plan for me is to work for the royal family?"

"Yes, and I think you'll be just thrilled with the position we have in mind."

"And that is?"

"Choir director."

"Choir director?"

"Recently, Kyramay, the talented songstress who had directed the royal choir for quite some time, has fallen to illness. Sadly, she is not faring too well. Her departure has left a void in the choir's structure. Now, they desperately need a leader. Someone who is imaginative, talented and can sing the roof off a temple. Boy, I can't wait to see their faces when they hear you sing. Between this world and the other, I've never heard your equal."

"Do I get paid by the hour or by the song?" she asked facetiously. The Russian had a laugh.

"I know you speak sarcasm, Lex, but in this world, as in the other, money will not be something you need to worry about."

She was flattered by all of this and equally as overwhelmed. "That sounds wonderful," she admitted, "but will you allow me some time to get acclimated to this place before I start punching a time clock?"

"Of course," he said placidly.

"So do you have another role besides soldier and historian?"

"Two other roles to be precise," he announced with a pompous air. "Firstly, I am in charge of food preparation for the royal families. This one keeps me really busy. It entails planning, preparing and serving two meals a day. I see to it that the royalty, the Crow Soldiers, and the castle workers all receive brunch and dinner. It's a huge task, and by no means do I go it alone. I lead a crew of fifty who divide the endless yet satisfying labor. These days, I do very little cooking myself. Now, my duties include deciding what dishes are to be served, perfecting recipes and basically making sure everything is going as planned. As we speak, a massive feast is being prepared, and as you see, I need not be present for it to happen.

My other job, and my favorite, is orchestra leader. Royalty love to be entertained. These days, contrary to the way it used to be, which was one mediocre show a night, we plan one astounding extravaganza every tenth day. It's a tiresome job, choosing the music selection, leading rehearsals, coordinating it all, but music is my passion so it's all well worth it. And, should you choose to be the choir director, you and I will be able to work side by side. Just think of the caliber of shows we could come up with when we put our heads together."

"Cooking and music," Lex observed with a smile. "Basically, the same things you do on Earth A."

"Yep! And tonight you will get a taste of my talents," he stated with zeal, "both on your plate and on the stage. It is what I call, medieval dinner theater."

Lex liked the idea of dinner and a show. She loved to be entertained, even though her mind was not currently deprived of stimulation. She took a long drink, eliminating the remainder of the cool earthy water from her cup. Sevastian was quick with a refill. Just then, while looking upon the jubilant face of her friend, a thought ran across her mind. It was certainly a digression from the present subject, but she decided it was time to inquire about something that she had been oblivious to since high school.

"I have a question for you," she began hesitantly, choosing her words carefully so as not to come across as offensive. "Now that things are out in the open, and I've been invited and encouraged to ask any question, I've just gotta ask… where did you come from?"

"I'm not sure I understand your question." he replied with a befuddled side tilt of his head. "I am from St. Petersburg if that's what you mean. But you know this."

"Sorry, what I mean," she clarified, realizing that her question was ill construed, "what I mean is, how did you become involved with," she raised her hand and twirled it above her head indicating the entirety of this amazing new world, "all of this? My first memories of you go all the way back to our freshman year. While waiting in line at the cafeteria one afternoon, I overheard a conversation between several students making mention that a boy from Russia had come to our school. I remember this distinctly because the name Sevastian struck me as very unique. That very afternoon you showed up in communications class. I remember Mr. Stroum looking at me and saying, 'now there are two of you with an accent – two exotic ingredients in the great melting pot.' The next day I saw you climbing into your father's sedan after school. After that initial recognition, I don't remember a thing about you until the beginning of junior year when the Flock had begun their ascent toward Rose stardom. At what point did you, Jade and Charlie become the Rose Flock, and why?"

Sevastian beamed with beguilement as if her recollection rekindled a fond memory. He spent the next moment in silence, all the while caressing his chin with both thumb and forefinger as if in deep consternation of how to properly reply. He grasped the backrest of the chair adjacent to Lex's and slid into it with a stooped posture. He leaned his elbows and forearms on the table before addressing her with direct eye contact. "Do you know why I came to America?" he asked.

"Actually no," she replied.

"My father was, how do you say, a 'bicwic' in the diamond industry.

"I beg your pardon. A what?"

"A bicwic," he repeated, quite sure of his usage.

"Oh!" she realized with a giggle, "you mean to say a "big wig" in the diamond industry."

"Yes, sorry," he said before moving on with little evidence that he would remember the proper terminology for future conversation. "Out of all the many locations he could have chosen to build his new headquarters in America, Wichita happened to be the most conducive to his plans. I had always had a close relationship with him, so when he announced that he would leave Russia for some place called Kansas, naturally I opted to come along.

Would you believe that he began teaching me how to cut diamonds when I was just seven years old? Immediately I fell in love with the art and ever since I have worked for him. I became very, very good at cutting diamonds as you have seen. When he saw how much I appreciated the little stones, he slowly began teaching me the business side of things. Even now, I am on track to take over the company after he retires."

"Oh, I see," Lex spouted in a moment of epiphany. "Charlie needed you."

"All part of his master plan," he said, confirming her realization. "When he first approached me about his little business proposition, he had been back and forth between earths several times. He had heard through the grapeline…"

"Grapevine."

"Right – he had heard through the grapevine that I was a diamond cutter and that was when he had his brilliant idea. This idea was the beginning of his systematic quest to discover the secrets of the interconnecting earths, and ultimately unlocking some of the universe's unsolved mysteries."

Lex then continued her postulation of what had happened, quite enjoying this newfound comprehension. "In order for him to succeed in unlocking these mysteries," she said, "he needed a limitless supply of wealth. He needed to be able to afford the telescopes, the books, the boats, the planes, the traveling and everything else involved with a no limits search of both worlds in order to find his answers. He figured that the quickest way to obtain wealth would be to collect the abundant diamonds from this earth and bring them back to the other where he could sell them for a profit."

"Precisely," Sevastian substantiated with a sharp nod.

"So how did he first approach you about all of this?" she asked.

"I cannot remember the specifics of our initial conversation, but basically it went like this… 'I have a large supply of diamonds. I cannot tell you where they came from. I need someone to cut them. The finished products will be sold. I would get eighty percent of the profits, he gets fifteen. The remaining five percent will be reserved for equipment maintenance and business expenses.'"

"It was probably hard to pass on that deal," she observed before taking on the remainder of the cloudy water in her glass.

"Although I had always been financially well-to-do thanks to my father, I knew that this interesting offer put forth by my strange classmate could be quite lucrative, so I went for it.

At the time, Ella, Charlie's mother, had already passed away. His father, Robert, was sick and spent most of the day confined to his bed. The cornfields around the house were unattended and overgrown with weeds. It was a dismal scene at the Roanoke residence as the old farmer slept away his final months. But even though life was fading from the farm, that musty old basement was really hopping.

Every day after school, I met Charlie and Jade at the farm. Every day, they had pizza and iced tea ready for me. We ate our snack together, then went to the basement where our little diamond laboratory had been established. Our first round of equipment was old, but it was functional.

There was another part to this little arrangement. I was to teach Charlie and Jade everything I knew about the diamond trade; everything from cutting, to cleaning and weighing, to selling. So I did, and they learned quickly. As anyone could predict, the three of us became great friends. It's amazing how many enjoyable conversations you can have when you spend hours cutting diamonds together. As our friendship grew, so did our wealth. We started by simply placing our finished products in Internet auctions and selling to local jewelry stores. When things really got going, we partnered with my father. This, as you know, eventually grew into the worldwide empire we have today.

That September, when Robert Roanoke passed away, we gathered at the Vandervelde's farm after the funeral service. Even though there were a lot of social demands on Charlie and Jade that day, the three of us did manage to break away for a little while. It was then that Charlie told us that he was going to build a castle in his parent's honor; a landmark that would allow the Roanoke family name to endure throughout the ages. At the time, I didn't believe it was possible, even for Charlie. But, somehow, he pulled it off. He and Jade were very generous in allowing me to have equal input about the castle's design. At this point, we were all family and it was understood that we would be together in this diamond endeavor until the end, whatever that end should be.

After the castle's construction, the establishment of the ice cave, and our elaborate security system, Charlie and Jade came to me one evening with a statement that would change my life. 'The time has come to show you where we get our diamonds' they said." He repeated the words once more, reliving with obvious glee the implications of this life-altering statement to which Lex could fully identify. "From there," he said in conclusion, "the rest is history."

"Fascinating," she said, meaning it with all legitimacy. "But... do you ever feel as though they, well, used you?"

"I suppose you could say that," he replied without an inkling of disdain for apparently "being used." "It's true that Charlie and Jade did not befriend me by chance, rather out of personal gain, but," he chuckled lightly, and with much merriment, "as you can see, I have been more than repaid for my share. And now we are all equals, comrades. Sure, we have different ranks and responsibilities here in Crow, but the three of us, four I mean, are in a very close-knit and unique alliance in search of the big answers. There is no rank or pecking order amongst us. We are nothing more than four friends enjoying every second of this amazing journey."

Lex smiled at Sevastian's enthusiasm, but an eerie realization crept into her mind extinguishing her light-hearted grin. Charlie had not randomly befriended Sevastian. Clearly, he used him for his own personal gain. That night at Vincent's, when Sevastian and Charlie had offered their assistance with calculus, had always in Lex's mind seemed a little too convenient. Was this a way to lure her in, just as he had done the Russian some years earlier? If so, the idea perplexed her. Sevastian had a very unique skill that he and Jade required for their master plan to succeed. What then did she have to offer? What skill did she have? What could he possibly want from an average Joe college student? Was it really a random act of kindness or did he have other things in mind? She wanted to relay these premonitions to Sevastian, right now, flat out, but couldn't bring herself to do it. This was based on the idea that if it really had been a random act of kindness, proposing that there was a hidden purpose would be downright insulting. She would, however, keep this postulation in the forefront of her mind until more clues surfaced and the riddle could be answered once and for all.

51

Sevastian glanced at his bare wrist as if checking a watch. He usually wore one, an old bulky piece with a calculator on the face. Perhaps his gesture was just out of habit, or perhaps it was an intentional implication of a tight schedule. "Better get moving," he observed. He motioned for Lex to stand. She complied by quickly finding her feet, and to the best of her ability, stayed out of the way as he began a curious sequence of events.

He hurried to the windows, tacking a rabbit-pelt curtain over each little port, eradicating the possibility that a pair of wayward eyes from the street might catch a glimpse of whatever he was up to. Once satisfied with their concealment, he shoved the sturdy little table a few feet from its original location, fully exposing the dirty woven rug on which it had stood. Grasping a corner, he flipped the rug to one side revealing a little trap door. The door creaked noisily on its hinges as he tugged it open and Lex was once again looking at steps descending into darkness.

Go figure, she thought.

"There are many reasons why we must remain inconspicuous," Sevastian explained as he tactfully began his descent. "This is why we often use our system of secret passages."

Curiously, Lex followed Mr. Moskincov down the steep little stairwell into a dingy, cobweb-stricken cellar. She even took the initiative to pull shut the trapdoor door behind her. Sevastian had brought down an oil lamp. He used it to ignite another that was sitting at the base of the stairs, then handed it to Lex.

The cellar was no bigger area-wise than the room above. It did, however, lack height. The ceiling was so low, Lex felt the top of her hair skim against the ceiling, collecting a network of cobwebs as she went along. The place smelled of earth and rodent and she hoped this was not to be her bedroom. The walls were lined with shelves of vegetable-filled jars. A brown, tailless rat scurried across her feet and underneath one of these shelves. Once the furry distraction had vanished from sight, she refocused her regard to the walls. Just ahead, there was a singular bare area devoid of shelving, and she knew right away, though she couldn't yet see how, that it must be another way out.

"Abracadabra," Sevastian said as he took hold of a section of shelving. He gave it a vigorous tug and it slid toward the bare area, jars clanging violently against one another as it moved. Sure enough, a tunnel was divulged. Once the lamp light splashed in, Lex could see that just a few feet into the tunnel were two identical doors. The twins stood side by side, both constructed of weighty wood adorned with supplemental rods of black iron. Both of them had a glossy iron knob sitting directly above a keyhole.

"One to the castle, the other to the coliseum," he explained as he removed a skeleton key from the side pocket of his cloak. He slid it into the keyhole of the door on the right, which he had just indicated was the way to the castle.

The duo shuffled into the narrow corridor guided by the haunting luminosity of the oil lamps, and from there, it was all uphill – literally. Sevastian took the lead with Lex bringing up the rear. Their lamps provided sufficient brightness in the damp passage deficient of natural light. For the next ten minutes, all they would do was climb stairs.

"Very interesting," Lex asserted, breaking a silence that had consumed the majority of the taxing ascent. "A secret entrance into the castle. Based on the statements you made earlier about the castle's security measures, it seems as though this would be illegal."

Sevastian chuckled lightheartedly between bouts of heavy breathing. "Not to worry," he reassured her, "it was Charlie's idea to build them. If Charlie says it's okay to build secret tunnels, you better believe it's okay to build secret tunnels. Nobody questions

Charlie, not even the Queen."

"So where does this ultimately lead?" she asked, slightly robbed of breath as the travelers came to the base of the steepest and narrowest section of stairwell they had thus far encountered.

"To your room," he answered frankly.

"My room?"

He nodded with gusto before leading the way up the final portion of the passage. Finally, after Lex's leg muscles burned from climbing what seemed like several thousand stairs, they arrived at a dead end. The terminus of the stairwell was blocked by a canvas material.

Sevastian placed a hand near the middle of the canvas. "Okay," he said, turning to Lex, "On the other side of this canvas is a painting which obviously means you have a secret passage sneaking into your room. Charlie selected this particular room to be yours because he has a thing for alternate exits."

"Or entrances," Lex commented.

"Yes, but nobody will use this passage as an entrance as long as you live here. Charlie, Jade and I are the only ones aware that this secret stairwell exists. The door from the cellar is virtually impenetrable even if someone should ever find it. Your safety and privacy while living here are assured. No one will pop in unannounced. I swear it." With that, he gave the canvas a sharp push. It was hinged on one side and flew open like a door. Lex couldn't keep the smile off her face as she stepped from the dank corridor into the welcoming brightness of the chamber that was obviously meant just for her.

52

The room was very large with a high ceiling. The theme was flowers, and the walls told a story. Lex recognized Sevastian's artistic embellishments right away. Behind them was the canvas doorway that they had just come through. Upon it was a painting of two flowers entwined by their lengthy stems. One was a vibrant red rose with lush emerald leaves and mighty thorns. The other she did not recognize. It was, however, plain and unimpressive compared to the rose, with small, modest petals and a dreary brown stem. The painting continued off the canvas and covered the walls encircling the entire room. She followed it clockwise and watched as the rose grew bigger and more beautiful with every few meters of wall, while the other flower remained unchanged yet still pretty in its own simple way. On the section of wall directly across from the canvas doorway, positioned between two windows, the painting began to make an obvious change. As the rose progressed along the second half of its journey, it began to wilt. The other flower, remaining present along side of the withering rose, stayed exactly the same, and was starting to look better and better in comparison. By the time the mural had made its full encirclement back to the canvas, the rose was pure black, and undeniably dead. The other plant, unfaded and unchanged, was still in full, bountiful blossom. In the lower left corner of the canvas was the word, AESOP. Lex gave Sevastian a smile of sincere admiration, which he reciprocated.

In similar fashion to her quarters back at the mansion, the bed was the centerpiece. In this case, it was like a bright golden star that everything else in the room revolved around. Its frame was gold, and knowing the Rose Flock, it was likely real gold. Surrounding the bed were shimmering curtains of white lace, swaying with the gentle breeze that capered in through the paneless windows. In her opinion, the harmonious duet of gold and lace was disturbingly contradicted by the animal pelt bedspread.

To the right of the bed was a wash station. A golden shelf was perched below a gold-rimmed mirror. Atop the shelf was a porcelain water pitcher with a matching cup, a hairbrush, a bar of soap and glass vases containing various powders and colorful liquids. An artfully crafted stool of pure gold summed up the vanity area.

Next to the vanity was a white bathtub, spacious and deep. Its glossy surface bared the dancing reflections of the many oil lamps that had been placed around the bedroom. The tub was already filled with water and emitted an inviting steam. Cadmium flames promenaded vivaciously in a stone fireplace adjacent to the bathtub. A curious concoction of metal piping was rigged between the two and Lex figured it was some primitive way of maintaining heated bathwater.

Adhering to the theme of royal decadence, a golden wardrobe was positioned in the corner of the room across from where they stood.

"Go on, see what's inside," Sevastian persuaded. He did not have to twist her arm and she strutted excitedly across the room. If her suspicions were correct, the contents of the wardrobe would be nothing short of amazing. Passing the open windows on her way, she glimpsed a view of the evening sky now in its transition phase from milky blue to starry black. Below, a dark sea stretched to an indistinguishable horizon spouting out legions of white caps in random patterns. This room was extremely, extremely high.

She arrived at the wardrobe and ran her hand delightedly over the amber doors. Relishing the moment, she eased them open slowly allowing the light to spill in a little at a time. Gasping with rapture, she beamed at the vast array of stunning dresses, tunics, colorful togas and another three Glast sheep cloaks identical to the one she was wearing now. Sevastian looked on as his friend, in her height of joy, examined one garment after another holding them up to her body, evaluating each one's potential of fitting properly.

"Are you guy's trying to bribe me into doing something?" she asked as she twirled gleefully, clinging to a dazzling green and yellow gown as if it were a long lost friend. It may have just been her imagination but the quick expression of unease in Sevastian's face might have suggested that maybe it really was a bribe.

"You'll notice that the Crow crest is absent from your garments," he pointed out, "Sadly, because you are not royalty, you are not allowed to wear it on your clothing. Not that you'd care too much about that I'd imagine."

She shook her head, with the word 'bribe' still wailing like a siren in the forefront of her brain. Everything the Rose Flock had given her, and were still giving her – was there an ulterior motive? This concept seemed to be surfacing a lot lately.

53

An hour later, she paced impatiently in her room - alone. Sevastian had left her to bathe and dress for dinner. She had enjoyed a hot bath while experimenting with the contents of the glass vases to determine which were meant for cleaning one's body. Unfortunately, a thick-pink liquid, which she had determined from its smell and texture to be shampoo, turned out to be a healing jelly intended for use on skin wounds. After gooping up her hair, she quickly learned to read the inscription on the bottom of the vase before utilizing its contents.

Of all the astonishing items within the golden wardrobe, she had chosen to wear the blue halter-style dress. It was her favorite of the bunch made of azure silk and embellished with white lace. The neck strap was fashioned from smooth pearly seashells and they felt good, almost soothing, against her skin. Above all, she loved the way the short train shadowed her every movement as she strutted about. The garment was flattering to her figure, suggesting that perhaps Jade had had a hand in its tailoring. Modest though she was, Lex couldn't help but strike a pose or two in front of the mirror as she crossed paths with it during her impatient traipsing, but this self-flattery was only to pass time. She was becoming increasingly anxious. Where was Sevastian? He should have been here by now.

She pranced to the window. Never before had she been afraid of heights, but the altitude of the room pushed the limits of her comfort zone. The three moons were perched close together on the horizon beyond the sea, each in a different stage of its cycle. It was awesome to see three moons at once. And then it hit her – a forceful slap in the face by the hand of reality.

Three moons, she thought with reluctant realization. Up until this point, she was not entirely convinced that this was a different earth, but now, looking out at three lunar bodies over a nebulous sea, the doubt was extinguished from her mind. Not even Charlie can fake that, she told herself. She would spend the next five minutes staring unblinkingly at the hypnotizing trio of extraterrestrial orbs.

Pulling away from the window, she began to pace once more. It was frustrating to be left alone during what she considered to be a very crucial period in her indoctrination process. She plopped down ungracefully on the bed and ran her fingers through the thick animal fur. The idea of sleeping under dead things wasn't particularly engaging.

Trying to keep her mind occupied, she looked over the mural again, focusing on the word AESOP, written in small print upon the canvas doorway, and wondered what those five letters meant. Was it a word, a name, an acronym perhaps? That held her attention only for a moment until her eyes fixated upon the other door – the one leading out to the spacious stone corridor she had caught a glimpse of as Sevastian had exited – the one she had been instructed not to open until he returned.

Momentarily, her ear was planted firmly against the door, listening intently to the voices coming from the other side. After several minutes, she could deduce that various groups of people, royalty to be precise, were heading down to the great hall for dinner. All were speaking Greek. She felt comfortable enough in her bilingual abilities to face the challenge of conversation in this strange place.

After a long hiatus since the last assemblage had passed by the door, she confidently concluded that she had no qualms about disobeying Sevastian's orders.

"What will it hurt to get a quick peek outside?" she asked herself. Placing a soft hand on the cold brass knob, she gave it a gentle turn. She tugged open the door and found it to be

deceptively, if not obnoxiously heavy, but her view of the outside
was immediately stymied. She jumped backward in surprise.
Flabbergasted, and maybe a tad afraid, she gazed upon a giant ogre
of a man, glaring down at her with animosity. By the way he was
dressed, she recognized him as a Crow Soldier. A gargantuan
spiked ball on a chain hung threateningly from his leather belt. His
face had been the unfortunate recipient of several nasty scars, the
most prominent slashing across his left eye. His shoulder length
black hair and his overall appearance reminded her of a
professional wrestler. His voice was deep and powerful as he
spoke.

"Were you planning on leaving, girl?" he boomed
aggressively.

She didn't know what to say, a meek head-shake "no" was
all she could manage.

"Tomorrow, at the coliseum, the fight of fights is taking
place," the giant man went on. "Because of this, a grand feast is
being served, right now, in the great hall. The meat is especially
juicy tonight and the mead especially strong. Right now, an empty
mug and an empty plate sit in front of an empty chair." He
squinted his dark eyes in rage. "My chair!" he bellowed so loud it
caused Lex to gasp involuntarily with fright. "And why is this?
Because I have been instructed to stand outside your sleeping
chamber so that you do not leave."

"I-I'm sorry," Lex squeaked, still very much terrified.

The man looked down at her as if she were not good
enough to strap his sandals and uttered a low growl. "You will be
sorry if you open this door one more time! Stay here as you have
been told!" With that he slammed the door with such ferocity, all
the lamps around the room vibrated noisily, and the flames in the
hearth were momentarily flattened from the resultant draft.
Stunned, she remained paralyzed in a defensive stance for a
moment before her fear made a hasty transition to outrage. With
reckless abandonment and the feeling of nothing to lose, she
yanked open the door with full force to catch an astonished

expression from the man who, despite his insufferable ranting about missing the royal banquet, had not abandoned his post. With a, "what are you gonna do about it?" look, Lex, with all the strength she could muster, slammed the door in his face just to even the stakes. She then punted the bottom of the door so vehemently that a decorative jewel from her sandal went flying across the room. This brash action caused her to tumble backward and her tailbone met the stone floor with a thud.

She picked herself off the floor and limped back to the bed. With arms crossed in rage and the scowl of a ravenous wolf, she plunked down upon the furry bedspread and started to formulate some choice words for her captors. *Who do they think they are, locking me in a room with a guard?* she screamed in her head. *The audacity!* Just then, in the midst of her silent rampage, there came a friendly knock. The door opened and in came Sevastian with a happy-go-lucky expression, as though everything was just perfect in his world.

"Sorry it took so long for me to get back," he said coolly. "I got caught up in the traffic heading to the great hall. I felt like a fish trying to swim up-the-stream." He snickered at his own analogy but stopped in a hurry when he noticed Lex wasn't amused. "So then…" he said uncomfortably, rubbing the back of his head and evading further eye contact, "You hungry?"

54

The thrill of this unbelievable journey diluted Lex's disdain of temporary detainment – so she chose to forgive Charlie and the Sevastian. The assumption was, as with everything thus far, they must have had good reason. Aggravating yes, but she considered what Charlie had said about enjoying the moment, and that advice would ease her frustration.

Following Sevastian through this exorbitant castle on route to the great hall was a truly awe-inspiring journey. Its interior was beyond astonishing and beyond convention, demonstrating nonpareil architecture as old as the mountains that lay beyond Crow. Grand archways, enormous marble pillars, dazzling fountains spewing plumes of turquoise mist, vivacious rugs that stretched for a hundred yards at a time, and even rows of gorgeous, white-barked trees were just a few of the particulars that adorned the route they were currently traversing. Looming above it all were giant chandeliers and winged sculptures gazing down imperiously from the lofty ceiling. The faded paintings along the corridor walls, portraying the faces of prominent Crow figures throughout the ages, could likely tell stories many centuries old if only they could talk. This place was much like the Flock's mansion back in Kansas, only on a much larger scale.

The duo made their way down golden hallways and corridors, descended marble staircases, and passed through enormous rooms of superlative stateliness. During this journey, they crossed paths with other residents of the castle, all dressed in their finest attire, and all chatting overzealously about the upcoming festivities. The alacrity hung so thick in the air you could cut it with a knife.

As the crowds streamed onward in a river of vibrant hues, Lex took notice of the many eyes that fell upon her. She wasn't sure if all this sudden attention was desirable. Was it because she was an outsider, or perhaps an intruder? A commoner amongst royalty? Was it because she was being escorted by Sevastian who may be a local celebrity, a Crow bigshot? Whatever the reason, the weight of all those scrutinizing stares made her anxious and antsy.

"Sevastian, am I welcome here?" she finally asked in a quiet tone.

He did not answer right away but produced a bemused smile, as if the question triggered the resurrection of a happy thought. Nodding, he looked upon her with twinkling eyes and said genuinely, "Lex, you are probably more welcome in this castle than perhaps anyone ever has been."

From ahead, the droning sound from a large gathering became audible and increased in amplitude as they approached the high marble archway which marked the entrance to the great hall. Lex's first impression was that "great" was a vast understatement.

Demanding her initial attention, the three moons cast their glorious streams of lunar illumination into the great hall through a colossal oval-shaped window near the ceiling. These beams fell upon a polished mahogany stage and blanketed the Crow orchestra in a soft, almost heavenly glow. The musicians were still in the process of setting up and settling in. Instruments were being tuned as myriads of stray notes escaped the stage only to be lost in sound as they were swallowed up by the cacophony of the crowded hall. Those who were not engrossed in instrument preparation were hustling back and forth across the stage carrying costumes, piles of sheet music and other random props. They all looked hurried to get things underway. She saw a frazzled man scurry from behind a curtain, passing off a brass horn to another man who appeared relieved to acquire the instrument. He then ran off to shout instructions at another group of musicians whose chairs had not been arranged in the proper order. Hanging majestically on the wall behind the stage, was an immaculate tapestry bearing the Crow crest.

Below the stage, and the source of most of the commotion, were scores of long stone tables filled to capacity with royalty. They talked, they laughed and they drank from gold and silver goblets. The colorful array of dresses, tunics, capes and gowns rivaled the splendor of a flower-filled meadow on a summer afternoon. The table tops were loaded with decorative bird sculptures, pitchers of water, wine and mead, steaming plates of meat, giant bread loaves and heaping bowls of fruit. Legions of kitchen workers, dressed in white food-stained tunics, hustled to and from the kitchen carrying even more food and filling every inch of the table with edible bounties.

Surrounding the majority of the great hall in a horseshoe fashion was stadium-style seating. This high-rise arrangement, meant to accommodate enormous gatherings of spectators, had been erected with thousands of square blocks. Currently, many more hundreds of people, seemingly not royalty as could be inferred by their plain and unremarkable clothing, were filing into these seats from all directions. It was truly a grand to-do, one which Lex had never seen the like. Sevastian stood reposefully by her side, rocking casually on his heels as she took it in.

"Royalty on the floor, castle workers in the high seats," he said loudly so as to be heard over the all-encompassing racket. "The castle workers have the privilege of enjoying the show but not the feast. Not entirely fair but that's a monarchy for you."

Lex looked ahead and saw the most beautiful table of all positioned front and center to the stage. This one was different because it was fashioned from gold rather than marble like all the others. The encircling chairs were not bench-like in manner but individual, high-backed seats displaying the finest of craftsmanship. The table's mirrored surface was blanketed with food but completely void of people. She thought that one of those seats might just be reserved for her and Sevastian, at least she hoped this to be the case.

She took hold of her escort's arm and the pair began walking down the center aisle. A subtle movement from overhead diverted her gaze toward the ceiling. There she saw a series of long, vibrant tapestries, four to be exact, swaying gently with an overhead draft. Each was of its own individual hue, and each bore a symbol unique to all the others. Below each symbol was a name. She remembered what Sevastian had taught her about the royal families and how the royalty as a whole stemmed from four ancestral divisions. It was her best guess that each tapestry was representative of a particular family.

Perhaps even more demanding of scrutiny, were the three monstrous chandeliers placed at equal intervals along the ceiling's apex. These artistic light sources were rigged with hundreds of miniature oil lamps and connected to each other by an intricate system of thin metal rods. After studying the setup for a moment, she surmised the thin rods, which were connected to one big rod, allowed every little lamp on the chandelier to be dimmed or brightened simultaneously – an ideal lighting arrangement for a theater and an adept alternative to electrically controlled mood lighting.

"This is our table coming up," he announced as he pointed to, not the head table, but a partially filled one near the kitchen entrance. "It is reserved for guests of the royal family. Believe it or not, I myself usually sit with the high council at the head table, but as you are not a member of the high council, we'll sit here tonight."

They arrived at the table to claim two vacant seats directly adjacent to a freshly cooked goose emitting a tantalizing aroma. Besides offering the occupants first dibs at the succulent bird, the seats also allowed Lex and Sevastian an unhampered view of the stage and the whole regalia. Sitting across the table with a smile of unfledged jubilance plastered to his face, was a plump man with a patchy white beard and wayward gray hair. His "kid-in-a-candy-store" expression was near comical and demonstrated his utter delight to be participating in such a clambake. He wore an off-white toga brandished with multiple areas of various discolorations. The woman sitting next to him, whom Lex guessed was his wife, or perhaps his sister, was equally as plump and had a kind, nurturing face. She too had the look of a child who just arrived at Disneyland for the first time. Her toga and its blemished condition was nearly identical to his, and Lex came to the conclusion that this less than flattering clothing just might be the best they had.

"A glorious evening to you, Sevastian," boomed the man from across the table. "And to the lady as well," he said, with a fond acknowledgement to Lex.

She reciprocated with a sheepish smile as she was still plagued by a bout of social anxiety in this strange new environment.

"I'm pleased you finally made it to the great hall," Sevastian replied. "And of all nights to earn a place at this table, tonight is certainly the one."

"The gods have been good to us," the plump man declared while sliding an arm around the woman sitting beside him. "We have only dreamt about sitting in the great hall. The famed royal feast, the Crow Theater – it is more than we could have ever hoped for."

"Alexis, this is Itys and his wife Niobe," said Sevastian. "They are farmers from Taras Argos.

"It's nice to meet you. I'm Alexis Lunden."

"Two names?" Itys said with absolute astonishment. "I've never met anyone with two names."

"I've never met anyone from Taras Argos," she said frankly. This statement drew a blank stare from the couple.

Sevastian chuckled, "Alexis is not from Crow." He then turned to her and said, "In Crow, as in every great city, we undergo a sacred ritual at the end of every growing season to honor the gods of Olympus to show our appreciation for the food they have bestowed. During this ritual, an animal sacrifice is made. This animal must be the most perfect in the city. Every livestock owner competes for the honor to have their animal chosen for the offering. This year, the chosen animal is a bull, and the bull is owned by Itys."

The bubbling couple, looking humorously giddy, was literally bouncing in their seats with enthusiasm as he continued. "Whomever raises such a creature to appease the gods, is rewarded with an invitation to a royal feast."

"A personal invitation from the queen herself," Itys interrupted, as if Sevastian had overlooked a crucial detail.

"In light of the epic Trigonous battle tomorrow, Itys and Niobe could not have been invited at a better time."

"So let me get this straight," Lex began, addressing Sevastian. She could feel her mother's tree-hugging attitude begin to percolate from within. "A city that is particularly fond of a goddess who protects animals, kills one to appease her? Is there something I'm missing?"

Sevastian was noticeably uneasy after the inquisition but forced an awkward smile as others in earshot, including Itys and Niobe, stared flabbergasted at Lex. "Eh, er, yes, Alexis," he stammered, "But there are other gods besides our beloved Artemis who may think differently. And remember our discussion about time-honored traditions?"

"I'm sure the bull would have had something to say about tradition," Lex said, looking Itys directly in the eye causing him to look away awkwardly. She knew she may be overstepping her boundaries, but she couldn't help it. The barbaric notion of animal sacrifice turned her stomach. But what else could she do, at least for the time being, but accept this sickening cultural atrocity? With a moment's deliberation, she conjured up the Greek words for "congratulations to you and your prize animal."

"Thank you, Alexis," Itys replied gratefully, now beaming again as if the preceding conversation had never taken place.

"See how beautiful she is," Niobe commented to her husband, as if admiring a piece of art on the wall. "What city do you call home, Alexis?" she asked "Alphenia? The most beautiful women are always from Alphenia."

Lex and Sevastian had not yet discussed an alibi as to where she had come from. Common sense told her not to blurt out the word Kansas. Her dawdled response bought him some time to invoke an effectual topic change. "Alexis has been chosen to lead the choir," he quickly announced. Apparently, this news was quite earthshaking as a hush fell over all those sitting nearby. All of the other occupants of the guest table ceased their conversation and focused their regard to this anonymous outlander.

"Is it true?" said the dark-headed man in an emerald tunic sitting to Lex's left. "It has been said that Sevastian was searching every village and city in the world to find a suitable replacement for Kyramay."

"Can you sing as well as she?" a blandishing young woman called from the far corner. Many more questions rang out from up and down the table. Lex was hearing them from all sides and did her best to translate each. Before she could respond to anyone, Sevastian rescued her from the surging current of inquiries.

"Silence! All of you!" he sternly ordered. They complied without question and he continued. "This is a secret known only by few. Not even the queen is aware that she is here. Alexis is meant to be a gift to our mighty ruler. Be thankful for the privilege of knowing this first, and above all, do not ruin the surprise." His announcement abated everyone at the table as they were now exclusive recipients of classified information. They smiled slyly at each other and gawked delightedly at Lex. It was interesting, she thought, that everyone had abided by his demands, falling silent at the drop of a hat on his request. To what extent was his authority? How far did the long arm of Sevastian reach?

55

Suddenly, from somewhere near the hall's main entrance, a powerful horn duet rang out and the room fell immediately noiseless. Again they sounded and this time, every person in the great hall rose to their feet. Lex followed suit. Despite the hundreds in attendance occupying every nook and cranny, the silence was so complete you could hear a pin drop. Her heart raced in expectation as the horns sounded for a third time, heralding the entrance of a most impressive entourage.

Leading the royal procession was Charlie. Lex's first impression was that he looked imperial. His outfit consisted of a full length tunic, deep crimson in hue, grazing the stone floor as he walked. A cape, matching the aesthetically appealing tone of his tunic, swayed behind him as he strutted onward. On the back of the cape was the patriotic Crow crest, the emblazoned symbol enhancing his supereminence. Ensuring the tunic's proper fit, he wore a glossy black belt around his waist. Attached to this belt at a point that was obscured by his cape, was that baneful double-bladed staff that Lex had the fortune, or misfortune, of observing earlier that evening. This time, the handle was not collapsed, rather, it was fully elongated and protruding in an oblique fashion from either side of his cape. His overall appearance demonstrated leadership, importance, and above all, an individual not to be affronted or trifled with.

His right arm swung relaxingly by his side while his left arm cradled a helmet that identified him as a Crow Soldier. The most prevalent feature of the helmet was the mohawk-like horsehair crest that ran along the top. There were two menacing eye slits that comprised the lateral borders of a central nose piece. Symmetrically occupying the forehead portion was a threatening embossment of a crow. The bird's wings of intimidation spread all the way to the far sides. This headwear was not unlike those that were worn by the soldiers of ancient Greece or Rome. Although differing in some manners, Crow as a whole, as Lex had thus far ascertained, was the spitting image of these iconic civilizations.

She was admiring him now much as one would a celebrity. Even though she knew him so well, at this moment he seemed so magisterial, so out of reach from any common person. He truly appeared godlike in her eyes as he led the royal party onward toward the head table.

Her excitement was quickly extinguished when she took note of who was following right behind. Her eyes narrowed into slits of malice, casting an evil glare toward the terrible goliath that had detained her like a caged animal, and treated her as though she were some kind of petty aggravation. He moved along with a strut that was most certainly a display of egocentric snobbery - at least as it appeared to her. Since they had last encountered, he had slicked back his long black hair and donned a cape. His entire outfit was black, much like his heart she thought, and he looked like a warrior that had ascended straight from the fires of hell. His menacing appearance was punctuated with the skull-shattering spiked ball that dangled pendulum-like from his beefy leather belt.

Another half dozen soldiers strolled into the hall forming a symmetric perimeter around a kind-faced old man. He shuffled along in the company of his guards with a gentle smile and a pronounced hunch. He wore a bright white toga with golden trim and leather sandals. A crisp ivy halo sat evenly upon his snowy hair. His white beard, squinty eyes, and cordial smile relayed an air of kindness. One wrinkled hand gripped tightly around the head of a polished blackthorn walking stick while he utilized the other hand to wave thoughtfully in all directions as to acknowledge his citizens.

"Who is that man?" Lex whispered into Sevastian's ear.

"That's Theophilus," he whispered back. "He's the most accomplished acanthar in the world. His knowledge is one of Crow's greatest advantages over all other cities. He is also Charlie's teacher."

A chill of excitement shot through Lex, immediately erasing her urge to further question Sevastian about the old acanthar. Her exhilaration was catalyzed by a thunderous explosion of praising cheer as the most formidable woman she had ever laid eyes upon crossed beneath the archway into the great hall. "Palas! Palas!" the crowd chanted in unison, displaying their high regard for this unique woman. The scene was electrifying, and deafening, and downright surreal as the queen made her entrance.

At first glance, Queen Palas could not have differed more from Lex's idea of a supreme female sovereign. It all started with her face, and her expression alone conveyed so much. She was not arrogant or consumed by the investiture of absolute power; rather she was virtuous and compassionate. Her clothes were not loud and flamboyant, but simple and elegant. Falling just above her knees, an off-the-shoulder dress of clean white shrouded her lean body. The simple garment was accessorized only by two white seashell clips holding her polished raven locks neatly behind her ears. She wore no jewelry, no decorations, not even shoes. Her soft feet met the cold stone floor with nothing to prove. She seemed young, perhaps forty.

The queen smiled warmly and waved her hand in an entrancing fluid motion as the large group of soldiers escorted her to the head table. Though outwardly stunning in her natural guise, there was much more hidden within Palas's dark eyes. This was something Lex could see so clearly though there was no physical manifestation of these invisible truths. Behind the queen's warm smile were emotional scars of hardship, struggle, perhaps the lingering burdens of past wars. Her ascent to power had not come easy, nor was her time as ruler always a smooth voyage. Lex had no idea the depth to which these truths extended, nor could she pinpoint the source of this unseen conveyance of the woman's history. She just explicitly knew that Palas was someone who had earned every measurable unit of praise that was being abundantly hurled at her from every citizen in the great hall.

The only person staggering enough to steal her attention from this magnanimous monarch was Charlie, who flashed a covert grin and an eye wink as he passed. This catalyzed a spontaneous burst of energy and Lex began cheering loudly with the rest of the city as the members of the head table took their seats.

The feast began, and along with it, the music. Soft notes from the Crow orchestra filled the room with a calming background melody for the opening part of the meal. Though the food was extraordinary, Lex didn't eat much. Between the steady adrenaline pump and the greasy rabbit legs from the kapeleia, she hadn't much appetite. Instead of keeping her eyes glued to the musicians like most others, she found herself straining to see the head table and what Charlie was up to. He was positioned between Palas and that giant man and spent much time in conversation with them. What could they be talking about? She despised not knowing, and she had gotten a good dose of that lately.

Sevastian wasn't much help either. Throughout the meal, she had quietly pounded him with a good deal of questions only to receive one of two answers: "Lex, we shouldn't be talking about this here," or "I'd better let Charlie explain that one." It was obvious that even in his absence, Charlie had an authoritative reign on the situation and it was agitating.

The lights were suddenly dimmed. The music stopped only to resume a moment later with amplified volume. The fiery horn section blared a stunning introduction for twenty or so female dancers. The olive-skinned beauties twirled onto the stage with lacy garments of flowing heather shadowing their movements. The horns mellowed then faded, giving rise to a soothing melody provided by the group of instruments that most closely resembled woodwinds. This spellbinding performance combined the grace of Swan Lake with the passion of Romeo and Juliet.

As the clan of barefoot performers glided in sync to the music, a sudden cannon fire of kettle drums initiated. The audience gasped in momentary surprise as several more women, this bunch clad in vibrant cherry capes, dropped from the ceiling. Each was tethered to a thick rope as they proceeded to perform an air-acrobatics routine to the perpetual oohs and ahhs of the crowd. It was clear by the complex choreography of the performers and the cohesiveness of music with dance, that Sevastian had been busy with this one. She could basically see the satisfaction spilling from his eyes as he watched his creative genius in action. This ancient-day Cirque du Soleil went on throughout the course of the meal.

When the vivid dance performance wrapped up, the red-caped flyers were seemingly sucked back into the ceiling and the floor dancers quickly shot off stage. Music was replaced by the rustling of sheet music, as the musicians leafed through their respective piles in preparation for the next selection. Then, a large group of children filed onto the stage. The reaction of the crowd reminded Lex of every wedding she had ever attended where the bashful flower girls shuffled irresolutely down the aisle to the awws and giddy laughter of the admiring adult spectators. In this situation, she herself couldn't help but giggle approvingly because, well they were so darn cute. The youngsters all wore little white tunics with gold trim. The boys had holly-leaf halos upon their heads and the girls wore matching seashell necklaces. With a little confusion, they finally managed to position themselves into three rows, shortest in front, tallest in the back. A little boy in the front row was fiddling with his outfit, and Lex tried to suppress laughter as a stagehand ran to assist the child before the whole thing fell clean off his body. The room fell silent as a nervous girl from the front row stepped forward.

"The city of Crow would like to thank our beloved queen to whom we dedicate this song," she stated deliberately as if she had spent the last three weeks memorizing the line. Palas smiled charismatically and gave a go ahead nod as the girl stepped back into place. There was a second of silence before the entire orchestra commenced with a soothing serenade. The children began to sing a song that sounded to Lex a lot like a national anthem. It was pretty, powerful and patriotic all at the same time, illustrating glorious victories of olden days and Crow's steadfast strength. They sang of the Olympians, though not one in particular, and praised them for their generosity and protection. This particular song proved to be a good history lesson in Crow lore.

The children's choir received an explosive applause from the audience and even a standing ovation initiated by Palas herself. They all bowed and ran excitedly off to stage left.

"They were terrific," Lex mentioned to Sevastian as the applause was winding down, "not to mention adorable."

"Not as terrific as the next performer," he said.

"Who will that be?" she asked curiously. He didn't have to say anything. His sly grin told her all she needed to know, and for the hundredth time today, her heart felt like it would break through her sternum. "What, you mean...me? Why?"

"You don't mind public performances, do you?" he inquired. "We thought this would be a nice surprise."

"Sevastian, I'm through with surprises today," she replied with a mix of sternness and apprehension. "I can't perform in front of a queen or an entire city in a world I know nothing of. What am I supposed to sing? What if I can't translate the song in time? I'll look like a fool. What... and, and why...?"

"You'll sing "River of Love and Life" and you'll sing it in plain English," he said calmly, placing a hand on the shoulder of his flustered companion.

"Why that song?"

"Because it is the most beautiful song ever written," he said as though it was an undisputed fact. "You even said it yourself once."

"But why must I sing? Why me?"

His easy-going attitude then made a swift transformation. He looked directly into her eyes, reminding her of the times long ago when her mother was about to tell her something very important.

"Alexis, you have a gift. You were born with a voice that would make the gods fall to their knees in envy. When you sing, a sort of contagious and undeniable peace looms over all who are in audible range."

"Well, when you put it that way," she said, taken aback by this compliment.

He continued, even more seriously now. "I realize you don't know this yet, but a new age is upon us, a dark age. The balance which we maintain in this world may soon be compromised. We can't take what we have for granted because it may not last much longer. I'm talking about peace. I for one choose to cherish every moment of glorious peace while it exists in such abundance. I don't mean to frighten you by all of this. The future is still, like always, unknown and hopeful." He paused to cast a cautious glance toward Charlie making it clear that he probably wasn't supposed to be talking about this matter. He ran a fidgety hand through his thick hair and continued. "All I'm trying to say, Lex, is that this world has never heard a voice like yours, and by sharing your voice tonight, the peace we still have will most certainly be reinforced."

She wasn't sure how to take his confounding monologue. It was like a pending death sentence mixed with a flattering compliment.

"Are you telling me our lives are in danger?"

"I'm sorry, I shouldn't have brought it up. I'm probably making things seem worse off than they really are. The last thing I wanted to do was alarm you the first day here. I guess sometimes my passion for this place clouds my reasoning." This was as emotional as she had ever seen him. Charlie will go into more detail when the time is right, but in the meantime, please keep this conversation between us."

"I will," she agreed.

She wondered what danger was out there. Why did Sevastian passionately and somewhat uncontrollably divulge this information to her? Why did he and Charlie impulsively react to the creepy girl in the alley? They had even appointed a guard to stand watch outside her door. With all these protective measures, she just couldn't help but feel the bite of trepidation.

"Just where do you think you're going?" she asked as Sevastian began an unexpected departure from her side.

"Wait right here. I've got a little speech to give."

"But…" And that was all she had time to utter before he was hustling excitedly away.

"I know I speak for this entire glorious city when I say that the youth singers performed wonderfully tonight," Sevastian announced when he arrived at the center stage. Applause of agreement ensued and he waited until it settled before continuing. "This will be a time to remember. Not just this night or tomorrow's event, but this age of our beloved city. Crow has endured through much and we are stronger now than we have ever been. We always have and will continue to persevere through any situation, any threat and maintain this gift of power the god's have betrothed upon us during our ongoing journey through time."

The faces around Lex were etched with pride, determination and even a few tears as he spoke.

"With Palas as our ruler…"

Applause and cheering surged throughout the room.

"Charlamos and his soldiers…"

The volume of commotion surged even louder now.

"We have on our side the great Theophilus, the wisest acanthar since Manult…"

The entire crowd, including a bewildered Lex just going along with it all, leapt to their feet bellowing out a deafening cry of loyalty. Sevastian was barely audible now.

"So, with that I say – let this peacetime endure, and let any opponent of Trigonous fall hard at his feet!"

It took all Lex's will not to cover her ears. The decibels from the electrified crowd were so loud that it bordered on painful. Sevastian had never seemed so commanding. People were standing on benches jumping up and down. This obstructed her view of the stage, but between the flailing bodies she could still catch snatches of her artsy friend who was at the moment a motivating, audience-controlling authoritarian. And the people ate up his every word.

It took several minutes for the masses to quiet themselves and sit back down. Sevastian stood proud and serious as they did so. He then, just for an instant, turned his gaze to Lex and smiled before again addressing the room.

"My friends, in light of the wonderful peace the gods have allowed, I have a gift for you. For all who have gathered here this night, may you graciously value your good fortune." Lex observed Itys and Niobe avert their attention from Sevastian so that they could briefly grin at each other. Charlie turned back to catch Lex's eye with an anticipatory grimace. She could feel the weight of other eyes the heavy gazes of those sitting around her, whose dumb luck permitted that they be prematurely briefed on this big surprise. Never so tense about singing to an audience, she nervously ran a clammy hand over her goosebump-riddled arm. In no way could she comprehend the significance of what she was about to do.

The lights suddenly dimmed and from the main entrance, a parade of women in snowy gowns strutted purposefully down the center aisle bearing brilliant burning torches. Their beauty in conjunction with the placid fire illumination injected an inexplicable sensation of tranquility throughout the crowded hall. The torch-bearing angels positioned themselves in rehearsed points around the room. Convinced that those sitting near were distracted by her thundering heartbeat, Lex crossed her arms over her chest attempting to muffle this imaginary phenomenon. Her time had come.

"It is with great pleasure and honor," Sevastian resumed, his voice saturated with delight, "that I present to the kingdom of Crow… your new choir director - Alexis, daughter of Olivia."

Her body had never felt so heavy as she irresolutely stood. She had been through so much already today and now this. Her mind was fatigued, and nervousness shrouded her like a woolen blanket. Stepping back over the bench, she felt eyes, hundreds of eyes, thousands of eyes, peering curiously from all directions. Next came the whispers that stirred up suddenly like an autumn wind; it was utterly overwhelming. Much to her reprieve, Sevastian hurried down and motioned for her to take his arm. Feeling as though she was dreaming, she allowed him to escort her to the stage.

As the two made the short journey, she saw everything and everyone in the room melt together in a virtual blur. The lights, the stage, the faces all dissolving into one colorful haze – even Charlie and Palas were indistinguishable. This had happened the very first time she had ever performed for an audience. She was to sing England's national anthem before an arena of soccer fans at a local college championship match. That night she aced the song and though sometimes she still got nervous, she had never again been outright afraid of public singing. Since then, she had performed many, many times. She thought she was now beyond the "blur effect" as she called it, but tonight rekindled an apprehension once thought to be long gone.

"They are going to love you," Sevastian whispered reassuringly, rousing her from the discomfited trance. All whipped back into focus and she hastily concluded that she had better make the best of this performance because it seemed so imperative to her friends – whatever the reason may be. With deafening whispers still flooding the air, they paced swiftly onto the stage.

"I hope you're not mad at me," he whispered with a voice craving reassurance.

"No, it's okay," she replied, attempting to appease him,

though it wasn't entirely truthful. "So then, River of Love and Life?"

"Yes, yes," he nodded. "First verse and chorus only. The orchestra knows what to do. They will play in C major, for the best cohesion with your voice. The overture will be short and recognizable with a two-measure legato lead-up. Sing it in English because it will fascinate the audience and make it easier on you. I'd advise mezzo forte as the hall is large and we obviously have no electricity for amplification."

"Uh, sure – no problem," she stuttered ever unsurely.

Sevastian bowed deep and held it there for a moment, as if worshiping a leader. "Thank you. You don't know what this will mean to Crow," he said. He snapped around toward the orchestra and administered a nod of commencement, then scuttled off stage leaving her all alone – alone in the company of a thousand strangers.

The musical introduction initiated and like a miracle drug, alleviated all tension. She was born to sing and no matter how nervous she ever became before show time, the music would always call her home. She was in her element now and she knew it, felt it, became it.

The horns rendered a buccinal sonant as her euphonic voice flooded the great hall with hypnotizing perfection.

"Moonlight shines, the river winds. I follow this path forged by time…"

Lofty string sounds faded into the mix.

"A thousand miles, then a thousand more. Glowing cities on golden shores…"

The eyes of the audience were consistently becoming wider and jaws rhythmically began to drop.

"Further along we're greeted by dawn, where mountain forests urge us on. Through churning mist and rainbow walls, the essence of thy being calls…"

An atmospheric entrancement had now grasped Crow's citizens who were held captive by this new mellifluous voice.

Certainly, their stunned faces were tell-tale signs that the likes of Alexis Lunden had never been experienced prior to this night. The only exception to the majority expressions of amazement were the proverbial faces of Charlie and Sevastian, who each bore a discrete, "I knew this would be a huge success," grin. At this moment in time, she was no longer a stranger in the eyes of Crow, nor did she seem human. With each word, she rose higher above all people, all social classes, the queen and perhaps even the gods.

"My lifelong friend, we have reached the end. My heart is now free in the eternal sea."

She finished with a flawless B chord and held the note until the background music ceased, leaving the audience with a spectacular a' cappella finale that resonated from every nook and spilled out into the cool night through the overhead windows. Then silence. A silence so utterly silent, that it screamed to be broken. She presented a swift bow then seized the moment to observe the captivated faces of her audience. She couldn't help but gleam in the satisfaction of nailing a performance. A confident smile made its way across her face.

Seconds ticked by before Palas rose to her feet, but she was not smiling. Everything happened very fast after that. Dumbfounded silence was instantly converted to praising applause, thunderous and vociferous. The city was impressed and in love, but what was going on at the head table? In the midst of the chaos, she saw Palas say something to Charlie. She saw Charlie resisting her, shaking his head at whatever she had said. Palas looked confused, excited and…worried? Sevastian was suddenly there between Charlie and Palas, trying to say something, yelling. The applause was overbearing. There was certainly a disagreement, or at least a serious discussion taking place below, though Lex hadn't the slightest clue as to its nature. She felt nervous, alone and confused. She frantically yearned for someone to come to her side, so she wouldn't feel so exposed – the center of attention in this frenzied place. How long would she be standing there before her friends came and took her away?

And just like that, she had gone from drinking in her own superb accomplishment, to wishing for nothing else but to be in her own bed at Aunt Claire's lake house, safe and away from this outlandish place.

There was no time to dwell on that thought. Palas made a hand motion toward her. Big Goliath made the first leap in her direction then in the next instant she was surrounded by Crow Soldiers. Charlie shoved his way through the mass of men until he reached her. This time, somehow, his presence didn't ensure that usual sense of relief. This time, he didn't seem to have control over the situation. Through the ear-splitting applause and the commotion of the surrounding soldiers Charlie somehow managed to get right up to her ear. "Tell them you're from Alba," he said.

"What?" she yelled over the noise, not that she hadn't heard him but because his demand was befuddling.

"This is the queen's will," he shouted. "I'm their lead soldier but they are obligated to obey Palas above all. Just go with it. I'll straighten things out. Remember, Alba." He gave a stern look that meant this was a serious situation. The ogre man that she already had a disdain for took a firm grip on her arm and pulled her forward.

She had been led, no, forced out of the great hall toward an unknown destination. The roars from the crowd faded behind as the pack moved swiftly down hallways and up long stairwells. It was difficult to observe her surroundings as she was enclosed by a force field of soldiers. She felt like she had been helplessly caught in the inescapable current of a raging river. From the few achievable glimpses that weren't obscured by bulky arms, bronze spears, and mohawk helmets, she saw that this small army was following Palas and the white-haired man in the toga. What was his name?

She saw Sevastian intermingled with the many armor-clad men. To her right was the seven foot giant to whom she had assigned the name "Asshole." To her left, Charlamos, with a displeased look that bordered on angry.

The pace was rapid and the distance long. They had done a considerable amount of climbing, so much that her ears began to pop. After what seemed like endless kilometers of dark stairwells, the entourage emerged onto an open rooftop. They were so high that the puffy cloud line was below them. The air stream at this altitude was strong and cold giving her bone-shuddering chills. They came to a stop and a woman's voice called over the wind.

"Just the high council," the queen ordered firmly, "and the girl."

Asshole gave an uncomfortable tug on Lex's arm. His grasp was tight, cutting off her circulation. Angry, and at wit's end, she yanked her arm free of his grip. She felt tears grace her eyes. She wanted to run. Run so fast and so far; away from all of this.

"Don't you ever touch me!" she screamed at him, feeling nearly out of her mind. He looked taken aback. As if nobody had ever talked to him that way before. Charlie quickly stepped between them.

"Isidore, enough, please."

Isidore nodded and without question stepped aside. A powerful gust of wind flattened her hair against the side of her face with strands of it sticking to the tears. Charlie's cape surged violently behind him like a flag in a hurricane as he looked into her eyes with adamant sincerity.

He whispered into her ear, "I am so sorry. I swear to you, on my life and our friendship that I had a plan to ease you into this."

Palas called once again, "Charlamos, bring the girl to my chamber." There was a golden doorway ahead with enormous crow sculptures on either side. It was the entrance to a large marble-walled room, isolated from the rest of the castle and alone amongst the night sky. This was undoubtedly the highest room in the castle and Queen Palas' domain. The soldiers stepped aside making a pathway for Charlie and Lex. Waiting at the doorway was Palas, Isidore, the old man and Sevastian. Charlie nodded to

Palas but did not proceed until he had finished with his apology.

"You have every right to be upset," he continued with hurt in his eyes. "This little plan I had sort of backfired but it's alright. After I get this straightened out with the queen, it'll be just you and me for a while."

She was exhausted physically, mentally and especially emotionally. More tears came and they locked eyes. "I promise, just you and me," he repeated. If he was faking sincerity, he was sure doing a good job. He made a head gesture toward Palas who was waiting cross-armed by the doorway. He said, "This is my fault," then twisted the side of his face into a guilty grimace. "I wasn't expecting her to react to you this way. Just follow my lead and we'll be out of here in no time." She nodded timidly as he placed his hand on her shoulder. His touch was comforting. Here she was, yet again, helpless in his presence. She wondered why she should still trust him. There was a part of her brain that always came to his defense no matter what the practical part was advising.

The practical part said, no way can this be real. But somehow, she knew it was. The practical part said, He's lied to you in the past and he's lying now. He's using you, I just don't yet know why. But somehow, she knew his intentions were good and his reasons were just. The practical part said, you are not good enough for him. He will eventually break your heart. But she didn't care. It was time to stop lying to herself. She loved him. Yes, she truly and in all ways loved him and she was willing to take that chance. She wiped her tears away with her palm, straightened her dress and stood up straight. She took a deep breath and said, "alright then, I'm from Alba." His smile was warm as August and his nod of affirmation was laden with respect. Although his mouth didn't move, his eyes might have just said, "I love you too." Together they turned and walked side-by-side between the two rows of soldiers en route to the golden door. The wind swirled around them and starlight rained down from above. The high council awaited and Lex couldn't even guess how this was going to go.

56

University of Cambridge, England.

Dr. Benjamin Lucant was perched upright on his sturdy stool behind a polished podium. With hellfire in his eyes, he glared at his class over half-moon bifocals that made him appear years older than he actually was. The large auditorium was chalk full of students, all of whom emitted random bouts of pencil twirling, forehead rubbing and foot tapping – classic expressions of anxiety. The students were now an hour into their final exam, and the ninety minute time limit was encroaching a little too quickly for most. The frequency of frantic erasing and hasty page turning increased with each tick of the clock. Foregoing the current model of online test taking, Lucant delighted in keeping things "old school" with the trusty paper and pencil. He wondered just how many of these pathetic, uninterested little shits would actually pass, as the greatest majority of them had been lingering around the fail zone throughout the entire semester.

The class was Italian Literature 201, formally Italian Literature 412, and the subject was the works of the infamous Italian poet Dante Alighieri. Professor Lucant was the undisputed authority on Dante, and thus was his ticket into the prestigious Cambridge University twelve years ago. In his earlier days, as a witty and ambitious young scholar, he traveled the world at his editor's expense, attending book signings and headlining Dante conventions. Any speech he gave, no matter the location, guaranteed attendance from world leaders, top literary authorities and droves of others who were just obsessed with Dante. Even in the world's largest arenas, these lectures were assured to sell out, regardless of whatever ludicrous price was assigned to the admission.

The pinnacle of Lucant's legendary career came following the monotonous task of publishing a new English translation of Dante's Divina Commedia. His sheer genius on the history, the language and the subject allowed him to produce the most sophisticatedly accurate version of the famous epic poem ever to be reproduced. There had not been such anticipation for a new translation since Henry Wadsworth Longfellow took on the task in the mid-eighteen sixties.

With the monumental success of the new translation, a devout following of Dante fanatics, Inferno junkies and an impenetrable repute, Lucant had earned himself the nickname, "Son of the Italian Language." This name he cherished and figuratively hung upon his chest much like a military veteran would display a purple heart. This name was sacred to him because in his elitist opinion, there was only one man who exceeded him in greatness – the renowned "Father of the Italian Language," Dante Alighieri himself.

Eleven years ago, Cambridge all but fell to its knees begging Dr. Lucant to board the faculty train. They made him an offer he could not refuse, and with the mounting fatigue of international travel and lecturing to crowded arenas, he eventually agreed to take on a teaching position in the arts department. When he first assumed this position, Italian Literature 412 was the most sought after elective at Cambridge. Many students craving to learn his unique knowledge of the subject, applied to the school for this reason alone. At the time, only twenty of the most dedicated and "worthy" students were hand-selected by Lucant to study what he believed to be sacred material.

Now after more than a decade on the job, thanks to ongoing changes in the college administration, his class had gone from the most competitive literature elective on campus, to a mandatory prerequisite that all undergraduates must complete before earning their diploma. Each passing year, for reasons unclear to Lucant, the college board of regents continued to whittle away his original curriculum and replace it with their own general idea of how Dante should be taught to those not pursuing a language or literature degree. In essence, how could something as complex as The Divine Comedy, the accounts of Dante's journey through nine circles of hell, then purgatory and eventually heaven, be taught to an engineering or law student?

The class roster had gone from twenty in the early days to just over three-hundred, so here he was, back to the crammed lecture halls and this time, only a small percentage cared what he had to say. As the professor gazed across the silent sea of despondent faces, he cursed the worthless students, cursed the university and cursed himself for allowing life to drag him this far down. The only thing that had ever given him any enjoyment was studying Dante's works and relaying his expertise to inquiring minds. Now that "inquiring minds" had been removed from the equation, his motivation was fading fast. His life was becoming an empty void, a void he continually filled with bitterness and anger.

For years now, no one had witnessed him smile or display any friendly gesture whatsoever. When he wasn't teaching, he quarantined himself in his office so as not to be bothered by faculty or students. His reputation as a fifty-something antisocial nut job ensured his privacy, as nobody would dare interrupt his quiet time unless a most pressing matter arose. More often than not, any disturbance of the professor's afternoon Dante research would result in a brazenly frightening verbal onslaught. This rash behavior eroded his once shining reputation as he steadily made enemies with fellow faculty members, disgruntled students and parents of disgruntled students. It also earned him the nickname Lucifer, and considering the material which he taught, that name was entirely apropos.

Over the years, many attempts had been made to get Lucant booted out of Cambridge, especially as of late. On a regular basis, he appeared before the college board of directors and once before the city council, to defend actions or statements that he had made, usually regarding students. His classroom etiquette and teaching style were unconventional. He found great delight in storming about the lecture hall and singling out students who seemed bored, unprepared, or just downright terrified. Once a victim was selected, he would first determine whether they had read the assigned material by firing off a series of questions. If the student survived the round, he would get personal. Next would come questions about who they were, what they did behind closed doors and what their outstanding sins were. At this point, the student would become petrified, a fossil. Lucant's rationale was - if a student could recognize their own sins and place themselves in the appropriate circle of Dante's version of hell, it could only aid in their understanding of the Inferno, and just maybe pull them a little deeper into his own twisted world. It was the extremely pious that would be most offended by this method of teaching, cringing at the thought of seeing themselves in hell and of course, taking action to assure that such blasphemy would not continue to prevail. Thus was the basis of Lucant's continual defense trials. Despite the sheer volume of complaints and endless empty warnings from the regents, Dr. Benjamin Lucant never lost his job. Because of his reputation, tarnished or not, there never seemed to be sufficient cause to terminate the position of such an accomplished Dante scholar. At times he seemed invincible and impervious to the rules of the college, which in turn made him that much more deviant.

He had no qualms about failing three quarters of the class. Although the curriculum had been trimmed up and tamed down thanks to those administrative bastards, Lucifer was still able to inject enough of his own material so that only those who had the capability to depart with their own souls and walk through hell in the pilgrim's shoes would successfully reach their Paradiso. In this class, it was not enough to read, comprehend and memorize. The professor required his students to send their minds down a path of evil that any normal person would not soon venture. His mission statement was simple and straightforward – "Dante's works are sacrosanct, and without exception, you must engage them as such."

"Your time is up," he announced without concern for the series of moans that infiltrated the auditorium. The students reluctantly and with much disenchantment gathered their things and filed toward the front table to hand in their exams. Lucant could plainly tell that he had either succeeded in ensuring the difficulty of the exam or that most had come unprepared. It was likely that about eighty percent of the students saw this class as an inconvenience or a necessary stepping stone to their respective degrees – Lucant resented this. In addition, he believed it to be an insult to Dante, which in turn infuriated him further. He glared outward over his long nose and furrowed his brows in anger. When the last student had departed the auditorium, he stood and actually cracked the slightest of grins.

Tomorrow, the college closed for the holidays which meant that today was his last day of teaching – ever. He had been planning this for quite some time, but forced himself to wait until he had his ducks in a row. He had yet to tell anyone about this and desired to leave without giving or receiving a single, annoying, obligatory goodbye. The thought of a going away party or an honorary celebration was loathsome. Cambridge as a whole would be shocked by his departure and it would be a large dent in their armor. Individually, the faculty members would probably have their own celebration, not of course to commemorate the career of a great colleague, but to relish the departure of a man whom they reviled. None of these things mattered in the least to the cold hearted Lucant. His concern over other people's opinions on the matter amounted to a hill of beans. This place had sucked the life and the ambition right out of him, and he'd be damned if he let it continue. He knew how to rekindle the flame, and the plan to do so would be the basis for his early retirement.

A half hour later, he returned to his office. His precedence was a major advantage when he had requested the finest quarters the college had to offer. It was as if Cambridge could not say no to their esteemed professor, and thus, he got his wish. This was his sanctuary decorated with extravagant Turkish rugs, rare paintings and a gorgeous Italian-style desk pricier than most new cars. Behind the desk, an organized collection of the finest and most prominent books in classic literature sat neatly on dust-free shelves. There was a rosewood cellaret containing bottles of sloe gin and scotch so rare that only the most knowledgeable connoisseurs might claim recognition. A gallery tone painting of Dante Alighieri hung alone on the east wall as if to guarantee that nothing would take away from this prominent attraction.

The west wall was almost entirely window, bordered by thick auburn drapery and valances, allowing a bird's-eye view of the activities in the courtyard below. When he first moved into the office, Lucant enjoyed watching the convening groups of students, and did so with a measure of envy. How wonderful their lives must be. Young and ambitious, attending one of the best schools their parents could barely afford and having their whole lives ahead to be whomever or whatever their hearts desired. Now after sliding along a downward spiral towards ultimate bitterness, the professor could no longer care about any of them.

He stood in the doorway and surveyed the room one last time. Although there were so many decorous things, so many expensive possessions, even some with a degree of sentimental value, he would leave it all. There was only one item from the office that he would take with him, which is why he had made this little pit stop on the way out. He traversed the room with the old floorboards creaking under his feet. Arriving at his desk where he had spent countless hours over the past decade absorbed in research, he dropped an envelope which contained his letter of resignation. It was entirely insufficient for the monumental occasion of his departure, but at least the message was directly to the point. He then unlocked the bottom desk drawer and peered down over his bifocals taking full pleasure in beholding the item within. This particular drawer was large enough to hold about a dozen books, or perhaps a bushel of office supplies, but its storage potential was wasted on the singular military-style knife that resided within.

Between his master's degree and his PhD program, Lucant had served six years in the Italian Navy. He had volunteered for a special operations group called the GOI, and despite the brutal selection process, succeeded in becoming a member. For the remaining four and a half years of his military term, he operated as an elite commando who was lucky to escape with his life in almost every operation he was assigned to. And thus was the nature of the GOI – life threatening missions, perfect planning, much enemy bloodshed, live to tell the tale. Lucant not only participated in this group, he was the all-star. His kill-count was in the hundreds, and he was legendary for disregarding the assured effectiveness of an automatic weapon for the personal touch of his knife. There was not a sensation in the world that could compare with a razor-edged blade dragging across a man's neck or piercing a man's heart. This was the personal touch that a gun could not fulfill and Lucant craved it.

If it weren't for his passion for Dante's works and his ambition for additional knowledge on the subject, he might just have retired from the GOI after a long, bloody, gratifying stint. After leaving the Italian Navy, he returned down the path of higher education, earning his PhD in Italian literature and focusing all of his energy on The Inferno specifically. Just like everything else in his life, this path was one that he chose for a particular reason, in short, this path was the means to an even greater end. Every degree earned, every lecture presented, every award won, was all part of a plan that he had been hatching for years. Now, he had achieved his expertise, earned his fortune and would no longer be held back by financial limitations. The time had come to put his master plan into action, and the thrill of finally reaching this point was enough to rekindle his enthusiasm for life.

He lifted the nineteen centimeter blade from the drawer and handled it with such affection, it might as well have been his own child. He reflected on all the lives that this one piece of metal had taken – and it was not done yet. If he were to succeed in his plan, there was little doubt that more lives would be sacrificed for the cause. The road ahead was dangerous and the secret he was after would be well protected. But Lucant knew how to get what he wanted, for he was a genius according to his school teachers and a written IQ test he had taken ages ago. He could work the charm and he could work the blade. He had always achieved everything that he put his mind to and more. Embarking on a quest to resurrect an old demon would be no different, of this he was confident.

He had never forgotten how Papa had tried to kill his only son in order to protect the black book. Little Benny had somehow escaped, and the situation was so dire that Marcello Lucant had taken his own life just to be free from whatever calamity he was mixed up in. Benny never tried, never wanted to suppress these memories. Instead, he allowed them to remain fresh in his mind so he would not forget the eminence of the black book. This book had been his central obsession ever since he first laid eyes upon it all those years ago. Lucant knew that it was still out there somewhere and he would stop at nothing to find it. Anyone who stood in his way or withheld information would atone for their stupidity.

The path to enlightenment had already been laid out, and it began exactly where it had started – the Dante Museum in Florence. After years of investigative research via the Internet, phone calls and letter writing, Lucant had been infuriated to find absolutely no information on Papa's death other than a mere newspaper article announcing the suspicious death of a local man named Marcello Lucant. The investigators on the scene had commented that things were still under investigation. It would end at that. He was smart enough to know that attempting to obtain classified information from the authorities would be a useless ploy.

Investigating Papa's death was a dead end road. The only other snippet of information he had at his disposal was Papa's partner in crime – a man by the name, Paulo. One evening back in

Florence, Paulo had come to dine with Marcello at the cottage. As was his customary pastime, little Benny had been eavesdropping upon their conversation. Though he had been in a room down the hall and the conversation was muffled, he thought he had heard his father allude to the notion that Paulo operated a gym or had recently sold a gym. A mere scrap of information, yes, but this was the only thing Lucant had to go on. However, after extensive Internet research, after seemingly hundreds of phone calls to every workout facility within a hundred miles of Florence, he failed to locate this anonymous man. His search so far had been utterly unproductive, and even though there was another person involved, the tattooed security guard, he knew that without so much as a name to go on, it would be virtually impossible to track him down.

At that junction, there was one other possibility – the curator of the Dante Museum. Certainly, whoever ran the place would not have been oblivious to the secret meetings happening in his own building. But this was forty years ago. Had the man been of any significant age, he may very well be deceased. Lucant's first lucky break came when he found out this was not the case. A simple phone call to the museum posing as a tourist inquiring for information told him that the man who used to run the museum was now in his mid-eighties, confined to a wheelchair, but still mentally intact. In fact, the man's son, the individual whom Lucant had spoken with, was the current curator who took over when his father had become too old to properly maintain the place. He had also foolishly disclosed that the both of them lived together in a house directly across the street from Casa de Dante, which by description sounded a lot like the very building little Benny had used to conceal himself when spying on Papa. If the jovial man on the other line had only known the mistake he was making when passing along this information to the curious tourist. Little did he know that Lucifer would soon be knocking at the door.

Lucant knew two things with certainty – hell was very real and the black book would tell him exactly how to get there. If someone were to ask why he craved this information, why he desired to follow the same path Dante had tread over one thousand years earlier, he would not have an answer to give. This was because he himself didn't know. Perhaps it was to actually see the one place his entire life had revolved around, to visit a location that many believe to be a fairy tale, to look upon Lucifer with his own eyes and live to tell about it as Dante had done. There was no exact answer, only an unexplainable craving to stand in that dark forest like Dante and with the black book as his own personal Virgil, follow the path through the underworld. He gripped the handle of the knife even tighter. He closed his eyes and felt a renewed sense of purpose saturate his conscience.

Hand of Fate (part 2)

Staffordshire England - Olivia Lunden strolls briskly up the sidewalk, humming an upbeat tune that has been stuck in her head since last night. Turning the corner by an antique store, she reaches into her jacket pocket and removes a ring of jingling keys. When she arrives at the next block, she stops before crossing the street and takes an appraisal of the sandwich cafe. Below the cursive green letters that read, OLIVIA'S, is a tidy collection of wrought iron chairs and tables, charming fig trees pruned to perfection and a freshly painted yellow door that lures hungry passers-by with a welcoming appeal. She crosses her arms with a grin and nods in satisfaction - picture perfect. She hurries across the street and as she hops onto the curb, a white hybrid surrenders a series of short, friendly honks. "Morning Stella," Olivia calls out to the elderly woman waving amicably from the driver's seat. She glides through the iron gate and stands at the front door fumbling through the collection of golden keys before finding the one marked with a black "O". The dead-bold clicks.

The hinges voice their familiar creaking song in harmony with a little tinkling bell as she pushes inside. She closes the door, stops suddenly and sniffs the air with a curious expression. The café's usual aroma of bread and lavender has been prevailed over by a venomous blend of earth, embers and decay. The air is enigmatically thick. The little dining room that is habitually charming feels like a tomb. She surveys the area with incredulous scrutiny. The early morning has not put forth enough light to expunge the dimness of the interior and it's difficult to see. Just as she reaches for the light switch, she gasps when her eyes fall upon a person standing against the back wall. If it had been a man, she certainly would have made a prompt exit, but since the individual was quite obviously female, Olivia stays. Her hand is over her heart and she breathes heavily from the initial shock. Surprise turns to suspicion and there is a glint of displeasure in her voice when she asks, "How did you get in here? You'd better have a good explanation because I have a good mind to call the police."

Before she can say another word, the girl advances toward her. In that same instant, Olivia brings both hands to her neck, her breathing becomes labored. Her eyes widen as this young woman, dressed in cultish black attire, seemingly floats across the cafe. Her hair, black as the ashes of hell, skims the tile floor as she approaches. Olivia is drowning where she stands, forcefully inhaling and exhaling and choking from the effort. Her lungs are screaming for the oxygen that, in defiance of all logic, has become extinguished.

Their eyes meet and Olivia stares with fright into the hollow pupiless whites of this unearthly stranger. She is paralyzed and all she can do is continue to fight for air as the young woman's milky white hand ascends in a fluid manner. With skin as cold as ice, she places her palm on Olivia's forehead. Olivia's eyes roll back and her body shakes violently for a moment. An impossible wind hurls through the cafe, sending napkins and sugar packets amuck. The girl's mouth does not move but her three simple words echo in Olivia's brain as clear as glass.

"I need her."

She removes her hand. The wind ceases and paper napkins twirl to the floor like maple seeds. Olivia can breathe again but she still cannot move. The two maintain eye contact for another instant before the girl in black floats around Olivia en route to the door. When Olivia finally regains control, she turns around to find the girl is gone, though the door had not creaked nor had the bell jingled. Olivia, usually strong and poised, falls to her knees and sobs. "What the hell was that?" she screams between uncontrollable bouts of tears.

Two hours later, with youthful exuberance, young Alexis skips into the sandwich shop, ponytail bouncing in perfect rhythm with her pink backpack. She enjoys helping her mother take and run food orders and looks forward to this routine every Saturday. The little café is bustling and she finds Olivia behind the counter, perhaps a little more flustered than normal and uncharacteristically disheveled.

"Hello, little flower," Olivia says distantly. "Busy today."

"You okay, Mum? You don't look well," Lex observes.

"Yes, fine, just a little overwhelmed right now," she says without eye contact. She prepares a tray and hurries an order out to a table. Alexis watches with concern. She knows something is wrong. Despite her accurate intuition about her mother's current state of well-being, she could not have predicted that her entire world was about to shatter like a mirror.

Five minutes later, the sound of plates and mugs crashing to the ground brings a stunned silence to the café. The silence is replaced by panic as many rush to offer help to the owner who is lying unconscious in a heap of broken glass.

PART II
THE OBLIVION ORACLE

"And we come forth to contemplate the stars."
- Dante Alighieri

Sacrilege

Sister Imelda brings up the rear of the procession as the holy sisters file into the first two rows of pews. There is electricity in the air tonight as Advent draws to a close. As Christmas approaches, these evening services never fail to attract at least a hundred more bodies than the norm, and this guarantees a tight squeeze in this moderately-sized Catholic church.

In the very back pew, the location nearest the door, a strange man, one who has never before set foot in this church, glares through furrowed brows at Sister Imelda specifically. He takes not a glance elsewhere as his eyes follow her every movement. Perhaps it is the candlelight reflecting from his shaved head that first snags the eye of the young woman, because his presence and his unsettling gaze does not slip her regard. She shudders as she looks upon him then quickly shifts her attention front and center, where purple candles flicker just below a large wooden crucifix.

As the first hymn begins and the congregation rises to its feet, she timidly turns for another look. The man in the back, shiny head, warm winter trench coat, thick black brows, is not standing like everyone else, not singing like everyone else, and he does not blink nor turn away as Sister Imelda's brave backward glance meets his unyielding stare for the second time. She is noticeably uneasy.

Mass progresses. At the initiation of Holy Communion, the man rises to his feet and vacates through the back door. The sight of the available seat commences a sort of "musical chairs" game as four others who had no choice thus far but to stand along the back wall, make a mad dash to stake their claim.

The slightest of smiles skims across Sister Imelda's face

after braving a third and final appraisal of this devilish man to discover he is no longer there. His departure pleases her as told by her implicit sense of relief. As for everyone else in attendance this night, their absorption in the moment makes them unaware that the bizarre, unspoken exchange had taken place between timid Sister Imelda and the stranger in the back row.

She is one of the last to leave the church tonight. Since most of the other sisters had been eager to get home to their families, she takes it upon herself to assist Father Lorenzo in assuring all is in order for tomorrow's morning service. After the chalice had been disinfected, the tabernacle restocked, the candles extinguished, the poinsettias arranged, and the general vicinity orderly, she bids the elderly priest farewell. With the smell of incense clinging tightly to her clothes, she puts on a warm coat and slips out the side door, making certain that it is properly locked before walking onward.

A light snow collects on her hair as she carefully traverses the slick sidewalk en route to her father's home. She takes small, purposeful steps so as not to fall and damage the glossy-red package she carries under her arm. This is a Christmas present for her father, and the porcelain angel beneath the beautiful wrapping paper would not fare well if it were to be dropped.

She has lived in this city all her life, and though the streets are sleepy and lifeless, she shows no concern of walking alone amongst the shadows and the overhead lamps. Though the way is dark and the ground is laden with patches of ice, she travels with confidence.

There seems to be no conceivable reason why Sister Imelda suddenly comes to a halt as she passes a little side-street, black with shadow. There is no movement, no footprints in the snow, and no sound except for the breeze funneling between the brick buildings. Perhaps this is a testament to the unspoken connection, the relationship that exists on a metaphysical level between good and evil, love and hate, life and death. Or, perhaps she detects the faint odor of incense which could only belong to someone who had just recently departed the church.

Whatever the culprit, she stands motionless now, seemingly held in place by fear's paralyzing grip. The increasing frequency of the white puffs from her lips attest to her rising apprehension. Her eyes slowly turn to the side-street where nothing is currently visible except blackness.

She gasps as a gloved hand shoots from the shadows, quick as lightning. This gasp is the only noise she has time to utter as she is torn from the light. The red package plunges to the ground followed by the unmistakable sound of cracking porcelain. The white wing of an angel cuts through the paper and immediately becomes red as it receives a shower of blood.

57

Lex was at wit's end as the fierce wind pummeled her body. This was all just too much. The day had been fascinating but also mentally taxing to the extreme. When she had been unexpectedly, not to mention quite aggressively yanked from the stage at Crow's theater and swiftly conveyed to the castle heights surrounded by a mob of Crow Soldiers, the proverbial camel's back had been broken. It now took everything she had to restrain an all out breakdown.

The majority of the soldiers that had made the journey to the rooftop had retreated back into the castle. Four remained on guard outside Palas' chambers as Charlie guided her through the golden doorway. Although the men made every attempt to maintain a disciplined stature, there was no mistaking their inquisitorial glances at the new girl who had indisputably succeeded in capturing the queen's regard. Lex looked skyward to avoid eye contact. In doing so she saw the carving above the door…

LIVE FOR THE GODS, DIE FOR CROW.

Palas' chambers could only be described as mystical, or perhaps otherworldly. The room was cubical in nature, and like the rest of the castle, it had been constructed of glossy marble blocks. Immense pillars of polished sepia granite, ten in all, methodically encircled the room connecting the floor with the ceiling. Attached to each pillar, heavyweight torches cradled by iron wall mounts flung firelight upon two prominent centerpieces, one a chair, or more appropriately, a throne. Elysian wings of silver and gold extended laterally from each side with such ornate craftsmanship, they seemed nearly lifelike. The two golden armrests were fashioned into the mighty paws of some great beast. The throne's framework was upholstered with thick animal furs. This royal seat overlooked centerpiece number two – a rectangular floor pool situated at the exact center of the room. The liquid within was so still and mirror-like, that one might be tempted to just walk right across. Beneath the surface, an ambiance of dark blues and grays swirled like a witch's potion. In the water resided the reflections of three moons, just as they appeared in the sky tonight. This was achievable because of an open gap in the ceiling directly above the pool, equal in size and shape. To the back left of the chamber was another door to a small adjoining room. Probably the queen's bed and bath, Lex surmised.

She jumped as the doors thundered to a close producing a deep echo that lingered for several seconds before attenuating into the atmosphere. With a metallic clank, Sevastian secured the doors with a sliding iron pole and joined the others who had formed a semi-circle around Lex. Palas slid through the gathering and positioned herself face to face with the overwhelmed newcomer. The queen's hopeful eyes of vivid azure met Lex's emerald irises with a penetrating gaze. "Tell me with certainty, Charlamos, is she the one?"

"Yes," he replied with unwavering conviction. Palas seemed neither impressed nor convinced.

"What land do you call your home?" she then asked Lex.

"Alba," Lex answered, as surely as she could, upholding her promise to do so.

Palas seemed intrigued by this then said to Charlie, "Why did you not inform me of her arrival, or the means by which you found her and thus, leave me to draw my own conclusion?"

"The presentation that I arranged was meant to be a gift to

you," he said. "I wanted Alexis to be a glorious surprise. There would be no one else who would suspect that our new choir director is anything but a choir director. And now, after just one song, the city loves her."

Palas thought about this for a moment. Seemingly satisfied with Charlie's justification, she nodded with enlightenment, "Brave Charlamos, with one clever move you have pleased me beyond words while at the same time gaining, Alexis, is it? unyielding protection from the people of Crow." Her joy was spilling over as she looked Lex up and down. "You really found her. After all this time," she declared in star-struck wonderment. She reached forward and took Lex's hand into her own, eyes radiant as she spoke. "Alexis, the defender. I am Queen Palas, daughter of King Astrapedes. I am not yet familiar with how you came to this city but I look forward to hearing the story. You are an honored guest and are to be kept here at the castle as such. Whatever you desire, be it food, drink, shelter or weapons, we will accommodate your needs. All in this room will be your council. We will do everything in our power to help you succeed."

Then, Charlie spoke. "Thank you, my queen, as I'm sure Alexis will praise your generosity."

"It would be impolite to neglect the girl's right to speak in these chambers," said the snow-white queen. "Please, Alexis, tell us of yourself, your toils, troubles, travels and how you came to this great city. And most importantly, how you will handle the task of which the sacred oracle spoke."

Lex might as well have not been listening at all, because most of the preceding conversation made no sense to her. The strange dialect in conjunction with an unfamiliar language, made her wish for little magical subtitles to appear over whomever was speaking. Moreover, she knew better than to tell Palas of the other world, the pool and the stone. Charlie's desperate request to proclaim being a native of Alba told her that even the queen was being deceived. She looked to Charlie to handle Palas' inquiries because she surely couldn't be expected to do so.

He politely said to Lex, "Might I be so bold as to ask for a moment alone with our queen? Theophilus and Isidore, I wish you to stay as well." He finished with a subtle wink at Lex. Palas seemed puzzled by this but did not protest. Charlie nodded to Sevastian who then approached Lex and escorted her back through the golden doors to the blustery castle top.

She shivered as a cool gust shot through her dress stealing away the few remaining fragments of warmth. The Russian huddled close so that his body would provide shelter from the cruel wind. She appreciated that. They stood at the waist-high stone wall and looked out over the clouds. Lex noted but did not give a great deal of consideration to a giant black bird that skimmed the cloud tops below. It was a swan, or so it appeared. The creature glided majestically with the wind, not having to utilize a single wing beat. With a moon on either wing, it made a sudden dive into the foggy haze and vanished from view. Exhausted, Lex rested her head on Sevastian's shoulder and shut her eyes. She had no motivation to continue questioning and really, just wanted to go to bed and rest her mind.

They were many yards from the golden doors and the soldiers who guarded them. With this safe distance and the tenor moans of the wind, Sevastian must have felt confident enough to talk without the risk of being overheard.

"The old man who gave Charlie the stone," he began, "the one in the alleyway the night of the full moon festival, issued a warning." Lex was listening but made no effort to acknowledge him. He continued anyway. "Not too long after Charlie and Jade returned to this earth as teenagers, he came to both of them in a dream. At the time, they knew very little about acanthary, but looking back, Charlie and Jade swear with certainty that it was in fact a dream invasion. The warning was to never, under any circumstances, inform anybody in this world of the Manult stone, because the consequences would be disastrous. He and Jade were the only ones who knew, and it was to stay that way. Charlie guessed that the old man would have told them that night in the alleyway but the soldiers arrived before he had the chance."

"But he told you, and me," Lex pointed out.

"You didn't hear me correctly. I said they were warned never to inform anyone in *this* world. The old man said nothing of the other. Charlie and Jade strongly believe that the reason the old man gave them the stone, and therefore conveyance to the world in which you and I belong, was chiefly to acquire resources. Resources which include wealth, knowledge, and maybe most importantly, the two of us, eh? Our biggest challenge has always been keeping it all a secret, especially to the people of this earth. We have been forced to get very creative and we have been forced to lie - a lot. But there is no other choice unless we defy the old man's warning."

Lex lifted her tired head from his shoulder and nodded an understanding. She would pack that information into her brain along with everything else that she had learned during this incredible journey. She now longed for this day's voyage to conclude. Just then, partially muffled by the constant squalling breeze, the doors of the queen's chamber rumbled open. She turned to see Palas, Charlie, Theophilus and Asshole approaching.

When the two groups merged, it was Theophilus who addressed her first. He took her hand into his own with an elated smile and said, "Alexis, my name is Theophilus, son of Xenoclyus. My position in the city and this high council is to oversee all acanthary, as I have experienced much in its workings. I teach the Crow Soldiers this art, and in the coming days, if it will please you, I shall begin to teach you as well. First and foremost, I must now declare that you, Alexis, our honored guest, will have every asset at your disposal while you stay in Crow. I will do my part in making it so."

She didn't know what to say so a straightforward, "Thank you," was all that escaped her lips. Charlie's subtle nod assured that the response was fitting.

Theophilus' eyes glistened with joy as he released her hands, and with high-spirited words spoke, "Great Zeus, mightiest among Olympians, surely holds Crow in high esteem to deliver this girl, this defender to us and to trust her safe keeping here." With that, he bowed to her and stepped back, falling in line next to Charlie and Palas.

Before her overwhelmed and tired mind could even begin to dwell on that baffling statement, Asshole, the giant Isidore stepped forward, and the expression on his face just might have shown a trace of humility. "I am Isidore, son of Kastromenian," he said in a deep baritone voice, his black hair splayed behind him in the wind. I am Charlamos' highest captain and honored servant of the queen. Alexis, I beg you to forgive the manner in which I engaged you earlier. I knew not who you were, and even if I had, I must remember how a stranger is to be treated in this great city. It is no secret that I do not bear the gift of swift tongue or stately manners. What I do possess is the ability to excel in combat, whether it be hurling a bronze-tipped spear or swinging this flail. I hereby make an oath, by Father Zeus, Athena, and Apollo, that I will protect you until the life flies from my body." As he spoke, Lex could deduce that he lacked social proficiency but his words were genuine. She obliged him with a tentative nod.

Finally, Palas spoke. "Go now, Alexis, and find peaceful sleep among the warm furs on your bed, and know this – no harm shall come to you under Crow's watchful eye. Charlamos has taken every measure to ensure that this will be so. Though you call Alba your home, I hope that you will consider Crow to be as pleasing as your native land."

With that, the queen retreated back to her chamber, Theophilus and Isidore back down into the vastness of the castle, and Charlie, Lex and Sevastian were left alone.

"Well, that plan backfired," Charlie said to the Russian after the coast was clear and they could converse freely. "I didn't expect Palas to realize who Lex was, at least not right away. I certainly didn't expect her to freak out the way she did. But I think I've got it all straightened out."

"What did you say to them?" Sevastian inquired.

"In so many words I told them that Lex was probably tired and overwhelmed and that she needs some time to herself."

"That sounds about right," she happily muttered with the anticipation of a warm bed and some alone-time.

58

"Comfortable?" Charlie asked as Lex pulled the heavy bed linens up to her chin and fell back into a sea of fluffy pillows. The score of animal pelts were weighty and a trite unsettling, but they certainly did add much additional warmth. As he started to systematically extinguish the candles, she began to feel a little uneasy. She was no wimp, but there was something about this giant shadowy room that tapped at her nerves. She eyed the painted tapestry, the hidden door that connected this room to the Moskincov house. She wondered how many people could use that secret entrance to visit her while she slept, though Sevastian had assured her that wouldn't happen. Charlie disrupted her thoughts as he plopped down oafishly at the side of her bed. He had eliminated all light except the fire in the fireplace and the soft moonbeams rolling in through the windows.

"Why do I get the feeling that I'm not safe here? In this world I mean?" she asked.

"What makes you think that?"

She began to recall, "Well, there was the way you reacted to that strange girl in the alley, the way you appointed a guard at my door and that thing the queen said about no harm coming to me while I'm in Crow. I'm beginning to think I'm here for a reason." He appeared to be formulating a response. "And why does everyone refer to me as 'the defender?'" Since she could pretty much predict that his explanation would be just another abstract request to take everything one step at a time, she spoke up before he could, mostly because she was too tired to deal with more puzzling details. "Never mind Charlie, Charlamos," she said.

"What can I do but trust you? I know you won't let anything happen to me, I just want to know why I must be guarded at all times."

"By tomorrow's end, you will know everything," he promised candidly. "Until then, get some sleep. If you need anything, my room is directly across the hall. And yes, there is a guard outside your room so you don't have to worry about anything. As for the hidden passageway, Sevastian guards that entrance. Rest assured that you are safe." She nodded and slowly closed her eyes. He then said, "Thank you for putting up with all this. You're doing superb."

She forced a smile as he made for the door. After only a few steps, an alarming outcry from behind stopped him dead in his tracks. "Oh my God, I can't believe... Oh no!" She shot up in her bed, wide-eyed and distressed.

Charlie ran to her side nearly in a panic. "What is it?"

"Aunt Claire doesn't know where I am. It's in her nature to worry sick about me. Damn, I'm always doing this to her. By this time in her world, it must be Christmas morning, and she's expecting me for breakfast."

He sighed then calmly replied, "No worries, I've got it covered."

"What? How?"

"I wanted this to be a surprise," he went on, "but amidst the countless details and planning, I forgot about your aunt." She stared at him, desperately awaiting alleviation of concern. "Please, Lex, lay back, shut your eyes and allow me to tell you a quick bedtime story."

"What? But Aunt Claire, she... You say you have it covered?"

"Please. Just trust me."

She reluctantly complied with this request, cursing herself as her hair met pillow. Though it wasn't entirely her fault, in the midst of the recent thrill ride, she had once again neglected to appease Claire's obsessive desire to keep her niece safe. Claire had made this oath, to protect and provide for Lex, while standing over Olivia's coffin that black Wednesday long ago. Placing all faith in the person sitting at her bedside, Lex listened as he began his story...

Coeval

Many years had passed since Charlie and Jade departed the plains of Kansas and returned to the world they once knew. Since rejoining life on Earth B, much has happened and much has changed them. Invaluable experiences ranging from euphoric to horrifying, have shaped and transformed their personalities. In the end, it is the imperious swell of guilt that invoked the decision to return to Earth A - a place in which four special people are certainly consumed by incomprehensible anguish over their missing children.

Charlie and Jade find themselves standing at the edge of the cornfield, stalks chest high, fireflies abundant in the humid night air. They have just been through the pool, the church and the woods. A nervous feeling grips tightly due to the long accruing anticipation leading up to the moment they would once again face their parents and explain where they'd been for so long. The alibi has been rehearsed again and again, yet the likelihood that they would be forgiven for such an atrocious deed as disappearing off the face of the planet, quite literally, remains bleak. It is all the pair can hope for to find their elderly parents still alive.

It is a peaceful summer night. The moon's orientation in the sky is consistent with midnight. Across the sea of rustling cornstalks sits the Roanoke farm. The red barns exist only as silhouettes against the twinkling starscape. The old farmhouse is dark except for a faint porch light and a white glow from a first floor window - Charlie's room. It wrenches his heart to see that Robert and Ella leave his light on every night in case he should return. After all they had done for him, how could he just up and leave? He hates himself for it.

Together the cousins walk along a narrow corn row without exchanging a single word, both dreading what awaits. It's like a death march – slow and purposeful with an unwillingness to reach the final destination. When finally they breach the threshold between thriving crop and freshly cut grass, Jade says with a sigh, "Best of luck."

Charlie gives a melancholy nod as the two embrace in a hug.

"I'll call you tomorrow," he says watching his cousin head for the dark county road that will lead her to the Vandervelde farm. "If I can remember how a telephone works." She turns back to him for a moment as if about to speak, then shakes her head and continues on her way. He feels guilty for allowing her to walk a dark three miles alone, then remembers that this girl is far more dangerous than anything she could possibly encounter along the way.

It is now time for Charlie to face the music. Nearly every part of his brain is telling him to turn around, return to Earth B, forget about this world and be done with it all. But one area of his brain, the area that houses the ability to demonstrate consideration and integrity, propels him forward. His boots make contact with the creaking porch. There's the handcrafted swing. He used to spend countless hours nestled in its solid comfort reading his novels. That seems like forever ago. He takes a deep breath, nods to himself, and opens the front door.

He figures the least startling way to announce his return would be to softly call Robert and Ella from the living room. Barging into their room might scare them to death. Perhaps they would think it a dream, to hear the calls of their long lost son. Softly, "Mom, Dad?"

No reply. This time a little louder.

"Mom, Dad?"

There's the rustling of sheets then a lamp clinks on from Robert and Ella's bedroom, its light reflecting off the adjacent hallway wall. Then, a shadow of someone stirring – slipping into a robe. An exhausted Robert Roanoke shuffles from the room, white hair in tangles, yawning, rubbing his eyes as if disoriented. Charlie is delighted to see that his overall health seems fair. Robert stares wordlessly for a moment then asks, "What's the matter?"

Charlie is taken aback. Robert must be confused or perhaps sleepwalking. The expected reaction would be to stop dead in his tracks, drop his jaw, and stare in shock with teary eyes - perhaps run to Charlie and throw his thankful arms around him - call to his wife that their son has returned. Maybe Robert couldn't see. The living room is too dark for an old man's cataract-stricken eyes. With nervous haste, Charlie flips on the floor lamp. Robert's face is radiating confusion. He glances around the room, eyes settling on the wall clock before saying, "What's the matter, Charlie? You know tomorrow's a busy day. I'd appreciate it if you'd let me sleep."

This defies all logic. Charlie is so caught off guard that he just stands there like a mute head case.

"Well, what is it?" Robert beckons. His tone is not angry but hurried. "You sleepwalkin', Charlie?"

Charlie could only shake his head and attempt to relinquish his dumbfounded expression.

Robert rolls his eyes as if thinking, "teenagers." "Not sure where ya got those clothes but don't get any ideas about wearin' 'em all the time. No boy of mine's gonna parade around dressed like a Buddhist monk." Robert turns back to the bedroom, stops halfway down the hall and says, "Go to bed, buddy."

Finally, Charlie blurts out, "Is Mom alright?"

"Of course she's alright, that is until you wake her. Please try and keep your voice down. Bacon and eggs will be on by five tomorrow. I want to get an early start at painting the barn." With that he retreats back into the bedroom and terminates the light.

Painting the barn? Charlie recycles the words in his head a dozen times. It was so long ago, so very long ago, so infinitely long ago, but he can just barely recall that on the night he left for Earth B, the plan was to help Robert paint the barn the next morning.

Charlie dives for the remote that sits on the floor by the

couch and quickly clicks to the Weather Channel. It can't be – July 24. What an extraordinary coincidence that he and Jade should return the same date that they left. How many years had gone by? A practical guess would be at least nine, ten maybe? Unless...

He bounds to the kitchen where the daily paper would be predictably residing upon the table. When he notes the date, the month, and the year, he collapses into the nearest chair sending a teaspoon clinking off across the kitchen floor. At this point, after all his travels and experiences, nothing should seem impossible, but for some reason the fact that not a day had elapsed on this earth during the years he had spent on the other seems perfectly inconceivable.

Heart pounding, he shuts off the light and makes for his bedroom. There he finds the fluorescent desk lamp that he had left aglow, the good-bye letter that has not been read, and the ajar window that had not been properly closed after he had crawled out. He now has a new puzzle to solve on top of all the others that have been compiling over the years. The task – to assign an explanation to this perplexing defiance of time.

This thought consumes him as he lays awake in bed. He will certainly not sleep tonight. Just then, he realizes something that he had blatantly overlooked. This is something so obvious, so barefaced and lucid, he feels downright stupid for not having realized it. During all those years he had spent on Earth B, he had not once needed a hair cut, a nail trim, a shave, or any other form of routine personal upkeep. At the moment, his only assumption is that he had not aged at all. This exhilarating train of thought could have only been derailed by a rapid tapping at his window. It's Jade, and her enormous grin tells him that she too has figured it out. He runs outside to meet her. The two would converse excitedly until dawn about this unbelievable predicament. All their worries about returning home evaporate into the summer night.

59

The bafflement in Lex's eyes told Charlie that she had comprehended the significance of the story.

"Do you now see why Jade took you to get a manicure and a haircut?" he asked. "Since your hair will not grow here, we figured you might as well have it exactly the way you want it. And believe me, there's not a barber in this world that can operate anything beyond sheep shears."

"But how…?" she began to ask, but Charlie cut her off.

"I haven't yet solved the secrets of the pool and its ability to defy time. All I know for sure is that time stops on the other earth, Earth A, whenever someone travels to this earth via the pool. Time on Earth A resumes as soon as we come back. On the other hand, time on this earth, Earth B, marches on no matter what."

"Do you at least have a theory as to why that is?"

"Well kind of," he replied, as if uncertain how to proceed. "I have no idea how to confirm it but I have reason to believe that our universe has many dimensions, perhaps ten or more. We can easily observe three dimensions in nature but currently, there are mathematical calculations by some of Earth A's most brilliant minds that are close to proving these extra dimensions exist. Science seems to accept that if there are other dimensions besides the ones humans can physically observe, they would be folded so thin that only mathematical equations can explain their existence. So, if the space that these dimensions occupy is distorted beyond our realm of understanding, perhaps that holds true for time within these dimensions. Long story short, I think that either one of these Earths exists in a dimension we cannot see or the connection between them exists in a dimension we cannot see. Either way, time between the earths does not behave like we expect."

Lex had to grin at, as it seemed in her mind, the insanity of it all. He had now opened another can of worms and she decided to have a quick go at it, sleepy though she was. "If I were in Kansas, and watched you enter the pool with the stone, you would disappear beneath the water and instantly re-emerge?"

"Exactly," he concurred.

"No matter how much time you've spent on this earth? Even if it were a million years?"

"It would still be instantaneous," he assured her. "There is one minor exception. Every year or so, a few days will slip by on Earth A even if we're all here on Earth B. I'm embarrassed to once again admit I don't know why that is.

"What if I went back to Earth A and you stayed here?

"As soon as the Manult stone crosses back onto Earth A, Earth A time resumes and I would begin to age here on Earth B until you return with the stone. There have been many times when Jade, Sevastian and I have had to split up. One or two of us return to Earth A while one or two stay here. At this point, we all underwent normal aging until the stone came back to Earth B and we were back together."

"I wonder then," Lex said, "if you, Jade and Sevastian don't age while here on Earth B, doesn't anyone find that a bit strange?"

"I'm sure it won't surprise you to know that we've covered our tracks with a little white lie," he explained. "Of course, you understand, in our unique situation there is often no other choice but to white lie." Lex could certainly appreciate that statement as she assumed she had been the recent recipient of these "white lies." He continued, "In due time, I'll fill you in on our fictitious story of immortality."

Lex pressed on with her inquiries. "So how old are you then?"

He chuckled. "You don't miss a thing, do you?"

"Well?" she prodded.

"We graduated high school together, shouldn't you know?"

"Come on, Charlamos, how many years have you spent on this earth, you know, not aging?"

"Honestly, I've lost track. Maybe sixty."

She couldn't tell if he was serious or facetious. It was a fascinating phenomenon, living for free so to speak - living, but not aging. That is, if it were actually true. "Are you eligible for the senior citizen's discount at the Hilltop Buffet?" she asked, unable to resist a cheap shot.

He erupted in laughter. When he finally cooled down he said, "Good to see you're still with me." He turned to the door after bidding her goodnight.

Before he left, however, she had one more question. "Charlie, what happens if we all die in this world?"

His face went from cheery to sober. "Do you mean – will the other earth be locked in a standstill?"

She nodded.

"Well," he said after a contemplative pause, "let's hope we never have to find out."

When the door shut and she was alone, the swell of emotions returned. This time she was too tired to make an attempt at sorting them out. She wanted them to go away and knew that sleep was the only means to achieve this, though it was only a temporary solution. As drowsiness took hold, her final conscious thought was of Peter Pan and Wendy in Never Never land.

60

There was no dream invasion that night. Charlie had been considerate enough to allow Lex a full night of undisturbed sleep – and sleep she did. Dreamless, peaceful, perfect slumber, only to be intruded upon by distant rumbles of morning thunder and fluttery notes of music.

Her eyes cracked open to a chilly breeze that inconsiderately trespassed its way into the room through the open windows. A misty wind kissed her face as she sat up, yawned deeply and stretched. She took a moment to observe her surroundings and reflect on the events that had transpired up to this time. After such quality rest, her thoughts and feelings had become more organized and controlled. Slipping a heavy blanket over her body, she walked to the window. The stone floor felt cold against her bare feet. At the window, her eyes widened at a scene so grand, it may have only been outdone by the infamous full moon festival that Charlie had so vividly described the day before.

The morning was cool, cloudy and damp with rain. The harbor below was blanketed by fog and from her vantage point, she could make out only the tallest masts of the larger shipping vessels as they protruded from the mist like ghostly wings. Farther inland, the fog dissipated and the citizens of Crow were out and about in full force. Thousands crowded the streets as music and smoke deluged the morning air. An infectious excitement arose in her body at the anticipation of attending this wondrous spectacle – a spectacle that no one on Earth A could possibly hope to imagine.

"Breakfast?"

She wheeled around at the startling voice she knew so well - Charlie. He had in his possession a silver platter with fruit, bread and milk. His attire consisted of the Glast sheep garments, including full cloak and shoe covers for concealing those comfortable trail boots. The chilly, wet day would certainly call for such clothing.

"Sleep well?" he asked.

"As a matter of fact, best sleep I've had in a long time," she replied in perfect Greek. He carried the tray over to her and placed it in the windowsill. "Thanks," she said, plucking a few plump grapes from their stems.

"Normally we'd have a nice big breakfast in a private dining room downstairs or a cozy fireside meal at the Moskincov place – but today I thought an informal meal at the window would get us to the festivities quicker." He looked down upon the sea-side streets with a gleam of expectancy in his eyes. "It's going to be quite a day," he assured her.

"And the itinerary?" she asked between bites.

"First, you and I will walk the streets, mingle with the citizens, taste the food, and take it all in. This will give you a nice introduction to Crow's culture. Listen to the lingo, observe the behavior, become familiar with the markets, the buildings and the streets. Now that you're rested and have seemingly accepted your predicament, I hope you can now truly appreciate this experience. After that, there's only one thing left to do - watch some damn good sport," he said with an obnoxiously large grin.

She finished off a slice of buttered bread and observed a group of dancers below. From this height, they looked like tiny performing circus fleas. She was enthusiastic but still rightfully guarded. According to Charlie, she had "accepted her predicament," but this was not so; not yet anyway. There was still something missing and until she figured it out, this was too outrageous to be true and too strange to be good. In addition, much concern remained that Aunt Claire might worry herself to death if

Charlie's proclamation of stopped time was false.

61

"Why are we wearing these particular clothes?" Lex asked, referring to Charlie's choice to forgo his fancy habiliments. She was confused as to why he seemed so content to gad about as a commoner when every other member of the royal family strutted their status like narcissistic peacocks. The two had just departed from the castle via the connection tunnel to the Moskincov house and were now entering the bustling streets. A chilly rain began to fall. In unison, they donned their hoods.

"People are never themselves in the presence of royalty," he answered. "They'll feel intimidated, hate you, kiss your ass, or any combination of said ridiculous behavior. Trust me, disguised as commoners, our time here will be much more enjoyable."

"Do Crow's citizens not recognize you?" she questioned.

"Many will," he commented, "but for the most part my face is unknown to the general public. I keep it that way for two reasons. First, since I'm in charge of law and order in Crow, this under-cover approach allows me to witness first hand what goes on beyond the castle walls. Second, I don't want celebrity status. I have more in common with the so-called 'commoner' than I do with royalty."

She smiled respectfully, admiring his character. She reflected on the time that he had seemed celebrity-like in her eyes. After getting to know him, she came to realize that he was not a self-proclaimed big shot or a larger than life superstar, he was just captivatingly interesting and tactfully modest.

As the two found themselves merging onto the main street near the coliseum, it became too loud for friendly conversation.

Cheering and celebratory commotion inundated the air around them. Everywhere they turned, someone was playing a musical instrument. Horns, strings, winds and even deep wooden drums, competed for dominance amongst the hullabaloo. There were singers, jugglers, food vendors and dancers. The smell of smoke, perfume and a panoply of different foods permeated the air. The weather, which seemed much to Lex like a typical dreary day in England, was doing nothing to hold this party down.

Heeding Charlie's advice, she listened in on random conversations as they strolled casually onward. Not only was it helpful practice in sharpening her knowledge of the Greek language, but also an insight into the way people in this world spoke to each other. She noted that the lingo was very similar to that which Homer used to write his epic poetry. Charlie offered his arm and she happily took it. Getting separated would not be desirable in this fiasco. As they bobbed and weaved their way through the fiesta, he did a fine job of playing teacher. After a short while, she had ingested several heaping spoonfuls of Earth B knowledge.

She learned that the performing arts were valued above all other professions. If you happened to be a commoner gifted with the ability to sing, dance, act, tell stories, or play an instrument, this was your best chance at success – namely by way of marrying into royalty. Even if the performers did not win the hand of an admiring member of the royal family, working in the Crow theater was still the highest paid profession one could acquire. This was why the musicians that buzzed through the crowd, commoner or not, were never dressed in rags, but clean, attractive attire.

"Fascinating, no matter which world one finds themselves in," Charlie commented, "human nature is virtually identical. Put a man on stage, on television, on the pitcher's mound, and he is instantly regarded with favor. He becomes a celebrity, he is treated as a celebrity, and he is paid as a celebrity."

"True indeed," Lex concurred.

"There are four common beverages in this world," he said

as the duo passed a crudely assembled plank-wood booth that had seemingly been erected in about a minute. Within the booth, two men with thick black beards were toiling diligently to accommodate the relentless demand for their drink. The amber substance was stored within hundreds of clay pitchers stacked high within the confines of the booth. The bearded men worked as a team, one pouring, the other accepting coin.

"You see here," Charlie pointed at the booth, "we have mead." They continued onward at a relaxed pace. "Common beverage number two – wine. The nonalcoholic choices would be water of course and tea. There are several varieties of tea – virgin ghala leaf, troghorn, willow root, and our favorite, cicadaweed. Cicadaweed is rare and expensive, so you'll rarely find anyone but royalty taking part in its consumption."

She next learned that the common meats were those of pig, lamb, bird, fish, deer and rabbit. She learned that the animals on this earth were similar to animals on the other, but not exactly. The first example Charlie offered to illustrate this point was the size of horses here on Earth B – much larger than the Earth A variety.

"On Earth B, rodents are predominantly tailless with broader bodies, longer toes, and thousands of mini suction cup structures on the bottoms of their feet. This compensates for everything a tail would provide."

He went on to mention that all felines on this earth are similar in size to those on the other, but here they have sharp protruding incisors much like the saber-tooth cats of Earth A's prehistoric era.

"And of course, as I have mentioned before," he added, "there are those living organisms in this world that never existed on Earth A… nymphs, cyclopes, minotaurs, cicadaweed; but in my opinion, the most fascinating life forms live in our seas."

"How about crows?" Lex asked as she skidded to an abrupt halt, barely avoiding a tail-end collision into a noble gentleman. She found herself eye to eye with the ominous black bird on the back of his cape.

"Can't tell an Earth A crow from an Earth B crow," Charlie said matter-of-factly.

He explained that due to the stark similarity between the geography of both planets, their location to a sun, atmospheric components, climate regions and gravitational pressures, organisms on both earths evolved in a similar fashion. He postulated that the differences among organisms, whether subtle or excessive, were likely due to the major events in the individual history of each planet - meteor strikes, volcanic eruptions, earthquakes, ice ages and glacier activity to name a few. All of these entities, along with how much time a given earth had existed to allow for evolution to occur, played a large part in how life on these planets had progressed.

They walked on, Charlie hopping from one topic to another, and Lex absorbing everything like a sponge. Then suddenly, there was a hand on her shoulder. Startled, she wheeled around to the sagging face and crooked nose of a hunched old woman.

"Your voice could move mountains," she said to Lex in a high-pitched, scratchy tone. She bowed to the both of them, a raggedy cloth hood keeping the harassing drizzle from her frizzled hair. Charlie regarded the woman with an air of suspicion that Lex deemed unfounded. The old lady was frail, amicable, and the last person on earth that should be portrayed as a threat.

"Thank you," Lex said, in reciprocation to the woman's compliment. "It was an honor to sing for such a city."

"You were in attendance at the royal feast?" Charlie questioned.

"Yes, great Charlamos," the woman concurred. "The gods gifted this old widow the glorious opportunity."

"Please, kind woman, tell us your name," he said.

"Agatha, daughter of Euthalia," she answered with eyes cast downward, as if uneasy in his presence.

"Where do you call home?" he then asked. "Do you live within the city or reside elsewhere?"

"My cottage is on a vineyard in Taras Argos. My family makes wine for the citizens of Crow."

Charlie glanced around. His curious observation provoked Lex to do the same. In the span of three seconds, she deduced that the woman was a street vendor, selling cups of purple wine from a collection of wooden barrels stacked on the back of a rickety wagon. Her horse was old and mangy, but appeared entirely content standing by as his owner pedaled her product. By the look of things, she was doing rather well. In the general vicinity, nearly every person had a tin goblet and sipped the robust wine with approving smiles.

Agatha first addressed Charlie, "Allow me to convey my appreciation for dining within the castle Crow," then Lex, "and extend my congratulations to the new choir director." She hurried to the wagon as fast as her crooked legs would carry her and filled two cups to the brim with a polished mahogany liquid. Charlie and Lex looked at each other, Lex with a bemused grin, Charlie with a lingering dubiety. The woman returned and held out the drinks for the taking. "Some delicious wine to ease your thirst and wet your tongue. No need for payment."

"Thank you!" Lex spouted energetically, immediately diving her upper lip into the sweet beverage.

"Your generosity pleases us," Charlie said with reserved alacrity as he took the cup. He bowed his head. "May the gods bid you good fortune."

Agatha displayed her remaining four teeth as she smiled beholdenly, then turned back to the cart and resumed filling cups. Charlie and Lex traveled on, slipping through the crowd and somehow managing not to spill their drinks in the turbulent surroundings.

Soon, the main street ended and the masses of people were far behind. They now stood at an intersection of three roads on the outskirts of the city. One veered to the left and continued another hundred yards before it was swallowed up by a thick forest. Another turned right and snaked around a collection of rolling hills toward a little village on the horizon. Due to the location, Lex assumed that the village was Taras Argos, where Itys and his wife lived along with Agatha, the sweet old winemaker and, still to Lex's astonishment, Jade, with her husband, Elias. The other road of course would lead back to the coliseum and the immense gathering of eager spectators. Since she and her "captor," as she currently thought of him, were now practically alone, she decided to question him about an issue that had been tamping her brain. "Why did you not trust that old woman?"

"Was it obvious?"

"Yes."

"It's not that I didn't trust her. Experience has taught me to be leery of anyone you don't know. Especially now that you're…" he stopped himself but she knew what he meant to say.

"Why are you protecting me?" she demanded. He looked surprised by the fiery inquisition, or unprepared.

"I can't tell you yet," he replied… unfulfilling, but honest at least.

She continued pressing him, "If you are protecting me, why would you have me sing in front of the entire castle and make my face known to everyone?"

"A valid question," he said, rubbing his chin contemplatively. "My plan was to save this for after the Trigonous match, but there'd be no harm in getting a head start. We have some time before the fight gets underway, so let me take you to the book parlor."

"Okay then," she agreed with some sense of satisfaction. This was a step in the right direction. She was going to extract every secret from him if she had to do it one tidbit of information at a time.

62

They headed back up the main street and within minutes were drowning in a sea of pedestrians. The crowd's viscosity had increased tenfold during their brief absence. The progress to reach whatever destination Charlie had in mind was painstakingly plodded as it took a great deal of effort to navigate through the bodies. From the corner of her eye, she noticed a group of passing noblemen bow their heads to Charlie. They then averted their regard in her direction, eyeing her with vested interest. Even though the ugly brown cloak all but swallowed her up, she was still being recognized. This only fueled the conundrum – how was Charlie protecting her if everyone knew her?

The pair jumped from the main street into a damp stone alley. Ahead to the left was a dingy two-story building that looked as though it had been around since the city's beginning. Above the front door was a flat wooden board with the illustration of a book painted upon its weathered surface.

"Here is Crow's version of a library," Charlie pointed out as the two neared the building. "The difference is, you cannot borrow or buy the books. You may only read them within the confines of this building under the watchful eye of the overseer. In this world there are no printing presses, which means we do not have multiple copies of each book. Most are original and unduplicated, therefore we cannot take the chance of having them borrowed. Now mind you, the books that are available to the public are indeed valuable, but it would not be devastating if one should fall victim to a mishap. Some books, however, are direly important, and those are locked up in the castle.

"Why are you taking me here?" she asked.

"It's all part of the process. You asked if you were being protected. The answer is yes, as you've already deduced. Your next question is 'why am I being protected?' Well, the answer to that is not so simple. In order to understand more, there's something I'd like you to read."

"And that is?" she asked, head cocked in curiosity. They came to a stop at the bottommost of three wooden steps that ascended to the front door.

"Inside you'll find an elderly gentleman by the name of Amartus. Because of his notable achievements in acanthary and extensive book knowledge, I have appointed him overseer of the book parlor. Go in and find Amartus. Tell him you would like to read, The Oblivion Oracle. I think you'll have just enough time to buzz through the short manuscript before the first fight begins."

"The Oblivion Oracle. Right. And where will you be? All this talk about keeping me safe and you're sending me off alone?"

"No harm will come to you under Amartus' watch," he replied confidently. "Besides, I'll only be a moment." He pointed to the far side of the alley. There, patrolling along a row of trade establishments was a Crow Soldier bearing fierce physical attributes. Lex had not yet come across this particular individual; and surely she would not forget meeting a man such as this.

"That soldier over there, Lycurgus by name, is someone I've been meaning to chat with. Just have to fill him in on some new security measures."

Lycurgus had taken note that Charlie was looking his way and began heading in their direction. The muscular soldier was decked out in polished bronze armor with a heavy leather tunic beneath. He carried in his left hand a sturdy shield bearing a disturbing image of a demon crow. In his right, a long, bronze-tipped spear. A bundle of five additional flesh-piercing spears was tethered to his back. His right eye was missing and he wore no patch to conceal the disgusting mass of scarred tissue that remained.

Charlie eyed the approaching Lycurgus with an air of esteem. He said quietly to Lex, "They call him the harpy slayer. If anyone has stories to give you nightmares... Anyway, Lycurgus is next in line for head captain should something happen to Isidore, your favorite body guard."

Although she had graciously forgiven Isidore for his less than cordial treatment, she had no desire, at least currently, to meet another of Crow's hard asses. Therefore, she decided to slip quickly into the book parlor before Lycurgus arrived.

"Oh, Lex," Charlie said as she was just about to shut the door behind her. "There are two things that the people in this world hold sacred - the gods and those with the gift of song. Last night you demonstrated that your gift far exceeds that of anyone who has ever set foot in this great city. This means you are now sacred to the citizens of Crow. As a result, you have an army at your back. Be it a king or a thief, the highest noble to the most vile murderer, every single man and woman in Crow now worships you and would give their lives to protect you." He flashed a warm smile then turned to greet Lycurgus.

So that's why he put me in the spotlight, she thought. In this case, recognition is protection. Interesting.

63

The book parlor was dimly lit and downright spooky. The place was overrun by cobwebs, dust and a lingering musty smell. Hopefully, she thought, Charlie isn't paying this Amartus fellow too high a salary. Perhaps this overseer compensates for his pitiful house keeping with book knowledge.

It was laid out much like a small library with many rows of shelving, shadowy aisles, an occasional stepping stool and a few tables here and there. Near the back wall, a stairwell led to the second floor. There was an eerie silence except for the pattering of rain and the muffled conversation between Charlie and Lycurgus from outside the door.

"Hello?" she called out accidentally in English. Correcting herself, she called out once more in Greek. Neither yielded a response. There was a doorway to the left, but the darkness from within led her to believe the chances of finding Amartus were greater if she ventured upstairs.

Foreboding though it was, there was still something mysteriously alluring about the old parlor. She had certainly seen grander book collections, the library in the Flock's mansion to name one, but never a collection so old – ancient. It was a book enthusiast's paradise. As she moseyed down the center aisle en route to the stairwell, she noted that some of the books along the top shelf had nearly an inch of dust sitting upon them – neglected, deteriorating. Many of them pertained to the gods of Olympus and the history of the world's cities. As an avid reader and self proclaimed book junkie, she hoped for the opportunity to come here again and study up on the literature of this fascinating earth.

The stairwell creaked under her feet, shouting its defiance at bearing additional weight as she ascended to the second floor. When reaching the top, she was disappointed to note that this room was even darker, dustier and more disorganized than the lower level. Had a hurricane come through? A raging bull perhaps? Books were strewn helter-skelter on the floor, piled haphazardly on tables and literally hanging off shelves. This again begged the question - what in the name of Sir Isaac Newton did Amartus do all day? A bookkeeper with poor organizational skills? That's like a farrier who's afraid of horses, she thought.

With no windows to aid her vision, she had to rely on a single candle, nearly burnt to a nub, sitting carelessly on a teetering stack of books. As far as she could tell, there was no one up here either. Perhaps Amartus had decided to hurry off to the coliseum with everyone else. She shrugged her shoulders and turned back to the stairwell, but just as she did so, something caught her eye. Was her mind playing games? She turned slowly toward the back of the loft. The candle's light only penetrated about halfway down the center aisle, but there lurking amongst the shadowy recesses, she thought she could just make out a human figure.

"Hello?" she called. "Excuse me - hello?" There was no answer but as her eyes adjusted to the dark, she became convinced someone really was there. With a pinch of apprehension, she crept slowly toward the aisle. "I'm looking for Amartus," she stated nervously. With each step, the figure became more apparent. It wasn't until she was but a few yards away when words finally arose.

"You are brave to have come here," said a girl's voice. Her tone was chilling, and sounded as though there were two people talking rather than just one.

"I beg your pardon?" Lex asked uneasily.

The figure stepped, no, floated into the light. Lex's tension meter skyrocketed. She promptly recognized this girl as the same one from the alley; the one who had projected that haunting phrase the night prior. She had also been the one standing next to the stone well at the marketplace and had seemingly vanished into thin air before Charlie had been able to spot her. Before the shadows had lifted from the girl's face, Lex decided that she was indefinably pretty in a "children-of-the-corn" sort of way. As she further observed this disconcerting stranger, pretty was swept under the rug, and mortifying quickly moved in as the dominant impression.

The girl, presumably equal in age to Lex, wore a ragged black dress that skimmed the ground as she moved. The unflattering garment veiled all but her porcelain face and frigid bony hands. Her hair, much like her dress, was long, black and extended the length of her body stopping just short of the dusty floorboards. When the candlelight kissed her eyes, Lex had to repress an alarmed reaction. Her eyeballs were devoid of pupils making her look very much like a demon.

"He should not have left you alone here," the girl stated.

Is she talking about Charlie? Lex was confused. She wasn't sure how much information to disclose and had no desire to loiter in conversation with this unholy stranger. "I'm here in search of a particular book," she finally said after thinking of nothing else.

The girl smiled and replied, "Wait here and I'll fetch you the book you seek." She whipped around and floated soundlessly into the darkness.

The whole situation was knotty. Lex hadn't even relayed the name of the book, yet this peculiar girl, who may or may not be human, had gone off to find it. Out of courtesy, she was about to call out the title, but then, as quickly as she had vanished, the girl reappeared in possession of a book. The manuscript cradled within the zombie's cadaverous hands looked so old, Lex was leery to touch it for fear that it might crumble at her embrace. The words on the cover were indistinguishable as they had been eroded by time and touch.

"Do you like poetry?" the girl asked, staring unblinkingly with those ghostly eyes.

"Well, yes I do, but I'm here for a book called The Oracle..."

"Poetry is prophecy," the girl brazenly interjected. She opened the book and flipped through a few pages before settling on something. She forced the book into Lex's palms with tenacity. "This is the one."

At the moment, Lex just wanted to high-tail it out of there and get back to Charlie, but that would be impolite seeing as how the girl had gone to all this trouble. Just to be appeasing, she lowered her eyes to the fragile pages and began to read the faded words...

Crow

Bright winter moons above bare trees,
Snow covered ground and a lonesome breeze.

The forest was dark yet I desperately,
Searched for the child night had taken from me.

Suddenly from above a melancholy cry,
A crow appeared from the cold starry sky.

I stopped as it perched upon an icy pine limb,
It shrieked and it cried then flew off again.

With hope fading fast I had to decide,
Should I follow the bird? Should I confide?

With tears in my eyes I blindly ran,
Chasing the crow across frozen land.

I came to a clearing in the middle of the wood,
Upon an old hollow stump the black bird stood.

Then with the wind it softly came,
The voice of the child calling my name.

I ran to the stump where my child lay,
The bird shrieked once more and flew away.

I fell to my knees as she closed her eyes,
And there by the stump my child soon died.

Off in the distance from the cold dark sky,
I heard the crow's lonely cry.

"It's such a sad story," Lex mentioned as she glanced up from the book to discover that the zombie had disappeared. This incomprehensible vanishing act left her ill at ease. As if right on cue, a monstrous clap of thunder shattered the silence and she nearly jumped out of her skin. After shoving the book into the nearest opening on the shelf, she swiftly vacated the second floor. In the midst of her escape, an alert sounded in her brain – a red flag. The poem had been written in English.

Just a matter of minutes ago, the first floor had seemed dingy and uninviting, but compared to the second floor, it now felt like a resort. She hoped that the mysterious girl had remained upstairs so there would be no more encounters. Just then, an urgent voice penetrated the air.

"Lex! You've gotta be more careful!" She jumped and spun around in one fluid motion to catch Charlie hustling toward her. At the moment, she did not appreciate the sneakiness.

"What's the matter, Charlie?"

He cautiously scanned the room and, in a whisper, said,

"Your shoe cover is half off."

"You've got to be kidding!" she said with irritation. "I just ran into an old friend upstairs and you're bothered over a shoe cover? What's the worst thing that could happen if somebody saw our fancy boots?" She didn't intend on being so snippy, but the incident upstairs had rattled her nerves.

"You're right," he said, placing a hand on her shoulder. And just like that, she became calm. It was as if she were a pot of boiling water and someone had turned off the stove beneath her. Charlie always had this ability to kill the heat. He politely knelt and fixed the shoe cover, then asked, "So who was it you met upstairs?"

"The girl you tried to catch last night – the one from the alley," she whispered, vigilantly eyeing the ceiling. Instantly, he became serious.

"The same one? Are you sure? Is she still up there?"

"I'm not sure…I…"

"Lex, is she still up there?" he repeated jarringly. This made her feel inadequate and downright mental for not having a good explanation as to the girl's whereabouts.

"I don't know," she blurted dejectedly. "She sort of disappeared but I suppose if there are no other exits, then she must be."

"Not surprising," he said as he began backing toward the front door tugging her along with him, "she's proven to be quite good at that. She either slipped out a first floor window or she's still in here somewhere. I've been near the front door, the only door, the entire time. Since you've gone in, no one has come out."

Suddenly, a drowsy mumble arose from behind the door, the one Lex had neglected to search earlier. She and Charlie ran toward the sound and plowed through the doorway into a small, dark storeroom.

There, lying amongst a pile of papers and books was Amartus, the overseer of the parlor. He was rubbing his forehead and seemingly recovering from a fainting spell. His puffy white hair was in disarray and his face was etched with confusion. At first, Lex thought that he might have injured himself during the fall because there were several pools of dark red liquid dotting the floor. A closer look revealed that the liquid had been spilled from a flask that lay near the doorway. She and Charlie immediately helped the shaken man find his feet.

"Thank you," Amartus began with a raspy voice. "You must believe me, Charlamos," he said, voice pleading, "I have not partaken in wine or mead. My flask contains only boreberry juice to help ease my sickness."

Charlie glanced down at the red liquid mess, eyeing it suspiciously. Kneeling, he dipped an index finger into the sticky contents. Ever so cautiously, he tapped the finger to the tip of his tongue. This provoked a sour expression ensued by a bout of what appeared to be drunken teetering. Just as Lex reached out to stabilize him, he shook his head with absurd rapidity and popped out of his bizarre stupor declaring, "Someone has poisoned you."

Amartus' beady eyes narrowed in outrage. He and Charlie looked at each other with shocked expressions, then they simultaneously vocalized their conclusion, "hornanthus!"

The urgency exhibited by the two experienced acanthars told Lex that this hornanthus, a plant with some degree of toxicity, had been slipped into Amartus' flask. Was this all part of some diabolical plan? Was someone trying to get to her? Such was her initial hypothesis as she considered the encounter with the girl upstairs. In her mind, it was all connected – somehow.

Charlie must have arrived at the same conclusion. Springing into action, he bolted across the front room. Arriving at the door, he flung it open and summoned Lycurgus with a sharp whistle and a frantic arm wave. A moment later, Lycurgus thundered into the book parlor in all his warrior-like glory. The forceful entry nearly split the door in half. With residual raindrops trickling over his gnarled eye socket, he clinched his spear with a deathlike grip. He then spoke with battle ready anticipation, "Awaiting your orders, Charlamos."

"Lycurgus, I need you to stand watch at this door, and for the time being, do not let anyone enter, and more importantly, do not allow anyone to leave."

The soldier nodded obediently, then met Lex's gaze with his good eye. In that momentary exchange of acknowledgment, she had inadvertently disclosed a hint of discontent with his presence. It was his likeness to Isidore that made her do it and she felt bad because there was something different about this man. She swore she detected a hint of sadness as he quickly looked away; as if he knew his hideously scarred face would frighten her. In a blink, he regained composure and stood stoically at the door determined to carry out his orders to a tee. A strange feeling, although diluted and inconcise, crept into her conscience – pity.

"One more thing," Charlie said, addressing both Lycurgus and Amartus, "I have a feeling that whoever poisoned the flask is still here," he gestured with a chin-cock toward the second floor. Lycurgus, with predatory instinct, nearly abandoned his post as he took a few impulsive strides toward the back stairwell.

"Lycurgus, the door," Charlie reminded him as the giant warrior came to an abrupt halt. He quickly back-stepped to the door following an apologetic grimace.

"I'll call if I need your aid," Charlie assured him. With that, he bounded up the stairs putting Lex in the company of two strangers. She decided that these two must have earned the implicit trust of the great Charlamos. Certainly, he wouldn't leave her with just anybody.

64

Stepping lightly amongst the foreboding shadows of the second floor, Charlie grasped tightly to the weapon beneath his cloak ready to call on it at any moment. His manner resembled a wolf on the prowl. He cocked his head, sniffed the air, and took a few more silent steps before repeating this process. He stopped abruptly, eyes widening. In a flash he wheeled around and there before him, just inches away, was the girl in black.

"You needn't bother with your weapon," she told him in an echoing dialect. "I'm unarmed and do not pose a threat."

"Somehow I find that untrue," he coolly replied. "Whether or not you intend me harm does not alter the fact that you are the first to successfully sneak up on me, and with that I draw the conclusion that you either possess an extensive knowledge of acanthary or you have undergone elite training."

Rather than confirming or denying these accusations, the girl simply stared with hollow eyes as if waiting for him to go on. If Charlie was uneasy in her presence, he did a good job of concealing it. He slid into a nearby chair, crossed his legs comfortably, and looked her over shrewdly. With his arm resting on the wooden table, he tapped out a couple off-beats with his index and middle finger then said, "If you don't mind, I have a few questions for you. I would appreciate it if you took a seat." With his foot, he pushed out a vacant chair, sliding it across the splintery floor in her direction. As he did so, a stack of books plummeted to the floor. Despite the clamor, neither of them, perhaps mistrustful of each other, broke gaze. When she made no motion to sit,

Charlie lounged back, rested his hands behind his head, and took control of the conversation. "Before I ask if you were the one to poison Amartus, I would like to know who you are and where you call home – by the authority of Queen Palas of course."

"You left the girl downstairs. Do you trust the men who watch over her?"

Charlie regarded this question with a beat of inquisitive silence. "I do. But why is her safety such a big concern of yours?"

The zombie-girl smiled, and as if it were common knowledge said, "Alexis is everyone's concern you know."

This observation was enough to bring him to an abrupt stand – his tranquil composure now compromised. "I'm not going to play guessing games with you," he threatened in a domineering tone, "so if you will, tell me how you know Alexis and what you want with her."

"Do you like poems?" asked the girl as she produced a withered old book seemingly from thin air.

He glared, eyes narrowed as if trying to decipher the optimum approach to this situation. Finally, with feigned optimism he replied, "Why yes, I love poetry. I suppose you have a poem for me to read."

"Take heed," said the girl in the most haunting voice yet projected, "satire will not serve you well."

He remained steadfast in his poise although he couldn't conceal a disgruntled glower at the stranger's disregard to his authority. Without so much as glancing at the book, she opened to the desired page and held it out for his retrieval. Guardedly he took it from her. With one eye on the passage and the other on this ghostly girl, he began to read. Before venturing farther than the title, he closed the book and said, "The story of King Uros. I've heard this poem more times than I can count."

"As I'm sure you have," the girl replied, unwavered by his lack of compliance. "Then, if you will, relay to me the significance of the passage."

"I'll humor you," he impatiently responded, "for sake of

time and the fact that I refuse to miss the Trigonous rematch, I'll forgo all the lead-up events and get right to the point. King Uros finds himself faced with the impossible task of having to choose between his city and the woman he loves. If he chooses the woman, the city will fall. If he chooses the city, the woman will die. In the end, he could not reach a decision and as a result, both met an untimely end."

The zombie nodded approvingly. "Very good, brave Charlamos."

"Is this supposed to mean something to me?" he asked, tossing the book onto the table.

"Keep that story in your head and your heart," she instructed. "The time will come when you will have to make a similar decision."

"I'm through with this game," he growled. "I don't have the time or desire to muddle through this riddle. You know more than you should and I want to know how."

Unfazed by this sudden onslaught of brutish demands the girl simply replied, "Now you know how she feels."

"How who feels?"

"Alexis. She too desires information, yet you keep her in the dark."

Charlie went white and slid a hand beneath his cloak for the weapon.

"There's no need for that, Charlamos."

He took a breath and suppressed his unease. "Since you seem to know so much, what would you have me do?"

"I know everything," she confirmed. Charlie made no motion of argument rather just waited for her to explain. "Time is short. You must tell her this day."

"And what of the poem?"

"That poem is a glimpse into your future," she said in a loud voice that sounded like three or four people talking in macabre dialect.

"My future? How?"

"Oh Charlie," she went on now smiling demonically, "you're a smart one. Do I need to spell it out for you?"

"How do you know to call me by that name?" He was now crossing into the realm of furious. The stranger's body-length hair began to rise hauntingly, as if it had been caught in a wind gust – though there was not a hint of breeze in the room.

"You must decide which sacred possession to give up and which to keep. In the end you will only get one. Be careful that your decision is not a selfish one."

Charlie jumped in. "There are many things sacred to me, so why don't you tell me what you're getting at."

"Your two true loves," she obliged. "Your city, and the girl."

"The girl?" questioned Charlie obviously taken aback by this. "You mean Phaedra?"

"Is Phaedra your true love?" the ghastly thing inquired.

He did not answer this directly. He stuttered for a beat then said, "So you're saying I will have to choose between the girl I love and Crow's demise?"

"That is indeed your fate, but not until it comes to that," she said in winged words. "In the meantime, it is your duty to protect and fight for both of them until the time comes to decide."

His face was now cloaked with anger. "How dare you speak down to me. Who are you to give me orders?"

In blithe disregard for his elevating temper the girl continued. "You have so far done your part to protect this city but fail to adequately protect the girl." Charlie teetered on the brink of rage as she continued. "Who do you really love, Charlie? If it is Phaedra, she has been beyond your watchful eye for nearly a year. On her voyage to Eubos, she is accompanied by a clan of soldiers, many of whom would sacrifice their lives not for her protection but for her heart." Charlie's hands involuntarily drew into fists. "And if it is Alexis," the girl went on, "right now, for the second time in this parlor alone, you fail to keep her within sight."

"I have a staggering revelation for you," he declared. "I am always watching over Alexis. As much as you think you know, I know more. As clever as you think you are, I am better. I was watching your encounter with her. I saw you give her the book and heard every word you said. 'Poetry is prophecy,' you told her. You had her read a poem - a poem she deemed to be sad. I did not come to her side right away because I didn't perceive you as a threat and I was curious what you would say. Since I now suspect you of poisoning our good overseer, I very much consider you a threat. Don't ever suppose that my eye is not on her. I am a born spy." He took the tip of his right foot and placed it upon a mangy maroon hardback that sat on the floor. Sliding the book to the side revealed a small fissure in the floorboard and a bird's eye view of Lex, Amartus and Lycurgus directly below them. "You see, I watch her at all times."

The girl offered an approving smile. "Very good, Charlamos," she said, turning away and slowly starting to glide toward the shadows of the back aisles. "You said I was the first person who has ever been able to sneak up on you and now you have succeeded in being the first to prove me wrong...or have you?"

Glowing with confidence from this perceived verbal knockout, he resumed his commanding conduct. "Do not turn away from me. I'm not yet finished with you."

The girl stopped and whirled around to face him. As if what he had just said was irrelevant to her, she offered a comment contrary to expectation. "It is now clear who you truly love." She smiled to herself as if bemused by her own formulations. "In love with one and courting another. Your city would fall if that ever got out."

The fury swept over Charlie like a gale force wind. "Blasphemy is good enough to land you in Tartarus!"

From the first floor came the muffled yet distinctively concerned voice of Lycurgus - "Charlamos?"

Charlie did not answer. In less than a heartbeat his bladed staff was revolved into full extension and rested threateningly on the skin of the demon's throat. She cackled insanely at the gesture. Suddenly, from seemingly nowhere, she conjured a whirlwind of such ferocity, it lifted every book from the table hurling them through the air. In seconds, the scene resembled a snow globe of chaos. Charlie was pelted violently with books and whapped repeatedly in the face by stray pages. It was all he could do to block the assaulting objects that were flying from all angles with excruciating velocity. Then, her fanatic laughter stopped. The books halted in midair and dropped to the floor in an earthshaking clamor. Resuming an expression of dire seriousness, she said, "Choose wisely."

"You are under arr…" Charlie yelled but it was too late. In a sickening and terrifying display of spontaneous combustion, the girl went up in flames then disappeared amongst the very fire that consumed her. Just smoke and ashes remained in her wake. There was no longer any trace of the black-haired, porcelain skin girl.

Lex, Lycurgus and Amartus appeared at Charlie's side, the latter two bearing weapons. They were just in time to witness their beloved leader hurl his own weapon to the ground in rage.

"Son of a bitch!" he cried out breathlessly, disregarding his own rule of foregoing English. Quickly, however, he regained poise upon noticing the others standing there.

65

Right away, Amartus began the tedious task of reorganizing the upstairs area following the events that had transpired between Charlie and the hollow-eyed girl. The books and pages had been strewn about in such a manner that reorganizing it all seemed unfeasible. All the while he emanated a feeling of guilt, as though he had somehow let Charlamos down. Several other Crow Soldiers had been summoned to assist with anything from perimeter guard duty and parlor search to clean up.

Charlie would not disclose to Lex, Amartus, or Lycurgus the details of his encounter with the zombie girl. His explanation for secrecy was that the high council must first be consulted. While waiting downstairs, they had heard raised voices and several sporadic thumps, but beyond that they were oblivious to the altercation. One thing was certain, whatever happened had truly shaken him up. The belligerent dispersal of his weapon and the swear word that ensued was the first time Lex had ever witnessed him lose his cool.

The first order of business had been to locate the poem of the crow. Though Lex remembered definitively where she had put it before fleeing with her tail between her legs, the book, of course, was no longer there. Charlie found this to be of little surprise.

While Amartus and the half dozen Crow Soldiers turned the premises upside-down for any clue as to who the girl was or how she managed to escape, Charlie sat Lex down and questioned her about the poem she was instructed to read. Of course, he had been clandestinely observing the confrontation, staring upward through a floor board separation while perched atop a bookshelf on the first floor. At that time he had been unaware that the girl in black was the one Lex had seen in the market and then the alley yesterday. He had just assumed that she was just some ordinary, innocent citizen who had been visiting the book parlor. While he gazed up through the floorboards, he had his bladed staff in hand, ready to plunge it through the ceiling and skewer this stranger if the situation had called for it. The only puzzle pieces he lacked were the words Lex had read silently to herself.

Though she could not recite the poem verbatim, she did well at recalling the premise of the melancholic story - someone running through the forest searching for a lost child, following a crow, trusting the bird to lead the way. The child is found. The child dies.

"That's pretty much it," she said, driven by nervous energy to sit completely upright in her chair.

Always the antithesis to Lex's proper English posture, Charlie was slouched tactlessly in his chair with both outstretched legs resting on a stack of books. He held his now collapsed weapon out to one side, twirling it in his fingers like a baton. He shook his head and replied, "I tell you, Lex, I'm truly baffled. What significance, if any, does that poem have in regard to you? Who is this girl? Of all my years studying acanthary, I've never seen such a disappearing act. I never thought it possible."

Lex threw out a clay pigeon, "Maybe she's a god." To her surprise, he didn't shoot it down.

"Whatever she is," he replied, "I don't think she's human."

She couldn't argue with him on that presupposition. "Oh," she remembered with a flare of avidity, "I forgot to mention that the poem was written in English. Is that of any importance?"

He went still, eyes widening. "Impossible," he uttered, falling immediately spellbound. "Are you certain?"

"Of course I'm certain."

"Impossible," he repeated. "English just doesn't exist on this earth. It's…well impossible."

"I think that on this earth, 'impossible' has a different

meaning," she acutely informed him, remembering how she could not get the word out of her brain after coming through the pool yesterday.

He actually cracked a smile at this and said, "A new mystery to add to the pile of old mysteries. The others will love to hear about this one."

"Are you worried? About the girl I mean?"

"No," he answered right away as if anticipating this very question. "As far as I can gather, she meant neither of us harm. I have reached this conclusion in light of the fact that she could have attacked either of us while we were alone with her, but as you know she made no such threat. Also, as I have already mentioned, her ability to vanish in flames defies any act of acanthary that I or my teacher, Theophilus, have ever seen or heard of. This makes her an anomaly and a powerful one. That kind of power, or ability if you will, could have been used against either of us, but again, it wasn't."

Lex nodded in understanding and said, "That makes sense. But if harm wasn't her intent, what was?"

"That's the million dollar question," he said. "I feel that it's safe to say neither encounter was coincidental. Those who have accrued such a vast knowledge of acanthary do not randomly haunt dark, dingy book parlors just for something to do. She was waiting for us and had predetermined which poem we were to read - yours about a crow, and mine, the tale of King Uros."

She knew it would likely be a waste of breath to ask him who King Uros was. He had already made it clear that everything that had happened was confidential until further notice. She opened up the filing cabinet in her brain and placed "King Uros" with all the other unknowns.

Following a thorough search of the book parlor, which frustratingly revealed nothing about the mysterious girl, her mode of entry or exit, or the origin of Amartus' tainted boreberry juice, Charlie and Lex found themselves back outside in the alley following the sounds of a roaring crowd toward the main street.

"Besides," he had said to Lex as they first stepped back into the rainy outdoors, "there's not much more I can do but bring up this matter to the high council."

Oddly, Lex had, dare she say, enjoyed this little book parlor incident. Realizing that she had probably underestimated the significance of the situation, she couldn't help but extract from it a bit of excitement, almost as if she had found herself caught in the middle of a medieval mystery novel with the privilege of witnessing it unfold first hand. Though the girl in black had been quite frightening to look at, Lex had not felt as though her life was in danger during their encounter. Her instincts were saying that this gothic stranger was not necessarily a friend, but neither was she a foe. She also knew she could be dead wrong about that.

The air was saturated with precipitation. She observed her breath puff out like smoke then quickly dissipate until the next followed suit. Water spilled over the brim of her hood and down onto the muddy, rutted alley way. Despite Nature's tormenting conditions, she remained comfortably warm and dry as a bone. She couldn't help but once again bestow full appreciation upon the amazingly utilitarian clothing Charlie had given her. So far they had lived up to their high expectations.

Just ahead, the alleyway opened to the main street where a thick wall of people had formed across the mouth of this intersection. Hearing excited banter from above, she looked up to observe dozens of people lining the rooftops. It didn't take a genius to determine that there must be or was about to be a parade of some sort. Meanwhile, Charlie was busy assessing the quickest route to get to the roof.

"This way," he instructed eagerly, taking her by the cloak sleeve and pulling her toward an assortment of random items piled next to a horse stable. With commendable effort, he arranged three bales of hay, five paneled barrels, an empty wooden cart, and a pile of rocks in such a fashion that a make-shift staircase was created. It was impossible for Lex to disregard the wobbliness of the structure but recounted many times in her life when she had undergone braver exploits.

Suddenly, like an explosion of dynamite, the crowd burst forth with a mixture of applause and screaming. It was then that she began to feel the ground rumble. Within the water puddles at her feet, ripples appeared reflecting the earth's vibrations. A scene from Jurassic Park flashed through her mind.

Charlie bounded onto the lowest hay bale of his improvised staircase and reached out for her hand. "Lex, hurry," he beckoned. "We must get to the roof. Trust me, you don't want to miss this."

66

Lex attributed her successful ascension onto the slippery rooftop to the agility acquired from years of gymnastics. On the final athletic leap from the highest wobbly barrel, the entire structure had collapsed. The ruckus caused several previously preoccupied spectators to wheel around at the commotion. Charlie was there to grasp her arms and stabilize her teetering body against the possibility of a backwards tumble.

"You will find a ladder in the back," a man quickly mentioned before refocusing his attention to the street. Charlie looked at Lex with a guilty grin and shrugged.

The wet wooden shingles were slick as snot making her thankful for the functional traction of her modern trail boots. This was a luxury others on the rooftop did not share as they stood stiffly, unwilling to make abrupt movements in trepidation of plunging right over the edge. What was going on, she wondered, that necessitated such a risk to secure this high perch? In an instant, the answer was clear.

At first sight of the cyclopes, she inadvertently clung to Charlie's arm in fear that their lives might be in danger. These creatures, possibly several hundred of them, formed a massive unit that snaked off into the misty horizon. They shook the earth as they marched through the deafening gauntlet of Crow spectators toward the coliseum. She could only infer at the average height of this monstrous race, deliberating nine feet to be a valid estimate.

They walked erect like a man, their gargantuan ape-like arms extending to their knees to meet watermelon-sized fists. Brown and black fur covered their bodies with trace evidence of pale skin beneath. Their stern faces, reflecting no other emotion than the business at hand, bared mouths of crookedly pointed teeth surrounded by a perimeter of black lips. Large pointy ears, flattened noses mostly obscured by fur, and small elliptical foreheads summed up the cyclopes' facial anatomy. And of course, the predominant trademark - a single nefarious eye residing directly in the mid-forehead.

Approximately half of the motley clan wore clothing, mostly in the form of leather toga-like garments saturated with rain and spattered with mud. The other half, chiefly male, paraded along completely naked, that is if you weren't counting thick beds of matted hair that did little to conceal enormous genitals that swayed like metronomes, keeping rhythm with their respective owners' lumbering pace.

"Cyclopes and man have always maintained a stable, yet fragile coexistence," Charlie explained to Lex, who was still adjusting to the shocking spectacle, jaw locked in the dropped position. "One of my goals upon constructing the coliseum was to strengthen the ties between us."

"It doesn't make sense," she stated. "How can the bond between humans and cyclopes be strengthened if they arrive in Crow only to be booed, then defeated in the arena?"

"You've got it all wrong, Lex. Listen to the crowd," he instructed. She did so and realized that the majority of the audience did indeed greet the parade of monsters with a welcoming ovation. Only occasionally did a stray boo rise up amongst the cheers. "You can't control every idiot out there, even if you impose consequences for discourteous behavior. As a majority, the citizens of Crow understand the importance of accepting the cyclopes into our city with open arms."

"Why so delicate an alliance?" she then asked.

"You'll probably find this interesting," he said. "Do you remember the part in Homer's Odyssey, where the ship of King Odysseus runs ashore on the land of the cyclopes?"

She indeed remembered that part, primarily because it

stood out in her mind as a disturbing and violent encounter between man and beast. If her memory was accurate, Odysseus and several of his crew had been held prisoner in the cave of the Cyclops, Polyphemus, following an unsuccessful attempt to befriend the beast. Polyphemus had gone about his daily business as usual, breaking routine only to torture, kill, then eat his captives. One by one Odysseus' men fell victim to this doom until the few survivors hatched a desperate escape plan. Lowering the gullible beast's guard with wine, the men blinded Polyphemus by driving a fire spit through his eye and by doing so, made their escape.

"And that is where it all went sour," Charlie said after Lex had recounted these events aloud. He was talking very softly in close proximity to her ear. "This of course is regarded as mythology on Earth A, but here on Earth B, the story can be found in every history book. Just one more indefinite connection between the two earths, and another miniscule piece of a larger-than-life puzzle."

After several exciting minutes, the tail-end of the cyclopes parade emerged from the foggy distance. This was when she saw him for the first time and knew exactly who he was without a word from Charlie. Standing a half meter taller than the other cyclops, Xenogorus tromped violently down the cobblestone street. Anyone who met his angry gaze turned away apprehensively. Horses whinnied and high-stepped in a panic as their owners scrambled to calm them. Urgent dog barking could now be heard over the subdued clamor of the masses. A restrained hush fell over the crowd as he passed, so as not to attract his unwanted attention.

Besides sheer size, there were other demoralizing features of this perilous beast that set him apart from the others. Xenogorus displayed a physical build such that each bulging arm resembled a bag of bowling balls, and each gargantuan leg, a silo of boulders. He was also shaggier than the rest of his breed, with a thick mane of gristly black fur. Instead of fingernails, this Cyclops had razor-like claws that were prepped for just such an occasion.

With bulky metal armor strapped to his chest, thighs and forearms, Xenogorus had committed little effort to concealing a grotesque, scabbed symbol carved deeply within the flesh of his back. This was the reminder of his loss just two days ago. He carried in his hands a rusty, or bloody, linked chain that, once unleashed, could cover a vast radius with devastating possibilities. The way he clutched the limb-shattering weapon verified that he had no intention of suffering another defeat.

From Lex's unease, an influx of admiration and intrigue crept in. This Trigonous, she thought, must be the very definition of brave. She herself couldn't imagine ever engaging such a creature in combat. She simply marveled at the one who could, and did, and will again. The idea of standing in a coliseum with a frenzy of eyes staring down as she stood before the grizzly brute, was enough to send a cold shiver down her spinal column. It would also be enough to give her nightmares.

There was no sleigh-bound Santa being toted by a gaggle of reindeer at the conclusion of this parade – only a hellish one-eyed gorilla bent on retribution. Once the monsters had passed, the masses of Crow citizens, including Charlie and Lex, shuffled through the downpour and under the grand stone archway of the coliseum. Many around them cursed the weather but showed no sign of abandoning to the warm dry refuge of their homes. The cyclopes had already gathered in a menacing collection of fur and eyes, occupying a portion of seating Lex likened to a visitor's section. The rest of the coliseum was filling rapidly as people filed in from every angle and doorway, from arena level all the way up to the gray sky.

The lower levels offered optimal viewing of the muddy battlefield, and of course this is where the bright hued clothing of the nobles congregated. Many of these sections had granite overhangs to shelter the fortunate ones from the elements, making all who had to endure without this luxury, ravenously envious. In comparison to last evening in the great hall, this gathering of human and Cyclops was bigger, louder and even more intense.

Electrifying commotion inundated the senses.

With a hand on her back, Charlie guided Lex across the arena toward a section of seating where white marble faded into lustrous gold. This roomy, elegant, protected section housed Queen Palas, Theophilus, a score of soldiers, and much to Lex's delight, Sevastian. The high council members sat upon weighty marble chairs, endowed with cushions and garnished with decorative engravings of vines and leaves. Several of these royal seats were currently unoccupied and it could be assumed that she and Charlie would soon alter that status. Climbing a flight of slippery rock stairs from arena level, the pair arrived at the golden dream seats and took a load off between Theophilus and Sevastian.

"Brave Charlamos, ever refusing to embrace your noble roots," Theophilus observed with a twinkle in his eye.

"My friend," Charlie replied, "I was showing Alexis around the city, therefore as it is made obvious by this unwavering rain, these cloaks of Glast sheep wool were the ideal choice for just such a day."

Theophilus, with a happy grin winked at Lex and said, "I do not know whether it is worse to allow our honored guest, this lovely girl of song, to walk about the city dressed as a commoner, or provide her with gleaming garments only to have her shiver."

Queen Palas, who was casually overhearing the exchange added, "Alexis may of course dress however she desires, wise Theophilus." Theophilus, who had selected a brilliant auburn robe for the occasion, nodded agreeingly. Lex couldn't help but feel a bit cheerier at the sight of the great acanthar's unrelenting happiness.

The queen, she observed, looked even more beautiful this rainy morning than she had last night, if that was even possible. Again, Palas opted for white, but this time it was a heavier cloth dress that shielded her arms and legs from the elements. A separate hood-like garment, laced with soft white fur covered her head, as vibrant curls of midnight-black hair poured outward. Her only accoutrement was a silver necklace with a green leaf charm resting upon her chest. As Lex was taking this in, she couldn't disregard the curious and joyful way in which Palas and Theophilus reacted to her presence. They made no effort to be discrete about this, smiling in reverence every time they met her green eyes.

Heavy thudding footfalls arose from the overhang above. Their magnitude sounded as if a Cyclops had wandered over to the Crow section. Not quite a Cyclops, but just as perilous, Isidore peered over the edge and down upon the elite inhabitants of this golden viewing section. Charlie shot him an acknowledging nod of the head. Isidore then stood erect, arms crossed authoritatively so that all in the arena could see that he alone had the privilege of watching over the high council. The beastly flail-bearer resumed a statue-still stance as cold rain plummeted upon him like millions of kamikaze bombers. Lex, not yet entirely warm to this man, couldn't ignore the feeling of relief that he would not be sitting with the rest of the high council during the exhibition. And yet, she did appreciate the idea that Isidore, seemingly an impenetrable wall of a human, was standing over her like a personal guardian angel - only not a beautiful angel like her childhood fairytales would have her imagine.

The coliseum was now beyond capacity. The citizens of Crow were squeezed into any available seat they could find. Many women sat atop the laps of men and many others were forced to stand along the stairways, offering company to the soldiers already posted there. The last seats to fill were those in close proximity to the cyclopes. Those who chanced sitting there were afforded a meager yard or two of buffer space between themselves and the hairy giants. Lex decided that being packed in like sardines would ultimately elicit added warmth to the majority of unlucky souls without shelter. This thought, however, was perhaps a justification to mask the guilt she felt while observing those outside the golden overhang shivering miserably as water poured down their faces into saturated garments.

Despite it all, anticipatory excitement spilled from the structure out into the misty gray sky. To her left, Theophilus and

Palas were now in conversation. Even though the exorbitant background noise made their discussion inaudible, Lex could tell that they were likely talking about her as could be inferred by the countless side-glances. Redirecting attention to the right, she found Charlie updating Sevastian on the book parlor situation. The Russian listened wide-eyed and speechless, racking his brain for an explanation but coming up short.

"And the book of poetry from which Lex read, was nowhere to be found. If that isn't enough to boggle your mind, get this - the book was written in English," Charlie informed him, wrapping up his account of the events.

"Finding this girl in black should be our primary focus moving forward," Sevastian concluded. "We must leave no stone returned."

"Unturned," Charlie corrected.

"An entity which can vanish in flames," Sevastian continued, "may very well be some sort of a god."

Lex chimed in, "That's what I said."

"But if that were true, how can an Earth B god possess a poem written in an Earth A language?" Charlie uttered. "And she…it…whatever, called me Charlie, my Earth A name."

"And she clearly knows all about Lex," Sevastian added with a hint of alarm in his tone.

"Poetry is prophecy," Charlie whispered to himself several times. "What the hell is that supposed to mean?"

Confusion befell the three and the choking grip of perplexity confined them to momentary silence. Upon bearing witness to Sevastian's reaction, Lex felt even more fearful about the possibility of someone trying to get to her. It wasn't until the crowd suddenly erupted in raucous excitement, when they were finally pulled from their thought-filled trances.

It was interesting how rapidly Charlie and Sevastian kicked their concern over the book parlor incident to the curb, as a huge golden gate directly below them was hoisted open by means of a pulley system. Xenogorus thundered into the arena in a terrifying display of intimidation. The citizens of Crow forced accepting applause as the chilling roars from the ferocious warrior echoed throughout the coliseum. The loudest ovation was from the cyclopes section, which filled the air with low, dreadful roaring. With malevolence in his eye, Xenogorus swung his sinister chain through the air with such velocity, it clipped the side of a nearby pillar, splitting it right in two.

"He's irate this day," Sevastian commented to no one in particular.

In the next moment, he and Charlie were wagering how long it would take for Trigonous to bring the monster down. Sevastian ventured that it would all be over in about twenty minutes, postulating that Trigonous could do it sooner, but would opt to toy with Xenogorus, as he had done the day before last. Charlie, on the other hand, reminded his companion that it was just such toying that caused Trigonous' near defeat and speculated that the cloaked warrior would end it much sooner. The wager was not gold or money, as this was of no benefit to either of them. Instead, of course, it was food – a full-fledged home cooked meal of the victor's choice.

Lex on the other hand, decided not to join in on the wager. For one thing, if it hadn't been for Xenogorus actually losing two days ago, she wouldn't have believed it possible. Today he was more angry and probably more motivated. She couldn't see the sense in gambling on his defeat. Furthermore, she couldn't shake the incessant feeling of nervousness that had been clinging to her ever since arriving in this world. This feeling coupled with the violent battle about to transpire, was enough to make her queasy.

67

Eventually, the chaos died down. This was when the queen, full of authoritative grace, rose to her feet. Lex, following the example of the other high-council members, also stood. Charlie pointed out to the masses of spectators who all followed suit. "This is how we demonstrate our respect to Trigonous," he whispered as everything fell astonishingly silent. Lex watched with interest as thousands of eyes darted this way and that, all determined to be the first to spot the hero. She remembered what Charlie had told her about Trigonous' surprise entrances.

A pearly white serpent, as majestic as it was malign, slithered toward the center of the muddy arena from an undetermined origin. Sevastian was the first to spy the ivory creature and wasted no time pointing it out. Thousands watched with interest as the snake approached Xenogorus, stopping just outside of his chain's deadly reach. Soon another came forth exactly like the first, appearing from somewhere around the opposite side of the arena. As if Medusa had just received a haircut, legions of white serpents began swarming through the sloshy earth toward the coliseum's core. Without altering his stone cold expression of vengeance, Xenogorus looked on as the snakes congregated into a living mound of alabaster scales, crimson tongues, and slitted eyes.

"This is a new one," Charlie whispered to Sevastian with a

smirk of sheer amusement. A ferocious thunder clap rocked the atmosphere and the black clouds above unleashed a cataclysm of trenchant rain. That was when Lex saw Trigonous for the first time.

A black hood appeared in the middle of the snake congregation. Then a figure slowly arose, shrouded in pure black, ascending through the floor of reptiles as if rising from hell. Giant serpents entwined themselves upon the body of Trigonous, slithering over the shoulders and around the neck of this hooded spectacle. Beneath the hood resided a haunting emptiness, a faceless black void, as if this person or creature lacked basic elements essential to life - like a head. In his black-gloved hands, were two sleek double-edged swords.

Lightning shot through the sky in networks of blinding arrays. Basking in Zeus's electric illumination, Trigonous raised both weapons high into the air so that Crow may acknowledge their hero. As he did so, the city reciprocated with an eruption of praising applause to such a degree, that Lex had to shield her ears from the painful decibels. A split second later, praise was washed away by an influx of terror.

While Trigonous had his back turned, Xenogorus seized the opportunity for a rancorous cheap shot. As if it were happening in slow motion, Lex watched the devastating chain weapon of the Cyclops swing back over his head, then accelerate toward Trigonous. As the bloody end of the chain came within centimeters of the hooded hero's extended arm, he dodged the bullet by leaping over the sea of snakes and double-rolled across the muddy soil. He sprung back to his feet facing the monster with both swords at the ready. Crow roared.

Missing the intended target, Xenogorus's chain sliced into the mound of snakes sending scales, blood and vertebrae airborne in all directions. With cadenced chants bellowing from the crowd, the giant Cyclops made several more attempts at dismembering Trigonous. Each time, Crow's hero allowed the last deathly link to come within a finger's length before quickly throwing his head to one side. It was as if this masochistic warrior enjoyed death whispering in his ear.

Sickeningly absurd, Lex thought as she took it all in with a racing heart.

Xenogorus, doing nothing to mask his mounting rage, tried once again for a successful strike with his chain. This time, during the split second when the chain hung in limbo between its maximum extension and initiation of retraction, Trigonous, with unbelievable hand-eye coordination, reached out, caught the chain, and yanked it with such force that the Cyclops lost his grip. As quick as the lightning zapping above, Xenogorus dove head first through the air and was able to recapture his weapon before it became custody of Trigonous.

The Cyclops was pelted with stinging rain and pummeled by berserk wind as he dexterously leapt to his feet. A vivid lightning bolt and a bone rattling thunder clap ushered in Trigonous's trump card. Lex watched with an upturned stomach as the hooded warrior launched both swords spinning through the air with such surgical precision, that they simultaneously lodged themselves into the giant's knee caps. Xenogorus roared in pain. His legs gave out and he fell to the ground so hard, Lex swore she felt the earth shake. The wounded beast instinctively allowed his right knee to make initial contact with the ground in an attempt to break the fall. This action drove the sword so far into his knee that the silver tip popped through the skin on the other side bringing with it streams of arterial spray. Xenogorus's chilling roars had now faded into gut wrenching moans of pain, like a deer after being struck by the hunter's arrow without the luxury of a speedy death. Moving in step with the echoing chants from the audience, Trigonous circled the Cyclops like a wolf. The rain was pouring so hard, their images were nearly lost in obscurity.

For the first time since she saw him emerge from the foggy horizon, Lex felt pity for Xenogorus. Empathy was always her greatest virtue, but if she wanted to survive in this world she thought, it would certainly be a weakness. She harbored this notion while Trigonous, apparently lacking any kind of mercy, kicked the downed beast in the face so forcefully, that the Cyclops flipped backward spewing a throng of muddy droplets into the air. Charlie and Sevastian were now jumping in celebratory joy. Lex couldn't contribute to the enthusiastic cheers of the masses, it just wasn't in her. She was beginning to realize that she was not cut out to witness such violence. Seeing this brutality in person was much different than watching it from behind a bucket of popcorn at the movie theater.

The rain eased, prepping the stage for the final act. Trigonous ripped the sword from Xenogorus's left knee causing him to howl in agony. The cyclopes in the visitor's section were quiet, heads hung at the impending defeat of their own hero. Xenogorus raised his hand to Trigonous – an obvious sign of surrender along with the unspoken message that enough was enough. In a tyrannical display of ruthlessness, Trigonous looked down upon his opponent with an outstretched arm, palm up as if he wanted something. Lex thought she caught a look of fright in the eye of the black beast. After a moment's hesitation and the crowd's resounding roars pouring down on him like anvils, Xenogorus grasped the handle of the sword still buried in his right knee, closed his eye, and yanked it out as blood and synovial fluid squirted in all directions. To his credit, he succeeded in restraining another wailing outburst. The Cyclops accepted defeat by placing the blood-caked weapon back into Trigonous' hand.

Lex didn't want to watch Trigonous' next order of business but couldn't peel away her gaze. Xenogorus obediently lowered himself into a prone position on the sloppy arena floor. He shamefully pressed his face to the ground in anticipation for a torturous déjá vu.

Charlie whispered to Lex, "Just remember, this is better than death - maybe." She nodded in understanding, then winced as Trigonous set to work, ripping open the scabs on his opponent's back with the sword's tip, and retracing the identifying symbol that had only just begun to heal. With his face buried, the Cyclops emitted muffled moans of misery and suffering as he was made an example of in front of thousands… check mate.

And that was that. Whether from pain or excessive blood loss, Xenogorus had fallen unconscious. Trigonous had yet another victory notch on his belt. Charlie had won the bet against Sevastian and Lex became the inauspicious recipient of an upset stomach. A handful of cyclopes lumbered out to lift Xenogorus off the battlefield. Trigonous made a quick exit through a golden doorway below. Praising chants from Crow's ecstatic citizens followed the hooded hero until he faded into the blackness of the coliseum's underworld. The golden doors thundered shut, barely audible amongst the vociferous tumult.

68

The Moskincov house was dark and chilly as Lex, Charlie and Sevastian stumbled in through the front door. They had avoided the congestion of the mass evacuation by utilizing a convenient stairwell located behind the seat of the Queen. This took them along a torch-lit pathway to a guarded door at the back side, and a stone's throw from Sevastian's little residence.

Before parting ways, and out of earshot from all but the high council members, Palas had said to Charlie, "It is uncertain how much time remains before the final divination comes to pass." She looked at Lex as she spoke, indicating that this bamboozling statement pertained to her in some way, shape, or form. "You have volunteered to take this in your hands, Charlamos. I know that you will do what needs to be done."

All eyes were on Lex before Charlie replied, "I will make certain she is informed today." After this concise exchange, Palas and Theophilus had been escorted back to the castle by a squadron of Crow Soldiers, and Charlie, Lex and the Russian made for the Moskincov house.

Instead of discussing the thrilling highlights of Trigonous' seemingly effortless triumph as expected, the boys jumped immediately back into conversation regarding the book parlor and the girl in black, the strange hauntress who defied their understanding of normality. This perhaps illustrated the urgency of the situation. Sevastian muddled about the house nervously, drawing curtains over the windows and locking the door. Charlie seemed especially tense. Intuition told Lex that her time was coming, to finally find out what the hell was going on and to break free from the confining chains of unawareness.

She stood near the bed, arms crossed and looking rather stern. Her evident frustration, an intended beacon of desired enlightenment, was on the table. At the moment, nobody spoke. Sevastian gathered some wood and kindling that had been neatly stacked by the hearth and proceeded to build a fire as Charlie slid the table away from the rug that covered the trap door to the cellar. She wondered what their intentions were.

Suddenly, there was a distinct noise from below the floorboards. Everyone stopped dead in their tracks and listened. The sound they had just heard was the bulky shelf of rattling jars sliding to one side, this much Lex knew. The question – who's down there? She had assumed that the only ones who were aware that the secret passageway existed were standing right here in front of her.

With haste, Charlie ripped back the rug and Sevastian flung open the trapdoor. The boys snatched oil lamps from the mantle and motioned for Lex to join them as they stampeded down the steep stairs to the cellar. Straight away, she saw a dark figure standing motionless in the tunnel's opening, the silhouette vaguely familiar. But it couldn't be, could it? In the next instant her suspicions were confirmed and out of fear, she stumbled several steps back up the stairs. Sevastian raised the oil lamp and the dancing firelight eclipsed the sinister black cloak of Trigonous.

69

"I can see by the look on your face that they have told you little of Trigonous," Jade said as she stepped forward pulling the hood down to reveal her painted face of ebony. She darted over to Lex, who remained petrified as a fossil. There was coagulated Cyclops blood on the black cloak, reflecting the torch beams with a metallic sheen as Jade threw her arms around her friend. The boys doubled over in laughter at Lex's flabbergasted expression.

"If someone would have told me an hour ago that I'd be hugging Trigonous, I would have thought them mental," she declared in a quivering dialect.

"I felt so bad for you the other night," Jade said, proceeding to disrobe the disguise, "in the kitchen, remember? You happened in on us while we were mending Sevastian's arm. I wanted to tell you everything right then and there, but you would have thought I was insane. You see that now, don't you?"

"I certainly would have," agreed Lex, who was just thrilled to have Jade back in the picture, convinced that she would be more straight forward than Charlie and Sevastian had been. "But I can't say I find you any less insane for going one-on-one with that Cyclops," she went on to mention.

"Yeah, you're probably right about that," Jade replied. "But it's just so invigorating."

Lex had to laugh out loud at that one. "Invigoration to me is a brisk walk on a winter morning, not skydiving without a parachute," she proclaimed. She then had an appraisal of the two doors in the cellar. "One door leads to my room, one door leads to the coliseum," she said, recalling aloud what Sevastian had told her the day prior. "Makes a bit more sense now."

Jade tossed Trigonous' cloak haphazardly into the dingy corner, then slid the shelf back over the entrance of the secret passageway.

"Surprised?" Charlie asked Lex.

"I should say so," she replied, finally starting to loosen up.

"The snakes were a nice touch," Sevastian commended. "Where did you learn such acanthary?"

"Saving it for a special occasion," Jade proudly remarked. "You're right, Sevastian, Xenogorus is certainly more menacing when you're standing face to face with him."

He chuckled lightly, "I saw no problems from your end. In fact I was hoping you'd stick it out a bit longer, just for our viewing pleasure."

"The pressure of being undefeated is heavy and honestly, I just wanted the win," she explained. "I let him whip that chain around for a while - tire himself out. When I saw his endurance fading, I just went for it."

"What made you choose to ignore the cardinal rule of combat?" Charlie asked Jade as they all tromped noisily up the stairs. Thanks to the fire, the living room was now brighter and pleasantly warm.

"Cardinal rule of combat?" Lex interjected, desiring an explanation before the conversation further progressed.

"Never part with your weapon during battle," he clarified as he dropped the trap door back into place and helped Sevastian roll the rug back over it.

"Hey, it worked on the Chimera, right?" Jade said nonchalantly. "I had a good feeling about it." She then turned to Lex. "Important to remember, if you're going to part with your weapon, better be damn confident in your ability to hit the target." Lex nodded but couldn't imagine when this lesson would ever pertain to her.

"I can't believe *you're* Trigonous," she said, as the girls took a seat at the table. Charlie sat as well while Sevastian placed a kettle of potatoes on the fire.

"Sometimes," Jade answered vaguely.

"Sometimes?" But before an explanation was offered, the pieces flew together in Lex's keen mind. Two days ago, Xenogorus and Trigonous faced off for the first time. Trigonous had nearly been defeated as a result of an arm injury. A scene flashed through her memory – Sevastian sitting on the kitchen counter, Jade running stitches through his bloody arm wound. When did the kitchen incident take place? Two days ago. Then, when she had questioned Charlie about Trigonous, he had told her that Crow's hero fought with three weapons. Three weapons – three - tri. Her startling revelation was that the number three was not about the weapons, but rather the number of people that assumed the role.

"You're all Trigonous?" she asked in bewilderment.

Charlie administered an approving nod and a golf clap, his usual means of congratulations, before saying, "And of course that is why Trigonous' identity must be confidential. Only the high council members are privy to this information."

"I know the disguise reveals little, but really? No one notices?" she wondered aloud. "What about the height discrepancy between you and Sevastian?"

"Are you calling me short?" Sevastian snorted while adding a palm-full of salt to the potatoes.

"Barring recent events, one hundred days pass between fights, so an outsider has difficulty taking Trigonous' height into account. Also, Sevastian wears some thick-soled boots when he fights to even him out." He made a smirk while ignoring a spiteful eye from Sevastian.

"But why," Lex prodded, "do you subject yourselves to such risk? Why do you voluntarily battle the best warriors in this world?"

"Practice," Jade casually replied as she used a wet cloth to wipe the black paint, or whatever it was, from her face, "to keep our skills sharp."

"Why?" Lex pressed. "Crow isn't at war, right? What are you training for?"

"We're not sure yet," Jade answered, "but as I'm sure you've gathered from the oracle's final divination, something big is about to happen."

"The who's final what?" Lex asked as confused as ever. At this junction, Charlie's face turned white as a sheet. If looks could kill, he would have been dead on the floor, sliced in half by Jade's razor glare.

"You haven't told her?" Charlie's hesitation provided enough time for Jade to fly from her chair in fury. "What is the matter with you – with both of you?" she shouted, flipping the relaxed mood one hundred and eighty degrees to tense. "You promised you'd tell her as soon as she arrived." She then turned this unexpected verbal onslaught upon Sevastian. "You always go along with my idiot cousin, even when his decisions are poor. "And you," she snapped, turning back to Charlie who was slumped down in his chair like a frightened child, "Are you planning on waiting until her fortieth birthday? For god's sake, Charlie, her life, her whole life will be altered by what you have thus far refused to disclose."

"Look, Jade," he said, forcing himself upright in a seemingly valiant attempt to defend his position. "I know what we had agreed to, but if you'll just hear me out, I know you will concur with my decision."

Jade eyed him threateningly as she slammed her body back into the chair facing him. She tapped her mud-caked fingernails across the table with an allegro cadence. "Go on then," she said.

He then proceeded with a lengthy recount of everything that had happened since Lex had awakened on the grassy hill, sparing not a singular detail. He spoke of her fainting spell at the forest pool, her exchange with Delias, her exchange with Isidore, her performance at the Crow theater, Queen Palas' reaction to the new soloist, the congregation in the Queen's chambers, the mystery girl at the market and her reappearance in the dark alley, then the book parlor. He painted Jade a vivid picture of a stranger's introduction to a new world and how the stranger's logical mind refused to accept the new world as a reality. Even Lex, who had carried the burden of frustration over Charlie's insufferable secrecy, could now appreciate his decisions thus far. Jade listened with a surprising amount of patience, interrupting not once. When all had been told, she sat in silence for a moment deep in thought, staring unblinkingly at the dripping candle in the center of the table.

Finally, she said, "Okay, Charlie, I see your point. I'm sorry to you, and," she looked to Sevastian who was casually slouched against the wall by the hearth, "I'm sorry to you as well." They each nodded their forgiveness. "But most of all," Jade continued, "I'm sorry to you, Lex. You've been tossed overboard and expected to swim. We all kept secrets from you, and though we believed we had good reason to do so, we felt terrible about it. This is why our initial plan was to tell you everything as soon as you stepped through the pool. But, as Charlie has pointed out, and as I'm sure you can see, things were not that simple. You've had to swallow a lot, and I'm afraid you must now swallow even more, because the biggest secret can no longer wait. Brace yourself, mentally I mean. I cannot promise you'll be thrilled."

"Please," Lex beckoned, pulse quickening, "tell me whatever you need to tell me. I'm ready."

"Like the ice cave," Jade replied, "this secret is better for show than for tell. There will be no more delay, save a brisk walk from here to the castle. Come on, we're leaving this instant."

"What about the potatoes?" Sevastian asked meekly. "Lunch is nearly ready." Jade did not respond to this verbally, but her sharp look provoked him to hastily remove the kettle of steaming spuds from the hearth and scurry to the front door to join the others who were already on their way out.

And that was how Jade operated - no-nonsense, to the

point, tell it like it is. Lex appreciated that approach, but the comment about bracing herself mentally made her strikingly aware that the time for answers was at hand. This made her nervous, but damn it, how long had she waited for it all to come out? Charlie's step-by-step technique, though reasonable, had been doggedly agonizing. This grand unveiling was what she had been waiting for, yearning for. She forced her jitters into submission and nodded resolutely to herself. Let's see what this is really all about, she thought, secretly wondering if she would be ready for whatever was in store.

70

The short time spent indoors was enough for the weather to make a notable change for the better. Although it was still damp and chilly, the melancholy gray was transitioning to soft blue and the ominous dark clouds had cleared out leaving wispy white puffs to assume the post. The streets were overrun with people and mud puddles. The cyclopes had departed for Harond with their tails between their legs, beginning a long and disappointing journey only to return with news of not one, but two losses in Crow. The word on everyone's lips was the fight. Multiple gatherings of Crowans, both commoner and noble, emitted excited banter recounting play-by-play details as Jade, Charlie, Lex and Sevastian made quickly toward the castle.

Here's your Trigonous, Lex thought to herself feeling pretty important to be strolling beside the very individual whom everyone was praising. She enjoyed being in on this little secret, but her mind wouldn't allow itself to stray far from the matter at hand. She knew something was up just by the way Charlie's eyes kept casting nervous glances in her direction. Jade trudged along with her head down, and Sevastian seemed to be avoiding eye contact altogether. Jade's hand rested on Lex's shoulder, meant for comfort, but only enhancing her anxiety. How many times over the last few days had she assumed that Charlie had finally told her everything only to discover that it was just another stepping stone? Was this too just a detour? She didn't think so, not this time, not with Jade driving.

"Lex," Jade said quietly as they strolled swiftly along, "I want to apologize for not being with you yesterday when you first arrived in this world. I don't know if you know this yet but…"

"I know. You're married," Lex informed her. "Charlie told me. A belated congratulations to you." She was genuinely happy for Jade, however, under the given circumstances, her enthusiasm was forced. She hoped there would be a time in the near future when the two of them could congregate over a fruity cocktail and every detail of this story-book marriage would be told. But for the time being, her brain could only focus on one significant event at a time.

"Thank you," Jade said, expressing gratitude with a slight bow of her head. "I wanted to be there with the boys to welcome you into this world, and to help you get acquainted. But between the olive harvest and preparing for today's big fight, I just couldn't get away. I'm sorry."

"It's alright, really," Lex replied. "If it's any…" she really had to strain for the Greek word, "er, consolation, I know how you can make it up to me."

Jade smiled inquisitively, "And how is that?"

"Please make sure before the day is through, that I know everything about this unusual situation I seem to have found myself in."

"I promise," Jade replied sincerely. Her response was gleeful, but in the next instant, as though someone had flipped a switch in her brain, the happiness morphed into a sort of focused apprehension. The four of them were now barreling across the drawbridge toward the castle's main entrance. Jade pointed straight ahead and said, "Your answers lie within the castle."

The guards stood erect offering no resistance to the high council members, only discreet stares of interest. The castle's immaculate courtyard was surrounded by endless vertical walls, half of them glistening from the sun's golden rays, half of them darkened by shadow. There were a multitude of statues, life-size re-creations of Crow's legendary ancients, situated in random locations. Lush trees thrived along the main thoroughfare.

Sparkling pools and fountains were neighbored by emerald holly bushes. Numerous marble pillars, hugged by vast networks of green ivy, offered structural integrity to the castle's interior boundary.

On a quiet evening or an early morning, the courtyard would be a peaceful sanctuary – a place to read a book, to meditate, or to take a leisurely stroll. Not today. Nearly every member of the royal family had been drawn here to join in the celebration of Jade's victorious walloping of the Cyclops. They congregated in groups, gadding about in boisterous jubilation while drinking wine and laughing loudly. The Flock pressed on, weaving through rowdy gatherings, keeping their heads low and gazes fixated straight ahead. This was not a time to get caught up in distraction.

Voices echoed from above. Lex looked skyward to observe even more people grouped together on stairwells, balconies, and stunning arched bridges that connected higher areas of the castle. On a bridge high above, a group of young women, dark-haired and dark-eyed, had taken note that Jade was passing beneath them. Leaning dangerously over the side, royal blue tunics fluttering in the breeze, they called out, "Jadenhara, join us." Jade made no acknowledgment, only quickened her pace.

Another voice rang out from behind, this time aimed at Lex, "There goes, Alexis, the girl of song!" This statement was followed by pleading requests for an audience with the new choir director and comments of praise for last night's vocal performance. At the same time, several people were calling to Charlamos, offering him wine in exchange for his company. All requests were openly ignored. It was not typical for the Rose Flock to be smug or ungallant, and to Lex, this was an indication of the situation's urgency.

"Perhaps the favorable weather is an omen," Sevastian offered unexpectedly.

"Perhaps," replied Charlie.

"I'm not going to lie, you guys are making me nervous,"

Lex said, nearly breaking into a jog to keep up with the hurried pace.

"I normally do not admit this, but I'm nervous too," Jade replied, blunt as a spoon.

Soon, the crowds were behind them as they followed the stone path through a narrow corridor of high walls to a segregated part of the castle. The area in which they now traversed was a surprising transition from raucous commotion to a calming tranquility. Although still very much inside the castle, it felt to Lex as though they had entered into a forest. There was a wooden sign posted to the first tree on the left and although she didn't recognize it right away, a moment of concentration led her to believe that it said something like – restricted.

The trimmed grass path led straight through a thick crop of trees. Situated between many of these trees like silent guardians, were statues of pure gold - the gods of Olympus. She marveled at each one feeling just a little smaller in their presence. Flocks of crows occupied the twisty branches overhead, their unmistakable cries intermingling with the whispering breeze and the rustling leaves.

A half kilometer later, the foliaged pathway opened into an intriguing area that also happened to be a dead end. To the right and left were colossal walls that touched the clouds. Directly ahead was another wall, except this one contained two stone doors of such height and mass that it was trivial to Lex how they could possibly be opened without the aid of modern electrical power or hydraulics. Perhaps it would be a combined effort of the twenty or so Crow Soldiers that were currently patrolling this secluded vicinity of the castle. Most of them, each bearing their respective weapons, stood or paced just in front of the monstrosity of a doorway. The others were perched atop the granite archway that encompassed the door's superior border.

At the sight of the approaching high council members, every soldier sprung to attention. Lex and company did not slow their cadence. Charlie moved to the front of the pack. He raised his hand over his head and moved it in a circular motion indicating that he wanted the doors to be opened immediately. The unspoken request was clearly understood as the soldiers on the ground rushed to comply. They divided themselves, half a dozen on each side, and took hold of a thick chain fastened deep within the stone of each cumbersome door. With commendable effort, they yanked the chain. Every muscle in their bodies bulged as the doors cracked open with an earthshaking rumble. Sandals fought furiously for traction in the wet grass as the men inched backward, heaving with all their might. When there was enough of an opening to squeeze a body through, three men on each side abandoned their position on the chain and scurried to the back side of the door to push. This expedited the process and the doors opened just in time for the Flock, and Lex, to pass through without breaking stride.

The only one to stop was Charlie, who made a quick request to one of the soldiers, "Aragos, in several moments, close the doors behind us. Remember, only the high council may enter."

Aragos nodded, "As you wish, Charlamos."

71

Everything was musty and dark, cold and damp. Jade led Lex and the others to the exact boundary where daylight from the open doors met pitch black. Mounted on the wall to the left were rows of peculiar metallic cylinders. Each was open at the top and filled to the brim with a dry plant-like substance. A small pipe exited from the bottom of each and coursed along the wall until it disappeared into the darkness.

"Welcome to the catacombs of Crow," Sevastian said with more gusto than one would expect for such a foreboding place.

"Would you believe that there are approximately fifty kilometers of catacombs beneath Crow castle?" Jade asked Lex. "In the ancient days, these catacombs were used for different reasons. Originally, they were a burial site for royalty. For the first few millennia of the castle's existence, they served this purpose. In that amount of time, thousands of bodies had been laid to rest down here, so needless to say, with almost every step, you'll be treading over someone's grave. You'll notice the floors are made of large, flat slabs of stone. Lift any one of these and you're sure to find human remains.

Eventually, burials were discontinued at which time the catacombs became a testing device for the ancient Crow Soldiers. It became a tradition, a cruel one in fact, that in order to achieve soldier status, the prospect had to survive the catacombs. He would be blindfolded, and taken to the far depths, left there, and expected to find his way back to the stone doors in complete darkness. With over fifty kilometers of possible pathways, I'm sure you can imagine what a daunting task this was. There was no other option than to succeed, and once you were left alone, alone was how you remained until you found the salvation of the doors or you died of hunger or hypothermia. During these trials, it was common practice to release wild animals into the maze with the soldier. Giant cats, wolves, serpents, and yes, even minotaurs. We believe this may be how the infamous stories of the minotaur and the catacombs came to be. Charlie has no doubt explained the mystery of how the history of this earth has somehow leaked into Earth A - this is just another example.

Many a prospective soldier lost their lives attempting to survive the catacombs. To this day, the tangled web of passageways and corridors are littered with bones of the unsuccessful. You'll also find the remains of wolves, snakes and other various creatures that unwillingly gave their lives to test the will of man. The few that made it out alive became legends. Completion of this colossal feat turned mortal men to gods, at least in the public eye. This is where the reputation of the Crow Soldier began - a reputation that is strongly upheld to this day. Charlie has not only made sure of that but has improved the quality and effectiveness of the training program.

After losing so many good men, the traditional survival test was discontinued and the catacombs were locked. They remained this way for thousands of years. The violent history made the catacombs a place to be feared and ultimately avoided. Not even the prospect of tomb robbery was enticing enough for the bravest of criminals to venture down here. It wasn't until our intrepid pioneer, Charlie, decided to reopen them for another purpose. The purpose of protecting the most sacred thing this castle possesses."

"Actually," Charlie said in clarification, "what we have hidden down here is the most sacred thing man possesses."

"And that is?" Lex prodded, fascinated by the history lesson, but also desperate to get on with things.

"That is what we are about to show you," he said, "but in order to see it, you must know how to get there." He directed Lex's attention to the metallic cylinders along the wall. "Sevastian, our mechanical mastermind has single-handedly devised a simple, yet ingenious strategy in what he calls, the cylinder system."

"It took me over three years to finish," Sevastian explained, "I spent a few hours each day down here mapping out every inch of this unbelievably complex maze. I can't say that I didn't enjoy it. How many archeologists on Earth A would sell their soul to be the first to walk through a tomb that has been sealed off for thousands of years? It's thrilling to stare into the faces of the ancient Crowans who rest down here. So many of them are surprisingly well-preserved, and many were buried with their possessions – it's really fascinating.

Once the map was complete, I then began routing a lighting system along every wall. Without the convenience of electricity, I resorted to a useful fuel source - droughts wood. Droughts trees are relatively common in the forests around Crow. Just strip the bark, grind it into a powder and add fire. This stuff will burn bright for several days before its molecular fuel supply is diminished." He walked over to the mounted cylinders and pointed, displaying them proudly as if he were about to present a science fair project. "You'll notice that there are three rows of thirty. Each cylinder is filled with droughts wood, as is each pipe connected to the cylinders. Apply a flame to the top of any cylinder, and the fire will spread through the pipe and down its associated route through the catacombs. Every meter, there is a dime-sized hole cut in the top of the pipe. This is where the flame escapes to emit light, and also where I can easily refill them with droughts wood.

Here's the cool part," Sevastian continued with ramped enthusiasm. "The cylinders act as a combination system. For example, say you want to visit the tomb of King Aradios. Simply light the second cylinder in the first row, the fifth cylinder in the second row, and the twenty second cylinder in the third row. This combination will illuminate the exact path to his resting place. Interested in checking out Charlie's decaying relatives? – five, eleven, twenty-six."

"That is brilliant," Lex agreed, "but how does one know which combination to light?"

"I'm happy to show you," he replied. There was a hand torch lying against the wall beneath the cylinder system. Beside the torch were two flat stones. Sevastian snatched the stones and struck them together overtop the torch. The torch received the shower of orange sparks and burst into a robust blaze. His timing could not have been better. No sooner had the torch been lit, when the giant stone doors came thundering to a close behind them. The sound made Lex jump. It gave her the heebie-jeebies to be closed off in such a location. With the supplemental firelight, she could now see the parts of the room that the sun's light had not been able to reach.

The ceiling was high, maybe eighty feet. Surrounding the room were many open passages leading onward to undesirable, deathly, darkness; except of course if you were Sevastian, who actually seemed to find the deathly darkness desirable. Metal pipes originating from the cylinder system snaked along the walls eventually entering into their respective passageway. Five hefty wooden barrels were stacked in the corner behind them. At some point in time, one of these barrels had fallen to the floor and cracked open. This allowed Lex a peak at their contents – droughts wood. The only other item of interest in this otherwise lifeless room, was a scroll sitting atop a rectangular stone slab near the cylinder system.

Sevastian lifted the scroll from its resting place. He held firmly to one end and let the rest plummet. When the paper hit the stone floor, it unrolled several more yards. Lex now understood what he was trying to illustrate. The scroll contained hundreds and hundreds of Greek words, names actually, followed by a three number combination.

"This is how we know who is where," he said. "There are still many names and combinations to add to the list. Believe it or not, the majority of the tombs are yet to be explored."

"So, is this a hobby of yours?" Lex questioned in disbelief

that anyone could have the desire, let alone the courage, to travel these dank corridors alone, unless you counted dead people as company.

"A hobby turned passion," he replied earnestly. "I guess I was born for archeology."

"Sevastian's explorations have produced many new insights into Crow's past," said Charlie. "Ancient kings and queens with previously undocumented existences have now become known. Light has been shed on long forgotten traditions. Astounding collections of artifacts telling stories of the past have been discovered."

"I cannot tell you that this isn't fascinating to me," Lex admitted, "but I'm curious to know why you've brought me here. And let me just say that I have no interest in becoming a Crow Soldier so please don't ditch me."

"No worries," Charlie said reassuringly. "We didn't plan on doing that."

"The only ones allowed down here are high council members," Jade added. "This means we won't run into any unexpected company. The passage in which we are about to travel is top secret, so you won't find its combination written on the scroll."

"Top secret. Of course," Lex repeated with an implication that she was not at all surprised as everything seemed to be top secret with these three.

"Three, nine, twenty-seven," Sevastian said. An easy way to remember is that the combination is three to the first power, three to the second power, and three to the third power – simple algebra." He proceeded to set flame to the droughts wood fuel in the three mentioned cylinders. Lex watched as small flames began popping up from the connected pipe. The pipe arched over several rectangular passageways before diving into the tunnel closest to the left corner. The tunnel now glowed in a manner that was almost welcoming.

Charlie took a deep breath, noted by Lex as an uneasy one.

"Shall we then?" he asked.

72

It felt to Lex as though she were taking a tour through a fabricated haunted house - as if it were nearing Halloween and she had paid her fifteen dollar entry fee in order to acquire a cheap thrill. This feeling arose because it was almost phony to see an entire, intact skeleton slouched in the corner with a ten thousand year old sword still clutched in its bony grip. She came across several of these unfortunate souls as she followed Jade, Charlie and Sevastian along the fire-lit pathway through the terrifying place that was the catacombs of Crow.

The first few bodies they had encountered had been so close to the entrance. If these men had just persisted a little longer and a little further down the path, they would have reached the stone doors and went on to fight, to be worshiped, to live and to die like a hero. Just a few more steps, one more blind turn of a corner, and there, waiting, would be everlasting glory. Instead, they lay defeated in their task and forgotten by time.

There were bones everywhere, and not just from humans as Jade had pointed out, but of large animals as well. The remains of a giant dog lay next to a grab bag pile of human bones which had probably sustained the beast until it too had finally passed on. Below the bone-littered ground were tombs. With every step, Lex was mindful that she was treading over ancient bodies buried beneath the floor stones. Death saturated every crevice. This unsettling particularity in conjunction with the low ceilings, the dismal lighting, the musty aroma, and the utter filthiness of the place, beguiled her to wonder what in the world the high council kept hidden down here.

"This valuable possession you speak of," she said, "I can see why this would be the optimal place for it. I can't imagine anyone, besides Sevastian of course, who would voluntarily roam around down here."

"That's the idea," Charlie agreed.

"While we have just a little way to go," Jade said to Lex as the group rounded a corner and started down another skull-strewn tunnel, "I must explain about the Oblivion Oracle."

"You mean the book I was supposed to read?" Lex asked shakily, in the process of regaining balance after stumbling over a stray femur.

Charlie caught her arm to steady her as he nodded, "Yes, but the Oblivion Oracle is a person. I meant to have you read a book about the Oblivion Oracle so you can fully comprehend this situation you're in. Thanks to our little friend from the book parlor, you never got the opportunity. Jade, would you like to do the honors?"

Jade nodded and began, "This earth, Earth B as we call it, differs greatly from Earth A geographically. First of all, based on a multitude of factors, we believe it is approximately two thirds the size of Earth A. We've also figured the land to water ratio at one to one. One side of the earth consists of solid land and the opposite side is a vast sea."

"So, the other side of this world," Lex asked, "is nothing but ocean? Really?"

Charlie took this answer. "This is our assumption based on weather patterns and water currents. However, it's hard to know for sure due to the dangers of maritime travel. Over the ages, there have been numerous expeditions to explore the seas and expand our boundaries of knowledge. We told you before, the waters of this world are treacherous and many explorers have sacrificed their lives to establish what would eventually become nautical safe zones – take the word 'safe' with a grain of salt. No matter which of the four seas you launch your ship into, the safe zone ends just a stone's throw offshore. Ships that dare venture beyond the sight of land rarely, if ever, return."

"What happens to them?"

"There are some freaky things out there," he replied darkly. "I'll just leave it at that for now. My point is, we can only assume based on man's unsuccessful seafaring history, that beyond this massive plot of land lies a vast sea, encircling the entire back side of the planet until it meets the opposite shore. This unknown abyss is simply called, the oblivion.

Charlie sent his cousin a visual tag team and Jade took the wheel. "The story I'm about to tell you is one of the oldest surviving tales. It dates back nearly fifty thousand years to the beginning of documented human existence. The exact events that occurred on that fateful day were recorded by one of the men who was actually there to bear witness to them – the very first king of Crow. His original documentation is one of the oldest and most valuable manuscripts we currently possess. Of course, we keep it safely locked up in the castle. Before hearing the story, and to fully comprehend it, you must know that a very long time ago, long before man walked this planet, the gods of Olympus erected a temple in honor of their beloved brother, the sea god, Poseidon. This temple was named Pantheon. Pantheon resides at the very northwest tip of land – the boundary between rock and water. This is also where the temperate waters of the western Sea of Poseidon meet the icy waters of the northern Charybdis Sea. This temperature clash makes the entire area one big storm zone. Pantheon is this world's oldest known structure. It has existed for so long, that even fifty thousand years ago, it was considered ancient ruins."

"Have you ever been there?" Lex asked her.

"Yes," Jade replied with an arcane hesitation. "We all have." She exchanged glances with the others and the overall impression was that this trip, for whatever reason, had not elicited pleasant memories.

"How long does it take to get there?"

"Forever, and nearly twice as long to get back," Jade

answered, seemingly mulling over some disturbing memory.

This unspoken behavior made Lex curious, as if she wasn't already packed to the gills with unquenched curiosity. She wanted to pry into the details, to ask why the very mention of their trip to Pantheon inspired such dismaying reactions. She decided that this could wait until another time. First things first, "So the Oblivion Oracle?" she said, prompting Jade to get on with the story.

"Right," Jade conceded. "The oracle. Sevastian, our well-studied historian, will give you a quick overview on the "big three," then I will begin the story."

Sevastian began to speak, and his dialogue was so smooth and concise, Lex guessed that it had all been premeditated for the very purpose of explanation. He said, "In the beginning, the gods of Olympus created man. Man was granted three slots of land in which to establish three great cities. For hundreds of years, humans labored to fulfill their obligation to the gods and thus, the big three were established. The first city to be completed was Alphenia, residing on the western coast of land along the Sea of Poseidon. This city was established on the foundation of power and dedicated to Zeus, ruler over all Olympians. It became known and is still known to this day as the City of the Thunder God.

Next to reach completion was Crow, a city which prided itself on both understanding and keeping the balance between humankind and the natural world. The goddess Artemis took special interest in this particular establishment and helped guide Crow's founders in the city's layout, construction and purpose. Because of this symbiotic relationship between man and goddess, there is not a city in this world which holds their particular Olympian to such high esteem and personal sentiment. From the vantage of the rocky cliffs to Crow's west, or the dark waters of the Andromeda Sea surrounding the city's harbor, one can observe a multitude of temples built in Artemis' name. It's no wonder that the name Crow is synonymous with – City of the Moon Goddess.

The last of the big three to reach completion was Eubos. Established in the northeastern outcrop of land, where the Channel of Nasilia empties into the Andromeda Sea, Eubos is the first place that human eyes may look upon the rising sun each morning. Because of this unique relationship with the star of life, Eubos dedicates itself to the sun god, Apollo. Eubos was erected on the foundation of wisdom and despite earning the nickname 'City of the Sun God,' Eubos shares its devotion with the clear-eyed Athena, goddess of wisdom. To this day, the world's greatest thinkers and philosophers congregate there to exchange insight and discuss all things that pertain to the mystery of their own existence.

The story of the Oblivion Oracle takes place in the earliest stages of man's existence dating all the way back to the original three kings of the original three cities." He punctuated his synopsis with a sharp nod of his round head.

"Thank you, Sevastian," Lex obliged. "That was nicely put together."

"And with no further ado," Jade announced, "I bring to you the story of the Oblivion Oracle."

Desperate to be anywhere but here, Lex allowed Jade's words to fill her head. A vivid imagination pulled her conscious back through the ages and let her escape, if only temporarily, from the dreadful catacombs.

Impartment

Jagged white cliffs overlooking a cold dark sea provide the foundation for the mystical Pantheon. The supernatural temple stands rigid against the fierce wind and relentless bombardment of sharp precipitation.

Three kings emerge from the wispy mist of the dead forest and look upon the ruins of this sacred temple with a mixture of awe and relief. One man sits atop a white horse and wears a crown of ivy and royal blue robes torn and mud-stained. Compared to his companions, he looks fresh and healthy, for he is the king of the western city, Alphenia, a mere forty day ride from Pantheon. The other two kings appear more like beggars than royalty. The luxury of a short journey had not been theirs. The haggard men, kings of Crow and Eubos, bear only fragments of their original garments along with lengthy beards, bloodied extremities and limping footfalls indicative of injury or extreme fatigue. They have been traveling tirelessly for hundreds of days to arrive at this place at this time. Their bravery and skill have gotten them here alive, as they've endured foul weather, beasts of the wilderness and unthinkable physical exhaustion. They have accomplished the majority of this journey on their own two feet as their horses had been taken by predators along the way. Their orders had been simple – arrive at Pantheon the day that Archea, Artemis and Enuma are altogether full, come alone, tell no one.

What force could lure these men from high thrones in powerful cities? What motivation could a mighty king have to risk his own life in order to arrive at this given location at this given time? The answers to these questions reside only in the minds of three kings and would be buried with each of them.

An unwelcome surge of northerly wind makes certain that even the last few steps of this long journey are testing. Three kings ascend the ancient marble steps and stand side by side amongst the impossibly large pillars of this eerily beautiful structure. From above, a dreary sky spits intermittent cycles of rain and sleet. The vantage point offers a panoramic view as the men watch, listen and wait. Behind Pantheon to the east, are weather-worn alabaster rocks that slope gradually into the dead forest, where dark moss-covered trees extend their crooked black limbs upward toward the churning sky. Below the white cliffs, to the west and north, is a bitter sea. Water turns to indiscernible gray as it blends with the misty horizon and enters into the oblivion. The king of Alphenia, the king of Crow, and the king of Eubos stand together, huddling behind a marble pillar to escape the ruthless wind. They wait for a long time in silent entrancement.

An improbable image appears. The silhouette of a small ship materializes from the foggy sea. With the little energy that remains, the three kings navigate themselves down the jagged cliffs and onto the rocky beach to await the portage of this ghostly vessel. The ship skims to a halt some distance off shore. The anxious men stand ankle-deep in the sea. Swishing waves lick the caked mud from their sandals as they strain to observe any sign of life from the idle craft. Then suddenly, something quite peculiar ascends from the waves several meters away. This startles the men and they retreat backwards a few paces. A man, a woman, or maybe something else steps from the sea. The ethereal being is cloaked in a heavy hooded robe that is scarcely visible behind the twisted network of brownish-green seaweed that it drags from the water as it steps forward. The face is veiled by a polished ivory mask. An unsettling emptiness shows through the eye and mouth holes, making it impossible to determine if it has a face at all.

The only certainty this individual permits is the contents it carries within its seaweed-covered arms. Three heavy books, dry despite just arising from the water, are held tightly to the stranger's chest as it stands before the kings. Without hesitation, the mysterious being places a book in the possession of each king. As this bestowal occurs, the world, quite impossibly it seems, comes to a halt. The wind ceases and the waves die away giving the sea a mirrored glass appearance. In this new peaceful still, and without audible words, this visitor from the oblivion fills the minds of the kings with a comprehension of the value they now possess.

As quickly as they had evanesced, the wind, the rain, and all the sounds of Nature pour back into existence. Joining this symphony of chaos, a roaring wave, a monstrous wall of black, leaps from the sea. The kings make haste inland to avoid its fury, grasping tightly to their gifts as if their very lives depend on the book's safe keeping. They look back just in time to see the thunderous wave crash upon the mystifying stranger, swallowing him into liquid oblivion. When the blast of sea spray dissipates, the being and the ship are gone. Everything is now just as it was before – except…

The beach, which had been a barren stretch of jagged stones, was now covered with beautiful scarlet amaranth blossoms. The kings stare at this with unreserved wonderment. They enjoy this miraculous splendor for a few moments; one last easy breath before a long journey home with their new sacred articles. One king, however, would never return.

73

"And there you have the legend of the Oblivion Oracle," Jade said conclusively.

"Good timing," arose Sevastian's voice from behind. The unusual, yet familiar drawl of a Russian-tinged Greek accent zoned Lex back to the present where her gaze fell upon a single wooden door a short distance ahead.

"The carving is the symbol for cursed," Charlie pointed out referring to the deeply etched markings on the door's exterior. "It's a last line of defense in case anyone else besides the high council makes it this far. People of this world are very superstitious. Hopefully the intruder would have enough sense to turn around and try another passageway."

Lex was now more nervous than ever, and not because of the deterrent sketch, but because she knew that whatever was behind this door was of extreme significance. And if she had made the correct deductions, it would be especially significant to her.

"Before we go in," she said, surprised that she was now the one stalling, "which of the kings did not make it home?"

"The king of Alphenia," answered Jade.

"What happened to him?"

"No one knows."

"And his copy of the book?"

"Lost in time."

Lex took a deep breath before asking, "And what of the other two kings?"

"Made a safe return to their respective cities," Jade replied, "where they fulfilled their unspoken vow to keep the books safe and protected."

"This creature, this mysterious masked being is referred to as an oracle, why?"

There was no verbal response, instead three eager faces invited Lex to open the door and find out for herself. With a firm shove, she flung the door open and saw almost exactly what she had expected to see.

The room was rather small. It was simply the final few meters of the passageway that had been segmented off by the wooden door. Sevastian's lighting system encircled the room emitting an orange glow upon the stone podium in the center. The giant book, a fifty-thousand year old miracle, sat atop the podium in such pristine condition, it looked as though it had been bound yesterday. On the whole, there was nothing fancy about this particular room, still it was a sight to behold.

"What's with the weeds?" Lex wondered aloud referring to the piles of withered fawn-colored foliage spread about the room in obscure piles.

"Skackus plant. Sucks every ounce of moisture from the air hindering any possibility of water damage to the sacred book," said Charlie.

After he spoke, an uncomfortable hush fell upon them. No one, not even Jade, seemed to know just how to take the next step. Eventually, as if coaxed by the hands of fate, Lex took the initiative. She didn't even ask permission to approach the brown book and run a trembling palm over the unmarked cover. This is what she was here for anyway. Charlie, Jade and Sevastian watched with as much excitement as any three people could project as she lifted the cover.

"This is finally happening!" she heard Charlie's voice proclaim as if he were a million miles away. "Fifty thousand years and it is finally happening!"

As she pulled the book open, the stiff binding struck the stone podium producing a sound that could be heard from every corner of the world.

74

Silence was all-encompassing, but to Lex, this silence was deafening. The ancient voices of the dead seemed to scream from the primordial corridors as she began to examine page after page of the sacred book. A sensation took hold, a gripping emotion, an indescribable feeling of uncertain origin. It was like the pinnacle of a dream, where all of the unconscious thoughts and emotions surge together in one thrilling moment of absolute significance. She knew whatever was happening, whatever was causing this arcane swell of new feelings, whatever path she was now venturing, was the path she was meant to take. Her heart and mind were saying that this was exactly where she needed to be. Yet despite the sentiment of absolute certainty, there was something that was not so clear. She could not understand a single word in the book. She looked over her shoulder in hope that her friends might explain how she was supposed to read a language that was foreign to her.

Charlie said, "You'll remember, I'm sure, when I told you that the inhabitants of this earth did not always speak the Greek language."

"Yes, that's right," she confirmed. "We agreed that Homer was the likely culprit for its introduction but know little beyond that."

"Correct," he said. "A mystery we've been trying to solve for quite some time. In light of the current circumstances, this mystery can be put aside. For now, we must focus our attention on you, and your purpose in being here. In particular, what this book means to you."

"How is this book supposed to mean anything to me?" she asked as cordially as possible.

"This book," he explained, "was written by... well you heard the legend. Going on nothing else but the testimony of the first king of Crow, we can only assume that the legend happened just as he had described. The truth is, since this happened so long ago, we cannot be certain. Did three kings risk their lives on a journey to Pantheon fueled by some secret knowledge from some otherworldly source? Did a seaweed covered creature rise from the gray waters of the sea clinging to three precious books? It's equally as likely as it is unlikely. What we do know is that for fifty thousand years, this book has predicted every major occurrence throughout history. It has foretold the great wars, the coming of new cities, the fall of empires, the rise of legendary monarchs, and so on and so forth, all with astonishing accuracy. To put it simply, this book is a miracle. Sometimes, the oracle's divinations are simple and straightforward and other times they are difficult to decipher, and we don't understand what he is telling us until the event actually occurs. One can only speculate the book's purpose or why such a gift was bestowed upon man."

"What's your best guess?" Lex wanted to know.

Charlie's answer seemed a trite farfetched, but the conviction in which he spoke indicated that he believed his own postulation without the slightest reservation. "I believe that it was written for the purpose of saving this earth from a premature death."

"Right then, what does that mean?"

"You have come to this world at a unique time," he told her. "Our timeline now resides on the final page of the oracle's book. Two cities, Crow and Eubos hold the only known copies, and we have been collaborating tirelessly to comprehend the final page, because understating this page is the means to prevent the end. Please," he invited with an open hand gesture, "have a look."

"You'll have to translate it for me," she reminded him as she began turning the great volume of pages toward the finale.

"One step ahead of you," he said. She reached the end and saw a newer, freshly etched parchment attached to the back cover next to the original version of the final divination. "Before you read, Lex, you should know that this page is not like any of the thousands before it. Every prediction the oracle has thus far recorded is written as a declaration. The passages tell what event will happen and when an event will occur. The last page, the final divination, is more mysterious and not so cut and dry." He seemed anxious as he nodded for her to proceed. "You'll see what I mean."

The strange dream-like feeling inundated her consciousness as she read…

THIS IS THE FINAL AGE OF OLYMPUS. CROW REIGNS SUPREME UNDER ITS ONE HUNDRED AND FOURTEENTH QUEEN. WAR DAWNS ON OLETHROS AND NASILIA. THE BLACK WIND ARISES. A DARKNESS BLANKETS THE WORLD, DROWNING ALL INHABITANTS IN A SEA OF DEATH. EVERYTHING BECOMES FIRE AND ASH AND BLOOD. HISTORY VANISHES. THE END OF ALL THINGS.

A doomsday prophecy. This much was evident to Lex. What isn't straight forward about that? she wondered silently. It was scary, yes, especially since the oracle never faltered on a prediction. There was yet another passage, so she decided to read on before asking any more questions…

I SLIPPED INTO DEATH'S REALM IMPOSSIBLE TO PORTRAY. WEIGHTLESS AND CALM I WAS EMBRACED BY A WINGED BEING WHO WAS NEITHER HUMAN NOR BEAST. ITS EYES SPOKE TO ME. "AMARANTH," IT SAID, THEN TOLD MUCH MORE.

DEATH HAD TAKEN ME, YET I RETURN WITH A
STORY OF HOPE. A STORY THAT WAS TOLD TO ME
FROM BEYOND THIS WORLD AND TIME. THE STORY OF
THE AMARANTH.

FINDING THIS BEING IS THE MEANS TO ALTER
THE WORLD'S DOOM.THE AMARANTH LIVES DURING
THE FINAL DIVINATION. THE AMARANTH, THE
DEFENDER, COMES AT SIXTEEN PASSINGS, TEN
CYCLES, TWO THOUSAND TERMS FOLLOWING THE
DEATH OF THE GOD KING. BORN IN THE NEW CASTLE,
THE SIREN CAN BE FOUND LIVING AMONGST THE
ROSES FOLLOWING THE WITHERING OF THE LIFE-
GIVER.

Lex read through the prophecy again and again, slowly,
then quickly, backward, then forward. Her soft face was masked
by shadows and shimmering orange reflections from the flames as
she tried in earnest to make sense of these riddling words. Charlie
and the others made no attempt to disrupt her acute concentration.
A nervous tension hung thick in the dungeon coupled by a
haunting silence. There was no shaking the feeling that this was
what everything had been leading up to, though she didn't entirely
understand why or how. The prophecy was intriguing yet vague
and indiscernible. An amaranth was just a flower, that much she
knew. The only conclusion she could establish following the sixth
time through the passage was that the world was going to end, and
the only way to stop this from happening was to find a specific
flower, an amaranth flower. With a face stricken by perplexity, she
turned to the Rose Flock. "What does it mean?"

"What do you think it means?" Charlie redirected with
faint unease in his voice.

"How would you expect me to know?"

"I just need something to go on," he implored. "Please, I'd
really like your take on it."

Lex sighed then made known her conjecture of how the discovery of a particular flower would somehow save the world. Before she could finish, however, Jade intervened. "I'm sorry, Lex, but I just cannot tolerate Charlie's procrastination any longer," She met her cousin's eyes in a dead stare. "Either tell her now or I will."

Charlie radiated apprehension like steam from a kettle. Finally, with seemingly immense difficulty, the words finally came. "You are the Amaranth," he said. "That is why you're here." Then he exhaled a deep breath and waited for her response. He was gratified by nothing more than a blank stare. What could she say to that? "I'll not stall any further, nor will I sugar coat this because Jade is right, you've waited long enough and we've put you through a lot." He took a few steps closer and looked her square in the eyes. "People in this world have been looking for you since this book passed into the hands of man. There are no words to describe how the three of us felt when we finally found you." During this prodigious revelation, he all the while gawked at her as if she were the most treasured thing he had ever laid eyes upon. "Alexis Lunden, the girl from high school. The girl we always knew of, but never really knew."

At this, Lex erupted in laughter. She couldn't restrain this outburst because the whole thing was, in her mind, utterly incongruous. "And from that passage, you concluded that not only was this Amaranth a person, but…me?" she asked, words wringing wet with doubt.

"Yes," he replied.

"How?"

"I'll admit it wasn't easy," he explained. "It was a combined effort of everyone in this room."

"The process in which we found you would make a captivating mystery novel," Sevastian spoke up exultantly. "Maybe P.J. Stockton's next best-seller, eh?

"Well then, would you please explain it to me?" she insisted as civilly as possible, as she was ardently unconvinced.

"Because nothing in this final paragraph describes me at all."

"On the contrary," Sevastian said, "everything describes you. You just don't understand yet."

Charlie took the reins and charged full force into the details. "With Crow and Eubos possessing the only copies of the Oblivion Oracle's divinations, we knew that it was up to us to find the Amaranth and that this earth's fate depended on us doing so. That much was obvious from the passage. We also guessed right away that the Amaranth was not a flower because the oracle referred to it as a being. Once we were all in agreement that it was a person or creature we were seeking, we then broke down the passage into individual clues.

The first clue we decided to focus on was the excerpt, 'born in the new castle.' This seemed simple enough. We asked ourselves, which castle in this world was the last to be built, therefore the newest? Simple research revealed that it existed on Ivel, an island in the Andromeda Sea located several nautical days southeast of Crow. We sailed to Ivel many times but our efforts were fruitless. We hadn't the slightest idea as to who or what we were looking for. It was as if we expected the Amaranth to just jump out and say, here I am! Jade, Sevastian, Theophilus, Isidore and I, spent many days in Ivel. We must have interviewed every inhabitant on the island, attempting to make some sort of connection to something, anything in the final divination. After an ineffectual shot in the dark, we set sail from the city no farther along than when we started.

On the long sea voyage back to Crow we had nothing but time in which to contemplate our mystery. In particular, we focused on the line – The Amaranth, the defender, comes at sixteen passings, ten cycles, two thousand terms following the death of the God King. The biggest question on our minds was – what did the oracle mean by, 'death of the God King?'"

"Pardon my interruption," Lex said, bringing to a halt his high-paced monologue, "but what is this business of cycles and terms?"

"Oh yes, sorry. I forgot to mention that on Earth B, we calculate time differently than on Earth A. Here, a single day is called a passing and is thirty-two hours in duration. Next, we have the word cycle, which is comparable to a month. A cycle is defined by the amount of time it takes the largest of our three moons, Archea, to go from full, back to full – one complete cycle. Finally, we have a term, which is the same thing as a year. Just like on Earth A, Earth B has twelve months, or cycles in a year."

"Let me make sure I've got this straight before you go on," Lex said, desiring to understand every detail for no other reason than to have her ducks in a row when the time came to shoot down this crazy notion at which the Flock was currently driving. "A passing is a day. A cycle is one month. And a term is one year, consisting of twelve cycles. Is that right?"

"Perfectly so," Charlie agreed. "The reason I'm explaining this is so you can understand the relevance of the oracle's time references." He then recited once again and this time it made sense to Lex. "The Amaranth, the defender, comes at sixteen passings, ten cycles, and two thousand terms following the death of the God King.

On the ship, as we sat in judicious collaboration over the oracle's divination, we became obsessed with trying to decipher what was meant by – death of the God King."

"Would that be a reference to the king of the Olympians, Zeus?" Lex asked.

"Exactly our first thought," said Charlie. "Throughout this world's history, every set of human eyes that had skipped forward to read the oracle's final divination made the assumption that the god king, Zeus would somehow, I guess, die or something. Then about two thousand terms later, the Amaranth would come.

This idea was vague and frustrating. There had never been any evidence that Zeus ever vanished from existence, nor was there any evidence that he had not. We all agreed that there must be another meaning behind – death of the God King.

Our next thought was that the God King could possibly be

a reference to one of the past kings of Alphenia, because Alphenia is also called the city of the thunder god, but like every other idea so far, this led nowhere. Our path toward enlightenment next led us to consult the history books on the events that occurred in this world around two thousand terms ago. This little operation was headed by Sevastian and was quite tedious. We had to research every major occurrence, every notable individual in every city during this approximate time frame. After compiling mountains of information, we were still not able to make any connection to a God King or anything in the final divination. At this point, we were as close as we had ever been to throwing in the towel.

After that strike, we collected ourselves for the sake of this earth, and surged forward once again. We brainstormed tirelessly, determined to solve this mystery that had been eluding mankind for fifty thousand years. The high councils of both Crow and Eubos, who, again, each have a copy of the sacred book, spent months at a time held up in discussion about the final divination. Even representatives from Alphenia and other smaller cities made the long journey to join in the collaboration.

Then, finally, it was Sevastian who made the first crack in the armor. He noticed something within the passage that now seems so obvious, I cannot believe that we, or anybody before us, had never picked up on it."

Lex looked to Sevastian. "What did you find?" she asked him, now feeling the bite of suspense.

He answered, "I saw a redundancy within the final paragraph. Do you see it, Lex?"

She skimmed quickly through one more time. "No."

Sevastian approached and pointed to the second sentence, then read aloud, "The Amaranth lives during the final divination. The oracle then goes on to say - The Amaranth comes at sixteen passings, three cycles, two thousand terms following the death of the God King. The redundancy is that both of these statements describe the exact same time period."

"How?" Lex asked, a trifle confused.

He repeated, "The amaranth lives during the final divination. The final divination is right now. The very next sentence says, the amaranth comes at sixteen passings, three cycles, two thousand terms following the death of the God King – which is also perceived to mean, right now. Why would the oracle mention the same time frame in two consecutive sentences?"

"You've got me stumped," she admitted with a shoulder shrug.

"We've each read through the oracle's prophecies many times," explained Jade. "The knowledge we've accrued from studying his writings told us that he would not say the same thing twice without a reason. My hat goes off to Sevastian, our super sleuth, who finally figured it out. His theory seemed absurd and we all had quite a laugh when he first mentioned it, but we went ahead, pounded the numbers, and another door was broken open."

Lex again looked to Sevastian who stood smiling, his chin tilted high.

Charlie said, "The reason the oracle said the same thing twice, is because he was referring to two different earths."

"You're saying that the Oblivion Oracle was aware that there was an Earth A and an Earth B?" Lex asked just to make certain she heard it right.

"It seemed just as farfetched to us at the time," Charlie replied, "but we went with it, just to see where this new theory would take us. So just hear me out on this one. Now having Earth A to work with, our first order of business was to apply the time reference. So, tell me Lex, what happened on Earth A two thousand years ago?"

"Lots of things I'd imagine," she threw back at him, not catching on to the obvious.

"The landmark event in which a certain person met with death and changed the course of human history on Earth A? No? Let me save you a headache," he said politely, "because this certain person has many names; the Alpha and Omega, the Rose of Sharon, the Lamb of God, the God King…"

Lex's jaw dropped as it finally hit her. "Christ," she blurted, "the death of Jesus Christ."

"Don't worry," Jade said. "It took us a lot longer than it took you. In our defense, it never dawned on us that the oracle may have been talking about Earth A. Of course, at this point, the three of us were on our own. Heeding the threatening advice never to tell anyone on Earth B about the stone, we now had the added challenge of concealing our new theories to the others in the high council."

"So you came to the realization that the oracle was talking about Earth A. Why then do you not assume the Amaranth is one of you?" questioned Lex.

"Actually, we thought that right away," Sevastian chimed in. "I must admit I was excited about the possibility that it could be me." He chuckled, as if the idea bemused him.

"Like Jade said," Charlie continued, "once the concept of Earth A became a possibility, and we identified Christ's death as the oracle's reference, pieces of the puzzle began to fall in place. The first piece – sixteen passings, ten cycles, two thousand terms following the death of Jesus Christ. On Earth A, this translates to September sixteenth, approximately two thousand years C.E. Tell me Lex, when is your birthday?"

"September sixteenth, two thousand and… Okay, that matches up, but what about everyone else on Earth A born on that particular day?"

"That's where the other clues came in," Jade said. "We could now apply the excerpt, 'born in the new castle,' to Earth A. Rather than trying to find the newest castle on Earth A, it made more sense to set our sights on towns and cities that went by the name New Castle." Lex's eyes widened as her friend asked, "Where were you born, Lex," as if Jade didn't already know.

Slightly entranced, Lex recited her birthplace like a first grader. "Staffordshire, England, in the borough of Newcastle-under-Lyme." The three allowed her a moment to digest the information. She still didn't believe it; she didn't want to believe it. "I knew two people in Staffordshire with that same birthday," she contested.

Charlie wasted no time in commencing toward something she couldn't help but accept. All the while, he circled her slowly with arms hung casually behind his back like a professor pacing about the classroom. "Thank goodness for the Internet," he stated appreciatively. "Without it, the next task would have been so daunting, it might have just been impossible. So, Lex, if you were on the case to locate the Amaranth, and you concluded that, the new castle, was a city or town rather than an actual castle, what then would you conclude about the excerpt, living amongst the roses following the withering of the life giver?" He was now speaking with such vehemence that he didn't allow her time to take a stab at the question. "Via the Internet, which by the way it's scary how much personal information you can dig up on someone, we compiled a list of every person born in a New Castle. From that vast list of names, we narrowed it down by separating only those who are currently alive, and, with the said birthday. Needless to say, the list was still hundreds deep."

"How then, did my name stand out on that list?" Lex asked, nearly feeling like a helpless animal the way Charlie was circling her.

"In this world, and as it would have been known to the Oblivion Oracle, the life giver is the mother. Withering, of course meant the dying or death of. The next step would seem simple and obvious, but at the time we were trying to find you, it was a shot in the dark. The chore was painstaking and monotonous, but we finally managed to identify those names on the list whose mother had passed away. Even still, the list consisted of eighty seven names."

Lex was staring down at the book, deep in thought and trying to make sense of every word. Jade appeared at her side and carried on the mind-boggling story. "The most enigmatic part of the oracle's passage was the excerpt, "living amongst the roses." It seemed like a familiar take on Aesop's poem, The Rose and the

Amaranth. Sitting on the mansion's rooftop for hours, the three of us would brainstorm on what this particular part could mean. You wouldn't believe all the ideas we came up with. I think it was Sevastian who proposed the idea that we should find a community of remarkably attractive people, find the one amongst them who was plain-looking, and hope that person's name was on the list." Lex smiled with half-hearted acknowledgement. As her doubt was being replaced by reality, she grew increasingly uneasy.

"Other dead end ideas," Jade went on, "the possibility that this Amaranth worked at a place that sold roses, or had a house with an extraordinary rose garden." Lex knew where this was going so she spoke up just so the inevitable would suffer no further delay.

"If New Castle was a city or town, it would stand to reason that roses would be a reference to a city or town," she stated, confident in her proposal.

"Lex, you know I've always admired your quick wits," Charlie said with a warm smile. "You're exactly right. So, from the top, we started the list with everyone born in a New Castle, then removed those that were already deceased. We narrowed it down further by taking only those with a September sixteenth birthday and then removed the names whose mothers were still living. Then finally, we did some research to find who on that list had moved to a city or town with the word Rose in it. After the final step, there was only one name remaining - yours."

Lex was stunned. All the cards were on the table and the facts were unable to be ignored or argued with. Jade added, "There is no irony in the fact that the Amaranth lives in Rose, Kansas. After all, that is where the church and the pool are located. To put it plainly – the Amaranth was destined to end up in Rose."

"Makes you wonder, doesn't it?" Charlie commented. "So much had to come together to allow all of this to happen. I don't think it was a coincidence that a girl born in England would end up in nowhere Kansas just by chance. Remember our Christmas lunch conversation about your aunt? I asked you if Claire had ever told you why she decided to move from Los Angeles to Rose? Did you ever ask her how or why she chose Rose?"

"She told me that it was literally random," Lex answered. "Her story has always been that she and her husband unfolded a giant map of the United States, closed their eyes and let their fingers glide across the paper until settling on Rose. But as I've told you before, she always seems bothered when I ask and changes the subject rather quickly."

"It might be said that outside forces were guiding her finger," Sevastian hypothesized, "but the methods and the reasons remain unknown to us."

"All we know for sure is that we have found you, brought you here and now," Charlie said with excitement, "all we can do is wait to see how things progress."

"There are two more things in the final divination that we have not discussed, and this seals the deal," said Jade. "The oracle refers to the Amaranth as the defender. The origin of the name Alexis, in this world and the other, means defender."

"Alexis, the Amaranth, the defender," Lex mumbled to herself as if entranced, all the while shaking her head incredulously.

This was when it finally hit like a load of bricks – the realization that she was just a puppet. She felt as though she had been kidnapped from her life, her world and her sanity. The Rose Flock did not arbitrarily sit at her table at Vincent's restaurant that fateful summer night. The candy they left behind was not an act of unbridled benevolence, rather a dastardly ploy to drag her into their world. The calculus lessons, dinner with Claire, invitations to the mansion, and eventually a job and living quarters were all just part of this great big plan to bring her here so she could theoretically, somehow, save a world she knew nothing about. There was a sudden urge to cry. She repressed it, then asked, "What does the oracle mean by 'the siren?'"

Jade smiled warmly, apparently not yet keen to Lex's sudden influx of unhappiness. "Just one more perfect reference to you. In this world, possessing the siren means to have a voice that could bring armies to their knees. This is a very rare gift. There is a considerable difference between having a good voice and having the voice of a siren."

"That night back at the mansion," Charlie added, "when you sang "Gabriel's Oboe" – that was when we heard you sing for the first time. At that point, if there was any doubt remaining in our minds about you being the Amaranth, it was erased after the first note from your lips. You can recall, I'm sure, when you sang "River of Love and Life" at the feast last night. Remember Palas's reaction? Hearing your voice was proof in her mind that you possessed the siren and that the Amaranth had been discovered."

A low rumbling sound arose from somewhere in the catacombs, nearly an infrasonic drone recognizable mostly by the vibration it caused.

"It's the doors!" Jade informed the others with exigency. "Someone's coming. Remember, Lex, you must remember that everyone else in the high council believes we found you in Alba."

"Alba, I don't understand."

"Alba is our alibi," Charlie explained quickly and quietly, now keeping an eye on the passageway. "Remember, the man who gave me the stone came to me in a dream and warned never to tell anyone in this world about it. How then could I explain to the others in the high council how I found you? From Crow, a long journey southwest will take you to an establishment by the name of Alba. It is not so much a city as it is a small sanctuary of unparalleled beauty. It is nicknamed the rose garden, because the entire settlement is surrounded by breathtaking rose plantations. Alba has been isolated and self-sufficient since its birth, and nobody knows much about the place. Its inhabitants are all women of great beauty and youth. These women are said to be nymphs, or part goddesses. According to the legends of Alba, any man who ventures into the realm of the roses, will be enslaved by the nymphs who live there.

"Doesn't sound that bad to me," Sevastian observed with a

smirk.

"Jade left this earth and returned to Kansas," Charlie continued rapidly with interval glances over his shoulder, "where she stayed for several months. We told the high council that she had decided to make the journey to Alba to see if she might find the Amaranth there. It had to be Jade because it would be too risky to send a male."

"I spent the past six months in Kansas," Jade explained. "I did not come to this earth at all. My first time coming back was just recently, with the purpose of watching the match between Sevastian and Xenogorus and also to help Elias with the harvest. The reason I stayed away so long was so the rest of the high council would believe that I had left for Alba in search of the Amaranth. Of course, at that point, we had already identified you, but it was all in the name of establishing our alibi."

"We've got to wrap this up," Charlie said as he glanced nervously through the door down the fire-lit hallway, as if someone would round the corner at any moment. "Queen Palas, Theophilus and Isidore think that Jade spied on Alba for several days from the concealment of the surrounding forest. Day in and day out, she observed the maidens tending to the rose gardens, but one stood out. The one that sang while she worked. The one with a voice so perfect, the voice of the siren. This one had to be the Amaranth. Jade questioned you and discovered that your mother had indeed met an untimely end. She discovered your name was Alexis, the defender. She convinced you to come to Crow, where a great surprise was waiting. You agreed to this under the circumstances that you would be well treated and that you should return to Alba at your own discretion. This is something a nymph, a higher being, would likely say in the presence of a mere mortal human such as Jade."

"Wait, the high council believes I'm part goddess?" Lex asked in disbelief, growing tired of the seemingly endless string of deceptions.

"If you're from Alba, you'd have to be," he replied.

"Instead of directly telling the others we had found you, I had you sing last night. When Palas heard your voice and learned your name, she knew the Amaranth had arrived in Crow. Last night, in the queen's chambers, after Sevastian had taken you outside, I told them our made-up account of how we found you. The queen and the others, in all due respect to each, swallowed this story hook, line and sinker. I then gave my opinion that it would be a good idea to get you accustomed to our city before springing this Amaranth thing on you. I said it would probably be too overwhelming for you to be taken from your home, thrown into a foreign city, then to hear the news that you are the one who is supposed to save the world. This, of course, is how I really felt as you know."

The pertinent information was coming so fast, Lex wished that she had more time to grasp Charlie's every word and give each a good mulling over. This was not to be. Sevastian cleared his throat as a warning. Voices arose from the stone hallway, then shadows on the wall. A small group of people rounded the corner, making toward Lex and the Rose Flock with resolute strides. It was the rest of the high council with Isidore leading the way. Queen Palas and Theophilus trailed a few steps behind the burly soldier and… there was someone else.

A young lady in a radiant dress of the purest white followed the others. Like the queen, she was barefoot, stepping confidently and uncaringly through the bone piles with unprotected soles. Also, in likeness to the queen, she was outwardly beautiful. Her charismatic smile, feminine physique, and stunning face were topped off with thick brown hair fixed in place by vivid indigo ribbons. In fact, she was Palas' exact clone, only with two decades of youth to her credit. Lex heard Charlie gasp and Jade whisper, "I didn't realize Phaedra would be back so soon."

Princess Phaedra, the one and only daughter of Palas and heir to the throne of Crow. Lex knew this as soon as the name had passed the barrier of Jade's teeth. She had heard much talk in regard to the beloved Phaedra from chance conversations around the city. Last night at the great feast, Itys and Niobe were exchanging thoughts about her perpetual trips to Eubos and tossing around speculations as to what important matter might demand so much of the princess' time. Just this morning while perusing the streets before the big fight, Lex had overheard an assembly of noble men discussing Phaedra's incomparable diplomacy tactics, and how she might one day rival or exceed her mother's renowned leadership.

Then, during today's battle at the coliseum, there was that single empty seat in the high council's reserved section. Lex had noticed the vacancy, and even subconsciously recognized the princess' absence, but had been too preoccupied by the miraculous events of the day to question it. Now that Phaedra was approaching, she wondered why Charlie or the others had thus far neglected to make any mention of her. The other curious phenomenon was the ghostly-white pallor Charlie's face had suddenly taken on.

The newcomers swept into the room with an air of zeal and Lex saw the high council in its entirety for the first time. Isidore, as if feeling that this situation was too big even for him, slid off to the corner. Every single eye was on the Amaranth and it was Theophilus who spoke first.

"Never did I imagine that my eyes would behold such a vision," he said marveling at Lex with that unwavering smile. "The Amaranth standing over the great book. This is truly a definitive day in history." The words bounced around inside Lex's head, meaningful yet arbitrary.

Phaedra slowly stepped forward, and her dazzling blue eyes met Lex's for the first time. The great and powerful princess did nothing to hide the fact that she was simply spellbound in the presence of the Amaranth. She bowed her head and said, "Alexis, I am Princess Phaedra. I, like all others in this room, have spent a great deal of my life searching for you. Ever since the day I first read the oracle's book, I have dedicated all of my time to finding the Amaranth. We had a strong feeling that we might find you in Alba. Praise the gods that Jadenhara's quest was successful," she stated exuberantly. "Our great city and our beloved earth have been granted a new hope."

Lex diligently contemplated a suitable reply, but in the end, a reply could not be formulated. Instead it was Charlie who finally said, "Alexis, over the past ten cycles, Princess Phaedra has traveled to Eubos numerous times to work in partnership with that city's high council. As you know, the only other known copy of the oracle's book resides there. We decided that working together would not only strengthen the bond between two of the great cities, but also increase our chances of finding you sooner. But tell me, Phaedra," he said turning to the golden princess, "why such a hasty return?"

Phaedra smiled as she looked upon Charlie with what Lex immediately recognized as infatuation. "The Eubos high council and I were not reaching new conclusions on the Amaranth's discovery," she explained. "After a few cycles of useless deliberation, we concluded that the search for the Amaranth was lost. The oracle's clues were too vague and the Defender could not be found. It was agreed upon that we should place the remainder of our hope in Jadenhara's quest to Alba.

It was during the return voyage when standing on the bow of my ship, I saw the black swan floating in the starry sky above, certainly on its way to Eubos. I called the bird down and when it landed, I noticed the message tied to its leg. It was word from Theophilus telling that the Amaranth had been discovered in Alba. At this enlightenment, even Lord Poseidon's gift of a swift tail-wind could not deliver me to Crow quickly enough. I ordered the crew to drop oar and row. Our ship speedily skimmed the waters of the Andromeda Sea, so that I may have the privilege of looking upon our savior with my own eyes." She stepped close to Charlie and gently took his hand, looked him in the eyes and said, "Now that the Amaranth is found, we may yet have the chance to rule our adored Crow." She then pressed her soft lips to his with endearing affection. Lex was stunned, paralyzed, as the truth was revealed - Charlamos and Phaedra were to be married, which meant that he was destined to be king. What a fool she had been, to think for one second that someone like Charlie would settle for anything less. At the sight of the kiss, her heart had shattered into a billion minute fragments. This debilitating pain, this crushing hurt, trumped every other emotion, and for the moment, nothing else in either world mattered.

"You are a beautiful one," Phaedra said as she looked Lex over. "As beautiful as the deed you are prophesized to accomplish. My travels have never taken me to Alba, but I have been told that it is an establishment of great beauty, in both its land and its people. You, great defender, are indeed a testament to that."

Deep down Lex wanted to return the compliment, to offer her congratulations for the engagement and to tell the princess how lucky she was to have Charlie, but the words would not come. She was suddenly in another state of mind, floating outside of her body, hovering just above herself in this eerie back chamber of the catacombs. She looked to Charlie with sadness radiating from her eyes and his reciprocating expression of guilt was proof that he comprehended her current feelings. She wanted to ask him why, but why what? – she didn't know. Why had he not spoken of Phaedra? Why was an ordinary girl from England expected to save an entire world? And why could she not gain control over her emotions?

Then Queen Palas spoke, but the voice only resonated in Lex's head as an indiscernible reverberation. "Alexis, will you choose to embrace the oracle's prophecy and fulfill the destiny of the Amaranth?"

And that was the kill switch. Something inside Lex went off like an atomic bomb setting fire to every nerve, neuron and fiber of her body. The crippling blow of Charlie's engagement coupled with all this additional news of monumental proportion felt like taking a cannon ball at close range and manifested as giant tears spilling from her wide green eyes. None in the room were privy to this reaction. Before the lachrymal flow, she had departed, or rather shot from the chamber like a bullet. Running blindly through distorting tears, tripping through bones, falling to the grimy floor, finding her feet, then falling several more times, she finally managed to escape the haunting darkness of the catacombs.

She burst from the underground caverns into the sunset light so out of her mind and so aloof to her surroundings that she did not hear the voices of the guards calling to her, asking if she was in danger or required assistance. She sprinted down the wooded path with such unfocused swiftness that she did not notice the sky transform to black as hundreds of crows lifted from the trees, squawking and beating their powerful wings through the evening air. She did not feel the weight of every noble eye as she ran like a gazelle through the main thoroughfare, distracting the celebration with her urgent pace. Her emotion-driven energy made her eyes gush, her lips quiver, and her strong legs soar across the drawbridge, down the main street, and right out of the city. It wasn't until she arrived upon the sanctuary of the woodland lake when she finally regained her composure. Ironically, only a day ago, this was the location where her composure had been abandoned for the first time in her life. It was the quiet serenity of the forest that called her back to a rational mindset. The sparkling waterfall, the dewy grass, the lush trees of unthinkable size, and the bank of rough diamonds encircling this tranquil haven were all calming. No wonder Charlie came here so often.

75

With the rapidity of her breathing returning to normal, she took a seat on an onyx boulder at the water's edge and looked down upon her reflection in the crystal lake. She knew that the most important matter at hand was her role as this earth's savior, but whether it was envy, jealousy, or disappointment, the only thing that played repeatedly through her mind was the kiss between Charlie and the princess.

After seeing Phaedra, Lex felt so plain. The face mirroring back from the pool showed unexceptional brown hair, still damp from the rain, untamed and flat. Her lips were dry, her cheeks red from the wind and the bulky woolen cloak was hardly flattering. It was fitting, she thought, that she should be called the Amaranth, because Phaedra was certainly the beautiful rose.

A tear dropped to the water sending delicate rings coursing outward along the surface. Taking her by surprise, a familiar face appeared from amongst the ripples. It was the fair Daphne. For reasons that Lex could not explicate, the nymph's presence was comforting. The Naiads were very sympathetic creatures. She observed this during their first encounter the day prior, and now saw it once again in Daphne's consoling expression.

"Why is there sadness in your eyes, Alexis?" she asked. Before Lex replied, Iris's angelic face breached the surface.

"I'm not sure," Lex said solemnly. "It's a combination of things, I guess. I have never felt so lost."

"Please," Iris implored, "tell us so we may help guide you."

Lex realized that she probably shouldn't tell these creatures everything, but her desperation for a third party opinion prodded her onward. "It's just that…" she paused and tried to collect herself, not wanting to expose so much vulnerability, "a while ago I met the most remarkable person. We became, at least it seemed to me, good friends. Then from this friendship something greater began to blossom, at least it blossomed in me. I would not be telling the truth if I said I did not love him – loved him," she sniffed and fought back another round of tears, "but his friendship toward me was…" she searched her mind for the translation, "fake. It was fake and all part of a bigger plan he had. It turns out the only reason he pretended to be my friend was so he could bring me to Crow, and…" She decided not to say any more. Something told her she shouldn't. But even if she wanted to, it would have been difficult to talk with her face buried in her hands. Tears came once more, and the Naiads waited patiently for this projection of grief to run its course.

When she finally stopped sobbing, she apologized for her behavior. It was embarrassing to appear so pathetic, especially in front of strangers, demigods. At this point she had cried all that she could cry, and sorrow was being replaced by resentment. The resentment was not just toward Charlie, but Jade and Sevastian. They had all been a part of this great big scheme. Even if Charlie was running the show, it was cruel that the others had not bothered to mention that he was engaged to be married. Was that part of the plan, to allow Lex to fall in love with him so she would trust him and follow him here? As despicable as the notion sounded, she couldn't be entirely certain that this had not been the case.

"I cannot imagine our Charlamos guilty of these deeds," Daphne said sincerely, "especially in regard to his true love."

How did she know I was talking about Charlie? Lex wondered as Daphne reached out a wet palm. Flattered by the empathetic gesture, Lex took her hand.

"He speaks of you as if you were an Olympic goddess. He tells of your beauty and your heart. He tells us he would do anything for you and defend you as long as his heart beats."

"I'm sorry, Daphne, but I don't think you understand," Lex said. "I am not his true love. The one he loves is the princess of Crow and they are already engaged to be married." Daphne and Iris exchanged a look of uncertainty at this new testimony.

"Charlamos has never talked of marriage, or that his true love is a princess. Surely, she cannot be the one," Iris said with confidence.

"There is one way we can be sure," Daphne continued. "We have never set eyes upon the Princess of Crow. If you are able, Alexis, will you tell us what she looks like?"

"Her beauty is unique and eye-catching - like a flower blooming in the snow," she began. "Her long hair is shimmering brown like the sun upon the seashore. Her skin nearly glows, her smile is warm, and she has the queen's commanding blue eyes, ever vigilant and alert. It's no wonder he adores her so much."

Daphne then said, "Indeed Charlamos has described his love just so, except for one difference." Lex cocked her head in curiosity. "He describes his true love as having green eyes. Green like an ocean of emeralds. Green like – like your eyes," she pointed out, as if Lex had not already made the connection. She remembered Charlie had used that same poetic analogy the night he had given her the watch. She would never forget that moment and those words. It was the first time she had really noticed the indisputable chemistry between them, and the first time those flames of affection had sparked. She remembered how her heart thumped in her chest when they stood there on Claire's front porch and looked into each other's eyes. With this new revelation, she was now more puzzled than ever. A flicker of hope was rekindled in her heart.

From behind, the distinctive clip-clop of running horses arose. Iris and Daphne bid Lex good luck and a farewell before plunging to the depths of the crystal water. They obviously had no intention of intervening in the affairs of the high council.

Both mounted on stunning horses of imperial stature,

Charlie and Jade pierced through the sunset mist of the forest. When goliath hoofs met the diamond bank, the two dismounted. Lex slowly rose to her feet. She could not imagine what to say to these two people who had been posing as her friends. It was all she could hope for that Charlie or Jade would initiate the exchange. Perhaps deliver some words that might put everything into perspective and relinquish the uncertainty, but this was doubtful.

"I thought we might find you here," Charlie said as he took a submissive step in her direction, expensive trail shoes crunching the precious stones beneath his feet. Jade stood back several paces, uncharacteristically speechless and seemingly ashamed. Charlie stopped just short of the Amaranth and appeared to be in deep thought about the formulation of his words. After a moment of uncomfortable silence he finally said, "Look, Lex, I realize that your trust toward us has been extinguished. I only ask, no beg, that you allow me to explain." She looked at him as though he were a perfect stranger. There was no masking the heartache that his betrayal had inflicted. "What was I to do?" he asked, surprising Lex with the question. "In order to save this earth, the Amaranth had to be found. It was, and still is shocking that the Amaranth actually resided in Kansas, and even more shocking that the Amaranth is you, Lex. In my position, I had no choice but to bring you here, and you've seen what a delicate procedure that has been. As thoroughly as I thought I had planned for your arrival, in the end there was no way to prevent you from discovering that we were not entirely truthful with you. I just hope that I can help you to understand why.

I owe you an explanation along with a complete account of the truth. This is what you have been waiting for and what you deserve – so here it is. Once we identified you, we had to somehow get you to Crow. We couldn't just kidnap you," he reasoned. "It seemed irrational to tie you up, blindfold you, and toss you into the pool. It was more logical to befriend you, earn your trust, offer you a job, teach you Greek, and have you bone up on the mythology so that your arrival here might be more digestible.

The night that Jade, Sevastian and I came into Vincent's and left you that mint candy made from yebillok root was the beginning of your long road to Crow. I knew how incredible that dream would make you feel. I knew that after you experienced a vision like that, you would not forget us. The seed was now planted. We allowed that seed to grow for a month or two until the night Sevastian and I came back to Vincent's and offered to help you study for your exam. Neither of us had a profound knowledge of calculus like we claimed. In order to make that night a success, we came to this world for three months - uh, cycles. This of course stopped time in Kansas. We studied calculus the entirety of every day so that we could help you pass the class. We invited you places and went out of our way to spend time with you and included you in everything we could. We built up everything as an ongoing surprise, always keeping your interest and leaving you eager for more. We gave you an endless supply of wealth and attention, anything to keep your allegiance." He appeared to find his truthfulness difficult to express but continued determinedly nonetheless.

"Once you finally came to this earth, I realized that things would not be as easy as I'd hoped. There were too many details, too many questions that I could not answer until your true purpose was revealed. There was not enough time to get you acquainted with a new world before springing this life-altering news. I could not tell you of Phaedra, especially back in Kansas. If I had told you I was engaged to the Princess of Crow, you would have thought I'd gone mad. It's because of all this that we stand here now, me ashamed and begging for your forgiveness and you rightfully overwhelmed and upset.

For what it's worth," he went on, now spilling over with so much sincerity that Lex felt for just a moment that he might actually mean it, "what I said to you about being my close friend was not a lie. If you can find it in your heart to believe me, and comprehend the decisions I've made, please understand that somewhere in the midst of this extraordinary venture, we have become so fond of you. We truly consider you family, and just as much a part of - what is it they call us - the Rose Flock?"

Though she had listened to his every word, Lex couldn't bring herself to make eye contact. She stared down blankly at the diamonds on which she stood and watched as they faded together in a translucent blur. She couldn't decide if this confession was an act of veracity, or one last desperate attempt to reel her back in so that the master plan may once again move forward. Before she could reach a viable conclusion, he did something that surprised her. He took her hand, looked into her eyes, and said, "It would kill me, it would kill all of us, if we lost your friendship. As of now, we are all embarking upon new territory. Nobody knows what it means to be the Amaranth, or what you are supposed to do so that the prophecy may be fulfilled. I, however, vow to help you and stick by your side every step of the way." He slowly lowered to his knees, surely not an easy feat with sharp diamonds digging aggressively into his patellas. "I pledge my life to you, Lex. And above all, I beg your forgiveness for my decisions thus far." Then it was Jade who hurried to Charlie's side, and following his example, fell to her knees as well. And there they were, in the hazy dusk of the giant forest, Lex stood idly as the two most revered people she had ever met bowed before her as if she were sovereign over the entire universe. But in the end, it was still too much. She needed more time to think, to sort through the truths and the lies, to try to make sense of this madness. Impulsively, she pulled her hand away from Charlie's and she saw hurt in his eyes. He and Jade slowly stood and awaited her verdict.

"Please," she finally said. "Please take me home." There was a moment of cheerless silence as Charlie and Jade exchanged a glance of despair.

"As you wish," he answered desolately.

"Before you go," said Jade who was now the one to tear up, "I want you to know that I understand your decision to leave this earth. You are welcome to live in the mansion as long as you'd like, in fact I hope you'll stay. As Charlie said, it would be devastating to all of us to lose your friendship despite the fact that we don't deserve it."

Lex nodded and mouthed the words, "I'm sorry," but there was no voice to carry these words. She wasn't certain what "I'm sorry" meant, as the phrase had surfaced without thought.

Jade threw her arms around her in a heart-felt goodbye hug. "I will really miss you," said the dark-haired beauty, wiping a tear from her eye.

Lex asked quietly, "What will you tell the high council?"

"I'll think of something," she promised, before climbing back onto her gray horse. "Remember, Lex, we truly do understand." With that, Jade rode off into the shadows of the trees with Charlie's chestnut steed trailing close behind.

"There will be no further delay," Charlie said as he pulled the Manult Stone from beneath his cloak. He motioned for Lex to lead the way. In no time at all, they had arrived at the willow tree and she was once again taking a step into the water gateway.

76

The moment was surreal for Professor Lucant. This was the first time he had traversed these streets and gazed upon these buildings since he was a boy. After forty plus years, it was surprising how little had changed. The Dante Museum had a new sign, bigger, more visually alluring, and new windows. The back entrance had apparently been bricked over. The building next door to the museum, the one that had been vacant during his childhood, was now a bakery.

The house he now stood before, the one across the street from the museum, was in fact the same one that had concealed his peeping younger self while he spied on Papa all those years ago. It was this very house that made it possible for Lucant to make that life-altering discovery and now, he hoped this same house would provide even more answers. Although he had learned a great deal about Papa via snooping, there was still so much he didn't know. Lucant was confident that this would soon change as he zealously recommenced this quest that started when he was just eleven years old.

He took one more look around, breathing in the moment, before climbing three concrete steps and giving the front door an allegro quintet of raps. He aspired to make them sound as friendly as possible, not too hard, not to light, and with an upbeat cadence to give the impression that the visitor might just be amicable. Tonight, Lucant was in as high of spirits as he had ever been. His life was moving forward again and his purpose for living had been rekindled. This was little Benny standing on that top step, following his ambitions and searching for answers. He allowed a beaming smile to divide his lips. For his part, there would be no acting necessary. He would let his cheerfulness shine through to the man who was about to answer the door.

"No need to knock, come on…in?" a man's voice said as the door opened. The large man now standing in the doorway had abruptly ceased his greeting at the sight of his visitor. He was clearly puzzled by Lucant's presence, this much was evident. Lucant's ardent grin widened at the sight of him. This was not at all what he had expected signore Horry Gallo to look like. When the two had spoken via phone several months earlier, Lucant, posing as a tourist with questions regarding the museum, had pictured an individual of slight stature, frail, timid. The culprit for this mental mismatch was Horry's voice. His alto pitch accented with a feminine lisp was a distinct disparity to his big-boned figure. Though he was burley, he struck Lucant as awkward and uncoordinated. His face was comical, clown-like, with an obnoxiously large nose. He sported a bushy, black beard with a pate to match.

"I'm sorry," the man said after allotting Lucant a long, awkward stare, "I was expecting someone else."

"I hope you'll pardon my intrusion at this late hour," Lucant began apologetically, speaking in perfect Italian. The man's face relaxed just a tad beneath his coarse facial hair as he continued. "Unfortunately, my busy schedule allots me little time to attend to personal matters, which is why I am here at such an inopportune time for you I'm sure. Signore Horry Gallo, no?"

"Yes, I am Horry Gallo," the man replied. "And you are?"

Lucant was curious how his next response would be received. After all, the man standing before him was indeed the current curator of the Dante Museum. In this day in age, there was hardly a sentence that began with Dante that was not punctuated with Lucant. "My name is Benjamin Lucant," he stated in a straightforward manner, so his introduction would not be misconceived as a hoax. Horry Gallo's face twisted into surprise. This nonverbal reaction told Lucant two things; one, that Signore

Gallo recognized the name, two, he was quite dubious that his visitor was indeed who he claimed to be. This was all confirmed when he finally gathered himself to speak once more.

"You must understand when I say I cannot believe you," Horry said as a cold, uncomfortable breeze pushed in at him. "I have attended several of Dr. Lucant's lectures, and sir, you do not look at all like him."

"A man looks quite different without his beard," Lucant contested with a light-hearted chuckle. He casually removed a wallet from his inside coat pocket and took from it his Cambridge faculty identification card. He handed it to the big man in the doorway and said, "On nights such as this, one is easily reminded of the extra warmth facial hair provides."

Horry reached out for the card, taking it in his giant mitt, turning it over and over, looking from front to back as if to expose some flaw that would make this identification card stand out as fake. Lucant hoped this recognition process would not continue too much longer as it was quite cold tonight. To his great fortune, Horry's expression slid from cautious to enthusiastic so quickly it was nearly laughable. Before he uttered his first words of excitement, Lucant knew he had completed the first step and that it would be of no consequence for Horry Gallo to lead the way to the primary target, Horry's father, Salvatore.

"It might as well be the pope himself knocking on my door tonight," Horry exclaimed in delight, his voice even higher under enthusiasm's sway. He reached out and yanked Lucant's hand into a rough shake. "What on earth brings you to the house of Gallo?"

"As I'm sure you know," Lucant replied, happy to receive his hand back from the gauche grip of his host, "it's not so much what's on earth that interests me, it's what's below it." He wasn't entirely keen on lowering himself to deliver such a pathetic gag but decided it would appeal to Horry's character. He was right. Horry chortled at this pitiful joke like an oversized child. Lucant continued, "But my true purpose in coming here goes a bit deeper. If I may be so forward, might we further discuss matters inside? I admit the winter and I do not always see eye to eye."

"Yes, yes, of course," Horry said all but jerking Lucant through the doorway with a clumsy pull of the arm.

Once inside, Lucant brushed the hitch-hiking snowflakes from the shoulders of his coat. He shivered twice, pushing the cold from his bones before the warm air of the entranceway expunged the lingering chill in a soothing blast.

"May I take your coat and hat, Professor?" Horry asked, still grinning uncontrollably over this celebrity caller.

"If it is no bother to you, I would very much like to keep them on," Lucant replied. "At least until I can warm up a little, eh?"

"As long as you are comfortable," Horry said, nearly bouncing now and looking more clown-like with each passing minute. "Please, Professor, come with me, there is someone whom you must meet."

Jackpot, Lucant thought to himself. This poor fool is going to make this all too easy.

The house was dark and unimpressive overall. Dim overhead lights guided the way as Lucant followed Horry down the narrow hall, old boards creaking beneath their feet. Ahead, a brighter light could be seen and music could be heard. There was a small kitchen on the left, a narrow staircase leading up to the right. And now that Lucant could see the living room, he deduced that the only visible entrance or exit was the door he had just come through. This appraisal of possible escape routes was an old habit he picked up from his time in the Italian Special Forces. He did this every time he walked into any enclosure so it was second nature at this point. It was imperative to always know the quickest escape route, and maybe more importantly, the quickest way his enemy could escape. If things were to work out with his plan, this bit of awareness might be pertinent to the evening.

Somewhere between a brisk stroll and a skip, Horry entered into a comfortable living room with Lucant hot on his heels. The ear-soothing tenor of Andrea Bocelli was drifting through the dusty speakers of a very old compact disk player. There were two portraits hanging on the wall, Jesus on one side of the room, Dante Alighieri on the other. The furniture was old, ugly and stained. Brown curtains, drab and almost repellant to one's gaze, were drawn tight over a window, another escape route. The Holy Bible rested upon the coffee table in the center of the room. Beside the coffee table sat a withered old man in a motorized wheelchair – this was Salvatore Gallo.

Salvatore was hunched. His face was kind enough but also tinged with a hint of shrewdness. He was mostly bald, with a sparse rim of black hair encircling his head just above ear level. He wore a heavy sweater and navy blue pants with irregular stains upon them. The outlines of his legs were little more than twig-like structures, atrophied after years in the chair.

Scarcely in control of himself, Horry pressed pause on the CD player and began to blurt an introduction. "Father, this is…" but he was cut short by Salvatore's gruff voice.

"Dr. Lucant," he said, quite sure of himself.

Lucant might as well have caught a glimpse of the Loch Ness Monster, he was that surprised. This instant recognition by the old man was not necessarily worrisome, but mentally engaging. Had Salvatore overheard the exchange that had taken place a moment earlier at the front door? This idea was unlikely given his distance from the entryway, the volume of the music, and the average hearing ability of an eighty-seven year old man. The more obvious option was that Salvatore had an apt ability to identify facial features, much unlike his son, and recognized the famous Dante scholar beardless and hatted.

"Yes," Horry replied, "this is the great Benjamin Lucant." He then turned to Lucant and said, "My father's vision is not so bad for his age, eh?"

"Quite impressive," Lucant responded with a courteous head nod to Salvatore.

Horry then commenced, "Professor, this is my father…"

"Signore Salvatore Gallo," Lucant interrupted, keeping

friendly eye-contact with the frail man in the chair and rendering Horry zero for two at introductions.

"I am confused," Horry said, his tone still upbeat. "Do the two of you know each other?"

"We have never met," Lucant replied.

"Professor," Salvatore said, getting right down to business, "did you come here tonight for a tour of the Dante Museum?"

"No," Lucant replied frankly.

"Then my question is answered," Salvatore said, nodding to himself while turning his gaze to the portrait of Dante on the far wall.

"Your question?" Lucant repeated, quite puzzled.

"Yes, will you explain, Papa?" Horry asked. "I'm sure our honored guest is just as confused as I am."

Salvatore turned back to the two men standing side-by-side near the hallway's entrance and said, "Fifteen years ago, Horry came home with your first book. Each night after our dinner we would come to this room, he with his book, me with my book." He pointed to the Bible sitting atop the table as an insinuation that that was "his" book. "Unlike my son, my days of chasing Dante were long over, so I paid the book little attention – that is until I happened to catch a glimpse of your name on the cover. I remember thinking that the name Benjamin Lucant was a very impressive coincidence. Later that evening, I opened the book to find your picture on the inside of the dust cover. It was then I knew without a doubt that you were Marcello's son."

"Papa, what are you talking about?" Horry asked in near desperation. The big man had obviously been kept in the dark about his father's secret.

Salvatore shot Horry a disgruntled glance for interrupting, then continued. "I knew without a doubt that you were Marcello's boy because you are the spitting image of him." He let out a guttural chuckle. "As for your professional interests, the apple did not fall far from the tree. You see, because you bear such a strong resemblance to Marcello, I was able to recognize you as soon as you came into the room tonight. So, I wondered why Benjamin Lucant might come for a visit but you just answered that for me, didn't you?"

Horry shifted awkwardly next to Lucant, as if his father's shrewdness made him uncomfortable. Lucant on the other hand was quite impressed. What a worthy adversary Salvatore Gallo might make, mentally at least.

The old man said, "I thought to myself, the only two conceivable reasons that this man would visit here would be to see the Dante Museum or to seek information about his father. Since, as you have just proclaimed, you are not here to visit the museum, the purpose of your visit must be the latter." He slowly placed his crippled hands on the wheels of the chair, turning himself toward Lucant. "That is all I know, Professor. Your knowledge of Marcello's life is unclear to me. I am not sure what kind of valuable information I can give you."

"I am truly impressed, signore," Lucant said, meaning every word of it. "Your astuteness is noteworthy and entirely accurate. I have indeed come here to talk to you about my father. I hope my visit is not a bother to you."

Horry's air resided somewhere between wonderment and disappointment as he said to Salvatore, "Why did you not tell me you knew Professor Lucant's father?"

Before Salvatore could answer, Lucant said, "I found out for myself many years ago that there are some things fathers keep from their sons."

Salvatore's naturally squinted eyes widened slightly at this comment, before returning to their neutral state of sagacity. He seemed to be in deep thought as Lucant and Horry patiently awaited his response. Finally, he said, "Do you drink, Professor? Grappa?"

"Only if it is stravecchia," Lucant replied with a grin.

"Is there anything else worthy of soaking your palate?" Salvatore replied, still displaying that stern expression of a long-beaked bird peering down from a power line. "Horry, would you mind fetching drinks?"

Horry seemed reluctant to miss even the most trifling segment of this riveting exchange but complied without quarrel. He hurried out of the living room, thumping down the hall like an ogre toward the kitchen. "I invite you to take off your winter attire, professor," Salvatore offered. He gestured toward the arm chair directly across the table from himself. "And please, do what I do best and rest your legs."

"As I was telling your son," Lucant said politely as he sunk into a dusty armchair, "the winter has a way of getting into my bones. If it is no bother to you, I would very much like to keep them on."

Salvatore nodded with indifference as Horry made a notably speedy return with three glasses and a bottle of grappa sitting atop a wooden serving tray. He set the tray on the coffee table, poured the grappa, and handed the first glass to Lucant, then Salvatore before lowering himself onto the couch with his large thighs.

Salvatore placed his hooked nose over the glass and sniffed it. He took a sip and said to Lucant, "Your father was a brilliant man."

"I would not know," Lucant replied. "He did not spend much time with me when I was young."

"I am sorry to hear that," Salvatore replied. "Marcello was dedicated to his research. The truth is, I knew him almost five years before I found out he even had a son. The man was one to leave his home-life at home."

Lucant nodded in agreement. "Yes, and when he returned home each night, he brought his, what was it you said, 'research' with him. I do not think he was even aware that he had a home-life. Because of this, I know very little about him, and that, Signore Gallo, is why I am here."

Salvatore cocked his head to one side in curiosity. "I am curious, Professor, how did you come to find out that I knew Marcello?"

"Because I followed him," Lucant stated matter-of-factly. "I grew tired of his secretive behavior so I decided to follow him. Every day he came to the Dante Museum, which of course you were in charge of at the time."

Salvatore put forth a faint visage of unease when he asked, "Did your father ever tell you why he came to the museum every day?"

Lucant wanted to play this hand delicately. Papa had disclosed some information – right before he went trigger happy, but Lucant was now interested to see how secretive Salvatore was going to be, so his answer was, "No, he never did tell me why he went there. In fact, he was unaware that I had followed him. It would mean a great deal to me, signore, if you could shed some light on my father's life for me."

There was a long pause where Salvatore seemed to be thinking hard, and the only sound that could be heard was the rhythmic squeaking of the springs inside the couch as Horry, like a big child, bounced out his excited energy while he too awaited a response.

"I hired Marcello to help me out around the museum."

"Liar!" Lucant screamed in his head, without so much as altering his attentive expression of interest. To Salvatore he asked, "What did he do there?"

"He gave tours, answered the guest's questions, things of that nature."

"Really?" Lucant asked, allowing a tad of disbelief to show through. "That is what my father did every day? What about this 'research' you just mentioned?"

Salvatore nodded and looked away. "It was a long time ago," he mumbled, "my memory is not what it used to be."

Lucant now knew what he was dealing with. The single lie that Salvatore had just told proved that he had been in the mix of whatever Marcello was into all those years ago. This man was protecting a secret so vital, that a father would kill his own son to keep it. This thought sent adrenaline coursing through Lucant's veins, yet he remained as relaxed as if he were sitting on a beach watching the sunset. He would suppress his violent ambitions and proceed tactfully. Perhaps further questioning would expose a hidden truth. Perhaps the old man would slip up. Lucant proceeded in a pleasant, civilized tone as he casually leaned back in the armchair and crossed one leg over the other. "Please, signore, is there anything you can tell me of my father's death? You see, I was not home when he died, and without a single explanation, I was whisked off to the orphanage. Once there, I was visited by a kind woman who explained to me that there had been an accident and that my father was dead. She never said what that accident was, and I was too shy, or maybe too upset to ask." Lucant paused and pondered. All of this was actually true, except the part about not being home when it happened. He really had been enrolled in a boys' home where he spent eight years of his life before enlisting into the Italian military. A frumpy woman in a blue blazer really had taken him into a private room to deliver the news about Marcello's death. She had been the resident psychologist and made a living tending to the never-ending issues of parentless boys. And, he never pressed her for more information on what sort of an accident it had been as there had been no reason to do so.

Years later, once he had made the decision to hunt down the black book, he did attempt to locate the police files on his father. His search came to a frustrating end almost as quickly as it had begun. He was told that all old files had been moved to a storage warehouse. When he pursued that avenue, he came to find that the warehouse had burned down eight years earlier. He knew he really didn't need them. The files would not likely contain any new information that he didn't already know. Still, it was worth being thorough. He was truly curious how the hunched old man sitting across the room would answer this question.

"What do I know about your father's death?" Salvatore repeated, interlocking his crooked fingers and resting his chin on them. He thought for a long time. Lucant wondered if he was fabricating a reply or actually trying to recall an incident that happened three decades earlier.

"Marcello had been very sick," he finally said.

Well, at least this is starting out truthful, Lucant thought.

"On the day of his death, he did not show up at the museum. This was quite unlike your father. In all the years I knew him, he never missed a day of...work. He never came late. I knew something had to be wrong." His words were interrupted by a sudden coughing fit, where gurgled, phlegmy gagging rendered him momentarily unable to relay speech. Horry was quick to his feet to refill his father's empty glass with another round of grappa. Salvatore, with watery eyes, drank the liquid in two quick shots. Lucant waited patiently.

Finally, Salvatore was able to continue. "After I closed up the museum, I drove to his... your house. I'll never forget what awaited me. Police cars, men in uniform, yellow tape. My heart ached at the sight. I remember feeling very sick. I ran to a man with a badge and a trench coat and asked him what had happened. I told him I was a friend. The man, the bastard, with such an unconcerned air told me that things were still under investigation. Then he turned and walked away.

Eventually the newspaper ran a story on the incident. The single article would be the only thing that ever mentioned Marcello's death before the mystery was seemingly buried."

Lucant leaned forward in his chair, intrigued and equally as confused at the word "mystery." If Salvatore was telling the truth, one would be led to believe that there was more to the story then an old man who had committed suicide.

Salvatore went on. "Marcello was found at his desk with a fatal gunshot wound to his head. As far as I'm aware, it is still undetermined if your father's death was a murder or a suicide." A strand of saliva dripped down the side of his mouth. He wiped it away with his shirt sleeve before asking, "Am I telling you anything you do not already know?"

"You are telling me a great deal, Signore Gallo. I am very grateful for this information," Lucant replied, now consumed with utter fascination. He imagined himself as a crime scene investigator walking into that old den and seeing an old man slumped over a desk. There would be a gun in his hand or on the ground in close proximity. There would be a gaping hole in his head. There would be blood spattered along the wall behind him. Every piece of visual evidence would scream suicide, but Salvatore had just tossed the word "murder" into play. Feeling the rush of suspense he said to the old man, "Please, will you continue?"

"Your father was a close friend of mine, and you see, his death began to consume me. I never planned on solving the investigation. I simply wanted to know what the police had found and what they might be thinking. As luck would have it, I had a cousin in the force. We were not extremely close but," he chuckled, "as you know, in Italy, family is family. After much persistence on my part, I finally talked him into looking into the reports. What he found out was somewhat disturbing."

Lucant, with all of his practice in remaining calm during the most intense situations, was having trouble doing just that. With eyes keen with interest, he nodded for Salvatore to continue.

"Does it pain you to hear this information about your father?" Salvatore asked.

"Not at all." Lucant replied. "That, after all, is why I'm here."

With difficulty, Salvatore went on. "Marcello was found face down on his desk with a bullet wound in the right side of his head. According to crime scene investigators, the bullet fragments and the blood that resulted from a close-range gunshot wound were located as one would expect in relation to your father's body. The gun that he had used, which was later confirmed to have matched the bullet, was found on the floor next to him."

"An obvious suicide," Lucant stated.

"Not so obvious when you consider the rest of the clues," Salvatore said seriously. "The investigators discovered that two additional bullets had been fired from that gun before the fatal shot. One bullet was lodged in a nearby wall. The other had shattered a picture frame in the hallway. There was no evidence that these bullets had struck a human target, but one must ask, why had Marcello fired two rounds before taking his own life?"

Lucant, of course, knew very well the answer to that question. He said nothing as Salvatore continued.

"Perhaps the most incriminating piece of evidence alluding to foul play was what the police found upon Marcello's desk."

Lucant's pulse soared. The desk in that old den was the very last place he had seen the object of his absolute desire.

"The bullet had not passed through his head in a clean manner. It was, forgive me, rather messy. A great deal of blood had blanketed the desk, the floor, and the wall. According to my cousin, it appeared as though half of the desk had been painted crimson. Except…" he paused, looking uneasy. Lucant's thirsty eyes prodded him on. "Except there was an area upon the desk that had not received a single drop. It did not receive a drop of blood because something was there when he had shot himself. The bloodless spot was in the shape of a perfect rectangle."

"A book," Lucant stated decisively.

Salvatore broke gaze, looking down at his shaking hands with a nervous semblance. He took a deep breath, and very quietly said, "Yes, presumably so. But there are many items that are rectangular in nature, it could have been a cigar box or a…"

Lucant was in no mood to listen to Salvatore try to invent false possibilities when they both knew damn well that it was a book that had been taken, and not just any book. Lucant cut the old man short. "Which means that the book was removed from the desk after my father had been killed."

Horry, who had been listening in silent disbelief up to this point, mouthed some indistinguishable utterance of shock as his father wrapped up his memories of the incident. "There was no additional evidence found at the scene that the police could use to determine what had really happened. All they had was an apparent suicide, two stray bullets, and something that had been taken from the desk after Marcello had…. well, you know."

Lucant was mesmerized by this. Some of what Salvatore had just said was brand new insight into his search for the book. However, this did absolutely nothing to help uncover its current whereabouts. The room was silent. Horry was staring at Lucant, apparently in high hopes of a magnanimous response. At the moment, Salvatore looked frail and tired, but mostly sad. The clever and patient professor decided to play his next hand.

"Perhaps we can help each other quench our curiosities, Signore Gallo," Lucant stated in an avid tone, trying to inject some life back into the man in the wheelchair. "You have so graciously told me information that I have spent a great majority of my life wondering about. Already, my trip here this evening has been anything but a waste of time. In return for your kindness, and in light of this new information, I can now give you some insight to both of these unanswered questions."

Salvatore looked up, interested. "You can?"

"Yes, I can explain why there were two stray bullets and an item missing from the desk."

Salvatore shook his head. "I am not sure I want to know. Maybe I want to leave it be. It took me years to put it all behind me and return to the life I led before your father came into it." He stared adoringly at the Bible on the table. "I have been traveling a different path for quite a while now. I am finally content."

"I envy your contentment," Lucant said calmly. "Unfortunately, I am anything but content. If anything, Signore Gallo, I am envious of you. You have already achieved my greatest desire. You have had the opportunity to study the sacred pages of that one-of-a-kind book."

"I do not know this book of which you speak," Salvatore said as earnestly as possible, although these words came to Lucant's ears as a timid lie.

"I do not appreciate deception," Lucant said with a growl, looking the old man square in the eyes. It was now time to take control of this conversation and get on with things. Both Gallo men looked very uneasy. "When I was eleven years old, I began following my father to your museum every day. He traveled with a tall, younger man in a burgundy sedan. The two of them would be let in the back entrance to the museum by an armed guard. It would be eight or nine hours before they emerged. When Papa returned home each night, he spent the rest of the evening in his den. I spied on him through the keyhole and watched as he studied two books. Eventually, I came to find out that they were both ancient copies of Dante's Inferno. The day he died, I learned much more.

As you accurately recalled, he was very sick. This is likely the reason why he absent-mindedly left that black book on the desk that day. Perhaps it was foolish, but I seized the opportunity to look upon its pages. I studied it just long enough to know exactly what it was. I would have spent the entire day committing the pages to memory, but he came home. I had been caught."

"Dear God," Salvatore uttered, voice tinged with regret.

"For a while, we sat in the den and talked calmly, civilized. Like the foolish child I was, I thought for a moment that perhaps he might be proud of me for showing an interest in something that intrigued him so profoundly. That is when he took out his gun and tried to kill me."

Horry gasped from across the room.

"The only reason he missed, even at such close range, was the sickness that filled his head. I was halfway down the street when I heard the third shot."

There was a long bout of silence as Lucant allowed this information to sink in. By the look on Salvatore's face, this information was tearing at his very soul. His past had now come back to haunt him, or maybe worse. There was nothing that Horry could say. He was so dumbfounded by this unexpected turn of events that speechlessness was his only response. As far as Lucant was concerned, Salvatore was responsible for everything that was about to happen. Horry, who, for all his oafishness seemed like a pretty decent man, would unfortunately be a casualty of this war.

So too, for that matter, would be his daughter.

"Now you have your answers, signore," Lucant said, casually sniffing his empty glass, allowing the lingering scent of grappa to caress his sinuses. "I think we both know that the item missing from the desk was indeed Dante's own copy of his book and I think we can narrow the list of potential thieves down to one suspect. If your accounts of that day's events are accurate, you arrived on the scene during the investigation, so you could not have taken the book. As it happens, I have been highly trained in the art of lie-detecting. This was very helpful during my time in the armed forces. And, as it happens, I believe you are telling the truth about your arrival at our home that evening. That being said, the likely book thief was the man who drove my father to your museum every day." Lucant leaned forward in the chair, resting his elbows on his knees. He gave Salvatore a look of utter seriousness and said, "I am going to need you to tell me his name."

"Please, Professor," Salvatore pleaded. "This is something that should not be pursued."

"That is for me to decide," Lucant said.

It was Salvatore's turn to get stern, "No, you do not understand. The information within the book you seek would completely alter the world as we know it, but it would not be for the good. I dare say it would catalyze the apocalypse. Don't you see? This is why thirty years ago, our group acquired that book in the first place. We stole it from a place that did not guarantee its absolute safety. Our sole purpose in life was to look after it, to guard it, to understand it. That is why we paid the best security guard in Florence to stand watch day in and day out. That is why we all took an oath to protect it and to keep it secret no matter what the cost. That, my dear Professor, is why your father tried to kill you even though you were just a boy. He did what he had to do in accordance with our pact.

Our biggest mistake was our curiosity and our thirst for knowledge. Your father, myself and the other men you saw, were each of us scholars of Italian history with a particular interest in

Dante. When we first heard the book existed, we were in disbelief. When the book came into our hands, we were elated. But, because of our lust for knowledge, and our desire to unlock the secrets within the book, we did not destroy it. We couldn't bring ourselves to do it. It seemed like sacrilege to destroy an artifact so rare, so valuable and so full of unbelievable information.

In the beginning, there was much discussion about what should be done with it. The smart conclusion would have been to burn it and eliminate the possibility that it should ever fall into the wrong hands. When not one of us could bring himself to strike the match, we forged an agreement. The agreement was simply: keep the book an absolute secret, protect it with your life, and…" he paused, and looked away as if ashamed. "Kill anyone who found out about it – anyone. I am truly sorry, Benjamin, that you had to suffer the repercussions of three foolish men. I too am still suffering from my past mistakes. Believe me, Professor, the book will consume you. It's almost as if it has its own evil soul."

Lucant was smiling on the inside. He, himself, had fallen under the book's spell, and had submerged himself in the disturbing feelings.

"After the book disappeared," he went on, "I locked the basement where the three of us met. To this very day, it has not been reopened. I cannot face going back down there in fear that the memories of the book would again overtake me. It took many years before I could rid my every waking thought of it. When it had finally fled my conscious, I spent the remaining years, even up to this day, living in fear that my past would catch up with me. Well Professor, it finally has. Out of respect to you, I cannot aid your search for that book. My knowledge of the consequences will not allow it. Although I deeply desire that it had never happened, I still must hold true to our pact. The fate of humanity depends on it. So you see, Professor, I will take that man's name to my grave."

Lucant should have been angrier, but he was so damn intrigued by all that he had just heard, he was unable, at that moment anyway, to get upset. He still had some cards up his sleeve. Card one – civilized diplomacy. "Signore Gallo," he said, feigning insult. "I, like my father, am a devoted Dante scholar. It seems you had much trust for my father. Why am I not worthy of that trust?"

"I don't mean any offense to you, Professor. Your reputation as a Dante scholar speaks for itself. If anyone on this planet is worthy of owning that book, it would be you. However, I would not feel comfortable giving the book to God himself."

Lucant nodded with a facial expression that might portray understanding. After all, he did understand, and even respected Salvatore's devotion to secrecy. Lucant was no fool. The old man had spoken the truth when he made the claim that the book would catalyze an apocalypse if it fell into the wrong hands. Papa had understood this as well. It would be difficult for others, especially those who were unfamiliar with Inferno, to grasp how the world might erupt in turmoil should it become common knowledge that the story was in fact true.

The black book was proof that Dante had indeed located the entrance to hell and traveled through the nine circles of increasing horror as he descended the depths. Along the way he encountered broods of evil that would cause one's very soul to shudder. There were unholy beasts, demons and creatures that were only known by the ancient Greeks. At the very lower sanctum was Lucifer himself. Should this become public knowledge, at the very least it could produce widespread panic. A more likely scenario would be the curious humans who would overstep their boundaries to get a glimpse of this for themselves. Lucant knew that the entities that dwelled below the earth's surface would not take kindly to mortal intrusion. It would then be likely that hell could be unleashed on earth. That would be the worst case. There were, of course, many other scenarios that could play out, none of them good. That is why these men, Papa, Salvatore, and the nameless other, were defending the secret with such ferocity. This steadfast devotion to a cause so dire would certainly call for extreme measures on Lucant's part if he ever wanted to pry the secrets from Salvatore's lips. Quite unfortunately for the Gallos, the wise professor had planned for just such obstinacy. It was time to play the second card, and this one, would be the trump card.

"I am starting to warm up now," Lucant said to nobody in particular. At this, he removed his wool hat and stuffed it efficiently into his coat pocket. The Gallos seemed almost startled at the sight of his cleanly shaven head. The air on his scalp felt refreshing as he was practically boiling in his winter attire. In truth, he had not been nearly as cold as he had let on. Instead, his intention for retaining his coat was because it concealed a crucial bargaining piece. He directed his gaze to Horry and said, "Signore, do you know the current time?"

"Yes," Horry said, "it is nine-thirty."

"So she is quite tardy then?"

"Professor, I don't know what…" and then he got it. "Yes, I was expecting my daughter to arrive some time ago, if she's who you're referring to." He chuckled almost nervously. "I've been so wrapped up in the conversation between you and my father, her absence slipped my mind." His burley face then twisted with perplexity. "But how did you know?"

Lucant could have gone on to tell him the details of how he had paid an unlicensed yet reliable, black-market detective to spy on the Gallos for the last three months. This was of course arranged over an untraceable, disposable cell phone, using a fake name, and even a voice moderator to ensure absolute secrecy of identity. This man had done such a fabulous job recording and cataloging every aspect of the Gallos' lives, that Lucant had even gone as far as to pay in excess of the agreed upon amount. When the man was finally relieved of his services and Lucant had disappeared into a sea of eight billion possible culprits, the Gallos' private lives were anything but private. Lucant knew every pertinent detail about Horry and Salvatore's daily routines, visitors, habits and so on. Even not-so-pertinent details such as Horry's shoe size and his favorite dessert had been recorded. From this wealth of information, it turned out that the most useful tidbit was that Horry had a daughter. She, her father, and her grandfather were very close. In fact, she never broke her routine of visiting them every Tuesday and Friday evening at eight-thirty sharp. As far as Lucant was concerned, the fact that she was a holy sister at a Catholic church made the whole situation that much sweeter.

He could have told the Gallos this, but it was way more pleasurable to be mysterious. Instead, he removed a plastic freezer bag from the inside pocket of his coat and tossed it haphazardly upon the table. The object within produced a dull thud as the Gallos looked on with confusion. This confusion would hastily be converted to horror at the realization of just what was sealed within the bag. Lucant knew that Salvatore, being quick as a whip, would know the origin of the object right away. Horry, however, would likely be slower to recognize that the severed hand belonged to his own daughter, that is, until he saw the silver cross ring upon the finger. Blood pooled in the bottom of the bag, still warm from the recent harvest.

"You son of a bitch," Salvatore growled contemptuously, looking now like an injured wolf.

"What is that?" Horry asked, examining the bag from his location across the room.

Lucant's brain instinctively assessed the possibilities of the situation. The next ten seconds would be determined by Horry's ability to function under extreme stress. Once he realized that the hand belonged to his daughter, Imelda, he would do one of two things. Horry's best option would be to stay calm, let the situation play out, and perhaps attack at a more opportune moment. That's what a smart man would do. His other option would be to give in to blind rage and charge Lucant like a raging lunatic. Should he choose this irrational approach, Lucant had his trusty knife strapped to the underside of his left forearm. The nineteen centimeter blade could be retrieved in the blink of an eye and Horry would be in a losing battle with an elite GOI commando. Still, the man was quite brawny. The lumbering bull has been known to spear an overly confident matador from time to time. Lucant concentrated on all aspects of the situation. His guard was on high alert.

"Is that….is that Imelda's hand?" Horry asked with a glassy-eyed expression. Lucant met the big man's gaze with cold indifference and nodded. "What have you done to my daughter?" Horry demanded, this time with fury spilling from his vocal cords.

In the next instant, Lucant knew which avenue Horry would take. The raging bull, he thought to himself as he covertly readied his hand on the knife blade. Horry soared to his feet and flung the coffee table aside as if it were made of plywood. Lucant, the skilled matador, stayed calmly seated for just a second longer as Horry lunged across the room, hands clenched in tight fists.

At the last second, Lucant sprung to his feet, anticipating either a full-on frontal tackle or a fist to the face. Horry chose the latter and drove his large knuckles toward Lucant's nose. Lucant dropped low and to the side, using the big man's careless momentum to his own advantage. Horry's failure to connect threw him forward and off balance. Lucant kicked his feet from underneath him and Horry plummeted to the floor beard first and thudded like a sack of flour. The vibration from the fall rattled the picture of Jesus from its hook. It crashed down loudly sending shards of glass skating across the wood floor. Lucant was on Horry before the bearded man could get back on his feet - the savage wolf overpowering the much larger buffalo. The knife's point caught the lamp-light as it arced through the air, driving downward with ferocious velocity. With a wretched sound of metal on bone, the blade lodged into Horry's lower spine. His agonizing scream displayed the upper range of his ill-fitting voice. Salvatore looked on in horror, helplessly confined to his wheelchair, feeble and incapable of intervening.

Horry's raging bellows now turned to miserable whimpers. "I can't move my legs," he cried, "Signore, why are you doing this? Please, my father will give you what you want." He gazed up at Salvatore with a desperate expression. "Tell him what he wants to know," he said between breathless grunts and clenched teeth. "Tell him, for Imelda's sake."

Salvatore was shaking. His expression became distant as he said almost inaudibly, "She's already dead son. She's already dead. We are all already dead."

He really is an intelligent man. Lucant thought, enjoying his controlling hand in this situation. This would work better if the Gallos believed Imelda to still be alive. She was, in fact, a crucial bargaining piece. But there were other ways to acquire desired information, more sinister ways.

Salvatore continued with an air that resided somewhere between anger and hurt. "You do not suppose he would just walk out of here after I tell him the secret I've been protecting my whole life do you?" He was clearly addressing his paraplegic son but looking at Lucant as he spoke. "You do not believe that once he knows the secret he'll just stand up, thank us for the grappa, and walk out the door? He's no fool. We know his identity. He would have every law enforcement agent hot on his trail the moment you or I could get to the phone. No, my dear boy, my wonderful son, he means to kill us. This was his plan before he even set foot inside our home." He leaned down and retrieved the Bible that had come to rest by the wheel of his chair after Horry had upended the coffee table. He rubbed his hand over the cover with a distant look in his eyes. "I have been ready to meet God for quite some time. Perhaps it is fitting this night, as we celebrate our savior's birth, that an old, tired man should die." His eyes filled with tears as he surveyed his son helplessly pinned beneath Lucant's knee with a knife in his back. "I am truly sorry, my son, that you, and Imelda have to die for my past deeds."

"Papa, please just tell him what he wants to know," Horry pleaded, now drained and weak.

"You do not seem to understand," Salvatore said. "This man will kill us regardless of what I do or do not tell him. I will not sacrifice all humanity for a fate that has already been determined for us. Thirty years ago, I made a pact with Benjamin's father to protect this secret. Tonight, this burden will finally be lifted from my shoulders." Tears dribbled down his face as he said to Horry, "I love you, my son, and I loved your beautiful daughter. Please forgive me." He cradled the Bible to his bony chest. "We will all be together again very soon, in our Father's kingdom."

Lucant took a deep, impatient breath. Of course he planned on killing the Gallos, assuming Salvatore would have given him the information he sought in hope that it would save the life of his beloved granddaughter. Obviously, the sly old bastard saw right through that charade. An elite GOI commando, however, was never without a plan B, or a plan C or D for that matter. His only regret is that plan B would take longer. How long, he could not say. The answer would depend on how long these men could withstand some good old fashioned physical pain. Lucant was not a psychopath. He received no pleasure from torture, but by the same token, he felt no regret either. He had a mission, and within this mission there were obstacles to overcome. Salvatore's defiance was the first big obstacle, and if the response was to take him apart piece by piece, that was what he would do. Plan B would hurt these men, and they would experience pain beyond anything they could have ever imagined. Lucant glanced at his wristwatch. Damn, he thought, this may take a while. I was hoping to be halfway to the gates of hell by first light. This was not the first time in his life that a wrench had been tossed into the spokes. Fortunately for Lucant, and quite unfortunate for Salvatore and Horry, improvisation came second nature to the brilliant professor.

He tried one last card, a card that served the symbiotic purpose of showing mercy to the Gallos all while saving himself the time and hassle of incremental body part reduction. He addressed Salvatore, with a tone that meant business, "Bravo signore, I commend your insightful outlook on this situation. If I am to be honest, it pains me to take the lives of two noteworthy colleagues, two men that share my passion, but alas as you say, it will be done. I will give you one last opportunity to spare yourself and your son a slow, painful death. Tell me what I wish to know, and I will kill you both, quickly and relatively painlessly. If you continue to hold out, you will have the pleasure of watching me remove Horry's organs right here and now. If he passes before you talk, you will be next, and I'll be sure to take twice as long with you."

"Please," Horry kept saying over and over, now sobbing with his nose pressed into the wood floor. It was uncertain which of the two men he was pleading with, perhaps both of them. Despite the desperate wails from his son, Salvatore said nothing, but began trembling so violently, that the Bible slipped from his hands and fell onto the floor amongst the shattered glass.

This silence gave Lucant his answer. With the precision of a surgeon and the grace of a figure skater, Benny withdrew the bloody knife, cut the shirt from Horry's back, and began to filet skin, starting at the neck and working downward toward the first puncture wound. Spinal vertebrae became visible, blood began to pool on the floor, and the excruciating, gut-wrenching screams from Horry became deafening. It was going to be a long night.

77

The return transport to Kansas was different from the initial transport to Earth B. Lex stepped into the water-like substance within the willow, instantly became drowsy, then fell beneath the pool in a peaceful, euphoric slumber. This time, however, there was not a puffy cloud holding her aloft nor did she fly through the cool night air like an eagle. There were no sparkling ponds, no dark distant mountains and no leafy willow trees. Instead, she felt as though she was hanging comfortably beneath the water's surface - warm, happy and content. Forgetting recent events, and the emotional havoc, the pool made her feel as carefree as a child. In fact, the prominent sensation that ensued from this wondrous voyage was the feeling of being held comfortably within her mother's arms.

It felt like hours. Curled up in this weightless embrace she felt safe, protected, and most importantly, a million miles away from any burdening care or concern. There was a certain love in the delicate way in which these invisible arms cradled her. It was not a mother's love, but perhaps something just as powerful. It felt like a dream. If she had been awake and able to see, she might have been flattered by the way Charlie was holding her there beneath the pool's glowing surface. It wasn't really water, so they could both breathe. He held her in his arms and stared unblinkingly at her placid face as if he could not admire anything more. Her head rested on his hand and her hair danced in step with the smooth dynamic flow of the pool. In that brief moment in time, they both achieved serenity; perhaps this was the calm before the storm. Just when it couldn't get any more perfect, she awoke.

Charlie had a firm grasp on her hand as he pulled her above the water – or whatever it was. His other hand supported her lower back. Her mind was hazy and her body unstable, but with his aid she found her sea legs and climbed from the pool onto the cold dirt floor. He quietly retrieved the watch they had left sitting upon the perimeter stone and handed it to her. "For what it's worth," he said.

She examined the timepiece - five forty-two pm, December the twenty-third. She wasn't surprised actually. There was no more doubt about the reality of the pool, the other earth, or any of the events that had taken place in Crow. She believed and understood that not a second of time had passed on this earth since she had last been here. Like an Olympic gold medalist standing on the podium, the concept of this unimaginable new reality was too grand to fully appreciate, but at least she had finally accepted it.

Still, after the plethora of fantastic new experiences, she could not get past the looming sorrow coming from within. Although she had gained so much, she felt like she had also lost. The kiss between Charlie and the princess flashed through her brain and reminded her exactly what it was she had lost.

What to do now? she thought. That was the million dollar question. Her world had been changed, rearranged, added to, then turned upside down. It was enough to make the most logical individual teeter on insanity. Here she was, standing in the secret basement of a mysterious ancient church with someone she might just love, who just happened to be engaged to a princess in another world. If that wasn't bleeding mad…

She needed time to organize thoughts and put everything into perspective. But how much time did she really have? Should her decisions be contemplated with urgency? On this earth, she had all the time she needed. On the other earth, time was running out, or so the prophecy said. One thing she knew for certain was that despite the downhearted look on Charlie's face, there was nothing she could even think to say to him. There was way too much to discuss, and before she thought it through, she did not want to venture down the road of conversation.

After departing the church, Charlie and Lex stood at the woods' edge, the bitter wind gusts slicing into their exposed skin like razors. This moment seemed surreal to her, as if seeing the snowy fields and the distant mansion on the hill was the first time it truly dawned on her that they had come back. It was nearly dark now. The deer family that had crossed their path two days ago, today actually, was still here, but only visible as dark shadows some distance off. The patch of woods was likely their winter home and the timid animals had been waiting patiently for the intruders to leave so that they may return to the sheltering refuge. Step after step, Lex matched her feet with each print she had made on the way out. The underlying symbolism of this action was the chronological manifestation of change. With each corresponding boot print, memories of her recent journey began to ignite through her mind. By this earth's time, she had left these prints only minutes ago. These several elapsed minutes, however, were sufficient for a drastic life altercation.

"Please, Lex," Charlie said as the two entered the mansion's back door into the dark, portrait-guarded hallway, "allow me to make you something to eat, anything you want. It would be the very least I could do."

She was famished, so hungry in fact that even the burnt rabbit legs back at the kapeleia sounded appealing. She now understood why the Flock devoured so much food every time they sat down to dine. The food in this world was far more advanced in terms of flavor and variety. The food in the other world wasn't bad, but in a primitive, no marinade, no seasoning, nothing fancy kind of way. Just pick it and eat it or kill it and eat it. She yearned for a satiating meal, and even more, to sit and eat with Charlie. Like the old times, when the two of them would perch next to each other upon wooden bar stools, taking slices from a mutual homemade pizza, sipping icy cola, and laughing about any silly thing that came to mind. She wondered if those fond interactions would ever return.

She shook her head at his offer, staying disciplined to her plan to think things through before talking with him. This was chiefly because she knew him all too well. He was smart, quick witted, and a smooth talker. More prominently, she did not want her feelings for him to get in the way of her own rational thought. Loon Lake was not far, surely she could hold out another half-hour for a meal.

He escorted her along the icy front walk toward her snow-covered car, staying close and ready for any possibility that she might lose her balance on the slippery cement. Was this a demonstration of his promised protection for the Amaranth, or simply his usual display of common courtesy? He always had, and still continued to watch out for her. She noticed and appreciated the gesture, but remained uncertain whether his constant consideration was part of the act. A memory re-emerged just then. It was Daphne's voice relaying what Charlie had said about his true love.

"Her eyes are green – like your eyes," the Naiad had stated so full of certainty, with millennia of wisdom to substantiate the claim.

"Green like an ocean of emeralds," Lex whispered to herself so quietly that there was no chance of Charlie hearing this. With a bare hand, he whisked away the powdery snow from the car's windows, then like always, opened the door for her. She climbed into the driver's seat avoiding eye contact.

"Just let me know what I can do," he offered. "Truth be told, I want more than anything for you to stay here with us. But if this is not your wish, I'll help in any way I can to get you moved back to the lake house, or wherever it is you desire. If there is anything you want, anything you need, anything at all, I'm just a phone call away."

"Thanks," she whispered, then quickly shut the door, turned the key and took off down the driveway to County Road 13.

Over the radio, a familiar old song was playing, "Can you feel the love tonight?" the man sang passionately. "It's enough to make kings and vagabonds leave the very best." Lex hastily turned it off, not appreciating the station's coincidental song selection. But the lyrics had stirred a thought - what kind of love would it take for the future king of Crow to leave the very best? This was Lex's first broken heart, over a boy anyway. She had no experience in dealing with such a thing, so the best she could do for now was to take solace in Nature's pristine white endowment.

Rarely had she experienced such a perfectly serene evening. On this December twenty-third, the black sports car crept slowly along the snowy back roads. There were no other cars out tonight, at least as far as she could see. In the distance, twinkling lights from farm houses shown like beacons on a snowy sea. Between them lay large voids of darkness. Plump snowflakes fell softly and gave the "warp speed" impression through the windshield as the car rolled onward. The tires made no noise as they eased through the powder, and except for a faint droning from the engine, all was silent. Lex used this time to let her mind recover from the recent stimulus overload and prepare for whatever decision she might make.

78

There was a classy sports utility vehicle occupying the driveway of Aunt Claire's lake house. Next to the SUV was a white luxury sedan. Roselyn and Linda were here - Aunt Claire's ritzy, pompous, and in Lex's opinion, annoying friends. For two middle-aged housewives that frittered the day away in tanning beds and massage parlors, Roselyn and Linda assumed a false identity of class and sophistication. They were always putting down the "simple folk" of the area, and constantly advising Lex to become more cultured – whatever that was supposed to mean. As it now stood, she might just be more cultured than anyone on the planet, having been exposed to an entirely new world. If she were to use these two gadabouts as a model for culture and class, then culture and class would mean watching celebrity television, sleeping with every man but her own husband, discussing the graphic details of her sex life, and looking down her nose at everyone who spoke in double-negatives. Providing no notable contribution to society other than keeping the local plastic surgeons in business, Claire's best friends were utterly worthless - two non-working, non-educated snobs with too much money because they had married wealthy men. Despite this, Lex's nature was to see the good in everyone. With that in mind she could at least appreciate how fun the ladies could be when they got in their groove. Unfortunately, tonight was not the time for her to endure their party-girl antics. All she really wanted was to spend some time alone with Aunt Claire. Maybe bake some gingerbread cookies or decorate the Christmas tree. She desired to partake in any of these traditional rituals, mainly for reassurance that her normal and familiar life had not been completely sabotaged. Claire had not been expecting her niece home until tomorrow night, so she could not be held accountable for having friends over in Lex's stead. It was all Lex could hope for that the two would be leaving soon, but this was unlikely at half past six.

"Alexis, darling!" Claire sprung from her leather armchair to embrace this unexpected visitor in a joyful hug. Roselyn and Linda waved hello, all the while offering repugnant stares. At first this was offending, then Lex understood why these looks had been cast. She was still wearing the wool cloak.

"I, I was in a Christmas play at the youth center," she lied. She absolutely despised lying but couldn't see any alternative given the situation. "I was the... the innkeeper."

Claire looked surprised and disappointed at the same time. "Lex, you should have told me you were in a play. I would have liked to see it. Who better than a professional to critique your acting, eh?" She gave a hearty snort.

"It was a last minute thing," Lex lied again. "Jade directs it every year and the original innkeeper came down with a stomach bug this morning."

"No acting experience required," teased Linda. "The innkeeper only has one line! - No vacancy!" she and Roselyn shouted together in a martini induced display of their irritating ways. "No seriously," Linda said, still giggling, "you look hot in that outfit. It's a wonder Joseph didn't leave Mary so he could shack up with you for the night."

Lex forced a convincing smile and even a laugh, but it was only a facade.

"How is the glamorous life with the Rose Flock anyway?" Linda asked through slurred words.

"Yes," Roselyn added, also fumbling through vocabulary. "We've been dying to know all about them. Please, do sit and tell us how they've become so rich."

Lex ripped into a Snickers bar with the civility of a hyena. Well, they travel through a mysterious pool of water which is really a gateway to another earth. On that earth, diamonds are everywhere. The Rose Flock simply collects the diamonds, brings them back to Kansas to a secret underground laboratory below the mansion where they cut them, photograph them, and sell them on the Internet. She could only imagine the stupid confused looks she would have received had she actually said this, instead she decided to humor them. "Ever heard of PJ Stockton?"

"The author?" Linda and Roselyn asked in unison.

"That's Charlie Roanoke," Lex explained with a mouth full of candy bar. She remembered that she had promised to keep this a secret, but this one petty cheap shot made her feel kind of good - as if she had gotten back at him a little bit. In the next moment she felt bad about this decision and hoped that the alcohol would erase this article of information from Roslyn and Linda's short term memory. This seemed to interest the cougars as they flashed crooked smiles at each other that seemed to say, "It makes me feel pretty special to know that little secret."

Any other night, Lex might have just made herself a cocktail and joined in on the fun, but not this night. Not with a burdened mind and a broken heart. Claire put a loving hand to Lex's cold cheek. The intuitive woman knew something was not sitting well with her niece.

"I wasn't expecting you home until tomorrow," Claire said with concern.

Lex nodded and regarded her warmly. "Christmas just isn't the same at the mansion."

"Aww, isn't that sweet?" Roselyn observed with mocking sincerity as half the martini found its way to her lap.

Claire ignored her inebriated girlfriend. "Please, Lex, will you join us?"

"Maybe after a while. I think right now I'll take a walk down to the lake – expend some energy, get some fresh air." She turned to the door and Claire looked on with evident concern.

"Don't go too far in that outfit," Linda called out. "Someone may try and return you to the homeless shelter." Lex stepped onto the porch and the last thing she heard before closing the door was Roselyn and Linda's drunken laughter.

In the spring and summer, the dirt path down to the lake was bordered by brilliant arrays of flowers; tonight there was only snow and ice. Lex followed this path across the yard, through the wrought iron gate and down the hill to the banks of Loon Lake. She took a seat upon a large tree trunk that had washed ashore sometime during the autumn. Snowflakes sprinkled upon the water which was not yet entirely frozen. High above in the windy sky, gray clouds rushed westward. She took a deep breath then sighed.

Perched on the log, trying to find a starting point in her quest to make sense of everything, she could not disregard a strange feeling. This was a feeling she had never experienced and could only define it as "the call of the wild." It tugged on her heartstrings, beckoning her to stand, to run, to follow the wind toward destiny. There was no mistaking that something was happening, something was taking over. This sensation had begun the instant she had opened the oracle's book. Charlie and the others had spoken on several occasions of outside forces at work. This force which filled her now, might just be what they were referring to. She put everything else out of her mind, closed her eyes and listened to her heart.

79

Charlie found himself the sole occupant of the mansion's library, in which he had miserably dropped into the center of the leather sofa. The black cushions swallowed him like a tar pit. He had just returned from Crow, a quick there-and-back, where Jade and Sevastian had been waiting for their retrieval. When he had seen Lex safely off, he had trekked back through the windy field of snow with downcast eyes all the way to the church. When he had recovered his two hitchhikers, who of course needed the provisions of the Manult Stone to make their return, it was like a melancholy parade of defeat back to the mansion. The three did not exchange a word during this downtrodden journey. Instead, they basked in a mutual despair over Lex's unexpected, yet understandable departure. Not only had a long and difficult search ended in vain, and fifty-thousand years of Earth B's history resided in its eleventh hour, but they had also hurt a close friend.

This was the very room, the very couch on which just a few hours ago, by this world's time standards, life was perfect. Lex had smiled so genuinely, even displayed glassy eyes as the brown wrapping paper fell from her favorite childhood book onto the white area rug. This gift, which had cost so little, had brought her so much joy. She had happily laid her head upon his shoulder, finding solace in his companionship before falling fast asleep.

He pulled himself upright from the cushion's quicksand clench and examined the book which still resided on the coffee table. On the cover, an adorable white mouse wearing a Santa Claus hat stood by a window watching a reindeer-guided sleigh fly off toward a yellow moon. He smiled as he looked upon the illustration, but the smile was graced with sadness. He gently took the book from the table and examined it, as if not wanting to miss a single detail of artwork. He grazed his hand over the glossy cover before letting out a dejected sigh. He fell back into the clinches of the couch hugging the book tightly to his chest. Of all his billions of dollars of material possessions, this little book was now the most sacred of them all. His eyes closed, and upon doing so, squeezed out one supple tear that slipped down his cheek leaving a wet streak in its wake.

"Charlie?" It was Jade. Charlie's watery eyes shot open.

"It's not often you show your sensitive side," she commented as she took a seat next to him, carefully cradling her trademark glass of milk.

"I wasn't aware that anyone would be joining me," he said without a tinge of embarrassment over being caught in a "non-manly" ordeal.

Getting right to the point she said, "Phaedra is a wonderful person - a beautiful person. One who is driven and passionate about her city and its future. This is a passion you both share. But amongst all of her diplomatic endeavors, she has shoved all else out of the picture, including you. I'm going to be blunt, Charlie…"

The faintest of smiles pushed across his face. "You know that's what I love about you. Never afraid to tell it like it is."

Jade continued, bluntly as promised, but with a pinch of delicacy. "Your engagement to Phaedra is a matter of convenience. Two members of the high council that come from separate divisions of the royal family. Two beautiful people with a common love – your city, and a common goal – saving your earth. Maybe you do love her or did at one time. Either way, it is crystal clear that you love Lex and this love shines through infinitely brighter than any affection you have ever displayed toward the princess." Charlie made no motion to object. He only continued to stare blankly at Molly the Mouse as his cousin pressed on. "Charlie, remember when I told you not to get attached to her? I said that attachment was, how did I put it, a confounding variable?"

He nodded.

"Well, we both messed that one up. We both got attached. But how could we not? Lex is the best person I know, and that's saying a lot."

"I won't tell Elias you said that," Charlie promised with a half grin.

"Thanks," she replied. "The point that I'm trying to make is that love is not something to be ignored. If you love her, which I know you do, then I believe you should pursue it."

He looked at her with surprise. "You do?"

"Yes. Right now, the best we can hope for is that Lex will come back to us. Should that happen, we are all entering uncharted waters. Excuse me for making this cheesy remark, but can you think of a better entity to guide us through these waters than love?"

"You're right," he said. "That was cheesy – but absolutely true."

She then said, "She is faced with a challenging decision, and now, so are you. You already understand what I mean, but I'm going to say it anyway. I know without a doubt that she loves you in return. I've suspected this all along, but it was confirmed when Phaedra kissed you. I've never seen such hurt as I saw in Lex's eyes at that moment. The sight of that was torture for her, and she clearly suffered tremendously, may still be suffering tremendously. Here's the problem. Phaedra is also in love with you. If you were to leave the princess for the Amaranth, it could very well happen that everything would be thrown into chaos. At the very least, the high council would crumble and the royal families would slip into a nasty, kingdom-splitting feud. It would be unlikely that Palas would accept this willingly. Remember, the queen has the highest authority and the final say. If you betrayed her daughter, worst case scenario, she could send you to…" The thought was so awful that Jade could not bring herself to say it aloud. Charlie however, finished the sentence.

"Tartarus," he said dolefully, "escorted by my own soldiers."

"That's the unfortunate truth of the matter," Jade agreed, "but know this, you have my full support in whatever decision you make. The practical decision would be to remain with the princess, marry her, become king, and fulfill your destiny as ruler of Crow."

"I've never really wanted to be king," he said, "you know this."

"Well then, this leads us to the so-called impractical decision – follow your heart, deal with each obstacle as it comes, suffer any consequences that may ensue." She stood, downed the final swig of milk, and began to leave. Before she departed the library, Charlie called out to her,

"What do you think I should do?" he asked.

"It would go against everything I stand for to settle for less than true love," she said with a convincing smile. "You needn't look further than the olive plantation in Taras Argos to know how I feel about that. With that said, I would choose door number two." She disappeared from the room leaving Charlie alone with a child's book and his thoughts.

80

After an hour of silent meditation, a layer of snow had accumulated on Lex's soft brown hair and during this time, the urge to go back to the other earth became increasingly stronger. She began to once again embrace the inner child. The excitement of adventure became irresistible. Whatever might be waiting on Earth B was hers for the taking. Though she did not understand why or how, there was an overwhelming certainty that the path she was meant to take was the path back to Crow.

There was something else. Something that she had been watching for the past half-hour. Swimming about ten meters offshore was a black swan. She had no idea where it came from, as it seemed to just materialize from the swirling snow. There was a flashback to the night with Sevastian, high above the clouds atop Crow castle. This was where she had first seen a black swan. Phaedra had said that the bird was a messenger. Lex wondered if the one she now looked upon was also a messenger, or maybe a sign. Up until now, she had only seen white swans in this lake and it seemed a little too unusual that tonight of all nights there would be one of solid black.

Almost hypnotized, the Amaranth observed as this unique bird moved subtly about in the icy water. Whether true to perception, or just her imagination getting the upper hand, the bird never seemed to take its eyes off her as it swam back and forth like a feathered pendulum.

A voice arose from far behind, riding down to the lake on the winter wind. It was Aunt Claire, checking to make sure her niece was alright. Lex shivered, realizing just how cold she had become while remaining idle for so long. In a dog-like fashion, she shook the accumulated snow from her hair and pulled the heavy wool hood over her head. "I'll be right up," she called out against the wind. She watched Claire's distant figure turn from the gate and hurry back to the house.

The sounds of the breeze and the sloshing of the icy water against the shore had offered just enough distracting clamor to muffle the engine sounds from the driveway. It wasn't until Lex crossed through the back gate, when she realized, happily, that the SUV and sedan had departed. With a shawl pulled tightly around her shoulders, Aunt Claire was watching from the front door's curtained window. Lex could pretty much guess that Roselyn and Linda had been purposely sent on their way, though it was probably against their will. She couldn't help but smile at the image before her. A cozy, snow-covered cottage on the eve of Christmas Eve. A warming fire glowed from within, and through the kitchen window, she could see a pot of cider on the stove and a sparkling, tinsel-endowed pine tree. Most comforting of all was the loving figure waiting by the door. This woman was forever putting her adored niece before anything and anyone. Lex's brisk walk turned to a jog, just so the inevitable hug would come quicker.

81

Once the cider had been poured and a plate of homemade fudge had been set on the coffee table, Lex, Aunt Claire and Ike, the affectionate ham of a black cat, found themselves nestled amongst the cushions of the comfortable fire-side couch with an old homemade afghan covering their laps. Claire had already explained that her friends had gotten way out of hand, and were therefore cut off, fed some strong coffee and sent packing. Of course, they were under the impression that Claire had suddenly come down with a splitting headache. Lex didn't hesitate to mention that a headache is probably a pretty common side effect when palling around with those two.

"Besides, it's not every day I get a surprise visit from my favorite niece," Claire said as she took a sip of hot cider and winced from the scalding drink. Although so much had recently changed, some things never would.

Lex had found an easy and consciously satisfying way to answer all of her aunt's questions without lying or saying anything that might elicit a call to the local psychiatrist. When asked what she had been up to yesterday and today, she simply described the things she had done according to this world's timeline. Yesterday she had made some advertising-based phone calls for the diamond company, ran on the treadmill for about forty-five minutes, finished a book, ate a plate of spaghetti with Sevastian and then watched The Christmas Carol with Jade. The part of the mysterious night walkers had been left out. Today she went to the salon and then to the store to buy some new trail shoes. She described the glorious Christmas feast Sevastian and Charlie had prepared and the relaxing nap that followed.

"Everything seems to be going wonderfully," Claire observed, "but tell me this, Alexis, why do I sense that something's bothering you?"

Lex was not prepared for the question and scrambled within her brain to find an answer. The lengthy pause seemed to prove to Aunt Claire that her suspicions had been confirmed.

"You can tell me anything Lex, you know that right?"

This was true. Lex had always felt that she could tell her aunt anything – until now. She had been sworn to secrecy and even if she blabbed every detail, there would be no chance that Claire would believe a word of it. The only solution she could devise was to be truthful about the big issue and disregard the inconsequential details of Earth B. "If you must know, and I admit it feels good to get this off my chest, I've been having some feelings for Charlie and I'm not sure what to do about it."

With a sparkle in her eye, Claire said, "My dear, that's no secret. I've known all along that you've had feelings for him. When a girl is in love, she makes it obvious in so many ways."

Lex nodded and wondered how obvious she had made it to Charlie.

"I do see your problem," Claire continued. "How do you tell someone how you really feel, when they are already in a relationship with someone else?"

This observation stunned Lex. The first and only obvious thing that came to mind was that Claire was talking about Princess Phaedra. But that was impossible. How could...?

"And how do you pursue a relationship with Charlie without jeopardizing your friendship with Jade?"

Oh she's talking about Jade, Lex thought, suppressing the urge to laugh. Claire, like everyone else assumed Charlie and Jade were a couple. Now speaking aloud Lex said, "I guess I never told you. It turns out Charlie and Jade are cousins."

Claire's eyes doubled in size as this information intrigued her, just as it had intrigued Lex when she had heard it yesterday.

"Then, unless they're kissing cousins, there's no competition," Claire remarked with a chuckle.

None whatsoever, Lex silently pondered, *just a beautiful princess*.

"Let me try again, Lex. You feel that you and Charlie are such good friends that telling him how you truly feel might endanger this friendship. Is this an accurate assumption?"

Lex considered this remark and did agree that there was a lot of truth there. Since it was true in a roundabout way, and she desperately needed something to go on, this became her alibi. "Yeah, that pretty much hits the nail on the head."

Claire, smiling, replied, "I've been around for a while. When you're as old as I am, you'll recognize these things too."

"So, what do I do?" Lex asked.

"That is something you'll have to figure out on your own. There are so many variables in these kinds of situations. I'll tell you this, Lex, you are the damn smartest duck I know. You and your mum are one in the same in that department. That being said, I know you'll find your answer when the time comes. Don't be hasty. That's what happened with Jonathan and me, we acted on impulse."

As sincere as this advice was, it did Lex little to no good. In fact, her situation was entirely different. It wasn't a matter of two friends maybe becoming more, it was a matter of a girl in love with a guy who was engaged. And what's more, the guy the girl was in love with, may or may not have used her, may or may not truly be her friend, and may or may not love her back. The entire situation was teetering on a sword's point, and for each sign that pointed one way, there was a countersign pointing the other. Oh yeah, there was also that thing about saving the world.

"I don't mean to get off the subject, Aunt Claire, but since you've brought up Jonathan, I was wondering if you could tell me again how the two of you ended up living here in Rose? Did you really just close your eyes and spin the globe?"

Claire chuckled nervously. "An odd topic you just pulled

from thin air, but… yes that's basically how it happened."

"Basically?"

"Well, no. The actual story is a bit strange so I typically avoid telling it."

"If you don't mind, I'd really like to hear it."

Claire shrugged and began with some reservation. "Okay, well as you know, before moving to Kansas, Jonathan had moved into my Los Angeles townhouse. You remember seeing pictures of the place?" Lex nodded. "After nine seasons of spending almost every waking moment on that bleeding set, we were both ready to call it quits. We had more than enough money to move away and live comfortably for the rest of our lives.

For various reasons, we had narrowed our living choices to Switzerland, New Zealand or somewhere along the coast of New England. We had been working closely with a real estate agent who just happened to be a good friend of mine."

"I vaguely remember this," Lex interjected. "Was her name Renna, or Rainah?"

"Rainah Newscome," Aunt Claire elucidated. "The reason you remember is because she died mysteriously. Rainah had worked hard on locating homes within our chosen locations and price ranges. The summer of her passing, Jonathan and I had an appointment. She was to meet us at my town home at noon, and the three of us would go through the final few selections over tea. But she never came.

We called both her phone and the real estate company numerous times but never could get in contact. At around two that day, there was a knock on the door." Claire shuttered as if the memory gave her the chills. "A young lady was standing outside with a packet of information in her hands. I'll never forget her, simply because she was a scary sight to behold. I think it was her voice that really got to me. She said, 'Rainah wanted you to have this,' as she handed me the packet. And that was it. She turned her back and walked away. Jonathan and I called after her, asking her name, who she was, and why Rainah had not given us this information herself. We took the packet inside, opened it, and found all the information for this house. Rose, an attractive suburb of Wichita, Kansas - a newly constructed cottage on Loon Lake, which was being offered at an unbelievable bargain. To Jonathan and me, it seemed too perfect, the price, the location, the view from the porch… and if a trusted friend like Rainah had truly found this for us, then why should we turn it down? We ended up taking a virtual tour and signing for the home that very day. As you can see," Claire pointed out with a circling hand gesture over her head, "everything worked out exceptionally well with this house."

"The story doesn't seem as strange as you made it out to be," Lex observed.

"Not until you hear the fine details," Aunt Claire said with nervous aspiration. "I must warn you, this part is a little frightening; hardly a heart-warming Christmas story."

Lex recalled for a moment the giant one-eyed monsters, the haunting book parlor, and her journey through the deathly catacombs beneath Crow castle. Her fear response was undergoing desensitization, so she believed she could probably handle whatever her aunt might dish out… or so she thought.

"Several months after we had moved into this house, Rainah's body was discovered in the San Bernardino Forest – she had been murdered, Lex."

"What happened to her?" Lex asked.

Claire took a deep breath, as if the memories were greatly troubling. "Fire. The autopsy report revealed that she'd been burned alive. Her killer was never caught. The motive never identified. I mean, what kind of a psychopath burns someone alive?"

"Who was the young lady that gave you the information for this house?" Lex asked with intense interest in the story.

"No idea, the girl was never found. The real-estate company had no clue who she was, how she acquired the information for this house, or why she contacted us to begin with.

L.A.P.D believes that the girl either committed the murder or knows who did. Neither I nor the real estate company could give the police any solid leads, so the only thing they could do was dust the packet of information for prints."

"And? Did they find any?"

"Not a single one. But believe me, Lex, the girl had her hands all over the plastic folder and I swear to you she wore no gloves."

Intrigued, Lex popped a piece of fudge in her mouth and chased it with a gulp of cider. It was a terrible story, yes, but interesting. It seems that someone had killed a real estate agent, informed Claire about this house, then disappeared off the face of the planet. "Wait. Disappeared off the face of the planet?" she whispered to herself in a terrifying moment of revelation.

"Why would someone go to such trouble to make sure you bought this house?" she asked loudly, as she now began to see how things were tying together.

Claire just shrugged her shoulders. "Something I've lost a lot of sleep over these past years. It worries me that this mysterious person, perhaps a murderer, knows where I live. If I had known what happened to Rainah before buying this place, I never would have bought it. Sometimes, especially on nights when you're not home, I admit I get nervous. Sometimes I regret my decision."

"Tell me," Lex said, jumping to her feet for no other reason than to ward off the swell of energy, "do you remember what this young lady, the one who showed up on your doorstep, looks like?"

Claire nodded, regarding her niece's odd behavior with a curious expression. "I'll never forget her. Appearance-wise she had long black hair that touched the ground and skin so white and smooth you could nearly see your reflection. Her plain black dress made it seem as though she belonged to a religious cult. But the one thing that I'll certainly never forget…" she paused, and shuttered. "Her eyes."

"What about her eyes?" Lex demanded.

"I don't think she had pupils, and… well, hollow would be the best way to describe them."

82

Pleasant chimes from the antique clock in the hallway indicated that it was now two. Lex had retired hours ago but had not yet been graced by sleep. Every time she found herself on the verge of slumber, her brain started revisiting recent events. Each rousing memory stirred her into wide-eyed wakefulness.

Her lake house bedroom was chilly, especially on winter nights. Circumferential bay windows, clear and unobstructed by curtains, allowed the occupant of the hand-crafted sleigh bed to watch the big flakes descend in a hypnotic frenzy. With three exposed walls, the bedroom had a tendency to be drafty. This effect was countered by thick flannel sheets that were stripped, washed and remade weekly by Aunt Claire whether or not Lex had actually slept there. She pulled the heavy bedding flush with her nose and stared blankly at the ceiling. Steady bouts of shivering consumed her, not from the cold but from a relentless nervous tension.

She knew the Flock would be very interested to hear that the girl from the book parlor had made an appearance in this world many years ago and was responsible for Claire's purchase of the lake house. She may also be responsible for the murder of a real estate agent. Somehow, for some reason, the girl in black made certain that Lex had gotten to Rose. The disturbing notion that she may have killed poor Rainah Newscome to achieve this soon sparked another horrifying theory. Did she also kill Olivia?

"Of course not," Lex told herself again and again as the minutes passed in an unconscious blur. "My mother died from cancer." But this was not reassuring. The girl in black had some great power, or knowledge of acanthary that baffled even Charlie. There seemed to be no boundaries to her ability, and she had already proven that taking lives was not off limits. As hard as Lex tried, she couldn't suppress the fear that steadily escalated inside her. The feeling of being watched, followed and manipulated by such a person, or creature as this demonic stranger was undeniably alarm-provoking. Expecting at any moment to once again look upon that distinctive porcelain face, she spent the next hour watching the windows nervously before finally falling asleep.

83

A recurring dream. Finally it had come again after a long three year absence. Lex desired this vision because it always filled her with a deep peace that even Charlie's dream invasion could not rival. She was very young when she first had the dream and it was her first taste of the splendors her unconscious mind could conjure. The second time it came was the night before her mother had collapsed from the cancerous lesion that would quickly take her life. Despite the timing, she had never associated the dream with death or discontent. It had occurred only twice more following Olivia's passing, and each time the placid images materialized in her sleeping head, she welcomed them with open arms.

The beginning never varied. Somewhere in the far north, she found herself pushing her way up a narrow path through knee-deep snow toward a rounded hilltop ahead. A coniferous forest lined the path on both sides. Residing between the rough pine trunks were soft, indistinguishable voices urging her onward. She had tread this path four times now, and knew very well the miracle that was waiting at the summit. Overly anxious to once again relive this wondrous moment, she attempted to quicken the pace.

A grim reality crept in as she came to realize that she was swiftly moving her legs yet making no forward progress. This was a first, and certainly an unwelcome alteration. Then another first - she heard footsteps approaching from the darkness of the surrounding pines. No, not footsteps, hoof steps actually. Startled, she gasped as the giant black horse stepped majestically from the pine forest. She had first become acquainted with this creature in

Sevastian's painting above her bed at the mansion. They crossed paths again in another dream the night before she had been introduced to Earth B. And here he was again, intruding on her personal sacred territory.

His ebony coat merged divinely with the starry midnight sky and his long mane of thick hair flowed dynamically with the north wind. The creature was larger than a Clydesdale, and could only belong to Earth B, where all the horses were this size. He approached Lex slowly. With a submissive head bow he passed on the understanding that she was his master. She reached out and stroked his fuzzy nose with the back of her hand and in doing so her ability to continue onward toward the hill was rekindled. She quickly came to realize that this creature was here to help her reach the desired destination.

The impossible task of climbing upon the horse's lofty back without aid could have only been accomplished in a dream. The next thing she knew, she was perched high upon the great animal and once again, thankfully, she was on her way to the summit. Although the events that had transpired before reaching the hilltop were different, the occurrence she had longed to experience upon arrival had not changed.

In her lifetime, she had never looked upon the northern lights with her own eyes. When she was a small child and this dream made its début, she had never even seen pictures of the Aurora Borealis in a book or a magazine. Even though real-world experience was lacking, her mind instinctively displayed perfect images of this phenomenon in all its radiant glory. The glowing streaks of viridian light embellished the heavens, raining down in magnificent luminosity as Lex on horseback took it all in. There was something magical about this moment, there always had been, when she arrived at this point in the dream. She never quite understood the connection between herself and the aurora, but unexplainably and undeniably a connection existed.

The atmosphere was emerald and sapphire and these bands of colors stretched from the star-speckled sky until they met the horizon of alabaster snow. There was a definite distinction between air and earth, and the dividing line looked to Lex like a good place to be. She was hypnotically attracted to the lights as they seemed to call out with an irresistible lure. This was the point in her dream where she always began to run toward them, letting gravity aid her descent down the rounded hill and across the snowy plains so she could immerse herself in the aurora's natural purity. Though this notion was deeply aspiring, it had never been achievable. Just as she would take the first few ambitious strides toward the northern lights, she would wake up. This is what always happened. But wait, this dream was different from the others before it. Instead of her own two legs, she now had a horse to carry her. She was under the impression that he was here to serve this explicit purpose. Her instincts told her that this time she would reach the lights. Just in case it didn't work and tonight would end just like all the others, she took a moment to savor the sights, sounds and feelings that her mind was generating.

She urged the black horse onward and the duo started down the hill. Each step was treading on new territory. The trot transitioned into a gallop, then a sprint. She drank in this wondrous moment as she glided across this barren, snow-covered plain at break-neck speed. Smiling uncontrollably in utter satisfaction, she opened her arms wide and invincible as the horse conveyed her onward.

The point in which the lights touched down was fast approaching. From here, it now seemed more like a porthole than the aurora. It bore a striking resemblance to the pool in the church, only orders of magnitude larger. Her anticipation was at its zenith as she realized that this was actually going to happen. Finally, she would make it to the lights. What this meant she did not know, but the way they called to her, had always called to her, she knew there must be some special significance involved. Squealing with delight, and the sheer thrill of it, she gripped tightly to the horse as he reached unearthly velocity. No longer a horse but a rocket, he catapulted his rider head on into the light as the sound barrier shattered and she experienced a pull of gravitational force too strong for any ordinary dream.

She was consumed by light and stardust. Atoms, beta particles, kaons, mesons, photons, every element from every universal dimension poured down over her head immersing her body and senses with immeasurable rapture. This only lasted for a short time before things began to take an unexpected and unwelcome change. The greens and blues began fading into burnt orange. The air began to get warm, then hot, then sweltering. Jagged rocks formed from swirling dust particles. The orange faded into red – morbid, wretched, bloody red. Shrieks of terror, or war, or torture shot through the air ripping into her eardrums like a jackhammer. Desperate to get away, to wake up, she covered her ears and closed her eyes. She felt hard rock beneath her feet. The ground was so hot, it scorched her soles. She opened her eyes praying for the lake house, but this was not to be. She was in hell.

She stood fearfully upon the banks of a bubbling river. The water was viscous and tinged with red, emitting a deathly steam as it crept along its blistering pathway. Behind her were barren plains of rock and fire. At the far reaches of the burning landscape, jagged black mountains jutted upward toward a sky of orange rock seemingly several kilometers in height. Fountains of lava shot from the earth at intermittent intervals and dark plumes of smoke crept through the baking atmosphere. Fires burned along sections of the ground with no apparent fuel source other than the rock on which they danced. Gray ashes drifted gently downward nesting atop her hair.

Across the river was another kilometer of the same barren, fire-rock plain. This vast expanse of scorching land terminated at the base of a hellish city carved entirely into a volcanic mountain. Directly in the center, unquestionably the main entrance to the mountain fortress, Lex saw cumbrous stone steps ascending to a fire-tinged metal door of leviathan bulk. This markedly disturbing establishment contained broad walls of charred stone, stairwells and watchtowers. Adorned throughout were satanic carvings and sculptures of human bodies contorted in postures and poses that could only be accomplished by demon possession. Doorways and windows were particularly vivid because of the hellfire that burned from within. Dark figures moved past the windows, or were they just life-like bellows of smoke? It was difficult for her to be certain from the distance she currently maintained.

Except for the unsettling babbling of the boiling river, the underworld was eerily quiet. She could not bring herself to move. She was bound to where she stood by a swelling trepidation and an all out uncertainty of where exactly she should, or could for that matter, go. Besides, the heat was the very definition of extreme. The exposure to this blazing temperature was beyond anything she had ever come close to enduring - so much so that breathing alone was at the utmost level of taxing. Her lungs toiled miserably to extract the trace amounts of oxygen from the underground atmosphere. All she could do for the present moment was to take in her surroundings, horrible though they were. Where was the black horse? Would he come back, she wondered, to help her escape this nightmare? How could something so perfect and beautiful transform so rapidly to something so undesirably horrid? How could the brisk tonic of the winter plains and the addicting hues of the aurora be swept instantly away by fire and rock? How, and why, did the wholesome white snow change so radically to fiery ash? She stared at the city in the distance as she searched for the answers to these intangible questions. It seemed to stare right back as though the city itself was a living being, a predator eying its prey.

A glowing flake of ash spiraled down from the air, landing most inconsiderately upon the nape of her neck. She jumped at the burning sensation and emitted a scream in the process. The sound that leapt from her voice box echoed throughout the underworld and caused the city to stir. She brushed the ash away from her neck and stood stone-still as she realized and highly regretted her folly. The metal door began to grind open, sliding upward into the rock as the mountain came to life. Flames leapt from the open entranceway, as if they were a pack of raging guard dogs seizing the opportunity to breach their confinement and run free.

Then from amongst the flames, an impossibility materialized – two impossibilities actually. Lex's heart thumped in overdrive as she looked upon two figures that were only discernible against the fiery backdrop as two women. As they were similar in height and build, they might have been twins, but she could deduce little else. They emerged outward as if stepping from an oven, and treaded several paces until they reached the top step. They stood, side by side, most certainly in the process of surveying the lone, trembling girl standing on the far side of the river. It remained this way for a moment, during which time Lex dug fervently to come up with some plan of action in this unpromising situation. Were these people friend or foe? There was no way to be certain. She thought of calling to them, and contrarily she considered running the other way. Every possible action was just as probable to produce an undesirable outcome as it was to result in her conquest over this petrifying dream.

"Why can't I just wake up?" she asked again and again, trying everything in her power to accomplish the means to this end. After all this desperate deliberation, she still had not moved an inch.

And then, a dreadful chain of events was put into motion. A voice arose from the silence that Lex understood to be emanating from the woman on the left. It was strange how her eerie tones were so easily audible given her distance. This phenomenon was akin to one which occurred just the other evening on the streets of Crow. While she and her friends had passed that dark alley, the girl in black spoke to her with words that somehow bypassed the ears of all others in proximity. This haunting voice came much in the same manner, as if the woman were talking directly into Lex's ear. The words were not welcoming, nor was the tongue understandable. A dark, ethereal pitch, a chant of sorts, articulated an ancient language that was all-out foreign to Lex's experience. Despite this lack of comprehension, there was no uncertainty that the words were threatening and evil in origin. Desperate to be rid of the unsettling vocals, she covered her ears. This proved useless as the voice, like the dream, was being produced by her own mind. She decided she would rather take a knife through the belly than listen any longer. Finally, the words ceased, and she was thankful. Again, silence reigned, but only for a moment.

Now, a new sound arose that was even more hostile in nature – a sadistic resonance of such terrifying degree, that Lex trembled violently at its initiation. This was the deathly roar of some unseen beast, coming from somewhere within the mountain fortress. It bellowed out from the entrance and echoed across the burning planes, over the jagged mountains and all the way up to the lava sky. This sound was the very definition of dreadful. The reaction it produced in Lex was an unmanageable, paralyzing fear like she had never felt. It was as if every shred of wickedness that had ever existed in the universe had been channeled into this one, savage bellow. She could not imagine what sort of creature could produce something of such sinister intent. She did not want to know. Never in her life had she been so desperate to not know something. In the ill-fated manner in which events were unfolding, she knew that she would not be so lucky as to escape this place without finding out. She was exactly, and most unfortunately, correct.

The two figures at the city's gateway stepped aside in opposite directions, parting from each other and creating a substantial gap between them. This gap was necessary to let escape the thing she would come to fear above all others.

With unimaginable swiftness, a deathly creature leapt from the flames, exploding through the gateway. It did not take its time in descending the stairway leading down to the burning plain, rather it cleared the entirety of the steps, shaking the earth as it landed. There was no wasted time and no doubt of its intentions. On two legs, this beast of supreme evil was sprinting directly for her with the very purpose of taking her life.

The horrid thing was enormous – at least twenty feet in height. Its girth too was ungodly colossal with an overall stature that dwarfed the Cyclops, Xenogorus. Its body was a sickening concoction of man and animal. With swinging arms and an upright posture it ran like a human, but the animal component demonstrated patches of shaggy black fur, patches of burnt fur, patches of burnt flesh, knife-like claws on the hands and hammering hooves instead of feet. And the head – the head was all animal, all bull. Adorned with slanted yellow eyes, the elongated face narrowed as it extended outward into two large nostrils connected internally with a heavy metal, ash-laden ring. The horns were the most unsettling feature, and this creature had not two but three of them. The first two, the ones that were located as expected on the lateral aspects of the creature's head, jutted out to the side before taking a menacing curve forward for the exact purpose of impaling prey with a head-on attack. The third horn was one in which Lex had never seen the equivalent. It exited the skull at the upper forehead region and then curved up over the contour of its head before shooting straight back into a razor point, ready to skewer any bold foe who was daring enough to wage an attack from behind.

It was a minotaur. Lex knew this right away, at least by the description conveyed by mythology. But the monster was something more than just a half man half bull. Though she couldn't comprehend the full extent of the beast's purpose, she innately understood this to be a design of the purest evil and the most ominous intent - the devil's spawn. Perhaps this was Lucifer himself. At any rate, it was drawing closer at a vexing speed and she was now forced to make a decision.

Her last hope was placed in the boiling river as it remained the only obstacle separating her from the demon. She hoped that the raging body of flesh-scorching liquid would deter him from making forward progress in her direction. But he was approaching fast and if he had any intention of skidding to a halt at the river's edge, he was certainly not showing it.

Her grim prediction became a reality as the minotaur leapt from the blistering earth and plunged into the water. His great height allowed him to fight and claw through the bubbling substance without actually having to swim or immerse his head. He ripped through the fiery rapids with the fierce determination of getting at Lex as expeditiously as possible.

The mystery of it all was the information that Lex's intuition was relaying. Yes, she had the mentality enough to know this was a dream, but as of recently, some deeper instinct, or ability had awakened within her. Her mind was becoming increasingly efficient at producing vivid dreams with all the lifelike sights, sounds, smells and feelings of actually being there. Perhaps this potential had been unlocked with her first dream invasion or the consumption of Earth B botanical substances. Her own brain was self-aware that this disaster-piece was only a dream, and at the same time it was telling her that this was a dire situation that required the utmost urgency. She knew that whatever was to happen in the upcoming minutes would be very, very bad. The minotaur emerged from the river, foot, by dreaded foot, and now, only twenty yards separated predator and prey.

She backed up quickly, terrified beyond explanation. She couldn't take her eyes off the demon but knew that there would be no chance of outrunning it by continuing onward in this ineffectual backward shuffle. The beast was closing in swiftly. She wheeled around to flee, praying she could somehow endure an all out sprint across a vast fire-consumed plain only to reach the foot of the nearest mountain which was uncertain to provide sufficient shelter or hiding place. The situation provided no other alternative. As she turned and took the first desperate stride, her toe sunk into a small fissure in the earth and she plummeted face first into a sharp bed of rocks.

Her fall was broken by the instinctive outstretching of her arms, but a terrible repercussion resulted from this action. The jagged end of the stone that made initial contact with her hand, ripped through her palm like a knife. She could see torn strands of muscle, damaged fibrous ligaments, and before the throbbing wound filled with crimson blood, even bone was visible.

The pain was intense and though she was dreaming, she somehow felt every bit of it. Her adrenaline-induced panic allowed her to fire back to her feet, but she was now flustered and disoriented. The demon thundered closer, now only a few paces away. Her legs catapulted her a few bounds forward at which time she mistakenly turned to evaluate the location of her assailant. As she turned, a fiery black fist caught her in the temple sending her entire body soaring through the air before slamming agonizingly against the unforgiving ground. She screamed in pain when she landed, but not because of the bone-shattering crunch, but the excruciating burns to her arms from landing in an area of fire.

Blood gushed from her forehead and flooded her eyes. She was blinded by her own life force and at this point she had a clear understanding of her fate and how this situation would turn out. The demon stood over her bellowing its hellish roar. She wiped her eyes, attempting to clear them of blood. This partially restored vision. Her strong survival instinct forced her to her feet one last time in an attempt to escape, an attempt that she knew would be in vain.

The next act seemed to happen in slow motion. The minotaur cocked his arm back over his head, then with iniquitous might, took a sinister swipe at Lex with razor claws fully extended. She leapt to the side trying to parry the blow but failed. There was contact and a shot of pain. Her body hurled through the air. As she spun through the smoky red atmosphere, she surveyed the ramifications of this last assault. It only took a split second to see that the demon's claw had slashed through her right arm just above the elbow. The pain radiated through every nerve fiber in her body and sent damage control signals to her brain. Her heart pumped at a dangerous tempo doing everything in its power to circulate revitalizing blood.

Her severed arm hit the ground before the rest of her body and rolled several times before coming to rest among a patch of dancing flames. Blood oozed from the sliced arteries and turned instantly black as it met fire. It was inexpressibly surreal to view her own detached limb lying on the ground, cooking sickeningly amid the flames like a piece of meat. At this point she had reached the height of terror. All she could do now was await the end. She channeled the trace amount of energy that remained into several beseeching screams of desperation, but these pleas for life were fruitless and the energy sustaining her cries was quickly drained. She was in shock now, lightheaded from blood loss and sick to her stomach from witnessing the mutilation of her own body.

The rest happened almost instantaneously. The demon charged toward her and leapt into the air. She screamed with everything she had left, a scream that could almost certainly be heard from every corner of hell. Her head fell back, her hair burst into flames. She felt the skin on her neck blistering under the intense heat. The last thing she saw was the demon's hammering hoof descending toward her face with brutal speed. She closed her eyes. There was a crunch. Her skull was crushed – and she felt every bit of it…

84

Lex's scream was shrill and continuous. Her nightshirt and flannel pants were saturated through with sweat, as was her hair, her face, and her sheets. Her body sprung from the bed as if it were being ejected from a plane's cockpit. Her bare feet made contact with the wood floor of the lake house bedroom. Her arms instinctively shielded her face in a protective manner, as if expecting another devastating blow from the black demon of her dream.

She screamed the word "no" over and over. Some quick and concise, some drawn out and blood curdling. The images were fresh in her mind and she was still trying to escape. She sank to the floor, back against the side of the bed. Her legs struggled to push her body backward. There was sweat covering the floor and her bare soles could not get a grip on the polished wood. Her terrified impulsive movements were driven by so much adrenaline that she pushed back against the heavy sleigh bed and it began rumbling across the floor leaving unsightly gouges as it scooted. The lamp on her nightstand crashed to the floor. The shattering glass could not be heard over the intense screams bellowing from her lips.

Claire burst into the room with a terror-stricken face. She swiped forcefully at the light switch and the room exploded with luminosity. She stood for a moment in shock, as if attempting to diagnose this horrid spectacle. There was a lot to take in. A shattered lamp, an entire bed relocated to the back wall, streaks of sweat on the wood floor, a terrified niece emitting raucous screams and moving in jerky, incoherent motions as if possessed.

"Lex, what's wrong?" Claire cried out from the doorway. At this point, Lex stopped screaming, but remained curled up on the ground breathing so heavily and so loudly, that Claire's words had not been heard. Claire bolted over, dropped to her knees and put her hand on Lex's back. At initial contact, Lex screamed again and recoiled backward until she hit the wall with a forceful thud. Claire was knocked off balance and toppled backward into the razor shards from the glass lamp, cutting her ankle in the process. Her blood dripped to the floor mixing with the salty lakes of Lex's sweat. The situation was chaotic.

"Lex!" Claire screamed. "Lex, get a hold of yourself!" She seemed reluctant to try another approach. She stood, slipping a little in the process, then determinedly limped over to her niece who had somehow squeezed her body between the nightstand and the bed weeping uncontrollably. This time Lex did not jump at her aunt's embrace. She looked up at Claire with the aghast stare of someone who had just experienced every detail of a brutal death.

85

It was morning. This much was evident from the light pressing in against Lex's closed eyelids. Below her eyes were dark puffy pockets either from excessive crying, lack of sleep, or the combination. She cracked them open to see that the darkness was gone, but the memories certainly were not. A momentary disorientation took hold as she wearily sat up in bed. This was not her room, rather, she had been fast asleep in Claire's bed. She looked over to see her aunt, the poor woman, sleeping soundly as last night's events had been quite nerve-racking and draining. She could see that Claire had been doing a bit of crying herself, as her sleeping eyes were outlined by a hue of blush red. Lex wondered what she must have thought of the whole unpleasant incident because nothing like it had ever happened before.

She did not remember much after awakening from the dream. There were fragmental recollections of sweat-soaked bedclothes, a broken lamp, and Claire's panicked expression. That was pretty much it. The nightmare that plagued her sleep was responsible for occupying the rest of her memory. She wasn't even sure how or when she had migrated to this room or this bed.

Many hours had passed since the hellish images played out in her head, yet she was still clinched tight in fear's unrelenting chokehold. She tried to understand the significance of the dream, certainly there had to be one. But, after much deliberation on the matter, there was no conclusion to be had. The only thing she was absolutely certain of was that she was terrified. Terrified to stay in this world, terrified to go back to the other, and especially terrified to enter into the realm of sleep where the evil of both worlds could easily find her. She was being followed, manipulated, and possibly hunted by the girl in black. Was this girl somehow responsible for the dream? Was the dream a warning that she was also being targeted by a minotaur? Was this creature the means to her end?

No, she thought. Ridiculous. But sadly, nothing seemed ridiculous anymore now that a whole new world of possibilities and unknowns had been brought into the light. She realized there was so much she didn't know. She had not known before last night that she could feel severe pain within a dream. The remembrance of her arm being disjoined from her body and her skull being crushed like a watermelon under the hammer-fall of the minotaur's hoof made her nearly sick.

As of now, she understood that there were three separate classifications of dreams, at least as she had thus far experienced. First, the "normal" dream, as she termed it. These dreams were the bits and pieces of abstract thoughts and images bunched together in an odd sort of arrangement. These were meaningless manifestations of recent short-term memories sprinkled with a touch of pure nonsense. Then, there was the ever desired dream invasion – desired because the only one she had so far experienced had been unreservedly delightful. In a dream invasion, one could experience an extremely vivid and realistic scenario that was being created by the invader. The third type of dream, the dream that occurred last night, was identical to a dream invasion in that it was so lifelike, it was difficult to distinguish dream from reality. The one and only difference between the two was that in this third dream state, the body retains its ability to feel. During this type of dream, one can feel with unconditional sensitivity the cold winter wind, the warm breath of a horse, the burning rock under foot, and the scorching blow of a demon's raging fist.

She again began to tremble as the minotaur's image settled itself into the forefront of her mind, and at this moment, something new came over her - a bold and exciting idea. This idea eased her tremors into submission and even brought the faintest of smiles to her face. There was an intense desire to no longer be afraid, to relinquish her fear, and this new scheme, she thought, was the means to triumph over it all. With this sudden newfound motivation, she hopped from the bed landing noiselessly on the floor. There was no need to wake Aunt Claire, not yet.

She returned to the scene of the crime, her bedroom, and noted that everything had been returned to its proper order, minus one lamp. The sheets had been changed and the bed had been pushed back to its original place. A whisk broom and dustpan sat beside a wastebasket that contained the shattered pieces of glass. The smell of floor cleaner hung thick in the air, the kind of cleaner that one uses to disinfect an area that has been bled upon. She recalled nothing of the cleaning process but knew that it must have consumed much of Claire's time. No wonder she was so wiped out.

Lex initiated her plan by tending to several routine practices. She went about her morning with the knowledge that this hot shower may be her last, that today may be the last opportunity to toast a bagel with an electric appliance, or that this may be the last time she would taste DentaWhite toothpaste on her tongue. In all honesty with herself, she knew this morning may be the final time that she would ever set foot in this house. It also meant that this may be the final time she would ever see her aunt, but this notion had to be forced aside for now so that she could make ready for her journey.

She brushed her hair until it was straight and shimmering then dressed in a pretty green sweater complimented by fitting jeans. Why not? Her mentality was - if she were to wear that damn cloak for most of the time henceforth, she might as well look nice for a short while longer. And as for the "damn cloak", it was stuffed into a duffel bag along with the appropriate undergarments, the trail shoes and the covers for the trail shoes. After she had eaten, showered, dressed and packed, she stood in the center of her room fighting the oppressive sadness. Ike, the friendly black cat, weaved in and out of her legs, rubbing his soft face against her jeans as if this were his way of asking her to stay. She looked down at him with a melancholy gaze. This moment seemed so much like good-bye.

She forced herself onward, down the quiet hallway toward Aunt Claire's bedroom. Holiday decorations adorned the walls and served as a reminder that this new reality had so completely stolen her attention from Christmas. Was it really December twenty-fourth? How different this Christmas Eve was from all the others. How insignificant it seemed. How little she cared right now. Today there would be no baking, no music, no "It's a Wonderful Life." Today, there would only be goodbyes.

Lex fell to her knees at Claire's bedside, stirring her aunt from slumber. It took everything in her power not to shed tears as she relayed her plans to leave the lake house for the mansion.

"We were supposed to wrap presents this morning," Claire said sleepily and with much confusion over her niece's abrupt change of plans. "What's going on anyway? What happened to you last night? Are you feeling okay?"

"It was just a dream," Lex said. "I'm so sorry for the fright I must have given you. Thanks for cleaning my bedroom."

"Must you really leave?" Claire asked despairingly while sitting up groggily.

"I have some…business I have to tend to with the Rose Flock," Lex explained using a vague depiction of the truth. "I will try to make it as quick as possible so I can…" she choked on her own words, "so I can get back and spend Christmas Eve with you. Please don't worry about me. I beg you to go back to sleep." She thought that Claire would offer another opposing statement in an attempt to keep her from leaving, but she was obviously exhausted and this would cut the battle short.

"Please hurry back," she whispered while laying her head back down on the satin pillowcase.

Lex nodded, then, despite her fervent desire to stay, departed the room quickly so Claire would not have to witness another round of tears. Forcing herself onward at that very moment was the hardest thing she had ever, ever had to do. As soon as she was clear from observation, the salty droplets plummeted from her eyes – this was because her gut instinct said that she would never again see her beloved aunt.

Ike followed her to the door and inadvertently became the recipient of a few tear drops to the head. She wrapped her fingers around the handle but did not open the door until she treated the lovable feline to one last scratch behind the ears. He purred delightedly at the gesture.

"Cheerio, my friend," she whispered, "you've always been my favorite of the bunch. Don't tell the others though. I'll miss you." With that she opened the door and made her final departure from the lake house.

86

With a gym bag slung over her shoulder, the Amaranth stood boldly in front of the mansion's front door. A determined look held tight to her face that the frigid breeze could not expunge. She was about to take a risky leap into the unknown – like standing atop a cliff overlooking a churning ocean. She had dedicated herself to take the chance, to dive from this cliff head first into dark water in which any skull-shattering, life-ending entity could be lurking just beneath the foamy surface. This decision to embrace her destiny was ultimately catalyzed by last night's dream. Had she thought about it for too long, she may have realized that going back to Earth B seemed counterintuitive, after all, it was most likely the planet on which the minotaur resided. If there was any unspoken truth to be extracted from the dream, it was that no matter where she was, fate would come for her. It would be pointless to try and hide on Earth A. Above all, she was being propelled by some unseen instinct that she could not pinpoint or explain. Never had she been in a situation of such uncertainty, yet she was entirely convinced she was embarking on a journey that had been waiting for her since the first light sparked in the universe. She raised a hand to the glowing doorbell.

The door opened before her finger had made contact with the ringer. She took a few paces backward as Charlie stepped out looking very tired. It was hard to read his face. His air resided somewhere between submissively reserved and cautiously optimistic.

"Were you watching for my car to pull up?" she asked in

consideration of his swift appearance at the door. She then remembered all of the security cameras around the outside and the alerts they sent to the phones of the Flock the moment a human or vehicle intruded one millimeter onto their property.

He averted eye contact and rubbed the back of his neck sheepishly. "Been watching for you the entire night," he answered. "I wasn't sure if you'd be coming back." It was obvious by his noncommittal tone that he had not gotten his hopes too high. For all he knew, she was just here to claim her belongings. He looked dolefully at the black duffel bag. "Are you collecting your things a little at a time?"

"Don't act so glum," Lex said with the slightest of grins. "It's pathetic." With that, she unzipped the bag displaying the contents within.

For the briefest of moments there was a spark of hope in his eye, but clearly he still wasn't sure what to think. "If you mean to give those back, I don't need them. They wouldn't fit me anyway… I…you…I mean…"

"Charlie," she interjected, cutting short his anxious rambling. "I brought them for Earth B. I'm going back. I'm…" she was thrilled to say it but equally as nervous, "I'm in."

He took a step toward her and his eyes were wide with awe. He was serious again – all business. "Lex, I need to know that you've had sufficient time to think this through, that you've weighed the options. You must understand that your destiny is uncertain should you choose to follow this path. This is not a decision to be taken lightly or made in haste."

"My destiny is uncertain no matter which path I take, and my choice to follow this particular path was made before I was even born," she said unfalteringly. Had this statement been directed to any other person in this world, save Jade or Sevastian, she would have been sent directly to the shrink without passing Go. But Charlie understood. He nodded and took one more step in her direction. They were now only inches apart. Their eyes locked.

"I swore that I would protect you along your journey to the

best of my ability. I mean to do just that." The passion in his voice escalated as he made the next declaration. "Lex, I have never admired anyone, on this earth or the other, as I admire you."

"That goes for us too!" Sevastian's voice bellowed in jubilance as he and Jade bounded through the doorway like giddy children on a playground. Their unexpected appearance caught Lex and Charlie by surprise.

"Ever heard of a little thing called privacy?" Charlie asked bemusedly.

"Oh please," replied Jade, sporting a beaming smile. "What did you expect us to do? Sit by and wait for you to 'ease us into' the news of her decision?" She bypassed him with a snappy wink, then leapt into Lex's embrace offering a mighty bear hug. "Thank you, Lex. You are truly noble."

"This will be the adventure of a lifetime," Sevastian stated overzealously, standing tall, cross-armed and ready for action.

"Well, my adventure started when I first stepped into the pool," Lex said, looking from friend to friend and trying to keep composed under all the praise. "And let me tell you – the plot thickens."

"How so?" Jade asked.

"I've got some news you will find most interesting." The Flock glanced confusedly at each other, then settled back on Lex longing for gratification. "I know why Aunt Claire moved to Rose."

87

All was silent around the dining room table except for the nervous clinks of Sevastian's fingernails against his empty teacup. The fire from the hearth blew out waves of soothing heat as the four sat wordlessly following Lex's description of the events that landed her aunt in Kansas. This seemingly premeditated ploy to bring the Amaranth to the gateway was enough to drive Charlie and company into speechlessness. The notion that the girl in black was moving at will from earth to earth had been especially confounding. This mysterious being was acting as puppet master and there was no conjecture as to why.

Finally, Jade spoke up. "Rainah Newscome was burned to death? Are you sure?"

Lex nodded while reaching for the teakettle and pouring herself a third cup of cicadaweed. She needed her mind sharp as a tack right now. "That's what Aunt Claire said," she replied assuringly. "I think that's the part that frightens me the most."

"Now there's not a doubt in my mind that the girl in black has traveled between earths," Charlie declared. "Remember, the poem of the crow was written in English, a language foreign to Earth B. Also, she had called me Charlie, my Earth A name."

"Does anyone have rational thoughts regarding this new information?" Sevastian asked around the table. There was no reply.

They returned to their hushed contemplation for a while before Jade said, "Alright, it's obvious that nobody has an explanation. For the time being, we must accept the fact that the girl in black, her abilities, her intentions, and her actions thus far are beyond our understanding. We can only hope that this new information might be used in the future as more puzzle pieces fall into place."

"So now what?" Charlie asked.

"We move on," Jade replied.

"Agreed," Sevastian stated energetically. "Jade's right. There's nothing else we can do right now with the girl in black. We've heard the story, reviewed the facts and still come up short. It's useless to deliberate on this any longer. We must turn our sights to the present and the future."

"Rest assured we will see her again," Jade added darkly, "and when we do, she'll either give us the answers we seek or I will force the information from her miserable lips."

"I'm not so sure," Charlie uttered timidly.

Jade glared at him. "Are you doubting me?"

"No, I don't doubt you for one second, but I've seen first hand what we're dealing with. She literally disappeared before my eyes in a ball of fire. A power such as hers does not suffer to a mortal human being."

A twisted smile crossed Jade's face. "Just makes me all the more eager to… to do what needs to be done."

Lex had to admire Jade's intrepidity and self confidence. At the current moment, this dark-haired warrior, this fearless soul that occasionally played Trigonous, seemed undefeatable. "Suppose she's on our side - trying to guide us perhaps," Lex submitted to the group. "Remember what you said, Charlie, after our run-in at the book parlor? You said she could have attacked either of us while we were alone with her. She could have used her supernatural powers to destroy us at any instant."

"And I hold fast to those postulations," he said, "but with Claire's insight, we can now assume that the girl in black literally burned an innocent woman to death. I don't care what anyone says, that's evil. It's almost as if she's playing chess and we're all pawns… and pawns are often sacrificed for the greater goal." He fidgeted uneasily in his chair before addressing the next issue, one of utmost sensitivity. "There's something else, Lex, that has crossed my mind that I truly hate to bring up, but just so it's all out there… I can't help but wonder if…"

She knew where this was going and completed his sentence, though it was painstaking to utter the words, "If the girl in black was responsible for my mum's death."

"I'm sorry," he said regretfully. "I see I'm not the first to consider that possibility. But had Olivia not passed away, I doubt you'd have come to Kansas."

"There's no way to know if there's any truth to that," Jade chimed in, "but if there is, that makes the girl in black an enemy."

"It most certainly does," Lex agreed with mounting anger. The idea sparked rage, and she desired to change the subject before it clouded her rational thought. "There's something strange that happened to me last night," she went on, recapturing the regard of her friends. "I don't know what to make of it. Perhaps it's nothing, but…"

"Well, what is it?" Sevastian pleaded impatiently.

She took a deep breath then dove into the events that composed last night's dream. Not a single graphic detail was spared. It was difficult to describe the second half while keeping the tremors from her voice. She had to stop several times while narrating the specifics of her own mutilation and death. The others were patient and supportive as they could easily tell that the mental experience had been beyond harrowing. Jade's consoling arm rested around Lex's shoulder. Charlie topped off her tea, and Sevastian cast quiet glances saturated with the utmost compassion. After all was told, including her waking reaction and Claire's intervening measures, there was another round of silence. This time the atmosphere was inundated with trepidation.

"It was just a dream," Lex said, putting an end to the hush. "I'm sure it doesn't mean anything." She said this in an attempt to ease the tension but knew very well that there was indeed a meaning.

"No," Charlie disagreed while remaining in his contemplative, fixed-eyed trance. "There are secrets and meaning within every dream. Anyone who has studied acanthary will agree to that. The tricky part is unlocking those secrets."

Sevastian's voice arose, listing the dream's key entities aloud. "A recurring dream, a black horse, the northern lights, hell, two indistinguishable female silhouettes and a minotaur. Lex," he said turning to meet her gaze, "do you have any idea what possible significance that dream could contain?"

"I have a theory," she said. "I needed the other world to unlock the second half, the evil half, of the dream. It seems to me that the timing is way too convenient to be coincidence. Remember, this was the fifth time I've had this dream, but only the first time of reaching the aurora and eventually the underworld."

"What could it all mean?" Jade asked, shaking her head in frustration.

Lex shifted uneasily in her chair as she put forth her best answer to this inquiry. "The dream is telling me how I'm going to die."

"Lex, don't say that," Charlie blurted objectionably. "I maintain my assertion that there are secrets within every dream, but I'm just as sure that dreams cannot predict the future."

"And I'm certain that they can," she countered. But there was no way she could explain how she knew this.

"Enough of this talk!" he declared in frustration. It was obvious that the very mention of Lex dying bothered him tremendously.

"You must trust me, Charlie. I have no idea how I know these things. The best way I can explain it is that ever since I crossed over to Earth B, I've inherited some sort of new instinct. Somehow a plethora of abstract knowledge has been implanted in my brain." Everyone eyed her with uncertainty, as though they could not properly respond to such a pronouncement. But she was convinced she could prove her point. Her next act would either confirm or deny everything she had just claimed. "When I was in the underworld, one of the women at the fiery gate spoke to me. Though she was far off, I heard her as though she were standing right beside me. This is what she said…"

She took a deep breath, closed her eyes, then proceeded to recite the exact chants and demonic syllables that had been articulated in her dream. There was no difficulty in remembering them because as she had just explained, the words were implanted. Something strange began to happen. A ghastly feeling gripped as she spoke. She became very hot, beads of sweat materialized on her forehead, yet she kept on, desperate to complete the dark message. The fire in the hearth grew noticeably larger, and it was scary that whatever she was saying seemed to be fueling this phenomenon. She began to feel lightheaded and nauseous but pushed indomitably to the end. When she finally finished, she felt as though she had just completed a run across Kansas. For some reason, as if the words were not meant to be spoken by a mortal human, she was drained. The fire regressed to its normal state of innocent dancing and popping.

"My god," said Sevastian. He stood, for no other reason than to demonstrate how downright shocked he truly was. "My god," he repeated.

This was all Lex needed to know. Her suspicions had been confirmed, though this was by no means a good thing.

"Sevastian, what's the matter?" Jade asked nervously.

"He's Earth B's most educated historian," said Charlie, "and as such, he recognizes the language. Am I right?"

Sevastian nodded. "Yes, though I don't know it well, or hardly at all. I am just familiar enough to know that Lex has just spoken the language of Dis." A hush fell over the room. You could almost hear the thumping of four hearts. "And unless someone has taught her this language behind our backs, there is no way she could have possibly known it."

"See," Lex said, more to Charlie than anyone else. "Now do you believe me?"

Charlie seemed to be in denial as he asked Sevastian, "By

what means did you come across this language?"

Sevastian started a restless pacing as he answered, "In the castle's book room, in the protected section, there is a manuscript that offers samples and translations of all, or at least most of the languages that have been known to exist on Earth B. It's one of the oldest in the collection. While studying it, I came across samples of this dark language. That is how I am able to recognize it."

"We need to get a hold of that book," said Jade eagerly. "If we can translate the words, we may get some more answers."

"So, the language from my dream, you said it was the language of Dis? What exactly does that mean?" Lex wanted to know.

"On Earth B, there is an underworld," Sevastian explained. "According to historical accounts, the city that resides there is called Dis."

"Yes, I think that's where I was," she said with confidence.

"That may be," he went on, "but unfortunately I don't think there's any way to be sure."

"Why not?" asked Jade.

"Because to my knowledge, no humans have been there. I went through a stage a while ago where I was greatly interested in learning about the underworld. I think I searched through every book in the castle and even the book parlor. There is such scant information about the place. In an eggshell… uh, nutshell, I have concluded that nobody has been able to find the entrance to the underworld, thus nobody has been there."

"How then did the language of Dis make it to the surface?" Jade asked with furrowed brows. "How do we even know there is a Dis? Someone must have been there to write about it."

"I'll look into it," Sevastian replied. "But as it is with most of our ancient documents, the information is so old, it's questionable if it's even valid."

Charlie stood abruptly. "Be right back," he said. He was followed by three confused gazes as he departed the dining room. He made a quick return with a sketch pad and a pencil. He placed the materials on the table in front of Lex. "I'm sorry to make this request of you," he said to her, "but the insight from your dream may be very helpful. Do you think you can write the words, not that I'm worried that you'll forget them, but so we can have them as a visual reference for translation."

She nodded irresolutely.

"Obviously you couldn't know the exact spelling," he continued, "but if you can write out the message phonetically, I'm sure we can manage a translation."

She lifted the pencil from the granite tabletop and began to write, her hand trembling just a bit as she did so. She hated these words, hated them with all her heart. When she finished, she ripped the page from the sketchbook and handed it to Sevastian. She then set immediately to work as her pencil began marking the next blank sheet.

"Might as well," she said to the others without lifting eyes from her project. "You know, while the images are fresh in my head." She was no Norman Rockwell, not even close. In fact, her drawing skills were duller than an old spoon. Nevertheless, she focused like a first grader, tongue hanging out of her mouth in total attentiveness, as she gave her best effort at sketching the monster that had haunted her dream. It took a while, and the others made no motion to interrupt as she included every detail – hooves, claws, eyes, horns, fur. As the picture took shape, she glared at the lopsided minotaur in loathing, but kept on going. Finally, she set the pencil down and took a concentrated appraisal of her work.

There's something missing, she thought. But what... oh yes. She went back to include one very important modification that she could not believe had been disregarded. With a heavy hand, she sketched the monster's third horn.

Again, it was Sevastian who turned the mood from anxious to tense with his phrase... "My god. It cannot be." All looked to him with expressions that demanded gratification. "I... I've seen this creature," he said with conviction.

"Where...?" Charlie began to ask, but it was too late.

Sevastian made a b-line for the exit.

"Where the hell are you going?" Jade demanded, very displeased to be left without an explanation.

"I'm going to Crow," he called out over his shoulder. "There are two books that I need to acquire. I'll be quick."

"Wait!" Jade ordered. "First tell us what you know!" but it was too late, he was on a mission and not stopping for anyone.

"Let him go," Charlie said. "I understand what he's doing."

"And that is?" Lex asked curiously.

"Apparently he has seen your minotaur," (Lex did not much care for the creature to be referenced as 'her minotaur,') "and needs one of the books in the castle to be certain, or to prove it to us."

The idea was remarkable to Lex, that Sevastian would make a quick jaunt to the other earth as if it were located right across the street instead of somewhere across the vast universe, and bring back with him two books totally alien to this earth. In addition, his little trip would seem surprisingly speedy to the three in the mansion, as time would stop here on Earth A the moment he stepped into the pool. When he said, "I'll be quick," he truly meant it, as his absence in the eyes of the others would consist only of his dash from the mansion to the church and back again. Probably fifteen minutes at most. Once on Earth B, he could take all the time he wanted to retrieve the books from the castle and it would be all the same to those waiting back on Earth A. Much like the other night, she recalled, when she had seen the night walkers from the upstairs window. From her perspective, they simply walked across the field and into the trees where they would re-emerge several minutes later despite the large expanse of time spent on Earth B. She couldn't help but allow her thoughts to be momentarily diverted as she imagined how nice it would have been to know about the pool during college. To have all the time she needed to study, to catch up on sleep, or just to have a pleasant getaway when the stress of school was overbearing.

Charlie's voice pulled her back to reality, "While we're

waiting for him to return, do you think that you could draw one more thing for us?"

"The city right?" she asked while repositioning the notebook in front of her.

He nodded. "If you don't mind."

"I'll do my best," she said, starting to work. There was a lot to remember about the hellish city of Dis, if it really was that particular city - so many gates, walls, watchtowers, windows and stairwells to demand her acute concentration and clear memory. Again, the others allowed her all the time she needed without verbal interruption. Their eager eyes followed her pencil's every movement.

She had not quite finished before the sound of the mansion's back door could be heard echoing down the corridor towards the dining room. Yes, approximately fifteen minutes. Shortly after, Sevastian's heavy breathing preceded his appearance. He bolted into the room carrying two books, each wrapped carefully in the broad leaf of a fie plant. Lex ceased her drawing due to the strong interest in what he had discovered.

"What did you find?" Jade asked as he placed the books carefully upon the table and began removing the protective botanical sheaths.

"This book," he said, as he gently opened the thinner of the two, "contains information about all the languages that exist or did exist on Earth B including the history and translations of each." He arrived at a section near the back and pointed his stubby finger at the page. "The language of Dis." The others gathered around, including Lex who decided that even the letters of this ancient language were evil in appearance.

"I think I am going to need a translation for the translation," Jade concluded after giving the pages a good looking over.

Sevastian replied, "Have no worries, I know the old language well. I had to learn it in order to read all of the books that were written before Greek."

"You're a credit to historians," Charlie mentioned appreciatively.

Jade spoke up edgily, "Yes, yes, he is great. So let the great one get to translating so we can know what message was spoken in Lex's dream."

"Halt your horses," Sevastian said, shooting his impatient friend an intolerant eye. "I have some more information to tell all of you." The Russian was noticeably uneasy as he opened the thicker book with the same delicate consideration he had shown the other. It was clear by his twitchy mannerisms that whatever he had discovered within this particular volume was not good news. When he reached the desired page, he stood back so all could see. Lex's heart, as it had done so many times as of lately, exploded into thundering velocity as she looked upon the face from her nightmare. There before her, clear as day, was the exact minotaur which had so brutally crushed the life from her body. She staggered backward a few steps desiring not to be anywhere near the thing, even if it was just an old sketch.

"So that is the same one then?" Charlie all but concluded after witnessing her reaction to the image.

"Third horn and all," she substantiated without indecision. I promise I have never seen it, or anything like it until my dream. And to be honest with you guys, I'm very afraid."

"And we should all be afraid," Sevastian said, not sugar coating the situation. "This is the Pyredaim."

"Are you kidding?" Charlie exclaimed, shooting up from his seat. "The Pyredaim?"

Sevastian gave a confirming nod.

It was clear to Lex that she was the only one who had no recognition of this name. "Just what the hell is a Pyredaim?" she asked in desperation. "Well?" She swore to herself that she would become belligerent if they chose not to tell her or if they said something like 'we'll have to save that one for later.'

Fortunately for the well-being of the others, Sevastian quickly spoke up. "To begin with, this minotaur at one time had a name but I've never seen it recorded in our manuscripts. As the story goes, he became corrupt and betrayed the gods. As punishment, he was cast into the depths of Tartarus and frozen up to his chest in a lake of ice. Supposedly the Pyredaim, which roughly translates to 'fire demon,' was frozen to keep his acanthary at bay. He was said to have considerable ability when it came to controlling fire."

"Where and what is Tartarus"? Lex asked.

"It's a prison," Sevastian replied. "Reserved for the worst criminals with the worst offenses. Believe me, you'd rather be put to death than go there.

So let me start by telling you the little we know about minotaurs," he continued hesitantly after a go-ahead nod from Charlie and Jade. "First and most basically, a minotaur is not a half man half bull like mythology will have you believe. He is not a fifty-fifty mixture of two separate creatures, rather he is his own race. Yes, it has attributes that are akin to humans and attributes that are akin to a bull or cow, but the species did not come about by means of some bizarre mating between the two. According to the history books of Earth B, the minotaur race was created by Zeus himself, king of the gods, ruler of Olympus, to protect something that is imperative to the god's well-being."

"And that is?" Lex prodded.

He gave his upcoming explanation a good thinking over before commencing. "The reason why Zeus created the minotaur was to protect the food of the Olympians, nectar and ambrosia, which is the source of their immortality. You see Lex, Mountain Olympus is surrounded by a large, dense forest called Dirgen. Dirgen Forest is the only place on Earth B where nectar and ambrosia grow. This infamous food and drink will render anyone who partakes in their consumption, immortal. Of course, Zeus could not have mortal beings such as humans stealing it, so to assure this did not happen, he created the minotaurs to guard the forest for all eternity. This race was designed to be the ultimate protectors of Dirgen. Everything about them, from their cheetah-fast land speed to their cunning intellect to their spear-like horns was put in place so that no mortal creature could get their hands on nectar and ambrosia. As far as I know, no one ever has.

Zeus, as the story goes, was very proud of his creation and very grateful for the minotaur's vital responsibility. As a sort of thank-you, or reward if you will, he bestowed his permission upon the horned race to consume the sacred food."

"So the minotaurs became immortal?" Lex asked wide-eyed.

He nodded. "Yes, and there would have been no holes in the decision had the Pyredaim not come along. Because once he became immortal, he could not be killed. And believe me, he needed to be killed."

"So he is still alive then," Lex said drearily. "Where is he now? Is he still frozen in Tartarus?"

Sevastian shrugged. "No one knows,"

"How about the underworld?" she then suggested.

"Yes, this is what I would gather from your dream. But we need to determine just how to interpret a vision such as that."

"I'm confused," Lex sighed. "Are Tartarus and the underworld the same thing?"

"I've always wondered," Sevastian replied, "But I cannot say for sure. As I've said, as far as we know, no human has been to the underworld. Also, no one has escaped from Tartarus. Basically, there are scant records of both places. All we have to go on are ancient legends which may be really far from the truth."

"If he is in Tartarus, that is where he belongs," Charlie said to no one in particular, eyes locked on the book.

Jade then said, "Maybe Hades is using him as a... a weapon of mass destruction for lack of a better phrase."

"Hades, god of the underworld," Lex recited aloud. "Do you think he has anything to do with this?"

"Impossible to say at this point," Charlie said with unfulfilling honesty. "Hades has been missing in action, at least in human affairs, since the beginning of recorded history on Earth

B."

"Back to the Pyredaim," Lex pressed on. "If he is immortal, is it impossible to kill him?" She could hardly believe that she was harboring such a strong desire to take a life. Was this part of the new instinct that had rooted itself within her body as of late? The others offered looks of surprise, as if they too had not expected such violent ambitions from their gentle-natured friend.

Charlie was the one to answer her question. "Yes, it is possible to kill an immortal. To put it bluntly and barbarically, if a spirit's vessel is damaged badly enough, the spirit cannot remain within the vessel."

"In other words," Jade offered in clarification," to kill a god, to kill a nymph, to kill a minotaur, their physical bodies must be ripped to shreds. It's not enough to lop off their arms, legs, or smash them beneath a boulder. A sufficient means would be to stick them into a giant blender and push puree or remove their heads. Do you remember the story of Prometheus from your mythology book? He stole fire from the gods and gave it to man as a gift. His punishment for the crime was grizzly. His body was chained to a cliff where each day a giant eagle would come and rip his liver from his body. Because of his immortality, this would not be sufficient to end his life. His liver regenerated day after day until he was finally set free by Hercules. Here is a bit of information that favors our cause. There are documented stories throughout Earth B's history, though few and far between, of immortal beings brutally slain to the point in which their superhuman bodies could no longer sustain life. Now the good news. Sevastian, Charlie and I have all successfully killed an immortal, many immortals in fact, so we know it can be done. And there's at least one weapon out there that can kill an immortal with relative ease."

"Really?" Lex asked with a spark of revived hope. "Where do we find such a weapon?"

Jade had a rascally grin as she said, "Not only has the weapon been found, it belongs to me. Charlie told you about the night of the Full Moon Festival, right? Remember the old man in the alley?"

"Yes," replied Lex. "Wait a minute, are you talking about the silver sword?"

Jade nodded.

"The silver sword will kill an immortal?"

"With one simple stick," she confirmed with confidence.

"That's right," Charlie said. "We discovered the sword's little secret under dire circumstances."

"So the mystery man in the alleyway gave a little girl a sword that will kill immortal beings?" Lex asked, just to make sure she heard it all correctly.

The others nodded. "Before you ask," Jade said, "we ourselves do not have an answer as to why this happened."

"When we get back to Crow, I'll go have a long sit in that particular alley," Lex said. "Perhaps he'll show up with a sword for me."

"At least we know that there is the slightest of possibilities that the Pyredaim could be killed," Sevastian chimed in, with his typical "glass half full" perception.

"Look," Charlie politely interjected so as not to dump too much rain onto Sevastian's enthusiasm parade. "We're getting ahead of ourselves. All of these things are just assumptions. Now it's clear that Lex's dream was not a coincidence, and as I said before, I believe that there is a certain message that we are supposed to take from it. But until we know more, we cannot benefit from sitting around devising plans on how to kill an immortal being. We're not even certain that the Pyredaim is our problem."

"He's definitely my problem," Lex said with all the conviction in the world. "And I want you to tell me his story so I know just who I am dealing with." There was no arguing with her and everyone knew it. After seeing that Charlie had nothing else to add for the moment, Sevastian pointed to the book that contained the terrifying illustration of the three horned monster.

"This book will do the story much more justice than I could," he said. "It was written between ten and fifteen thousand years ago. The author is anonymous and frankly, quite unimportant to our current situation."

Lex pulled the book close to her and snapped it shut rather maliciously. She did not desire to look upon her enemy's ugly face any more for now. "Reading this book will be one of my tasks when I get to Earth B," she assured the others. "In the meantime, let me finish this god-awful sketch of the underworld city and we'll go from there."

At the conclusion of these proclamations, a smile of respect arose on Jade's face. "I can see the Amaranth coming out in you," she said to Lex, who was a trite bewildered by the unexpected remark.

"How do you mean?"

"You're really taking charge here. Though you have just been thrown into this crazy new reality, you seem determined to do what needs to be done, to get to the bottom of this mystery."

Jade's observations had been valid. Lex did feel as though she was finally stepping up to the plate. Before now, she had been sort of lagging behind the others, along for the ride, following the pack. This subordinate position was the only choice she had been allotted, until now. At this point in the game, all four of them were sailing side-by-side into uncharted waters. And, following last night's vision, she could now for the first time offer her own helpful insight to the cause – whatever that cause was. Yes, she was still wrenched with fear over what might be, but her current motivation was derived from her necessity to make every detail of her dream known to the others so they could in turn help with her quest to better understand her own path. Acknowledging Jade's comment, Lex nodded to her, then once again put pencil to paper.

All the while she was adding the finishing touches on her best attempt at an accurate depiction of the city, Sevastian had been acting, well, odd. He hovered obtrusively over her shoulder, seemingly taking a marked interest as the sketch neared completion. More than once, he mumbled to himself in Russian as his eyes were fixed to the page in confusion or concern, maybe both. He was fidgety and breathing heavily. He seemed uncomfortable, restless. He paced about in close proximity to the artist, never venturing far from her side and not once breaking gaze from the drawing. The others, except for Lex who was now dotting the I's, regarded him as though he was going out of his skull. Charlie and Jade's heads turned in unity following his incessant tempo, back-and forth, back-and forth, as if a tennis match were taking place right there in the dining room.

"Are you about to have a heart attack?" Jade finally asked after his edginess had apparently tapped at her last nerve. "If you are, I'll donate your body to the zoo. Certainly, your corpse could sustain a whole family of lions for several months."

"I just may be," Sevastian replied impervious to the insult.

"What's going on with you anyway?" Charlie wanted to know. "I can see the wheels spinning in your head from over here."

"Done," Lex announced. Sevastian snatched the drawing from the table as quickly as if it had been the last slice of pizza.

"Seriously, Sevastian," Charlie said, "is there something you need to tell us?"

He replied in the affirmative, his fingers running anxiously through his thick tousled hair. "Yeah, but you won't believe it. And I can't be sure… no, yes I am sure… I have seen this city before. And not on Earth B."

"What?" said Charlie, his singular word dripping with skepticism. "I'm sorry, my friend, but that I cannot believe. Where do you think you've seen this city?"

Sevastian looked perplexed as he answered, "In a book my father owns."

Anamnesis

It's a late summer evening in St. Petersburg, Russia. One half of the sky is a dazzling purple and orange cocktail, an atmospheric dreamscape. The eye-catching ambiance above is slowly being swallowed by dark thunderheads rolling in from the Baltic. The warm breeze whisks off the water and up to the mainland carrying with it the familiar scent of marine life and the promise of rain. The elegant Moskincov house is the first man-made structure to be greeted by the salty winds as it nests atop a cliff overlooking the white-capped waters. It is a sight to behold with its gated semi circle driveway, well-groomed landscaping, gleaming white pillars and sleek marble staircase all accentuated by the high-priced backdrop of the Baltic Sea.

Pavel Moskincov's freshly waxed sedan turns into the driveway. The iron gates click open with an electric hum in operational obedience toward the sensor in the car. The sedan rolls to a gentle stop in close proximity to the front door and a large man with a shiny bald head and a dapper black suit squeezes out from the driver's seat. At first glance, he could be a bodyguard, or an ex shot-putter, but closer inspection might offer an opinion to the contrary. The dress suit has been professionally tailored, and the large sum of money he spent in doing so has given him the privilege of appearing as though he were an avid powerlifter as opposed to a flabby man with a fanatical taste for vatrushka. Though he could be intimidating to approach, Pavel Moskincov has a heart as big as his beloved city. He is a grizzly bear by appearance but a teddy bear by nature.

He has spent the entirety of today in business meetings surrounded by swarms of wealthy, gray haired men in black suits. Throughout the day, he has given three presentations, signed his name to twenty-something documents, shaken hands with every prominent executive in the area, and most importantly, he has made tremendous progress with the plan to expand his diamond trade to North America. Mr. Moskincov's company is number one in the Russian diamond market and he himself is the chief with the nickname "The King of Diamonds." He is a business-minded wizard, but not necessarily self-made. His own father had been the one to initiate the spark that would eventually set the company ablaze with prosperity. Pavel Moskincov senior, or P1 as he was often called, was a savvy entrepreneur who had begun with a humble, one room jewelry store in the coastal town of Kronstadt. Before his death, P1 had developed the business into three thriving stores of the highest reputation. This is where his son took over and did much justice to a father's legacy. Once the company went online, the wealth and success poured like Niagara Falls.

With a leather briefcase in hand, he walks the steps to the front door. For a man of his build, he has a youthful spring in his stride. His content smile when looking upon his own residence is perhaps the ultimate illustration that he is glad to be home. Anna, his all-in-one hired hand, greets him as he enters. She smiles devotedly and hands him a vodka and tonic with lime. This little request had been made via mobile phone during his drive home, and Anna, per usual, had not let him down.

Anna was reminded daily of how she was worth every ruble. Ever since his wife left, Pavel had been expected to undertake the impossible juggling act of running a company, managing a big house and raising a young boy by the Moskincov standard of excellence. Realizing that he could not possibly manage these tasks riding solo, he had put forth the most thorough of searches for the perfect nanny. After nearly seventy interviews, he settled on the snappy thirty-something school teacher from Ukraine. She cooked, she cleaned, she shopped, she landscaped, she folded laundry. Best of all, she made sure that his only son was kept well abreast with his chores and studies. She had a perfectionist work ethic and an agreeable personality. Pavel was so reliant on her services, he would gladly at any moment triple her already bloated salary just to keep her aboard.

"Would you like dinner at the table tonight, Mr. Moskincov? Or if you have work to do, I can bring it to your study. Which will it be, sir?"

"Neither, Anna," Pavel says with a temperate smile. "I ate a late lunch with a few associates today, and would you believe that I, the greatest of eaters, am not currently possessing an appetite?"

Anna laughs at his self-criticizing declaration.

"No," he continues, "tonight the Stolichnaya will do just fine. Where is Sevastian? Has he behaved today?"

"Yes sir, he has been well-behaved as usual. As for his current whereabouts, I cannot be sure. I saw him only five minutes ago on the third floor balcony watching the storm come in. Should I call him for you?"

"No, leave him be for now," Pavel replies with a contemplative rub of his double chin. "I have been meaning to… to catch up on some reading. If you need me, you will find me in the library with my book collection. And if you could, another vodka in say, twenty minutes?"

"Very well, Mr. Moskincov," Anna says with a conceding head nod. "Shall I make the next one a little stronger?"

"It has been a long day. Stronger will be much appreciated."

Pavel's book collection is small, but quite commendable as he only seeks the most significant literary works to grace his shelves. For Pavel, significant usually meant rare, or one of a kind. This pricey collection is one of his many hobbies and he usually stops at nothing to acquire a new addition once his desire has been fixed upon it. Each of the fifty or so hardbacks that sit behind the glass display cases, have been obtained either by persistence, cunning, being in the right place at the right time, or parting with a large sum of money. Yet there is one book in the collection, the one he fetches directly after closing the door, that has not been gained by conventional means. Unlike all the others, this book has been acquired by bloodshed.

There is a small safe on the middle shelf situated dead center among a row of books. Pavel raises the protective glass from this particular shelf and begins spinning the little combination wheel on the safe. With a click, the door to the safe pops ajar. Expectancy twinkles from his beady eyes as he opens it and removes a black iron box from inside. This box too has a combination pad in the form of three side-by-side wheels. The box is set upon the reading table and unlocked. Before he proceeds any further, he places a pair of soft white gloves on his giant hands. He sinks into the cushioned swivel chair and it creeks insolently under his weight. The book he lifts from the iron box is wrapped in a delicate cloth, which is removed with attentive consideration. "It has been a while," Pavel grumbles to the thick black book as if it were an old adversary. His voice is tinged with contempt, as if this unique possession might have been, or may still be an enemy of sorts. He dons a monocular that had been hiding in his shirt pocket, cracks his knuckles, and turns directly to the back one third of the volume. He is shaking all the while.

Time passes and there is a soft quintet of taps on the door. It is Anna, punctual to the minute with the beverage delivery. "Please, Anna, place it over there on the end table," Pavel instructs, pointing to the little piece of furniture at the opposite side of the small room. It is clear that he is taking every provision to ensure that a clumsy mishap does not leave this black book sopping with vodka and tonic. Though Anna has never once proved to be anything but steady on her feet, he stands firm in his decision. She complies without question and asks him if he desires anything more. He shakes his head and returns his gaze to the book. The door closes lightly as Anna departs the room.

The door opens but a few minutes later, this time there is no knock. Pavel looks up to see little Sevastian and smiles at his intrusively inquisitive son. Though this is without a doubt an unexpected interruption, Pavel is happy to see him nonetheless.

"Hello, my boy," he says to Sevastian warmly. "How fares my favorite son this evening?"

Sevastian trots enthusiastically to his father, totally ignorant as any boy of six would be, to the sacred article upon the table. "Papka," he says, "what are you reading?"

Pavel sits in silence for a brief moment with an air of reservation regarding this question. But then he smiles and says, "My dear boy, my curious little Sevastian. Would you believe that many years ago, anyone who asked about this book, and I mean anyone, would be… well, I do not wish to scare you. Times have changed, and so have I." The little round boy cocks his head to one side as if confused by this declaration.

Pavel slides the chair back from the desk and gives his knee a few hefty slaps. "Come sit on my lap, Sevastian. I will show you something that very few have ever seen." Sevastian's face turns aglow and he scurries over to his father's side. Pavel hoists the youth to his knee with perhaps more difficulty than he had expected. "You must get your appetite from my genes," he says grunting and straining to situate the boy so as to elicit the least amount of discomfort to his thigh.

Once properly positioned upon his father's broad leg, the black book draws Sevastian's attention as though it were a plate of chocolate truffles. With naïve intent, he reaches his roly-poly fingers toward it. Pavel with perhaps more force than intended stops his son's bold gesture by yanking Sevastian's arm down and away from the desired target.

"No, Sevastian, you must not touch. You see how I wear gloves? This book is very valuable so you may only use your eyes."

Sevastian nodded with apologetic obedience then gently turned back to the black book with a comical delicateness, as if his gaze might inflict some sort of damage upon the exceedingly vital object. On the left page, there is a good deal of writing that he does not recognize or understand. It is not Russian or English. It is handwritten rather than typed. On the right page, there is a city either just at the base of a volcanic mountain or actually carved into the mountain. Running in front of the city is a river emitting little squiggles portraying steam. There is fire raging throughout the sketch. The way in which the city is depicted appears as though it is a large beast rather than a place of habitation. The central entranceway strongly resembles a massive mouth – the pointed projections from the ascended gate bear a resemblance to sharp teeth. Two crescent windows just above the main gate resemble an evil pair of eyes, each one with rampant fire bursting outward. Two cylindrical towers twist skyward over the mouth and the eyes, each ending in a sharp point. These towers resemble two great horns. Everything extending laterally from the central gate, the crooked stairwells, the bulky walls and the multitude of towers could easily be arms and claws.

"Does this frighten you?" Pavel asks as his son appears rather disturbed by the illustration.

"I do not like it, Papka," Sevastian replies with youthful honesty. "May I go now?"

Pavel chuckles lightheartedly as he helps his son down to the burgundy area rug. "Well, it frightens me too."

"Then why do you read such a book?" Sevastian then asks.

"Because it is one of a kind," Pavel answers, eliciting a non-satisfied look from his son. "You are too young to understand I believe."

"Okay, Papka," Sevastian says with fading concern for the whole situation. "I will go find Anna now. She has promised to teach me Eralash tonight."

"Eralash, well, that's a man's game," Pavel mentions importantly, making Sevastian all the more anxious to get on with learning it. He turns quickly to the door, but not before one more word from his father. "Sevastian, there is no reason to tell anyone about this book. It is scary and worth forgetting about. Do you understand?"

Sevastian shows no sign that he retains the slightest bit of care over the book or its evil content. As it is with children, their minds hop from one thing to the next without pattern or warning. Pavel seems satisfied that the matter will be laid to rest and bids his son a good night. Unknown by both of them at that current time, the image of the hellish city was permanently engraved in Sevastian's memory and would never, ever be forgotten.

88

"Are you absolutely sure?" Charlie questioned doubtfully as Sevastian concluded his reminiscence of the black book in his father's house.

"It was a long time ago," Jade added, staying congruent with the overall theme of skepticism. "You were very young."

"There's only one way to find out," the Russian firmly replied. "I'm going to call Papka. What time is it in St. Petersburg? Six in the evening? He should be home by now, or at least on his way."

"Will you put him on speaker phone?" Jade asked. "I'd love to hear for myself what he has to say."

"Yes," Sevastian said, "but I think it's better if he doesn't know everyone is listening in on the conversation. I have a feeling that this may be a sensitive subject, you know, based on the warning he gave me."

"I think we'd all like to hear this conversation but there's a problem," Charlie submitted to the others. "Pavel Moskincov speaks Russian as a first language and speaks to his son that way. If Sevastian were to initiate the conversation in English, he may become suspicious."

"No problem there," Sevastian said while removing a mobile phone from his pocket. "Translation app to the rescue." He rapped away at the touch screen and in no time had the desired program up and running. "Okay, Russian to English," he instructed the phone.

"Russian to English," the phone repeated in a smart British inflection.

"Gather around everyone," he said to the others as he propped the phone up against an empty tea cup. "Lex, this translation application will simply listen to what father and I say in Russian and display the conversation across the screen in English."

Lex replied, "Actually I have this app on my phone as well. It came in very handy the night I waited on a table of Japanese tourists."

Sevastian inhaled a nervous breath, "Call Pavel's cell." In the next instant, the line was ringing. A man with a deep raspy voice answered and…

The words, "Hello, Sevastian," darted across the screen of the translator.

The others read along in agonizing silence as Sevastian and his father exchanged pleasantries and caught up a bit. Lex guessed that it had been a while since they had last spoken to each other. They looked to Sevastian imploringly, desperate to come to a conclusion over the accuracy of his memory. After about fifteen grueling minutes of obligatory repartee about diamonds, hockey, Sevastian's perfected recipe for lobster bisque, Pavel's latest attempt at a jogging routine, Anna's vacation to India and the particulars about Sevastian's next homecoming, Lex, Charlie, and Jade finally got what they had been waiting for.

"I have a question that will seem strange to you, Papka," Sevastian said, trying his best to ease such an indiscreet change of topic into the conversation.

"Yes, what is it?" Pavel's deep voice questioned. The others held their breath during Sevastian's restive pause. The black vertical line on the screen of Sevastian's phone blinked rhythmically, awaiting the next words to translate.

"Many years ago, when I was just a boy of six or seven, I came into your book room one night and found you reading a book that I remember finding most interesting."

"You had visited me there many times throughout your childhood," Pavel pointed out. "I am not sure I can recall one particular time."

"Yes, I think you can," Sevastian advanced with determination. "The book I am referring to was the only one in which you wore gloves to turn the pages." There was a lengthy pause in which Lex thought she could actually feel the tension radiating through the phone. Sevastian spoke again before his father surrendered a reply. "That night, when I came in, the book was open to an illustration of a city – a city in the shape of a monster, a city that breathed fire. You told me that this book was one of a kind." There was again a hushed hiatus before Sevastian forced the ball into his father's side of the court. "You remember, don't you, Papka?"

"Yes, I remember," Pavel finally said, "One of my biggest regrets in life was allowing you to see that book. One of my biggest fears was that you might one day ask about it. Today my fears have been realized." The others exchanged glances of the utmost perplexity along with a round of shoulder shrugs as the voice on the other end of the line carried on with, "My hope was that you were too young and unconcerned about the book, but I forget how smart you are, even at that young age, you absorbed everything into memory. Why should the book be any different?" Pavel was stringing these sentences together with inarticulate precipitance as the unrest over his son's inquiry was becoming quite apparent.

"I'm sorry if I have upset you," Sevastian pushed on after looking to the others with alarm. "I am in a situation, one in which only you can help."

"How does your situation relate to the book in question?" Pavel asked with desperation in his tone.

"My investigation into this particular issue is ongoing," Sevastian explained, "therefore I hope you understand that I cannot speak of the matter until I fully understand it myself."

Pavel did not reply, but his breathing through the phone was becoming noticeably labored.

"Papka, I am going to send you a picture message, and I need your expert analysis. Please, look this over carefully." With that, he snapped a picture of Lex's drawing with his phone and sent it directly on its way to Russia. "It should be there. Did you get it?"

"Yes, your text just came through," Pavel confirmed shakily.

"Great," said Sevastian, "Tell me – is it, or is it not the same city from your book?"

All in the room waited in nail-biting silence as Pavel's long, wordless interval was presumably being used to open the text and review Lex's sketch. All held their breath - no one moved, no one blinked.

Finally, Pavel Moskincov, the Russian King of Diamonds, spoke with a very different tone. No longer was his voice trembling with fretful anticipation, rather it was commandingly stern. "I am going to tell you something, my son, and I want you to listen well. I do not know what you are up to or where you acquired this drawing. I do not want to know if you drew it from memory, or if it came from somebody else. It does not matter. The only thing you need to know is that you are digging into something evil. Leave it alone or you will most certainly regret it. For your own good, I am putting an end to this conversation here and now. I will not comment on your drawing nor will I give any information about the book. I will conclude by telling you exactly what I told you that night long ago – the book is scary and worth forgetting about. I will not tell you again."

Sevastian's expression was one of despondency as he gave it one more audacious go. "I trust your judgment on the matter and value your warning. If I told you my situation was one of life or death, would that alter your refusal of information?"

"No, not life. Death only," Pavel shot back aggressively. "Why can't you understand this?

"Papka," Sevastian pleaded, "I vow to you, on my life," he cringed as he uttered this lie, "that I will drop the matter completely, never again to mention or pursue it, but first I just need to know if the city I sent you is the same as the one in your book. Your answer will put all to rest."

"Damn your persistence, Sevastian."

"Papka, please, is it or is it not?" His eyes were closed, as this utter defiance of his beloved father pained him tremendously.

Another long silence, the most uncomfortable bout of hush yet to grace the conversation. Then, finally, "Yes, the city is unquestionably the same."

Sevastian's jaw dropped, as did Charlie's. Jade fell back in her chair and Lex brought a trembling hand up to her mouth, green eyes wide and troubled.

"Please, son, please keep your vow that you will now drop it for I will give you nothing besides what I have just foolishly said. Do not bother to come after the book, because I have gotten rid of it a long time ago."

"I will keep my word," Sevastian said as Charlie from across the table mouthed the words,

"Ask him the name of the book." Sevastian shook his head. He would not dare test his father to any greater extent.

"I trust that you will, for your own sake," Pavel replied, then abruptly disconnected.

Lex crossed her arms and slouched backward in her chair. This new development was as incredible as it was disturbing. The voice from Russia had just validated her claim that she had dreamt about a place that was already in existence, but one that she had never seen. Pavel had also made it obvious in so many words that this particular city was the devil's domain. At this junction, the others would have to take initiative in dealing with the matter. She didn't know Pavel Moskincov as they did so she realized that she would have little advice to give in dealing with his determined defiance of Sevastian's requests. She predicted that Charlie and company would eventually hash out a scheme to deal with the King of Diamonds. For her, there was a bigger topic, one that she had yet to bring up to the group. This was the plan to relieve some of the fear that had accrued from the days recently passed – the brilliant idea that came to her this morning while lying awake in

Aunt Claire's bed. If this plan was successful, she would be ready and able to defend herself against the minotaur the next time he came too close for comfort. After Pavel's abrupt hang-up, Charlie relayed his thoughts on the matter almost instantly, so Lex's idea would have to wait a few more minutes.

"Don't you see?" he said to no one in particular.

"See what?" Sevastian asked.

"The big plan, the outside forces. This is just another example, and now we know that Sevastian has a predestined role in all this as well."

"Riddles, Charlie. You are talking in riddles," Sevastian said with a flick of frustration.

Charlie stood and began pacing in circles as he often did when he spoke with tenacity on a given subject. "It's crystal clear. We have already deduced that someone or something made sure Lex got to Rose because she is a key player in this bigger-than-life situation. You," he sent an identifying head nod to the Russian, "have always assumed, as I have, that you were brought on board for your diamond expertise."

Sevastian was yet to catch on. "Yeah, so?"

"So," Charlie repeated with emphasis, "Claire Lunden came to Rose at the hands of the girl in black, therefore Alexis followed. Pavel Moskincov just happened to temporarily move to Rose so that he could establish his American headquarters in Wichita. Wichita? Really? Why not New York City? Chicago? DC? The answer is obvious – he came to Wichita because you had to get to the pool. I guarantee you if we dug deep enough into your father's process of coming to America, the girl in black would emerge somewhere along the way. Therefore, in conclusion, Sevastian is more than just a skilled diamond cutter, he too has been chosen by… whomever or whatever to participate and contribute to this quest. Just as it is no coincidence that a Hollywood star came to Kansas, it is also no coincidence that your father just happens to have a book that contains a picture of the exact same city that Lex saw in a dream."

Sevastian beamed with importance as Charlie's statement sunk in.

"There will be time in the future to discuss my ascertainments to a greater extent," Charlie continued, "but right now we have a serious problem to address. It's reasonable to assume, no, it's reasonable to say with confidence that this book will give us more answers. The problem we face is that our situation demands that we get our hands on it. Pavel Moskincov refuses us this information, yet it must, it absolutely must, be obtained."

Jade nodded in agreement and said, "This is indeed a problem. I love Pavel, we all do. He's a wonderful, caring man, a business partner; one who has done so much for all of us over the years and now, ironically, he's an immense obstacle in our path. If we are to succeed in saving Earth B, we must either obtain that book or find out everything about it from the man who owned it."

"My guess," Sevastian added," is that despite his comment about getting rid of the book, he still has it. I say this because he values his precious book collection over anything else he owns. If I know Papka, he would not part with presumably the rarest and most valuable book of the lot. As a matter of fact, when I visited St. Petersburg this past summer, I noticed that the safe in which he kept the book was still there on the shelf. Was the book still in the safe? I'll bet it probably was."

"I don't suppose you know the combination to the safe?" Jade asked.

Sevastian shook his head.

"Well then," she continued, "this will be a delicate task, won't it? We can't just sit the man down and explain our situation. And based on his adamant misgivings about Sevastian's questions, I'd say he will not willingly give in to our begging and pleading. So, this leaves us with two options, trickery or force. I can't bear to contemplate the second, but I think we would all agree that these two methods are the only way."

"We will not use force," Sevastian said quickly and quite

resolutely. "I'm sure we can come up with a plan without… well, without using force."

"Here's my concern," Charlie offered. "If you're correct and he hasn't gotten rid of the book, he may be more likely to do it now that you have inquired after it. It may be just a matter of time before he trashes it, sells it, burns it, whatever. My point is, we need to get our hands on it very quickly. If we cannot accomplish this before the book is out of our reach, we'll have no choice but to extract the information we seek from Pavel's own lips."

Lex interjected, cool and calm. "Well, we have time on our side, don't we?" The others turned their regard to her, as if they had temporarily forgotten that she was even there. "If I may, I'd like to propose a logical idea."

"Yes, please," Jade invited, giving Lex the floor.

"I agree with Jade, this will be a delicate situation, and one that may require much planning. I also agree with Charlie. If Mr. Moskincov still has this book in his possession, he may be more likely to get rid of it now that Sevastian has expressed interest in it. A state of affairs such as this will require a cunning plan and an even more cunning back-up plan. We will need time to devise this plan without giving Sevastian's father time to decide whether or not the book is worth keeping. Therefore, we should head back to Earth B and take advantage of "stop-time" on this earth. There, we can take as long as we need to figure things out."

"Brilliant!" Charlie exclaimed as he leapt to his feet, clapping his hands at the same time. "I love this girl," he declared with a wink in Lex's direction. "That's exactly what we'll do."

"Good thinking, Lex," Jade added to Charlie's shower of compliments.

"Can you believe how things are unfolding?" Sevastian said to all in the room. "Lex left us for only one night and came back with more new insight than we've ever had. Perhaps we are just a few steps away from identifying our antagonist. And once we know who or what we are dealing with, we might see to it that the oracle's final divination is altered."

"Well put, my friend," Charlie said. "Okay, let's fill our bellies before we leave. Who knows when we will taste pizza or tacos again."

Jade said, "I agree we should eat. But let's make it quick. We want to preserve as much time as possible in case we need it when we get back. Are you planning on joining us, Sevastian?" she asked after noticing that he had taken a seat at the table instead of making toward the kitchen like everyone else.

"You guys go ahead. I'm not really hungry." The others looked quite surprised but made no objection because they saw what he was up to. Positioning the book of translations in front of him along with Lex's phonetically transcribed syllables, he set to work deciphering exactly what was said to Lex in her nightmare.

"I now find myself more curious than hungry," Lex said as she turned back towards the dining room table. I can't pull myself away." The others seemed to share this opinion as they too stood in motionless limbo between a nourishing meal and a quench of their curiosity.

"Go. Eat." Sevastian urged. "This will likely take a little while. There's no good reason to go hungry just to sit here and watch me muddle through the translation. Go. I'll call you when I figure it out."

89

Brunch consisted of a giant vat of pasta – quick, filling and satisfying. Because of the necessity to hurry, to get back to Earth B so time here would be put on hold, the ingredients from this meal came from boxes and cans. This would normally aggravate Sevastian tremendously but he was tied up with other matters at the moment. It would have been his choice to create this feast from scratch using tomatoes imported directly from Italy, olive oil from Greece, and pasta handmade from the finest flour, but under the given circumstances, less was more. During the meal, there was little chatter. Sitting atop barstools encircling the kitchen's island countertop, the housemates twirled spaghetti noodles on soup spoons and ruminated silently within their own minds. Once in a while a noise arose from the adjoining dining room as Sevastian cleared his throat or readjusted himself in the chair. At the initiation of each random sound, all would perk their ears in hope that he had completed his translation. Finally, after many false alarms, the confirmation came, but the tone was not especially spirited.

"I think I've got it," he called, voice echoing from the spacious dining room. Silverware and napkins plummeted to the countertop and floor as the others made a mad dash from the kitchen. "I do not think it's exact," he informed them as they gathered around his chair, "but having only Lex's broken syllables to work with, this is as good as it gets. I'm sorry, Lex, but I don't think the woman at the city gate was inviting you in for tea."

She leaned in with Charlie and Jade to get a good look at

the sketch pad. The first three quarters of the paper contained scribbles, erase marks, and crossed-out words and letters. Near the bottom, all the trial and error began to flow into actual words, and the actual words into cohesive sentences. The bottom center contained the final product, and the message could not have surprised her less…

I SEE YOU AMARANTH
I KNOW YOU ARE HERE
HE IS COMING FOR YOU
YOU ARE THE HUNTED
YOU WILL DIE

She should have been more afraid, but after all that had recently happened, her lack of adverse reaction to the threat could be chalked up to acceptance. There was nothing in those lines that she did not already know or expect. Her motivation now was to delay this promised doom long enough to do her part – whatever that was. As the others shared facial expressions of rage and resentment, she decided that this would be the perfect opportunity to unveil the plan she had been harboring the entire morning. She said, "When I meet him again, the Pyredaim I mean, I will not fall so easily. And if he does defeat me, he will not do so without undergoing his own bit of suffering."

"Goddamn right!" Jade said, backing Lex's claim with glaring eyes and clenched fists. "I'll make a necklace from his third horn."

Charlie was a little more pragmatic. "Don't worry, Lex," he said with so much confidence that it would be impossible for anyone to doubt him. "We will be your force field. Crow will be your fortress. The soldiers will be your own personal army. That minotaur will not even come close to you."

"Yes, I have all confidence in that," Lex replied, "but I can't hide within the castle forever, and I can't always have several hundred soldiers by my side. Therefore, if the time comes when it is just him and me staring at each other from across the boiling river, I need to be able to provide my own protection. Therefore…"

"That will not happen," Charlie cut in. "There will never be a time when we leave you alone with him, or any enemy for that matter."

"Therefore," Lex repeated, silencing him with the fire in her voice. She drew in a deep breath and completed her sentence. "Therefore I must become a soldier."

Silence befell the room. All looked at her with their own individual airs. Sevastian was leery, Jade seemed almost proud. But it was Charlie who was unmistakably the most obstinate in his rejection of the proposal.

"I'm sorry, Lex," he said firmly, "but that is out of the question. For your own good, I cannot allow it."

"How is it for my own good if I can't defend myself?" she shot back, livid that he should blatantly decline.

"Lex, you must understand that my number one concern is your well-being. For this very reason I cannot condone your suggestion. Believe me, I see your point about defending yourself. Don't worry, you will be taught. But undergoing training to become a Crow Soldier may kill you before you ever get the opportunity to use the training."

"I don't understand," she said snippily, arms crossed in resentment.

"Here are the facts," he resumed. "Only the strongest, fiercest, most able-bodied men get selected to begin training. Of those men, one quarter will quit, one quarter will become severely injured and one quarter will die. Those are hard statistics."

"You forgot the one quarter who make it through and become the greatest warriors in the world," Lex reminded him.

"There are two of you in this room to attest to that, and we all know there should really be three." She said this with an insinuating glance at Jade. "Jade, please, you agree with me, right?"

Jade said, "Don't get me wrong, I've been well trained with the blades, and could give any of those boys a run for their money…" Sevastian nodded agreeingly to this, "but the fact of the matter is that there has never been a female soldier."

"Why not?"

Jade thought about this for a moment. "I guess because no female has ever wanted to."

"Don't you want to?" Lex asked, certain that someone with Jade's dominant personality would be chomping at the bit for overall superiority.

"Truthfully… yes."

"Then why have you not?"

"The law states that females cannot be soldier candidates," Charlie answered when Jade did not produce an immediate response. "I'm not saying I agree with it," he then added after taking note of Lex's disgruntled expression. Perhaps she had inherited some of her mother's feminist genes, because as of now, she was willing to wage an all out war in the name of anti-sexism.

"Let me guess. The law was written at the dawn of civilization by a bunch of men, right?"

"Well, yes," he replied a little uneasily, breaking eye contact as Lex drove forward.

"And because of Crow's value of time-honored tradition, this law has never been amended or made an exception thereto, right?"

He nodded.

"You are the head soldier, are you not? A member of the high council. You have the queen wrapped around your little finger, yes?"

"Look, Lex, I…"

"Amend the law," she demanded. "Charlie, the path that I

am taking will not likely be paved with blacktop. You know this. I'm asking this favor because I need to be an elite warrior just like you. I have to have the confidence and the ability to turn myself from the hunted into the hunter. Becoming a Crow Soldier is the optimal approach to achieving this."

He held his palm outward, almost as if he were surrendering under the onslaught of valid points and fervent pleas. "Like I said, I agree, completely. If you want my honest opinion here it is... I think the training will kill you." He turned to the others. "Am I being unreasonable? Do any of you disagree? Sevastian? Didn't you come within an inch of death during your training? Jade, you've heard his stories, you've heard my stories. How can we allow Lex to just step blindfolded in front of the firing squad?" He turned back to Lex and finished off with... "It's suicide."

Despite all of this, she remained stubbornly undeterred. "Yet you and Sevastian decided to 'commit suicide,' and here you stand, alive and well, and guess what? You are bloody soldiers! Why have you no confidence in me?" Once these words were set free, she could tell her dogged persistence might have just paid off. This came at the price of dumping a load of distress on Charlie.

He approached her slowly and said, "I have more confidence in you than I have in anyone else. We all do. I just don't want to see you get hurt or worse. You're right though. The path will be rough. You have seemingly accepted this. You also seem to have accepted that your well-being may be in jeopardy the minute you step back into the pool. As hard as this is, I too must accept it. You should be able to defend yourself. You need to be taught raw survival and lethal weapon handling. This is what you will receive in soldier training. Because there is apparently no changing your mind..." he paused and looked to the others who expressed their reserved approval with timid nods. He turned and locked eyes with Lex. "Against my better judgment, for you, I will try to have the law amended."

A smile the size of California shot across her face.

"What happens to you during training is out of my hands, and this goes against every vow I've made to protect you, but in protecting you I must also honor your wishes and let you take the lead. You are, after all, the Amaranth. Though I can't be with you during the actual training, I can at least see to it that you're well-prepared before you head off to your destined training ground. As soon as we get to Earth B, the three of us will work with you so that you'll have every advantage when the time comes to set off on your own."

"I think that's a splendid idea," she replied, noticing that Jade was looking at her with glowing admiration – like a parent whose child had just won the spelling bee or scored the winning goal. Despite the promise of ruthless brutality in undergoing this training, Lex felt an unwavering sense of relief. This was due to her understanding that her actual threat was not the training, but this unknown foe on Earth B. This of course, like everything else in the future, was a mere premonition. But the little voice inside her head, the one that had just started talking a few days ago, told her that this was to be. And, despite the guarantee of upcoming trials and tribulations, she had never felt a bigger sense of purpose, never felt part of something more significant, never felt so damn alive.

"I've got to admit," Sevastian said to all, "it feels good to have a little direction and some new goals – some new mysteries to crack open."

The atmosphere was suddenly inundated with motivation, except from Charlie's end as he still clung to concern over Lex's decision, or his own decision to go along with Lex's decision. Jade and Sevastian rallied around Lex, throwing hugs, patting her on the back, offering their undying support in the cause. The scene was akin to a locker room before the big game.

Then it was coach Charlie who settled the troops by constructively laying out the plan. "Alright, everyone. Let's meet at the back door in half an hour, changed and ready to go. As always, make sure those lists are updated."

"Wait a minute," Lex jumped in suddenly remembering yesterday, when she had first departed for the church, he had made the unusual request to construct a detailed list of future appointments. "I never understood your reasoning for making this list."

Smiling, he said, "Remember returning to school after holiday break and forgetting your locker combination after just two weeks? Try remembering to pick up your friend from the airport after one hundred days on Earth B. Trust me, the list has saved me on many occasions."

"Makes sense to me," she replied, fully appreciating his experience in the matter. "I'll see that it's updated." And when these words parted from her tongue, she again felt as though there would never be a time when she would again look upon that well-documented list of appointments.

90

In thirty minutes exactly, the Rose Flock decked out in the protective cloaks of Glast sheep's wool, assembled at the mansion's back door. There was an unspoken exhilaration in the air. Sevastian clutched tightly to his books while nibbling on a pound cake. Since the moment Lex came down from her bedroom, Charlie had not ventured more than two feet from her side. This was perhaps a demonstration of his promised protection.

"Maybe we should bring a shotgun," Lex suggested with intended sarcasm. "If the Pyredaim is waiting for me at the other side of the pool, we could just take care of him then and there."

"Actually, Lex, that reminds me," Charlie said with a flare of enthusiasm. "I think I'm yet to come clean about the ludicrous question I asked you this past summer. Do you know what I'm talking about?"

She tried to recall, but in the tangled web of all his ludicrous statements, she could not pick out one in particular. She shook her head in the negative.

"I asked if you had any metal in your body."

"Oh yeah!" she exclaimed as the recollection of that absurd and untimely question returned to mind.

"I was very nervous to ask you because you'd likely think I was a crackpot."

"Well, there's no changing my opinion on that now," she replied with a gleam in her eye.

He laughed at this then said, "Take a look at the eyelets of your trail shoes."

She knelt down and pulled back the covers, even though

she did not have the faintest inkling of his intentions. "Okay, now what?" she asked after noticing nothing out of the ordinary.

"When you first bought the shoes, the eyelets were reinforced with metal. Now you see that there are no metal reinforcements, only the leather lace holes. Bottom line, the pool removes every trace of metal from the traveler. When you suggested bringing a gun for protection, it reminded me that I had not made you aware of that point."

"That is interesting, if not a trifle inconvenient. Well, so much for pictures," she said in reference to the fact she now had to discard the cell phone concealed within the pocket of her cloak. She bashfully removed the item under an onslaught of snickers and set it on the nearby windowsill. "Just thought I could make the world's coolest scrap book if I ever make it back," she justified. The look on Charlie's face illustrated disapproval over her 'if I ever make it back' comment. She pacified him with a feigned mischievous grin as if she were only kidding around.

Jade surveyed the clan. "Are we ready?" The other's rendered a mixture of nods and thumbs up. "Well, off to battle once more," she declared metaphorically, or perhaps literally.

"Once more?" Lex questioned as they departed the warmth of the mansion to be bombarded by the frigid Christmas Eve chill. "Besides the coliseum, have you actually fought in a battle?" She said this while picturing in her head a vast open field with armies lined up on opposing sides, then charging voraciously at each other before coming together in a bloody clash.

Jade laughed and said, "The extent of it would boggle your mind. Lex, we have a lot to catch you up on. Don't worry, between your training, choir directing, helping with the plan to best Pavel Moskincov, finding the girl in black, learning acanthary, and saving the earth, I'm sure there will be some spare time for our thrilling war stories." Everyone chuckled amusedly at this, and even though it was all but certain that they were heading for troubled times, there was still a mutual optimism.

They set off toward the little patch of woods, side by side.

Four friends bound by fate, brought together perhaps by some greater power. They walked with heads held high. They walked with purpose. They walked with every intention of making certain the oracle's final divination would not come to pass. The fierce unbarricaded wind blew fresh powder over their foot tracks almost as quickly as they had been made. By the time four hooded figures disappeared into the trees, Mother Nature had erased all evidence that anyone had passed between the mansion and the old church. As the world around was making final preparations for its beloved holiday, as plump turkeys cooked in ovens, as the last gifts were being wrapped, as familiar melodies poured from stained glass windows, the massive home stood vacant against a gray sky. County Road 13 had never seemed so lonely.

THE END

THE STORY CONTINUES WITH BOOK II, FOOTSTEPS OF PROTUS.

www.ingramcontent.com/pod-product-compliance
Lightning Source LLC
Chambersburg PA
CBHW021153030726
47493CB00029B/1394